...avis is in top form with *Enoch's Ghost*. Blending elements of classical literature, mythology, biblical history, and theology, he's invented a wildly creative universe as richly populated as Tolkien's Middle Earth or Lewis's Narnia. Accessible to readers of all ages, *Enoch's Ghost* will delight Davis's regulars, as well as engage new readers, making them want to dive into all the other DIOM books wholesale. This is creative art that is godly and entertaining.

—**Kevin Lucia**, *The Press & Sun Bulletin*, A Gannett News Publication

Spectacular! A well-written sequel to the **Dragons in our Midst** series! I had trouble putting the book down. I felt like I was with the characters, experiencing every moment with them side by side. I will treasure this book and read it many more times in the future. After finishing *Enoch's Ghost*, I felt closer to God. The book painted a portrait of God's love that spoke to my heart. Bryan Davis has succeeded once again in writing an eye-catching, heart-wrenching novel that all audiences will love. Well done!

—**Gabrielle Schultz** (Age 14)

All I can say is "Wow!" Words cannot describe *Enoch's Ghost* by Bryan Davis. If you've read his **Dragons in our Midst** series and *Eye of the Oracle*, you will want to read this book. You'll love it! It was so gripping I didn't want to put it down! This book really inspired me to pursue my faith in God!

—**Nick Battaglia** (Age 18)

Extraordinary! Mr Davis brings imagination to life in the **Oracles of Fire** series. He opens the gateway to another world with vivid descriptions and memorable characters, creating a tale of faith, love, and adventure while masterfully distinguishing the battle between good and evil. You'll be rapidly turning the pages until the end! *Enoch's Ghost* is possibly his best book yet. I highly recommend it for all fantasy-lovers looking for a good read!

—**Sarah Holloway** (Age 15)

I have had the opportunity and privilege to read all of Bryan's books. I have found them to be written in such an interesting manner that I am unable to lay them down. God has endowed Bryan with the gift to write mysteries of bygone days, weaving sp..pecially pleased with the message in ....ls over all evil.

ge 78)

Enoch's Ghost is a great Christian book for everyone! I'd read it again and again. It was FANTASTIC!

—**Hannah Webb** (Age 11)

Enoch's Ghost is Mr Davis's best book yet. It's full of suspense. You won't be able to put it down! It has plenty of thrilling adventures and compassionate sacrifices. You never feel as though you're reading a book, because it feels like you're living the story right alongside the characters.

—**Michelle Albert** (Age 17)

I have never read a book that captivated me as much as *Enoch's Ghost* has. As soon as I started reading the very first chapter, nobody could get this book away from me. Mr Davis uses his amazing talent in such an awesome way! I encourage anyone to read Mr Davis's books!

—**Hannah Meyer** (Age 14)

Enoch's Ghost combines a great group of characters and a great storyline, making it an unforgettable read! Unlike many books I've read, in the **Dragons in our Midst** and **Oracles of Fire** books, Christianity isn't just implied – it's the theme!

—**Ariel Hicks** (Age 16)

Enoch's Ghost is an awesome book! I loved it! Not just an exciting read, it also has a depth of story that is astounding. All through it, I could see biblical truths and God's love and power at work in the lives of people, which have inspired me. *Enoch's Ghost* is simply amazing!

—**Hannah Sharp** (Age 14)

This book is as good as *Eye of the Oracle*. If you are a fan of dragons, you will like the whole series. Bryan Davis is one of the best Christian authors out there.

—**Alex Kahale** (Age 16)

Enoch's Ghost was even cooler than *Eye of the Oracle*, and it was very suspenseful. It clears up a lot of things from *Tears of a Dragon*. I can't wait for *Last of the Nephilim* to come out!

—**Tony Laudadio** (Age 12)

Bryan Davis's books are on top of my list, and I'm reading them constantly. I don't know anyone who can combine such a compelling and awesome story with Christian values as well as he can.

—**David Webb** (Age 15)

Enoch's Ghost

ORACLES OF FIRE®

CANDLE
BOOKS

Enoch's Ghost
Copyright © 2007 by Bryan Davis
This edition published in the UK in 2010 by Candle Books
(a publishing imprint of Lion Hudson plc),
Wilkinson House, Jordan Hill Road, Oxford, OX2 8DR
Tel: +44 (0)1865 302750 Fax: +44 (0)1865 302757
Email: candle@lionhudson.com
www.lionhudson.com

Published in the USA by Living Ink Books,
an imprint of AMG Publishers
6815 Shallowford Road
Chattanooga, Tennessee 37421

Distributed in the UK by Marston Book Services Ltd,
PO Box 269, Abingdon, Oxon OX14 4YN

Enoch's Ghost is the second of four books in the youth fantasy fiction series,
Oracles of Fire®.

Scripture quotations are taken from *The Authorized (King James) Version.*
Rights in the Authorized Version are vested in the Crown. Reproduced by
permission of the Crown's Patentee, Cambridge University Press.

ISBN 978-1-85985-872-1

ORACLES OF FIRE and DRAGONS IN OUR MIDST are registered
trademarks of AMG Publishers.

This book has been printed on paper independently certified as having been
produced from sustainable forests.

Printed and bound in Great Britain by J F Print Ltd., Sparkford, Somerset
First printing 2010
10 9 8 7 6 5 4 3 2 1 0

For every child who fears the darkness, for every father who plunges into the darkness in search of the lost, and for every hero or heroine who carries a flaming beacon that dispels the shadows – this story is for you.

ACKNOWLEDGMENTS

To my best friend and biggest fan of all, Susie – hearing you read my book out loud is one of the blessings of life. With every breath from your lips, you bring life and love to my words and remind me that God has blessed this effort. You are a treasure.

To my AMG family – Dan Penwell, Warren Baker, Rick Steele, Dale Anderson, Trevor Overcash, Joe Suter, and all the staff – even if I were to thank you a million times, it wouldn't be enough.

As always, I thank God for his Amazing Grace. I once was lost but now am found, was blind, but now I see.

Last, but certainly not least, I thank my departed father for his role in inspiring me to include a powerful theme in this book. Even as he lay on his deathbed, his feeble yet deeply meaningful words ignited an amazing string of miracles. Now I know the meaning behind the twelve people, the ten faithless wanderers, and the two precious copper coins.

AUTHOR'S NOTE

Enoch's Ghost is the second book in the ***Oracles of Fire*** series. It is a sequel to the ***Dragons in our Midst*** series and picks up the story where *Eye of the Oracle* and *Tears of a Dragon* ended.

Here is how the stories line up in chronological order. The ***Oracles of Fire*** series is in boldfaced type.

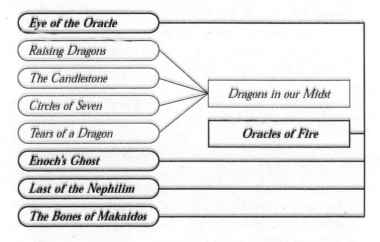

Readers who have not delved into *Dragons in our Midst* or *Eye of the Oracle* will have no trouble understanding and enjoying *Enoch's Ghost* if they read the recap at the end of this book first. This story extends earlier adventures that will lead readers into a multidimensional land, a fascinating journey guided by the *Oracles of Fire*.

CONTENTS

CONTENTS

x

ENOCH'S ORACLE

When fathers, sons, and daughters part,
When hearts are cut and hewn,
No solace can replace the love
No song can bind the wound.

For blood that spills from shredded hearts
Can never be restored
When love is lost, when trust is torn,
When shattered faith is poured.

Will pride forever break the bond
Of love that spawned a birth?
Will memories of death be lost
When life sprouts new from earth?

O what will soothe betrayal's pain
And what will smooth the scar?
Can sacrificial blood rain down
The healing from afar?

A witness goes to spy the land
With nine more flaunting pride,
But giants seize their quaking hearts,
And faith is cast aside.

Yet two bear witness to the truth;
They trust in God afresh
To catch their souls and take them home
Should giants slay their flesh.

These giants born of demons' seed
Will cast a net to snare
The holy city high above
And snatch it from the air.

O who will stand within the gap,
And who will sacrifice?
O who will bleed for love alone,
And who will pay the price?

A widow lays her copper coins,
Two mites, her treasure store,
While hypocrites parade their gifts,
Mere sweepings from their floor.

The humble gift restores anew
The hope when life began,
When fathers, sons, and daughters clasp
Their hands of love again.

But will the daughters take the gift
Of coppers from the king,
The wounds that pour his saving blood
To heal the family ring?

PROLOGUE

The great dragon's eyes glowed with blood-red luminescence, and his voice rumbled like distant thunder. "Mardon, the time is short. When will the giants awaken to bring about our final victory?"

"Soon, very soon." Standing on the edge of a precipice, Mardon held a shining rope of gold, as taut as a harp string and almost as slender. It stretched across a chasm that lay before him, the canyon path of a magma river far below. A mere stone's throw away, a nebulous figure held to the golden line from another precipice, too far to detect any features of form or face. The barest of glows emanated from the slow-moving river, casting reddish light and illuminating the rutted walls and jagged ceiling of their underground cavern.

"Sapphira's latest use of her power," Mardon continued, "has allowed me to draw Earth and Hades so close, only a mere thread of dimensional space separates them. A few more pulls should bind them as one. Even then, I cannot guess how perfectly the two dimensions will combine. The dead souls should eventually

1

become as they were when they were alive, but we might have to wait for the merged realms to reach a state of equilibrium before everything settles." He strained against the line again, letting out an almost inaudible grunt. "That's why the synchronization has to be precise. The realms must not touch until the timers are ready to expire and the escape route for our giants is complete."

The dragon beat its wings and joined Mardon at the edge of the chasm. "Leave the escape route to me. The giants will need to loosen their muscles after such a lengthy nap, so I envision a staircase that will lead them to the light."

Mardon pulled the line, drawing the other precipice a few inches closer. With every painstaking inch, the ground trembled, raising the crunching complaint of stone grinding against stone. "An excellent idea," he said. "Many steps to strengthen their resolve ... and their anger."

"And then our next step."

"The greatest step. When I finish creating my tower to draw Heaven down to Earth, my plan will be complete."

"*Your* plan?" The dragon's eyes blazed. "I sowed the seeds of this plan long before you were born, the seeds of Eden that I gave to Samyaza's wench, Lilith. It was she who first cultivated the Nephilim. You merely took her place in my grand scheme."

Mardon averted his eyes and focused on the narrowing chasm. "I see. Morgan never told me where the seedlings came from."

"Giving credit to others was not in her nature."

"True enough." Mardon turned back to the dragon. "I am therefore pleased to give you credit. When Heaven meets Earth, and I am installed as the mediator of the final covenant, you will be a chief prince."

The dragon flashed an odd smile, toothy enough to be menacing, yet it carried a hint of amusement. "Beware of overconfidence. There are forces, human forces, that can stop us."

Mardon shook his head. "Sapphira's power is insufficient without her sister, and no one has seen Acacia in years."

"Do not underestimate an Oracle of Fire. You consider Sapphira a mere seedling who has outgrown her pot, but she is far more powerful. She has already meddled in too many of my affairs for my liking."

"Trying to kill Sapphira is dangerous," Mardon said. "It means death to any who shed her blood."

"We need not kill her as long as she remains ignorant." The dragon raised his head and looked into the cavern's dim upper recesses. "Yet, there is another who could ruin our plans. She is capable of discerning the meaning of your need for building a vortex connection between Heaven and Earth."

"Thigocia's child?" Mardon laid a hand on his head. "I have forgotten her name."

"Ashley Stalworth. If she alerts her mother, then all is lost."

Mardon pulled again. The rope vibrated, shaking off golden sparks that floated into the chasm. "Do you have a remedy?"

"Divide and conquer. While you build your tower, I will deal with Thigocia."

"And what of Ashley?"

The dragon's eyes flashed once more, this time with a glow of triumph. "For now, she is under my control. Fear has kept her from the light, and I intend to keep it that way."

3

CHAPTER

RETURN OF THE DRAGON

D ragon riding isn't all it's cracked up to be," Ashley grumbled. As she retied her hood, a thick cloud bank enveloped her in white mist, dampening her coat sleeves and drawing a shiver from her chilled arms. She clutched Thigocia's protruding spine with a gloved hand and slid forward, ducking under the streaming fog as she reseated herself. Wearing long underwear and thick denim jeans turned out to be a lifesaver. After over a thousand miles of flying, dragon scales felt like broken concrete under her backside.

She lifted the GPS locator in her palm and brushed a layer of mist from the display with her thumb. On the playing-card-sized monitor, a red dot pulsed in the middle of a blue splotch on the map. Each beat of Thigocia's enormous wings jostled the screen, but she managed to hold the unit steady enough to figure out their ground position as they flew a few thousand feet above Montana's highlands.

She swung her head around to the pair of teenaged passengers seated behind her and shouted through the whistling wind, "I think we're right over Flathead Lake!"

Thigocia dropped suddenly through an air pocket.

"Whoa!" Ashley yelled, squeezing her legs tightly around the dragon's neck.

Finally, Thigocia caught stable air with her powerful wings. "Sorry about that!"

"No problem," Karen shouted. "I lost my breakfast an hour ago!"

Walter pulled down the bill of his baseball cap and regripped the spine between him and Ashley. Scrunching his thick, wet eyebrows, he peered down into the blanket of clouds. "Any sign of attack jets coming to greet us?"

"No worries." Ashley rubbed the dragon's thick hide, still yelling to overcome the roar. "Thigocia's scales would skew the radar echoes. She probably looks like a wandering albatross on the screen."

Karen, sitting behind Walter, the wind whipping her dampened red hair around her freckled face, pulled on his sleeve. "We're more likely to see gawking bird watchers than attack jets."

"Too bad. I was kind of hoping to get a jet to follow us." Walter leaned to the side and pointed past Thigocia's swinging tail. "Can you imagine how a pilot's eyes would bug out if he came up behind us and—"

"Hey! Not so far!" Karen grabbed Walter's back scabbard and pulled him upright. "I only have you to hold onto."

Ashley pressed the GPS unit against her chest. "Walter! Don't scare us like that!"

"Sorry." Walter's blue eyes sparkled, and a wide grin spread across his boyish face. "I guess I'm not cut out to be an albatross."

Rolling her eyes, Ashley turned her attention back to the locator. After flying so far, mostly in the middle of the night, and having to endure Walter's never-ending jokes and Karen's constant fretting over his safety, it was time to get their feet back on the ground for good. Yet, even at ground level, life had been a pain – drinking water from streams, eating berries and nuts as well as wild game Thigocia would capture and cook, and wearing the same clothes for days on end. Everyone was ready for a change.

Walter sighed. "So how far is it to the mountain?"

"We're coming up from the south on this path," Ashley said, tracing a line on the grid with her finger, "so, if we don't have to take a detour to stay in the clouds, we'll probably get there in about ten minutes."

Walter leaned into the beating wind. "All I heard was 'ten minutes'."

"Right!" Ashley said, raising her voice to compete with the strengthening gale. "Give or take a minute!"

"Good!" Karen blew a strand of hair from her brow. "I'm getting soaked."

Bending her long, scaly neck, Thigocia brought her head close to her riders. Thin strings of smoke swirled away from her flared nostrils. "When we get there, I will give you the Sahara treatment. You will be warm and dry in no time."

"Unless it's raining," Walter added.

Karen shivered and slid closer to Walter. "Or snowing."

Ashley tapped her jaw with her fingers and spoke into the breeze. "Larry, what's the weather forecast for the Flathead Lake area in Montana?"

A computerized voice hummed through Ashley's tooth-embedded transmitter. "Cloudy and cool today, high in the fifties. Rain changing to freezing rain tonight, low in the thirties."

"Not good." Ashley pulled a soaked tissue from her jacket and wiped her nose. "I hope we can find shelter, or we'll all die of pneumonia."

"An excellent suggestion, O daughter of a dragon. The official forecast calls for a sixty per cent chance of precipitation, but that seems low to me. Based on

7

the satellite presentation, I calculate a sixty-three-point-seven per cent probability. On a scale—"

"No!" Ashley shouted. "Not another dragon scale joke!"

"Your mind-reading capabilities are working perfectly, O maiden of the mailed membrane. On a scale of one to ten, your mental perception rates a nine point two."

"I don't read minds!" Ashley moaned.

Walter laughed. "Good one, Larry. You slipped in your scale joke anyway."

Ashley swung her head toward Walter. "You heard him?"

"Barely. It sounds like a buzz coming from your ears, like the highest note in a bumblebee choir's scale."

"Cool!" Karen chirped. "Another scale joke!"

"Walter! Cut it out!" Ashley scowled at the GPS unit. "It's a good thing we're almost there. Another night of this craziness and I'd be ready to check into Arlo's psychiatric hospital."

Karen reached over Walter and patted Ashley on the back. "Well, they do have a vacancy now that we sprang Arlo, but you probably wouldn't get any treatment. Thigocia scared the workers so bad with that blast of flames, I don't think they'll ever come back."

"Yeah," Walter agreed. "I guess you could say Thigocia fired them!"

Walter and Karen gave each other a high five, while Ashley just shook her head and groaned. When Walter and Karen finally stopped laughing, Ashley called out to Thigocia. "Mother! Get ready to descend!"

Thigocia curled her neck back again. "Ashley, I am not a dog to be commanded. A bit of courtesy is always appropriate when addressing your elders."

Walter whispered into Ashley's ear. "And your mum is about as elder as you can get."

8

"Speaking of courtesy ... ," Ashley whispered back, glaring at Walter. She rubbed the dragon's neck scales and sighed. "I'm sorry, Mother. It's just that five days of flying with these characters has made me crawl right to the edge of sanity."

"I fell over the edge," Karen said.

"I jumped," Walter added. "And I can't seem to climb back up."

Thigocia's scaly brow wrinkled sympathetically. "We are all tired, but we will soon be able to rest without fear of being discovered. The mountain site is remote enough for us to remain in hiding, but we will have to descend quickly in order to keep our approach a secret."

"Bring it on!" Walter pushed his cap tightly over his head. "Riding a dragon roller coaster in the daylight sure beats all the slow night flying we've been doing."

He grabbed the spine with both hands, and Karen wrapped her arms around him. For the moment, except for the whistling wind and slow flapping of dragon wings, all was silent, allowing Ashley to concentrate on the map. When the blinking dot glided across the border of the blue expanse and into a green region, she raised her hand. "Okay, Mother, we should be right over it. Time to make your dive."

A low growl rumbled from the dragon's throat. "Ashley?"

She winced and leaned forward. "*Please* make your dive?"

Thigocia began folding in her wings. "Hang on!" As she angled downward, her scarlet laser eyes pierced the clouds below.

Ashley hugged the spine and lowered her head. Suddenly, it seemed that the whole world fell out from under her. Her body floated upward. Her stomach squeezed the breath out of her lungs. With streams of cloudy vapour whipping by, she tightened her grasp, forced in a chest full of air, and shouted into the gale. "You two okay back there?"

"Yeah!" Walter choked out. "Except I lost my cap, and Karen's strangling me!"

Ashley ducked lower. "Just hold tight!"

When they broke through the clouds, Thigocia pulled up and banked to one side. "I sense a hint of danger," she said as she coasted into a circular descent.

"Where?" Ashley yelled through the swirling breeze. "How far?"

"It is difficult to measure. The intensity is low, and the location seems vague."

Ashley peered at the mountainous terrain below – wooded peaks, plunging slopes, and two river valleys nestled between high, uneven ridges. Autumn had stripped many trees to a few stubborn brown leaves, while bushy firs and ponderosa pines infused the mountain with lush greenery. "Should we land?"

"Yes. We must fulfil our reason for coming, and if a battle ensues, I cannot fight with three untrained riders. Besides, our warrior needs firm footing if we expect him to use his weapon."

Ashley glanced back at Walter. His expression had hardened. His eyes flashing, he reached over his shoulder and grabbed Excalibur's hilt. He slid it out part-way, as if checking its readiness, then returned his grip to the dragon's spine.

As Thigocia approached a mountaintop, her eyebeams sliced into the shadowy, forested slopes. The blanket of clouds hovered low as she drew up her wings to angle sharply toward a small grass-covered clearing at the very top of the rounded peak.

Holding her breath, Ashley leaned into the dragon's dive, trying to duck under the torrent of fog-soaked air. Seconds later, Thigocia thumped against the ground, making a loud squishing noise as she skidded through a carpet of wet grass.

Walter slid down her damp scales, avoiding her beating wings, and landed feet first. He whipped Excalibur from his back scabbard and pivoted slowly, firmly gripping the hilt of the sword with both hands. Although no sunlight penetrated the low cloud bank, the blade shimmered, emanating an aura that coated the silvery metal.

Thigocia lowered her head to the ground, making her neck into a stairway. Ashley grabbed a duffel bag strap from her mother's spine and clambered down the scaly ladder, followed closely by Karen. They rushed to Walter's side, turning with him as he scanned the encircling line of denuded trees and tall conifers that lay only a stone's throw away in every direction. Although a hint of wood smoke tinged the air, no sign of fire arose from the thousands of acres of forest that spread across the distant hills.

"I don't see anyone," he said, twisting back toward the dragon. "Do you still sense danger?"

Thigocia's ears rotated, like satellite receivers searching for a signal. "Something sinister ... not close at hand ... perhaps among the trees, but I saw nothing in the forest as we descended."

"Something invisible?" Karen asked. "Maybe a demon of some kind?"

"We destroyed the Watchers." Thigocia snorted twin plumes of smoke into the air. "I doubt that any other demons would be foolish enough to seek a confrontation."

"As long as the danger stays on the sidelines," Walter said, lowering Excalibur's point to the ground, "let's get started on what we came here to do."

"But first ..." Thigocia blew a hot dry breeze toward the three humans.

Walter spread out his arms, letting the desert-like wind flap his wet sleeves. "Ahhh! The Sahara treatment!"

Ashley and Karen stripped off their coats and basked in the drying flow.

"Can't beat this with a stick," Karen said, squeezing her eyes closed. "Ashley, I'm glad your mum is so full of hot air."

"Good one." Walter pointed at Karen and winked. "And it's a good thing she doesn't need a breath mint."

As Walter and Karen continued trading jokes about hot air and halitosis, Ashley rotated her body slowly and basked in the

11

luxurious breeze. She winced now and then at the heat and the inane jokes as she watched Walter playfully jabbing Karen. Would he ever grow out of his childish ways? He was a valiant warrior, but at times he seemed like such a kid. Still, it would be fun to join in, kind of let loose and laugh with them. She closed her eyes and shook her head. No. Someone had to be serious around here, so it might as well be her.

After a few minutes, the girls put their coats back on, now warm and dry. Walter patted Thigocia on her side. "You're better than a thousand hair dryers, and we didn't have to worry about popping a circuit!"

"Time to get to work!" Picking up her bag, Ashley strode through lush, calf-high grass until she reached a thinner section with only a short carpet of greenery. Something underneath had obviously stunted the growth. She scuffed her shoe across the soil, exposing a solid foundation. "There's a slab here," she said, looking back at her mother. "Was this our home site?"

"It has to be." Thigocia flicked her tail toward a tall oak. "That tree was next to your grandfather's bedroom window."

Ashley walked under the oak's dripping branches and ran her hand along the trunk's rough bark. Her fingers traced a deep furrow until they came across the outline of a heart. Stooping, she gazed at the initials carved in the centre but could only make out the first letter of each pair – T and H.

"Timothy and Hannah," she whispered.

A trickle of memories seeped into her mind, a lanky man lifting her into the tree's lowest bough. As his brown eyes gleamed, a smile radiated from his noble face, but as thin veils darkened the scene, he backed away, his body fading as he withdrew. With her little bare toes wiggling in front of her, she reached out a pair of chubby hands, and a childlike voice squeaked out.

"Daddy!" Ashley said softly, tears welling as she dug a fingernail into the bark. "Daddy, come back!"

Her mind's eye still watching from the tree, a window came into view, white drapes drawn closed on the inside. Her thoughts drew her into the bedroom, and, against the adjacent wall, she found a single bed covered with a blue downy quilt. Another man, an older man this time, sat on the edge and gestured for her to come to his lap.

Ashley whispered the nickname she gave to the man after her father died. "Daddy!" He had become a replacement daddy, a kind but sickly old man who assuaged the pain in a little girl's heart. After a few seconds, the image of her departed grandfather also faded away in darkening shadows.

New memories flowed. As a two-year-old girl, she leaped into her grandfather's outstretched arms, a book tightly clutched to her frilly nightgown. He took the huge volume and opened to the first page, squinting at the opening lines. "Are you sure you want to read this? It's really dark and scary."

She ran her finger across a sketch of a solitary man walking in the midst of a gloomy forest. The black-and-white drawing seemed so real, she could almost hear his feet shuffling through the path's tangled weeds. "I already read it to myself, but I didn't understand all of it."

Her grandfather slid his hand over the drawing. "So you want me to explain it?"

Little Ashley nodded. "Especially the scary parts. They gave me goosey bumps."

Withdrawing a pair of reading glasses from his pocket, he sighed. "Okay, let's see what this says …"

Midway in the journey of our life,
I came to myself in a dark wood,
For the straight way was lost.
Ah, how hard it is to tell
The nature of that wood, savage, dense and harsh.

13

The very thought of it renews my fear!
It is so bitter death is hardly more so.
But to set forth the good I found
I will recount the other things I saw.
How I came there I cannot really tell,
I was so full of sleep
When I forsook the one true way.

Ashley nodded slowly, recognizing the words being replayed in her mind. "Dante's *Inferno*," she said out loud. That story had haunted her dreams for years, a plunge into the depths of hell where she witnessed the torments of the damned – souls who would suffer for eternity. With every succeeding circle of punishment, she pictured herself in the place of the tortured, stripped naked and pummelled by demons century after century without hope of rescue. Even her cries for mercy would be echoed by the mocking curses of Satan's henchmen – prayers answered by obscenities.

She shook the thoughts away, and her flow of memories jumped to another scene – the same bedroom, but this time her grandfather was rushing her across the room, carrying her in the crook of his arm. With his free hand, he thrust open the window and threw a duffle bag outside. Then, after lifting her over the sill, he whispered, "Wait at the tree!"

Toddling in pink slippers, she hurried to the oak and peeked out from behind the trunk. Her grandfather scrambled through the window, snatched up the duffle bag, and caught her into his arm as he passed by, barely slowing down at all. Seconds later, they were standing at the edge of the forest. As little Ashley watched the house, puffs of white colouring her excited breaths, her grandfather pulled a cap, two boots, and a pair of mittens from the bag. "It could be a long hike," he said, "but we have to get to a phone to warn your parents."

14

He pushed one of the mittens over her stiff, frigid hand, and nodded toward a path in the woods where a matrix of spindly shadows criss-crossed a leaf-strewn trail. Her grandfather's breathing grew laboured as he stretched the ski cap over her ears, his own breaths puffing streams of white. "We'll follow it ... until we get ... to the creek bed ... but we have to throw them off the trail ... by walking through the water."

Ashley laid a hand on his chest. "Is your heart hurting again, Dada?"

He took a deep breath and covered her hand with his own. "It was, but it's getting better now."

As her grandfather replaced her slippers with boots, Ashley looked back at the house. One of the men came out and pulled a gasoline can from a car, then went back inside. "If those men catch us," she said, gazing at her grandfather again, "would they kill us?"

Raising a finger to his lips, he whispered, "I think they would. That's why we're hiding."

"If they find us, and kill us ..." Her lips puckered, and a tear rolled down her cheek. "Would I go to Heaven?"

He moved the clasped hands from his chest to hers. "I told you about how to get to Heaven. I've sung you to sleep with 'Amazing Grace' a hundred times, but you wouldn't believe me."

She wiped the tear, and her voice pitched higher. "I'll believe whatever you say. I just don't want to go to Hell."

"Of· course you don't, and you won't." He brushed away another tear with his thumb. "Just listen for God's voice and always follow the light, and he will lead you to Heaven." He kissed her forehead tenderly. "Can you do that?"

Sniffing, she gave him a slow, uneasy nod. "I think so."

He patted her on the head and inhaled deeply. "I think my heart is strong enough now." Picking up the bag, he took her hand, and the two hustled down the leafy slope. The forest darkened with every step – downward, always downward. Fear

15

gripped her heart as visions of Dante's demons haunted every shadow along the way.

Ashley's memories jumped again, this time resurrecting a dense forest, a dark starless sky, and the sound of her grandfather sloshing through a shallow brook. With her cheek on his shoulder, her gaze stayed locked on the bouncing trees behind them, each one seeming to draw a sword, just as those two intruders had drawn theirs, the two men who had invaded her home and chased her and her grandfather away.

Suddenly, a loud explosion rumbled through the woods. She jerked her head toward the sound just in time to see a huge fireball billow into the sky and then disperse in a million orange and yellow sparks. Glowing cinders flew in all directions and twinkled like copper-coloured stars.

Her grandfather covered her eyes with one of his big, soft hands. "It's going to be okay," he whispered. "It's going to be okay." But the despair in his voice said otherwise. It wasn't going to be okay, and even at her young age, she knew her life was going to change forever.

"Earth to Ashley!"

Ashley blinked.

"Come in, Ashley!" Walter waved his hand in front of her eyes. "Are you okay?"

Ashley gave him a brief nod. Walter's voice sounded like her grandfather's, an echo of love travelling across thousands of lonely nights, bringing comfort, yet drawing tears. *Are you okay?* the voice repeated, tugging at her heart as the memories streamed away from her mind. She firmed her chin. It was a terrible time to cry. She had to stay strong.

"You zoned out," Walter continued. "What's rattling up there in that souped-up brain of yours?"

She brushed away a tear. "I finally remember the night when the slayers killed my parents."

16

"Really? Any clues that'll help us find your father?"

She shook her head. "Not yet. Maybe searching around will trigger another memory."

"There's not much here to search through," Walter said, kicking a brick fragment. "Someone really cleaned this place up – no broken drywall, no plumbing, not even the kitchen sink, but your mother found where the fireplace used to be. She says that's important."

With Karen standing at her side, Thigocia pawed the dirt at a raised portion of earth on the opposite side of the foundation. "We hid the keepsake box under the hearth. If it is still here, it should be under one of the bricks."

Ashley pulled the bag strap higher on her shoulder and hustled with Walter to the site. While Walter traced the edges of the brick layer with a pocket knife, Ashley stroked her mother's neck. "Seeing this place brought back a lot of memories, including what happened the night you died." She pulled out her tissue and dabbed her nose. "I was in the woods when our house exploded."

Thigocia's ears twitched, and her eyes darted between the foundation and the forest. "When we finish here, I will tell you more about that night, but I dare not lose my concentration while I am monitoring the danger. It seems to be slowly increasing."

"I got it!" Walter called. He pried up the edge of a loose brick and began tossing fragments to the side. When the opening was about six inches square, he plunged his hand into a hole and withdrew a black metal case about the size of a music box, bent on the top and rusted along every edge. Rising to his feet, he handed it to Ashley. "I guess you should do the honours."

Ashley glanced at her mother and slowly opened the box. Inside, there were four compartments. One held a folded piece of paper; the second, a gold ring with a mounted red gem; and the third, three coins – a dime and two pennies. The fourth compartment was empty.

"Is that a rubellite?" Karen asked, pointing at the gem.

17

"That was my ring." Thigocia lifted her clawed hand. "I stopped wearing it when I realized that Devin was still alive and stalking me."

A breeze lifted the folded paper, but Karen pinched the edge and kept it in place.

Thigocia touched Ashley's back with her wing. "The paper is the telegram Gabriel sent to congratulate us on your birth."

Walter pushed the lid farther open, and it broke free from its rusty hinges. "Ooops! Sorry!" He set the lid carefully on the ground. "I was trying to get a better look at the coins. Why were you saving them?"

"When we left the hospital after Ashley was born, Timothy bought a newspaper and coffee from an elderly street vendor. When the man gave Timothy those coins in change, he closed Timothy's fingers around them, and I will never forget what he said. 'The dime represents the ten spies who quaked at the sight of giants in the Promised Land. They are chaff in the wind, a dime a dozen. But the pennies represent the two faithful witnesses who believed God would conquer the Nephilim. They are the widow's mites – copper coins, yet rare gems – a gift that Jesus declared far more valuable than the treasure of kings. Keep these coins and never forget God's promises.'"

Ashley plucked the dime from the box. "What should we do with them? We can't bury them now."

"Put them in your pocket," Thigocia said. "The box is worthless, so there is no sense taking it along. We can store the telegram and the ring in your bag's waterproof pouch."

After sliding the coins into her jeans pocket, Ashley handed the box to Walter, withdrew the telegram, and unfolded it. Holding the worn edges carefully, she read out loud. "Congratulations on the birth of your daughter. May she live in peace and learn the secret behind the Oracles of Fire. Signed, Gabriel."

As she scanned the logo and address at the top of the page, she tapped her jaw. "Larry, I need you to contact the Western Union office on Stephens Avenue in Missoula. Find out the data source of the request for the telegram Gabriel sent to my birth hospital on the day I was born. It says it came from Glasgow, but I have my doubts. If they won't give the source to you, go ahead and snoop in their database if you can. It could be a matter of life or death."

"Consider it done."

"What? No witty reply?"

"On a scale of one to ten, your tone of voice registers a nine point six on the 'I'm-totally-stressed-out' meter. It is not safe for man or machine to test your limits at this time."

"Good choice," Ashley said. "Give me your report as soon as you can."

Walter nudged Karen. "Larry sneaked in a scale joke again."

"Hush!" Ashley elbowed his ribs, but she couldn't keep a smile from breaking out. "Or feel my fire-breathing wrath!" She held back a grimace. Walter didn't laugh. Was that joke too lame? Shaking her head at her lousy timing, she propped the telegram in front of Thigocia's nose, but not close enough to risk singeing the page. "Does it make sense to you that Gabriel would reveal his location like this? Glasgow is huge, but why even give a hint?"

"It would not make sense at all, Makaidos ... I mean, Timothy and I asked that very question."

"Could it be a clue to where he really was?" Walter asked. "Some kind of family code? You know, maybe Glasgow means some other city."

"There was no code." Thigocia's red eyes seemed to darken as she recalled her story. "We left Gabriel near Glasgow with one of the Circle of Knights who took him to Patrick where he stayed for a time. We hoped he would be safe while we led the slayers to the States to get them off track. Patrick later told us that Gabriel disappeared, and before this telegram came, no one had heard from him for forty years."

19

Karen pointed at the note. "So what's that stuff Gabriel wrote about Oracles of Fire?"

Thigocia's draconic lips turned upward, revealing a gentle smile. "While he was in Dragons' Rest, Timothy met a girl named Sapphira who told him she was an Oracle of Fire, but he only knew that these oracles would bring about an end to Dragons' Rest. He never saw her again, but we know that Dragons' Rest was destroyed, so this girl might have had something to do with it. Maybe finding her is the key to finding Gabriel."

Ashley refolded the telegram. "Or maybe even finding my father." After sliding the paper into an inner pocket in her bag, she carefully lifted the ring from the box and laid it in her palm. "Mother," she said, arching her brow, "I already have a rubellite ring, but may I wear yours?"

"I would be honoured. I would have eventually given it to you anyway."

20

Ashley slid the band over her right ring finger, but it wouldn't pass her knuckle, so she moved it to her little finger. As she closed her fist, the rubellite seemed to glow with a deeper, more vibrant red. "Very strange," she said, passing it in front of her eyes. "It's almost like it changed when I put it on."

Karen pointed at Ashley's left hand. "Are you going to keep that one?"

"My other ring?" Ashley pulled it off and laid it in Karen's palm. "You can have it."

As Karen slid the ring on her finger, her face beamed. "I'll take good care of it. I promise."

Thigocia's ears jerked around. Her eyes flamed as she growled, "I sense an increase in danger. Our safety could well be in jeopardy."

Walter dropped the box and jerked out Excalibur. "Which direction?"

"There!" Thigocia blew a dart of fire, scorching the grass a mere ten feet away. "Where my living room used to be!"

Walter waved the sword back and forth. "I don't see anything!"

Ashley pulled up her bag, withdrew a photometer, and pointed it in the direction her mother had attacked. Tapping her jaw, she called out, "Larry, are you reading this? I estimate a distance of ten feet."

Larry's familiar voice buzzed through Ashley's mouth. "To quote an oft-quoted movie, 'There is a disturbance in the force'. The wave frequency resembles what we have seen in the wake of a cross-dimensional rift."

"The wake? You mean something just left this dimension?"

"Or is about to enter it. The strength of the field increases for point seven seconds, then lessens for the same amount of time before going back toward its peak — a sine wave."

Ashley clicked a dial on the photometer and frowned at the flashing digits on its tiny screen. "If it's sinusoidal, then the dimensional barrier is probably stable, at least for now."

21

"Affirmative. Stability, however, does not mean the barrier has not been breached. Something has triggered the dragon's sensitivity."

"You're right." Ashley laid a hand on Thigocia's neck. "Mother must be detecting danger from the other dimension. Something's getting through."

Walter raised the sword high. A brilliant beam of light blazed from the tip and pierced the low clouds. "I set Excalibur on deep fat fry, but I can't cook what I can't see."

As Thigocia sniffed the air, her eyes brightened again to fiery scarlet. "It feels strange – powerful ... crafty ... sinister."

Larry's buzzing voice spiked. "The curve pattern has shifted. The peak energy is growing rapidly, and the entire field is destabilizing."

"I see that!" Although her hand shook, Ashley kept the meter pointed at the same spot. "It's going nuts!"

Walter set his feet in a battle stance as he waved the sword's beam across the field. An explosion of light energy erupted from the ground. Streams of sparks spewed in arching tentacles that seemed to reach out for Ashley and company before falling to the wet grass in a sizzling shower.

As fountains of energy continued to shoot upward, Walter drew the sword back, ready to strike. A mass of blackness appeared in the centre of the fountain, eclipsing the brilliant light. Ribbons of smoke arose from the falling sparks and created stringy black columns that masked the growing shadow.

An acrid film coated Ashley's tongue. She coughed and spat. "Get back!" she shouted, pulling Karen's elbow. "Those fumes could be deadly!"

The three humans back-pedalled into clearer air. Thigocia beat her wings, fanning the poisonous stench toward the erupting sparks. The smoke seemed to attach to the central swelling mass, like black papier-mâché plastered on an inflating balloon. As it grew, limbs emerged – four legs, a wing, then another wing, and finally a long, spine-covered tail.

CHAPTER

FALLING

Karen grabbed Walter's sleeve. "It's a dragon!"

Walter stepped between her and the fountain of sparks. "It's definitely not a fireworks show."

With the smoke decreasing, Thigocia lowered her wings and shuffled back to join the others. "Its size would indicate a male, but I do not recognize him. He is covered with residue, and his form is indistinct."

"I assume the source of the danger has arrived," Ashley said.

"Definitely. But it is a strange sort of danger. It does not seem ready to attack and kill. It is more subtle ... much more subtle."

Walter set Excalibur's beam directly over the dragon's head. "Stay where you are!" he shouted. "Or this beam will turn you into dragon bacon!"

Amid the dying sparks, the dragon shook his body and cast off his black coat, revealing shimmering red scales. With its mouth wide open, its broad head shot forward. A flaming rope reeled out and snapped across Walter's arm, a fiery bullwhip that cracked like a rifle shot and shook Excalibur from his grip.

Walter lunged for the sword, but the dragon spewed out another fiery rope and popped the whip near the hilt as it lay on the ground.

Karen dashed forward and, sliding through the grass feet first, kicked Excalibur over to Walter.

"Way to go!" He snatched it up with his uninjured hand.

Karen leaped to her feet and rushed back to Ashley, calling out, "Fry him, Walter!"

Ashley wrapped her arms around Karen and kissed her on the head. "Don't ever scare me like that again!"

Shaking his wounded wrist, Walter took a step closer to his attacker. "What do you say, lizard? War or peace?"

"You do not need a weapon," the dragon growled. "I will not harm you."

Ashley pulled on her mother's wing. "Do you know him? Can you fight him?"

"I …" Thigocia stumbled backwards. "I cannot believe my own eyes."

A smile spread across the dragon's scaly face. "Surprised to see me, my long-lost niece? Or have you simply forgotten your beloved father-in-law after all these centuries?"

"Father-in-law?" Ashley squinted at the huge red beast. "Arramos?"

Arramos bowed his head. "At least my granddaughter knows who I am, and she has never met me before."

"If you mean harm to these children," Thigocia said, baring her teeth, "I will fight you to the death! If you are who you claim to be, then you know I am a warrior to be reckoned with. Even if I cannot defeat you, I will exact a toll from your flesh."

Arramos let out a deep-throated chuckle. "Now, Thigocia," he said, in a condescending tone, "this is no time for theatrics or

24

modern trash talk. I have come to bring enlightenment, not harm."

"Impossible!" A shower of sparks flew from Thigocia's nostrils. "My danger sense has never been wrong."

"You sense danger because you fear what I have to say." Arramos swept his spiny tail across the old foundation. "When you saw my familiar shape materializing, the sight of me chilled your heart, because you sensed that I would bear a message that would crumble the basis of your faith and plunge you into a chasm of doubt." His eyes flamed red as he edged closer. "Thigocia, what you fear is the truth."

Thigocia backed away a step. "I do not fear the truth! I came here to *learn* the truth, to find clues to what happened to my husband and my son."

Arramos seemed to glide toward her, closing the gap. "But have you forgotten your daughter? Why do you not seek for her?"

Thigocia blinked. "Roxil? She is alive?"

"Indeed, she is. Why have you forsaken her?"

"I ... I never forsook her." As Thigocia backed away again, thin smoke rose from her snout. "I thought she was dead."

For every inch Thigocia retreated, Arramos advanced two. "You thought the same about your husband, yet you seek him with all your heart. Have you abandoned your daughter because of her lack of faith in humankind?"

"Abandoned? But I never knew ... I mean—"

Arramos came within a few feet of Thigocia, his eyebeams now shooting directly into her eyes, seeming to lock the two dragons in visual combat. "Come now. You have been alive for thousands of years. You have seen the Maker rescue from floods, famines, and fire. Your own husband testified to the Maker's rescue from the futility of Dragons' Rest, yet you took no thought that he could do the same for your daughter." His red scales flashed. "Perhaps your love for her has waned because of her rebellion against you and your mate. Were you so wounded by her offence that you have turned your back on her?"

"I have not turned my back, I—"

Ashley stepped in between the two dragons, breaking the eye lock. "Mother, don't listen to him! He's attacking your character to deflect the focus from the question at hand. It's called *ad hominem*, an old debate technique."

Arramos cast his eyebeams on Ashley. "Ah, yes! My granddaughter, the genius anthrozil!" His smile returned, wide and toothy. "I must say that watching you through the years has swelled me with pride. Your amazing intelligence is becoming known around the world."

"And that's called bootlicking," Walter said. "You don't have to be a genius to see that."

"Exactly." Ashley stepped out of Arramos's eyebeams. "Why don't you just get to the point? Why are you here, and what do you want with us?"

"Very well." Arramos switched off the beams and moved back far enough to address them all. "I have come to lead Thigocia to her daughter so we can all search for Makaidos. When we have four dragons together, we will be able to bring order to the world."

"Bring order to the world?" Ashley set a hand on her hip. "How do you propose to do that? Four dragons can't possibly defeat modern armies. Besides, why would we want dragons deciding what's right or wrong?"

Arramos furrowed his brow at Ashley and slowly stalked toward her as he spoke. "Are the decisions of humans creating a Utopia? Are you pleased with constant wars, terrorism, and the killing of innocents for selfish gain? Humans are so self-obsessed, they lust after sensual gratification to the point of participating in the most debased and disgusting behaviours imaginable." He halted his approach and spat a wad of fire on the ground near Ashley's feet, igniting a clump of grass. "The vermin of this world refuse to stoop so low. Rats know better than to kill their own young. It is time for dragons to bring sanity to the world, and soon we will have the means to enforce our will."

Rubbing out the tiny blaze with his shoe, Walter scowled at the dragon. "I don't like the sound of that. Sure, there are a lot of rats in this world, but I wouldn't want a bigger rat telling them what to do."

"Your offence is expected. You are human and therefore destined to submit and obey." Arramos turned back to Thigocia and Ashley. "The two of you, on the other hand, will take your places as queens in the new world order. This is your reward for choosing to keep your dragon essence when you could have become human."

Thigocia laid her wing over Walter's back. "My husband was convinced that the Maker created us to serve humanity. Our son, Goliath, rebelled and made war against the human race. Makaidos was a noble dragon, filled with integrity and truth. Goliath, though he was our scales and bones, was a demon-possessed liar." As she drew her wing back from Walter, she spat her own wad of fire on the ground. "Whom do you think I believe and trust?"

"You do well to honour my son," Arramos said. "He was noble, pure, and filled with integrity. Yet, much has changed since you last saw him, events that he could not have told you." He unfurled his wings. "I know where Roxil is. Let me take you to her, and you will learn that I speak the truth. There is a great danger brewing that I will reveal once I receive your compliance, but I cannot wait long."

Thigocia stretched out her wings as well. "If Roxil is alive, I will find her myself. The Maker will lead me to her."

Arramos's voice sharpened, spiced with a growl. "The Maker sent me to lead you to her. This is the answer to a prayer you could not even utter. Do not cast aside his favour and forsake your daughter once again."

"I do not believe you!" Thigocia swung her tail around and

27

thumped it on the grass near Arramos. "I will learn the truth without you. You have no monopoly on knowledge."

"Do not let your ignorance be magnified by your arrogance!" Arramos brought his head within a few feet of Thigocia's. His eyes blazed once again. "I cannot force you to obey the Maker, but I can make it more difficult for you to refuse."

Suddenly, the foundation began collapsing underneath Karen. She fell forward, clawing for solid ground. "Walter!" she screamed. "Help!"

Dropping the sword, Walter dove for her, but just as his fingers touched hers, she plunged out of sight into the darkness of a manhole-sized pit. As his momentum carried him into the opening, Ashley leaped for him, wrapped her arms around his ankles, and slid toward the hole. With a lightning-fast lunge, Thigocia snatched Walter's jacket with her teeth and yanked him back to safe ground, Ashley still hanging on.

28

The two teens scrambled to their feet. Walter grabbed Excalibur and pointed it at Arramos, his face as red as the dragon's scales. "Where is she?!"

Arramos blinked casually. "She is falling, so she is quite safe. Frightened out of her mind, I am sure, but unharmed." A new toothy smile spread across his face. "Until, of course, she hits the jagged rocks at the bottom."

"Hits the jagged rocks?" Walter shouted. "When?"

"Fifteen seconds." Arramos turned to Thigocia. "Will you come with me? All I need is your word, because I know you will not lie."

"You mean if I don't come with you ..."

"She will die in ten seconds."

"But how will you stop her from falling?"

"Five seconds!" Arramos thumped his tail. "Will your doubts cause her death?"

Thigocia bowed her head. "I will go!"

A silvery tongue flicked from Arramos's mouth. "A wise choice."

Brilliant light erupted from the depths of the pit, then disappeared in a flash. From far below, a loud crunching racket churned closer and closer. A steep rocky path appeared in the dim light, climbing upward and winding its way around a central stone column that arose along with it. When the path reached the upper edge, it moulded itself into stairs – steep, uneven stairs that descended in a tight spiral and disappeared in the darkness.

"Just follow the staircase," Arramos said, nodding at the spiral, "and you will find the girl at the bottom, safe and unharmed, but she will need your help to ascend."

Walter's face blazed even hotter. "You're the monster that made her fall!" Excalibur's beam shot from the end of the blade. "Why should we do anything you say?"

Arramos slapped his wrist again with his fiery rope, knocking the sword from his hand. "Will you stand here stubbornly and play the foolish child? You are free to insult me until your useless anger is appeased, but that will not help your friend while she lies at the bottom in need of your aid!"

As Walter rubbed the welt on his wrist, the scarlet colour spread to his ears. He bent over slowly and picked up Excalibur, glaring at Arramos but saying nothing. After resheathing the sword, he stepped gingerly on the first stair and looked back at Ashley and Thigocia. "Seems sturdy enough. Who's coming with me?"

"Wait a minute!" Ashley set her hands on her hips and leaned toward Arramos. "Using your convoluted logic, now that we're worried sick about Karen, we should just do anything you say. Give me one good reason to believe that this isn't a trap to get rid of us, too."

"Allow your mother to check," Arramos half closed his eyes. "If her danger-sensing ability is as unerring as she believes, you will learn that the way is safe."

Thigocia scanned the pit with her eyebeams, then pushed her

29

head into the darkness as far as she could. After sniffing for a few seconds, she withdrew and looked at Ashley. "I sense no danger, but who can tell how long that will last? And I cannot go with you to warn of any approaching danger. The opening is much too narrow for a dragon."

Ashley crossed her arms over her chest and tapped her foot on the ground. Another life-or-death decision. Should she go with Walter or not? Her mother would be able to take care of herself, wouldn't she? Still, Arramos seemed to have a lot more power than any other dragon, so who could tell what he might do to her? But Walter could run into all sorts of trouble, even with Excalibur. He wasn't exactly a superstar swordsman yet, and could he take care of Karen by himself? Wouldn't Karen feel better with her adoptive sister nearby?

Finally, Ashley took a deep breath and touched Thigocia's wing. "Mother, I'd better go with Walter. You understand, don't you?"

"Of course I understand, but where will you go after you get Karen, and how will I find you again?"

Ashley leaned close to her mother's ear and whispered so quietly, she could barely hear her own words. "I'm not sure, but if we're not here when you come back, go to the Bannisters' house and find Larry. I'll stay in touch with him through my tooth transmitter."

Walter joined the huddle. "Don't forget. I have a cell phone in my pocket. I don't know what kind of signal we'll have, but it should work once we're back up here."

A large tear dripped from Thigocia's eye and fell to the ground, a line of vapour rising in its wake. "Take care, my daughter. Losing you again would be more than I could bear."

Ashley reached into her pocket for her tissue and clenched it tightly. Her voice trembled. "Don't worry," she said, patting Walter on the back. "I have a warrior with me."

Unfurling her wings, Thigocia turned back to Arramos. "You

have my compliance. Before we depart, tell us about this great
danger you mentioned."

The male dragon's eyes widened. Tiny dark circles formed at
the centre of his red pupils. "An ancient enemy is plotting to
merge Heaven and Earth, which will likely bring the most terrible cataclysm the world has ever seen. He is crafty and powerful, and humans will be unable to stop him, so we dragons must
go to battle against him before we can take our place as global
peacemakers."

Thigocia nodded. "Lead on, Arramos, if that is your real
name. If your word is true, there is no reason to delay. If it is false,
then I want to learn of your treachery as soon as possible while
keeping you in my targeting sites."

"O ye of little faith," Arramos growled. "Soon you will learn
the truth." He beat his wings and lifted off the ground.

As the two dragons rose toward the low-lying clouds, Ashley
and Walter gazed at their sleek, graceful forms. "Think he's telling
the truth?"

"About Roxil or about the so-called danger?"

"Either one." Walter's eyes stayed focused on the dragons as
they shrank in the distance. "That Heaven and Earth merger
sounds pretty drastic."

"The Roxil story could be true," she said, "but the Heaven
thing is too far-fetched to believe. Even if Heaven exists, you can't
lasso it and pull it down from the sky."

"Good point."

Ashley picked up the duffle bag and checked inside for her
photometer. Yes, she had put it next to her nearly empty bottle of
water. "You know, I still can't get over it."

Walter shifted his gaze to Ashley. "Can't get over what?"

"Well ..." She pushed her toe into the soft turf. "It's kind of
hard to explain, so maybe we'd better get going. Karen's waiting."

Walter took a step down into the stairwell. "Give it a try

while we're going down. I'll listen." He turned and marched into the dim passage.

Ashley followed, hurrying to keep up with his quick pace. "I guess ..." She paused as she tried not to let her voice bounce with her body. "I guess I feel kind of freakish. I can't get over the fact that I'm the daughter of a dragon."

"Actually," Walter said as he withdrew Excalibur from his scabbard, "I'd be surprised if you weren't."

"What?" Ashley jumped down two steps at a time to catch up. "What's that supposed to mean?"

Walter stopped and turned. "Uh ... It means you're strong and brave, I guess. Isn't that true of dragons?"

The light from the land above faded away, leaving them with only Excalibur's delicate white glow. She set a hand on her hip, trying to read his expression, but shadows veiled his face. "Are you sure that's what you meant?"

"Not a hundred per cent." He moved the sword, allowing the blade to cast its glow over their faces. His eyes gleamed. "Why do you ask?"

"Because you joke around a lot." Ashley shifted uneasily from side to side as she tried to avoid his piercing gaze. "I'm putting my life in your hands now, so please cut out the jokes for a while. I need to trust every word you say."

Surrounded by the dimness of the underground cavern, Saphira stepped up to the column of light, close enough to feel a gentle tingling. Swirling eddies of white radiance spun away from the tall cylinder and kissed her cheek, raising goose bumps all across her arms. Excitement spiked the chill. It was time once again to leave her abode in the depths of Hades and pass through the dimensional portal to the world of the living, but this time in the company of a dragon and the human son of dragons. She smiled at the thought. Now that Jehovah had infused her with internal fire, Hades could never feel like home.

She turned toward her companions, one dragon and one human, and spread out her arms. Tiny flames rose from her fingertips, her emotions igniting her gift of fire making. The sparking tongues of yellow and blue raised an odour of sulphur, but it quickly burned away. "Come closer," she said. "We probably can't all fit in the portal, but maybe I can spread out its light and envelop you."

Behind the tawny dragon, dozens of lanterns lined the exterior of a colossal, cylindrical building, framing her huge scaly body. The structure, the foundation floor of the ancient Tower of Babel, rose high into the upper reaches of the enormous cavern, scraping by one of the longer stalactites and disappearing into the darkness above.

Roxil swung her spine-covered tail forward and shuffled to the swirling portal, grumbling as she lowered her head to Sapphira's level. "I don't like the idea of just popping out in the modern world. I doubt that humans will take too kindly to seeing someone like me appear out of nowhere."

"That's for sure." Gabriel spread out both his human arms and his dragon-like wings. "I don't think anyone's going to believe that I'm an endangered bat species, either."

Sapphira touched a dagger tucked under Gabriel's belt. "I'm kind of nervous about taking that. It was Morgan's."

"I grabbed it while we were running in Dragons' Rest, so I didn't have time to get a look at it." He pulled it out and lifted it close to his eyes. "Merlin told me there's something special about Morgan's dagger." He pressed his fingertip on the blade. "There! See? The shape of a cross in the stone's crystalline structure. It's staurolite."

"Staurolite? What does that mean?"

"It's powerful and mysterious. Merlin said that when this dagger is used for evil, only God can reverse its damage, but when it's used for good, even its victims can receive mercy." He tucked it back between his belt and trousers. "I never really understood what he meant by that, but it might come in handy wherever we're going."

"Wherever we're going," Roxil repeated. She brought her snout so close, Sapphira could feel the hot breath on her cheeks. "Do you know where we're going?" Roxil asked with a challenging tone. "Do you have a plan for finding my father?"

"Cool it, Sis!" Gabriel reached over and shoved Roxil's head away. "If I know Sapphira, she's got everything covered." He turned to Sapphira, his eyebrows raised. "You do have everything covered, don't you?"

Sapphira tried to keep her gaze fixed on Gabriel, but out of the corner of her eye, she could see Roxil's red pupils blazing. "Uh, well, I'm not really sure where we'll come out, but I think we'll show up wherever we need to be. That's what happened the last time I went through. I showed up inside the rubellite gateway between Dragons' Rest and the world of the living, exactly at the right time to help Billy and Bonnie get into Dragons' Rest."

"So this is a random jump into space," Roxil growled. "You don't know if we will come out freezing on a mountaintop or drowning at the bottom of an ocean, do you?"

Sapphira frowned at Roxil. "Look around you!" She nodded toward the huge building behind them. "Jehovah used you dragons to make that museum drop right into this dimension, giving me scrolls for learning, fuel to keep me warm, rich soil for growing the tree that kept me from starving, and a portal to the outside world that helped me save lives." She pointed at the ground, her finger now on fire. "I lived in this hole for thousands of years, sometimes alone for centuries, and, yes, I doubted. I cried. I was so desperate I wanted to die. But Jehovah kept me here for a purpose, and I couldn't see it until exactly the right time. But it was perfect. I was able to help save Billy, Bonnie, and the faithful dragons. Jehovah was even merciful enough to use me to save a faith-

34

less dragon." She extended her blazing finger toward Roxil. "You."

Roxil backed away a step but said nothing.

"Maybe I can help a faithless dragon see the light." Sapphira waved her hand at the portal column and shouted. "Expand!"

The column rolled out into a bright screen, and the light particles scattered to reveal two dragons standing close to a teenaged boy and two girls, one a young redhead and the other a taller, older teen. They seemed to be on a grassy field, and the distant mountaintops indicated that they, too, were at a high elevation.

"Mother!" Roxil called out. "The female dragon is my mother!"

"*Our* mother," Gabriel corrected. "Do you recognize the male?"

Roxil moved closer to the screen. "It is Arramos. He is Makaidos's father and my grandfather. He is the first of the dragons and the greatest." Roxil turned back to Sapphira. "If we go through the portal, is this our destination?"

"I believe so," Sapphira replied. "At least that's how it worked last time."

"Then let us make haste! There is no reason to delay!"

Gabriel patted Roxil on the neck. "So seeing is believing, huh? I guess you—"

"Don't make sport of me with your sarcasm!" Roxil reared back, ribbons of flame spewing from her nostrils. "You might be my brother, as you claim, but to me you look like a human – a two-legged vermin!"

Gabriel stumbled backwards, but Sapphira caught him. At that moment, the younger girl on the screen disappeared into a hole. The portal flashed. A new image appeared, replacing the mountaintop view. A man standing on rocky ground pulled a thin golden cord held by a dark-winged humanoid who crouched just beyond a narrow fissure only a few feet away.

Sapphira walked slowly toward the screen, pointing. "I know him! That's Mardon, one of my old masters!"

As Mardon strained against the cord, the fissure thinned until it

35

vanished. The portal screen exploded, sending thousands of minia-ture tornadoes of light spinning across the chamber. Dozens of sparkling eddies covered Roxil and Gabriel, consuming them as they buzzed through their bodies. Every inch of flesh and scales trans-formed into light, pulsing and twinkling. Within seconds, the eddies vanished, leaving the radiant outlines of a dragon and a winged boy.

Breathless, Sapphira reached for Gabriel, but her arm passed right through his shoulder. "What happened?" She tried to hold his phantasmic hand. "Can you talk?"

His lips moved, but no sound came out.

"Can you hear me?" she asked.

He nodded. A radiant stream twinkled under his eye.

Sapphira tried to wipe his tear, but it was no use. This poor boy had only recently escaped being trapped in a phantom state, but now he had lost his physical form once again. She tried to hear his thoughts, like she once did when he was first translumi-nated back in England, but nothing came through.

She stepped around Gabriel and tiptoed up to Roxil. "Uh, Roxil, I assume you can hear me, too, right?"

The dragon nodded. She opened her mouth as if trying to speak, but only a few white sparks dribbled out. Her pulsing out-line made her expression hard to read, but she seemed frightened, more of a vulnerable appearance than her usual tough demeanour.

Sapphira raised her hand and tried to pat Roxil on her neck. "Don't worry. I'll try to figure out what happened. Mardon's obviously up to something, but I can't begin to guess what we saw on the screen."

She looked back at the spot on the floor where the portal col-umn had been, now dark. What could possibly make the path to the world of the living vanish like that? It was almost as if Mardon somehow intentionally moved the interdimensional passageway. But why?

She snapped her fingers. Maybe that was it! She dug her hand into her jeans pocket and withdrew the candy-bar-sized timer she had taken from the mobility room years ago. The digital counter read "0001".

Sapphira rubbed her chin. It was so close, maybe this explosion was the first step in awakening the giants, and Mardon was finally making his move to bring them to the world of the living. Maybe somehow they had already been transported to Earth's dimension, which would explain Roxil's and Gabriel's change to an energy state. Roxil had been killed centuries ago and was now an escapee from Dragons' Rest, so she had no living, physical body, while Gabriel only regained his body during his time in Dragons' Rest or one of the Circles of Seven.

Snatching up a lantern, she strode to the chamber's exit. "If you want to come with me, please hurry. I have a hunch." Without looking at the lantern, she said, "Ignite." The wick burst into flames.

As the light brightened, she picked up her pace. Slapping her bare feet against the stone floor, she dashed through the familiar underground corridors that led to the mobility room, the chamber where Mardon trained the Nephilim to walk and gain strength.

She leaped over the bones of the long-dead Nephilim carcasses that lay strewn next to the mobility room's entrance, then burst inside. Marching along the row of growth chambers, she eyed the giants suspended within the recessed cavities in the wall.

She whistled at the sight of these massive men, still amazing, though she had seen them countless times. The process that put them in these growth chambers seemed more miraculous than scientific. How could hulking giants begin as tiny humanoid plants, engineered from the genetic material of fallen angels? Who could have designed a scheme that would uproot those plants at a young age and place them into magnetic fields that suspended them in mid-air until their limbs were strong enough for walking? Why would anyone want to take so many years to train them as mighty soldiers?

And now they slept, awaiting a slumber-ending call that Mardon had programmed long ago. The digital counter embedded in the rock underneath each growth chamber carried the same "0001" reading as the counter Sapphira had taken more than eight decades earlier from under Yereq, the spawn she had nurtured as a seedling until he was ready for mobility.

She stopped in front of Yereq and gazed at his stern, bearded face. Although he was asleep, he seemed anxious, as if suffering through a bad dream. Even as a seedling, he had often dreamed, his tiny green face twitching and frowning, and she would wake him up with a soothing song. But those days were only a memory.

Although they had enjoyed a caring relationship when he was a mere spawn, the last time she had seen him awake, he scowled at her, having been trained in hatred by Morgan in preparation for his role as lead Naphil, the general of her conquering army.

With Morgan's death, however, and Mardon's disappearance, who could tell what was in store for him? Once the counter ticked to zero, would Mardon return from the strange precipice they had seen and somehow lead the Nephilim to the upper lands in the world of the living?

She longed to replay Yereq's days of innocence, to sing something sweet that would free him from this never-ending nightmare. But could it possibly help? Could her voice somehow call him back to wakefulness, back to a time when his heart wasn't cold? A song played in her mind, one of the few light-hearted melodies that Naamah, her slave-driving mistress, had taught her centuries ago. Stepping closer to Yereq, she let it emerge from her lips, soft and sweet.

'Tis time to rise my verdant child
And greet the day so warm and mild.
So sing with me, and we will dance
To show the world our sweet romance.

38

When Sapphira finished, she lifted the lantern to watch Yereq's eyelids. They twitched again. His lips moved as if ready to speak. Suddenly, he leaned forward and fell out of his chamber, crumpling to the floor face down.

Sapphira leaped to his side. "Yereq! Are you all right?" Pushing with all her might, she tried to turn him over, but he was too heavy. She sat down and shoved his body with both feet until he finally flopped onto his back.

She laid her ear against his chest. No breathing. No heartbeat. Pushing his chest with her doubled fists, she cried out, "Yereq! Wake up!"

No response.

Pressing her ear down again, she listened. Still no heartbeat. She opened his jaw and blew into his mouth, but her feeble breaths barely inflated his lungs. Again and again she tried to resuscitate him, but his body was so big and solid, and she was so small, she felt like a mouse pushing an elephant.

39

Finally, she climbed on his chest and jumped up and down, but after several attempts with no success, she gave up and sprawled over his body. "Oh, Yereq! I'm so sorry! My song woke you, but it was too early. Why couldn't I have waited? Maybe without Morgan around, I could have turned your heart back to love!"

She gazed at his lifeless face, dirty and scraped from his fall to the mobility room floor. Looking up at Roxil's and Gabriel's floating energy forms, she wiped her eyes. "I have to go to the springs." She climbed off Yereq and ran to the exit, lighting her way with a small flame in her palm.

When she reached the hot springs chamber, she grabbed a towel she always kept near the main pool and dipped it in the water. With the towel dripping a trail behind her, and one hand lifting a tongue of flame, she rushed toward the mobility room and met Gabriel and Roxil just outside the entrance. "I had to get a cloth for Yereq," she said, lifting the towel. She then rushed inside.

Kneeling at the fallen giant's side, Sapphira mopped his face, clearing dirt and blood. With each wipe, his skin briefly faded to green before turning back to light brown, reminding her again of his days as a plant, the early days when he would eat eagerly from her finger. He was so cute back then, his wormy meal dribbling from his lips, but now clotted blood smeared his chin, a far cry from his past innocence. Sapphira wiped it away. "I hope I get to see you in Heaven," she said, new tears welling, "but with all the hate you had in your heart ..." She couldn't go on. Straightening her body, she twisted the towel, wringing it out on the floor. As she wrenched the cloth far beyond need, her tears dripped down to mingle with the dirty, bloody water.

Gabriel knelt at Yereq's opposite side, pointing at the wall. Sapphira looked up at the growth chamber. It wasn't empty as she expected. Something else was there. Sniffing back a sob, she picked up the lantern and lifted it high, but its glow only rose to the occupant's knees. With a trembling voice, she spoke to the wick. "Give me all you've got." The light burst forth, revealing a young, redheaded girl suspended where Yereq used to hover.

"Who could that be?" she asked out loud. "She looks sort of like one of the girls we saw in the portal."

Gabriel floated between Sapphira and the girl, mouthing silent words and gesturing.

She tried to read his indistinct lips to no avail. Could he have met the little redhead while acting as Bonnie's invisible guardian angel over the years? A redheaded girl had participated in some of those adventures, but Sapphira's own view of those events had flashed by on her portal screen in rapid succession, so only a few faces stayed in her mind. Still, Gabriel might have seen how the girl got there. He and Roxil were waiting at the door while she was at the springs, so they might have seen someone come in.

"If only you could talk!" Sapphira groaned. "Now we're all

stuck here with a new mystery, and we'll never find our way out!"

As her voice echoed, repeating her plaintive call, she raised her finger to her lips and bit it. Maybe there really was no way out. Yereq was dead. Her exit portal was gone. If she really was already in the world of the living, how could she get to the surface? If Acacia were here, they might be able to work together to create an exit, but the only new portal she had ever made was in the presence of Enoch's Ovulum. And where was Acacia now? Was she dead, too? Lost and wandering with Paili in a strange dimension?

Grief flooded her mind. She gnashed her teeth and pushed her bare toes against the rocky floor until they hurt. Even with the phantom forms of Gabriel and Roxil hovering nearby, she felt more alone than ever, and their lurking presence made it worse. This wasn't just an underground tomb in the land of the dead. It was haunted by ghosts.

She stepped on the hearth that abutted the chamber and touched the ring on the girl's finger – a rubellite!

"Are you a dragon child?" Sapphira asked, giving the girl's wrist a gentle tug. "Wake up," she called in a sing-song voice. "Wake up, whoever you are."

She slapped her own hand. No! No singing! Waking her up might kill her, too!

Standing on tiptoes, Sapphira looked at her closely. There was no response. Her freckled alabaster face and pale pink lips stayed perfectly still, though her chest expanded and contracted ever so slightly.

Sapphira blew out a relieved sigh. Good. The girl stayed asleep.

As she continued gazing at her pretty face, she felt drawn to her, a strange emotional attachment to this sleeper from the land of the living. "I'll get you out of here," she promised. "I'll get us all out of here, so help me God!"

CHAPTER

ELAM'S JOURNEY

Elam waded through an ocean of knee-high wildflowers, scattering pollen from dozens of orange, purple, and yellow blossoms. A wash of delicate scents bathed him in perfumed air, but he hadn't come to this field to enjoy the sights and smells. He had to find the path and follow it.

Pushing aside a swathe of long-bladed grass, he searched the ground for a red petal. For the last several miles, a trail of red flowers, intermixed with a rainbow of other colours, had guided his steps, but they had suddenly ended about a hundred yards back.

"Follow the trail of blood – the red flowers," Merlin had told him. "Then enter the Forest of Molech and look for Glewlwyd, the gatekeeper."

Elam stopped and swivelled his head. Nothing but grass and flowers as far as the eye could see. Why would the trail of blood vanish? Could Merlin have been wrong somehow?

Pulling off his cloak, he trudged back to where the path of red flowers ended. After laying down a small shoulder bag, he plucked a blade of grass and sat among the flowers, glad to give his legs a rest. Since he wore lightweight khaki trousers and a short-sleeved tunic, the warm sun felt good on his bare arms, but the hooded cloak was ready at his side, just in case. Merlin had told him that nights in this land were unpredictable, sometimes muggy and warm and sometimes breezy and cold.

As he chewed on the end of the blade, he stared across the vast field, his eyes barely above the tiny blossoms. He had often heard about this land, the second level in the Circles of Seven. The Bible referred to it as Hades and sometimes Sheol, which was the name his father, Shem, and his grandfather Noah called it in their stories.

Smiling, Elam pushed his cloak under his head as he lay back. Those were the days! Noah was the best of storytellers. Always ready with tales of life in the ark – tales of riding out the great storm, feeding hundreds of squawking, baying, and howling animals, and helping them bear their young, including the delivery of a calf from a cantankerous elephant.

A yellow petal fell on his nose, jerking his mind back to the task at hand. Only his more recent memories would give him any clue to what he should do next. Had he missed a word, maybe a sign or a symbol in Merlin's instructions? The secret meeting that began this adventure was still clear in his mind.

Merlin had come to Sir Patrick's ready to send Elam out on a great journey ...

Sitting on a stool in the dim compass room, Merlin laid a strap over Elam's shoulder and patted the bag that hung at the bottom. "Water, bread, and a special device that might come in handy. It's a spyglass that my ancestors passed down through many generations."

Elam dug the spyglass out of the bag and looked through the lens, extending the telescopic cylinder to its maximum. He pointed it at the rectangular hole in the ceiling and gazed at the crescent moon peeking through a thin cloud. Then, turning it to the old portal screen, a shimmering window in the outer wall, he focused on the jungle-like trees on the other side. Rain dripped on the undergrowth, ferns, and vines that disguised a field of bones. "Does it do anything special?"

"I'm not sure. I found no use for it other than viewing things at a distance." Merlin pointed at an etching on the dark, metallic side. "But this Hebrew script tells me that it could have other attributes."

"It says, 'Enoch'." Elam rubbed his finger along the etching. "You mean this belonged to Enoch the prophet?"

"It did indeed, but in my brief encounter with him, I never thought to ask him what it does beyond the obvious." Merlin pointed at the portal window. "But it might be useful when you cross the field of the second circle. The grassland is so vast, at times you won't be able to see anything but grass and flowers all the way to the horizon."

"Is there a path?" Elam asked. "Markings? Landmarks?"

"Only one. You'll have to follow the trail of blood – the red flowers. Then enter the Forest of Molech and look for Glewlwyd, the gatekeeper."

Elam walked up to the portal window and touched it. The solid barrier sent a tingle through his fingers. "What does this gatekeeper look like?"

"I wish I could tell you precisely," Merlin replied, rising from his stool. "He is somewhat invisible."

Elam spun around. "Invisible? How can I possibly find someone who's invisible?"

Merlin joined him at the window. "Actually, I think semi-transparent is more accurate. If he moves, you will see him, like flowing water. So walk carefully or you might stumble over him while he is sleeping, and he can be quite irritable if he decides not to like you."

45

Elam collapsed the spyglass to its original state. "When I find him, then what do I do?"

"First, beware," Merlin said, raising a finger. "The forest is haunted by the Caitiff – the spirits of those who abused or murdered children during their lives on Earth. They wander there in hopelessness, waiting for the judgment of God. They know their penalty will be sure and severe, an eternal damnation that will make them suffer beyond all others. So, they are desperate and cruel, both to each other and to any lost soul who ventures among the perverse."

Elam shivered. "Why would the gatekeeper be in a place like that?"

"The forest serves as a barrier to those condemned souls who might try to leave the Circles of Seven. At the centre, there is an unusual gate that serves as the only dimensional exit that an unqualified person could possibly use, and Glewlwyd guards it. His transparency keeps him safe from the Caitiff, and he acts as a guide if a worthy seeker of the gate enters the forest, as Acacia and Paili did not long ago."

"So what do I say to Glewlwyd when I find him?"

"Tell him you are seeking Heaven's lower altar, and ask him for passage to the Bridgelands. He will likely test you in some way to prove who you are, but I cannot predict what the test will entail. Just answer his questions. If you pass, he will allow you through the gate." Merlin stroked his bearded chin and sighed. "Unfortunately, that's only the beginning of your trials. Since even Glewlwyd can be deceived, once you go through the gate, there will be another battery of tests you must pass before you get to the altar. These will examine the character of your soul rather than the cleverness of your lips, so all deception will be purged along the way."

Elam laid the spyglass in the bag. "How in the world could Acacia carry Paili through all of that? I mean, she had great character of soul, but what about the Caitiff? How could she get past them while carrying a limp body?"

"Joseph of Arimathea guided her, and he likely took over the burden of carrying Paili. He was a great warrior in his time, so he is strong, and the Caitiff fear him."

"Where is Joseph now?" Elam hiked his bag higher on his shoulder. "I mean, I'm no coward, but I wouldn't mind having him along if he's available."

Merlin untwisted the bag's strap and patted it down. "I have no idea what has become of Joseph. As far as I can tell, you will have no guide, but I'm sure you will find your way." He laid his palm on the back of Elam's head. "You have proven yourself worthy of every assignment I've given you, and this will be no exception. But you must maintain a confident mind-set in full assurance of faith, otherwise your heart might melt within you."

Elam kept his head straight, not wanting to disturb Merlin's touch. The old prophet's strong fingers felt good in his hair, filling him with confidence and energy. "I appreciate your faith in me," Elam said. "I'll remember what you told me."

Merlin pulled his hand away. "I know you will."

Turning back to the portal, Elam gazed at the jungle scene again. The rain had become a downpour. "Any last-minute instructions?"

"Indeed. I have saved the most important part as your final warning in order to firmly implant it in your brain." Merlin glanced at the doorway leading to the living quarters of Sir Patrick's house, and, leaning close to Elam, lowered his voice to a whisper. "I have learned that Mardon, Sapphira's old master, is behind a plot that could trigger a potential catastrophe so great, even Heaven and Earth would be destroyed. Yet there is a way to stop him. You must find Enoch, but you need not warn him of the threat. He knows of it all too well and is counting on your help to save the cosmos."

Elam pointed at himself. "*I'm* supposed to save the cosmos?"

"Not alone. You will simply be one of the tools God will use, like a commander leading the troops into battle. Enoch is mustering soldiers from Earth and from another dimension that you have never heard of." Merlin tapped his finger on Elam's head. "I believe you know the soldiers from Earth, a young man and woman named Walter and Ashley."

Elam nodded. "I know *about* them. I was called Markus back when they helped Billy and Bonnie survive the Circles of Seven, but I never had a chance to meet them."

"Their role is crucial," Merlin continued, "yet they have no idea that Mardon is trying to build a tower to pull Heaven down to Earth. It will be up to Sapphira and Enoch to guide their steps. If they fail to do their part, all will be lost."

"What about this other realm?" Elam asked. "How am I supposed to lead soldiers from there?"

"Only one man from there is involved, but you are not responsible for calling him to your aid, though you know him quite well." Merlin paused for a moment, his stare riveting Elam in place. Finally, the old prophet sighed. "Aren't you going to ask me who he is?"

Elam shook his head. "If you wanted me to know, you'd tell me."

Merlin chuckled and patted Elam on the back. "You haven't changed much, have you?" Pulling away slightly, Merlin kept his voice low. "Enoch sang a prophecy for me. I have not discerned whether or not it relates to the potential calamity at hand, but maybe it will give you wisdom."

Angling his head upward, he crooned in a soft, melodic tone.

The tree that bears the ark of God
Has flown to Heaven's narrow gate
To purge the serpent's fatal bite,
The fruit of Morgan's wicked hate.

A host of martyrs bends the knee
Behind the altar's sacred door,
Awaiting Elam, son of Shem,
To lead a march to holy war.

A path of light will lead the way,
A path the tree will soon ignite,
A path of sorrows, pain, and death,
A path to guide the mourning knight.

But still there lurks a dangerous foe
Who seeks to drink of Elam's life,
To take the fruit that burns within,
The flame that melts a subtle knife.

The journey takes him to a land
Of children once forsaken here
To battle altered tribes of war,
Deceivers masked to virgin ears.

And once that land is cleansed anew,
The tree must bring the ark to Earth.
Sapphira begs for borrowed bones,
The only way to bring new birth.

Sapphira bends, but will she break?
Depends on Elam's safe return.
For if he fails to bring the ark,
Her life is chaff and soon will burn.

When the last note faded, Merlin folded his hands and
watched the rain through the portal window. "After the song,
Enoch left to join Acacia and Paili at the altar, but I could not

follow, for I still have important business to take care of inside the Great Key."

"You mean creating the covenant veil for the dragons?" Elam asked.

"Yes. And then I will go to Heaven with my wife and never return to the Earth." Merlin clasped Elam's shoulder. "When you find Enoch, Acacia, and Paili, they will divulge the rest of the plan to stop Mardon and his schemes. I suspect, however, that there is much more going on than meets the eye. Mardon is, as were Devin and Morgan, a mere pawn in the devil's ultimate plot, so watch for something more sinister behind what you can see with your eyes."

"So you don't know what the rest of the poem means, that stuff about someone wanting to drink my life, bringing the ark, and marching to war?"

"I have ideas, but uninformed speculation is wasted effort. You will have to ask Enoch."

Elam shook his head. "Please pardon my frankness, Master Merlin, but sometimes I don't understand prophets like you and Enoch. Why can't you just speak plainly instead of using songs and poems?"

Merlin chuckled. "Sometimes we don't even understand the verses ourselves. We frequently offer our own reasoned soliloquies, but once in a while we speak exactly that which God bids us speak, word for word. Occasionally he reveals his thoughts in riddles and parables so that those who earnestly want to know the truth will seek it with all their hearts, even if it means struggling through dangerous journeys." He tightened his grip on Elam and gave him the gentlest of shakes. "This is how we prove the confessions of our lips."

Elam sighed, warmth flooding his cheeks. He let a timid smile break through. "I'll take that spiritual slap on the hand and get on my way."

50

"And I never saw him again," Elam whispered to himself.

While it was in reality only a few days ago, it now seemed like months had passed since that meeting. Time in the Circles of Seven was confusing at best, sometimes so sluggish even seeds from the heads of grass stalks seemed to fall to the ground in slow motion, while at other times life zoomed at a frenetic pace. Wildflowers sprouted, grew, and blossomed in seconds, and the sun raced the clouds across the sky.

Today seemed long. The warm sun perched at the zenith and stared at him like a big orange eye that refused to blink. Still, a cool breeze blew across the field, drying the sweat on his brow and making the grass wave and the flowers nod their colourful heads.

Rising to his feet with his cloak over one shoulder and his bag over the other, Elam pulled out Enoch's spyglass and pointed it toward the field for the hundredth time. Still nothing but grass and flowers, grass and flowers, and more grass and flowers.

51

He glanced down at the abrupt end of the path of red and muttered, "Should I just go in the exact direction the path is pointing?"

A deep voice replied. "That would make the most sense, son of Shem."

"Who said that?" Elam swivelled his head, searching for the source of the voice. "Where are you? How do you know me?"

No one answered.

He gazed up at the sun, avoiding a direct stare, then swept his foot across the grass, searching for any odd creature that might have spoken. Finally, he wiped his brow. "I must be going nuts!"

He glared at the last red flower on the path. "Okay," he said, reaching down and plucking it, stem and all, "I don't know if you're the one who spoke or if you're just the victim of my newfound insanity, but you're coming with me." He marched forward, his eyes picking out one of the taller blades of grass and, once fixed on it, he watched its waving head of seeds as the breeze continued to blow. When he reached it, he locked his gaze on another seed-pod farther ahead, then another, as he kept to a straight line.

After a few hours, the sun broke free from its lazy perch and began drifting toward the horizon. He laid the flower on his ear, drew out the spyglass again, and searched ahead. A low dark rise loomed in the distance. Finally! Could it be a line of trees? The Forest of Molech?

He stuffed the glass into the bag and clutched the flower. "I'd better get there before dark," he said, breaking into a jog.

The sun slid down the sky, and evening draped itself across the field, but not before the forest came into view of Elam's naked eye. Minutes later, just as darkness began settling over the land, he arrived within a few yards of the edge. The grass ended abrupt-ly, giving way to damp black dirt, pockmarked with squatty orange toadstools. The soil reeked of decay – rotted leaves and mould, and maybe even carrion mixed in somewhere.

He peered into the forest. With only a few stars twinkling above, he couldn't even distinguish one tree from another. As he continued to stare, tiny red lights blinked on and off deep with-in the woods.

"Eyes!" Elam said out loud. The pairs of red points gathered together, drawing closer by the second. Now dozens of eyes approached the edge of the forest, their glowing beacons shining brighter, harsh and hateful.

He back-pedalled into the grass and crouched, holding his breath. The eyes closed in, then halted at the tree line, but there seemed to be no shape or silhouette, no head or body surround-ing the lights. The darkness blended every movement into warped shadows.

He exhaled as slowly and silently as possible, but they must have heard him breathe, or maybe smelled his breath. The crim-son eyes began bouncing up and down, as if they were owned by excited monkeys. Grunts and shrieks erupted, but the creatures stayed put at the tree line. Soon, the din grew to a fevered pitch, and the creatures howled, some with pained wails.

Elam crouched even lower. Could they be fighting?

The howls suddenly stopped, and a strange soft light filtered into the trees. He glanced at the horizon to his right. A full moon peeked over the field, sending its yellowish beams across grass, flowers, and forest.

White vapour arose between him and the trees, like steam from a heated pot. It coalesced into a human-like phantom with long, elastic arms that reached toward the woods. The eyes scattered, blinking off as the creatures turned and ran.

Staying low, Elam caught a glimpse of what looked like human or ape-like legs in retreat, so whatever these things were, they must have been bipeds. But what could that vapour be?

As the moon's full disc appeared, the phantom dispersed, and the entire scene brightened. The trees looked like tall hardwoods with bushy tops and trunks stripped of branches to about head height. A few moonbeams illuminated the forest floor, which seemed bare, perhaps leaf-strewn, except for a strange lump at the base of one of the trunks. He studied the lump but couldn't figure out what it was. Another mystery, but it would have to wait for morning.

53

Using his cloak as a pillow, he lay down in the grass and folded his hands on his chest, still clutching the red flower. Although the surrounding air was still warm from the daytime heating, a tingle crawled along his skin, making him shiver. The strange creatures in the woods, their ghoulish red eyes, and their bestial wails were enough to give anyone a chill. Not only that, with its long, gaseous arms, the phantom had looked more like a ghost than a random cloud of gas, and anything that would frighten away those forest devils had to be more than just a passing vapour.

Elam closed his eyes and nestled deeper in his cloak. "It's still safer out here," he murmured. "It would be crazy to go in those woods in the dark."

As he closed his eyes and drifted toward sleep, a soft voice whispered in his ear. "Yes, son of Shem. When danger is near, always stay in the light."

CHAPTER

THE PRISM ORACLE

Thigocia kept her eyes trained on the red dragon in front of her, the creature calling himself Arramos. Staying above the clouds, they had flown rapidly for over an hour, faster than she had travelled since before her days as a human. To this point, her questions about their destination and time of arrival had been answered with, "You will soon learn," giving her good reason to believe what her sense of danger continued to blare – trouble lay ahead.

Arramos finally slowed and flew side by side with Thigocia. As their wing tips nearly brushed each other in their synchronized downstrokes, he blew a short burst of fire. "I must now use my flames to create a hole in the dimensional fabric that will take us to your mate's dwelling place."

Trying to keep her distance from the larger dragon, Thigocia descended a few feet and skimmed the tops of the clouds. "You said we would find Roxil and search for Makaidos with her."

"We shall. First we are going to the Bridgelands, the place where I believe him to be. Although I have scoured many of the fields and forests of that land, I have not been able to locate him. But the place is so large, it is impossible for one dragon to complete a search, especially since he could be on the move." He dropped down to Thigocia's level and flew close again. "Perhaps with your help and Roxil's, I can find him. Before we contact Roxil, however, I want to show you what is occurring in the Bridgelands so you will better understand our mission."

Thigocia set her gaze straight ahead. "Very well. Lead on."

Shooting another stream of fire, Arramos wheeled to the left, keeping a sharp angle as he traced a tight circle and aimed his flaming jets at a centre point. As the fire stretched downward into a tornadic funnel, Thigocia kept pace with him, her own wings fanning and twisting the flames.

Arramos flew faster and faster. Thigocia strained to keep up. The flaming tornado grew wider, hotter, brighter, slurping the clouds as it twisted. Soon, at the focal point at the top of the spin, the sky ripped open, a small hole at first, but as the cyclone expanded, the surrounding air crumbled into the hole, widening it into a black chasm.

"Follow me!" Arramos ordered. He dove into the dark void.

Thigocia flew around the flames, slowing her speed. Should she follow? Was it mad to dive into the unknown, trailing a mysterious, sadistic dragon that kept her danger alarm trumpeting? As she slowed, the hole began to contract, so she beat her wings faster, trying to keep the chasm entry open. What choice did she have? She said she would follow, and, besides, she didn't even know where she was or how to get back to Ashley. It would be unthinkable to give up on this mystery now.

Taking a deep draw from the sun above, she steered into the blackness. Instantly, the air supporting her wings vanished, and she floated in a vacuum, yet she still sensed forward movement at a dizzying rate of speed. After what seemed like several minutes, air began to fill her nostrils and billow under her wings. Light also returned, dim at first, but soon, a field of grass appeared below and a red dragon standing near a pool of water.

She descended in a wide circle, scanning the area for any movement, but Arramos remained the only sign of life. Purple flowers dotted the field, raising a sweet aroma, but with her danger alarm still pricking her brain, this was no time to savour any simple pleasures.

When she fanned her wings out to land, Arramos thumped the ground with his tail. "I was beginning to wonder if you had decided to renege."

Thigocia settled her claws in the soft grass skirting the pool and collapsed her wings. "Yet you waited."

"It was a mere passing thought. I have not so soon forgotten your integrity."

Thigocia dug her claws deeper into the turf. "It is sad that you have forgotten your own."

"A sharp tongue is unbecoming of a dragon queen, but I will overlook your indiscretion. Your fighting spirit will be of great benefit."

"I will not argue the point." She scowled, twitching her ears for emphasis. "Just get on with it."

"Very well." Arramos brushed the ground with the tip of a wing. "We are in the Bridgelands, a connecting byway between Earth and Heaven as well as between Heaven and Hades. It is likely impossible to conceive with finite minds like ours, but you might think of it like this." He dipped a claw into the pool. Black ripples scattered from the entry point, creating a dark expanse across the surface. "I brought you here so that you could see the plans of God and men. Many pools in the Bridgelands reflect invisible realities, but this one reveals the structure of the dimensional cosmos."

A Saturn-like shape appeared on the pool's dark canopy, but instead of rings around a planet, a large flat disc surrounded a

57

smaller, nebulous white orb. Three tiny moons adhered to the outer edge of the disc as it revolved slowly around the orb. "The centre sphere is Heaven, a realm that contains the holy city, the angels, and the saints. The wider disc around Heaven is where we stand now – the Bridgelands, a flat territory that connects Heaven to Earth and Hades, which are represented by those two smaller spheres on the edge of the disc. At one time, Dragons' Rest was also a sphere on the edge, but it no longer exists."

He set the tip of his wing near two of the outer spheres. "As you can see, Earth and Hades are very close to each other right now, dangerously close. The wall of separation between them is fragile and ready to collapse." He touched the pool again, and blackness swallowed the image.

"I saw a third sphere on the edge," Thigocia said, "on the opposite side of Heaven from the Earth. What was it?"

"Another world. I have never been there, but Enoch told me it is uninhabited. It may eventually be part of the Maker's grand purpose, but I am not privileged to know."

"So is Makaidos somewhere on the disc?" Thigocia asked. "The flat part?"

"He cannot be anywhere else. I have checked the Prism Oracle myself, and he has not entered either Heaven or Hades, and he is no longer on Earth."

Thigocia twitched her ears. "The Prism Oracle? Is that some sort of list of who is where?"

"Not really a list – a query. Access to this information is no secret in the realms of the dead, at least to those who know where to look." Arramos unfurled his wings. "Come. I will show you."

As he lifted into the air, Thigocia followed, staying close enough to listen to any further explanations but far enough back to watch from a safe distance. Clear skies allowed for brisk flying and easy scanning of everything on the ground. Beautiful meadows and forests abounded, with bubbling streams and clear pools nourishing the landscape for miles and miles. The male dragon descended and glided over a stream, casting his red eyebeams over its muddy shoulder. "Look closely, and you will see human footprints – fresh, not more than three days old."

Thigocia scanned the mud with her own eyebeams. "I see them. Two different sizes. What does it mean?"

"It proves that the Maker has placed humans here, though I have not seen any besides one I will tell you about in a few moments. Perhaps my son is also here in his human form, and he has found a companion."

She flicked off her beams. "A companion?"

"It is only a guess. He might also be alone somewhere else. For all I know, this pair of inhabitants could have human feet and the head of an ostrich. In any case, they hide well. And considering that we are likely a fearful sight to them, their scarcity in the open is no wonder." Arramos ascended again and flew on.

Thigocia beat her wings and caught up. "May we come back to this place and search?"

"We shall see. I have to make sure we meet Roxil on time."

After passing over a hilly plane that stretched from horizon to horizon, they plunged into a deep canyon where a raging river careened around a bend. After it straightened farther down its path, it hurtled into a steep ravine and splashed against a pair of huge boulders, sending up billowing clouds of mist.

The boulders diverted the river to one side but allowed a stream of water to feed a shallow pool on the opposite side where Arramos and Thigocia stood. As the river beat against the stone obstacles, water flew over the tops and drizzled in front of the dragons. Light sparkled in the prismatic droplets and painted a strange, full-circle rainbow – a halo with seven colour bands that hovered in the midst of the spray.

"This is the Prism Oracle," Arramos shouted, competing with the roar of splashing water. "The concept is quite simple, though I have no idea why it works. While gazing at the oracle, you walk into these shallows and speak a name. Because of your touch, the oracle knows the identity of the one about whom you are enquiring, and the colours merge to create his or her image. The appearance of the image tells us where the person is."

Thigocia peered at the marble-like boulders framing the halo and returned his shout. "How did you figure out the purpose of this oracle? I see no signs or symbols to explain it."

"What do you remember about Enoch?" he asked.

"In his battles with the Watchers, he proved himself a prophet of the highest order." Thigocia looked up at the sky, allowing the droplets to drizzle into her eyes. Their touch was cool and soothing. "I was very young when he left the Earth," she continued, still speaking loudly, "but the impression he left on me will last forever. I revere him and Merlin as the two greatest prophets I have ever known."

"Then you will have no problem with trusting this oracle, for Enoch himself established it. During one of my searches here, he hailed me as I flew over. When I landed, I recognized him immediately, and my heart leaped for joy at finding my long-lost friend. He already knew why I was here and showed me how the oracle could provide the insight I needed, the proof that my search in the Bridgelands was not in vain."

"What else did he say? Had he seen Makaidos?"

Arramos shook his head. "As human prophets often are, he was mysterious, and he said very little. After he explained the oracle to me, he seemed to melt into the river and flow away."

Thigocia moved her head closer to him, searching for a hint of deception in his eyes. "That story has the ring of myth. Who would ever believe such a tale?"

"Believe what you wish." He nodded at the calm pool at the edge of the splashing water. "But if you try it, you will know that I could not have conjured what you will see with your own eyes.

Say the name of someone you believe to be in Heaven, then one in Hades, and then one on the Earth. You need not shout, as I am doing. The oracle will hear you."

Thigocia stepped into the water and stared at the splashing chaos. How could a river striking a pair of boulders create an oracle that could see through the veils of the afterlife and show them to anyone who might ask? It made no sense. Still, the prophets had spoken of miracles just as strange, a donkey speaking to a mad prophet, and a voice in a burning bush commanding Moses to free the Hebrews in Egypt. Could the Maker also prepare such an oracle in this strange land? Who could deny his ability to do this miracle as well?

After thinking for a moment, Thigocia took a step closer and said, "Noah."

The coloured bands broke away from the halo and mixed in the centre. Then, as if painted by an invisible brush, a man appeared, the image of Noah at the age he had been while on the ark, the time when she knew him best. Backed by a golden sky and wearing a dazzling white robe and a crown of gold, he smiled, then faded as the colours streamed back to the edge and re-formed the halo.

Arramos raised his voice again. "He is in Heaven. According to Enoch, white and gold are the colours of Paradise, and the crown proves that the Maker has forgiven his many sins."

Thigocia glared at Arramos but decided not to challenge his criticism of the great ark builder. The task at hand was too important to allow for delay. She thought for another moment and said, "Ham."

The colours once again painted the image of a man, this time the son of Noah standing in front of an orange background, wearing a tattered orange tunic that barely fell past his hips and covered his loins. A black execution hood rested on his head as if placed there in preparation for the gallows but not yet pulled down over his face.

61

"He is in Hades," Arramos said. "Orange and black are the colours of destruction, and the hood is the symbol of all who will someday be cast into the Lake of Fire."

"Now someone on Earth," Thigocia said quietly. With a sad tremble in her voice, she whispered, "Ashley."

Within seconds, a perfect duplicate of Ashley stood within the mist. Dressed in jeans and a grey Montana-emblazoned sweatshirt, she carried a walking stick and hiked in place in front of a blue sky, moving but never leaving the oracle.

"She carries the symbol of one still on a journey," Arramos explained. "Whenever the oracle displays an Earth-dweller, he or she is always walking, for their path is not yet complete. Since you knew Enoch, you may speak his name. As one who never died, he has not yet established his abode, for he is God's dimensional itinerant."

Thigocia spoke the prophet's name. The oracle echoed his image, showing Enoch as an old man dressed in the style of his pre-flood days, a flowing brown tunic tied at the waist and leather sandals on his feet. He stood in front of complete blackness, without crown, hood, or walking stick.

"He seems to be floating in space," Thigocia said, shouting once again. "There are no colours or clothing that reveal his location."

"Exactly. Enoch told me that souls who are not in Heaven, Earth, or Hades would appear in this manner. He dwells in the lower altar inside Heaven's gate. Since he never died, he is not a resident there and is allowed to visit other realms." Arramos nodded toward the splashing water. "Speak the name of your mate – my son – and you will see why my search here continues."

She looked back at him. "Shall I say his dragon name or his human name?"

"Either one. The oracle will know."

Thigocia took another step closer and said, "Makaidos."

The banded colours once again painted a portrait, this time of a man who, much like Enoch, stood against a black background. He was dressed in beige slacks and a navy blue sweater, the same clothes he wore the night Devin and Palin destroyed their home and their lives.

"No crown," Arramos shouted. "No hood or walking stick. He, too, is neither on Earth nor in one of the afterlife destinations, so I believe he must be here in the Bridgelands."

As the image faded away, Thigocia heaved a deep breath and stepped out of the pool. The two dragons backed away to a quiet bend in the river where they could talk without shouting. "But why was Makaidos left here? If anyone had faith in the Messiah, it was he."

Arramos draped a wing over her neck. She flinched but stayed in place. "I cannot answer that question fully," he said. "Makaidos was unique. He died as a dragon but later left Dragons' Rest, his natural eternal abode. He was then born into the human race as an adult, the only one with faith in the Messiah already established, so he never aged, and qualified to avoid the curse of natural death." As he pulled his wing back, his eyes sparkled like polished rubies.

Thigocia swished her tail through the water. She wanted to ask about her own destiny, seeing that she was the only dragon resurrected from the circles to remain a dragon, but it was best for now to keep to the task at hand, finding her mate. "But if Makaidos had faith, he should have gone to Heaven."

"That part is a mystery to me. I have no answer, only my theory that he was given a unique destination when he was murdered. The oracle says that he is neither in Heaven nor in Hades, so on that we must rely. Soon, you will have an opportunity to question Sapphira, the Oracle of Fire. She can verify that Merlin confirmed this, for he, too, has queried the oracle."

Thigocia bowed her head. "Up until this point, I had thought you a liar, but your story no longer bears the marks of a lie." She gazed again at the boulders, now veiled by mist in the distance. "And this oracle seems to have no prejudice; it shows neither pessimism nor false hopes."

"Yet you still have doubts." Arramos reached his wing toward her again. "Why?"

"You have to ask?" Thigocia ducked under his wing and backed away, scowling. "Your treatment of Karen was cruel coercion. You stabbed us all with fear."

Arramos whipped his wing back. "It was the only way to convince you, but it was not cruel, for the child was never in danger as long as you were willing to yield to my God-given authority as king of the dragons." He extended his neck and looked her in the eye. "You must admit that I tried with gentler methods."

She jerked her head lower, avoiding his stare. "I admit it, but I reserve the right to continue doubting. A position of authority never gives licence to cruelty."

"As you wish. But when the time comes for battle, you must put your doubts aside."

"Battle?" She looked up at him. "What battle?"

"The danger I told you about. I am sure you remember King Nimrod's tower and how Roxil and I helped Makaidos knock it down."

"I remember."

"Another tower, far more dangerous and cunning, will soon pierce the skies. This one, constructed by Mardon, the son of Nimrod, threatens the very fabric of the cosmos. It has already brought Earth and Hades on a collision course, and if it is completed, it will destroy the Bridgelands and everyone in it, including Makaidos. There is nothing we can do to prevent the first collision, but we can stop the merging of Earth and Heaven and save the life of your mate … my son."

Smoke spewed from Thigocia's nostrils. "So our battle is against Mardon."

64

"Yes. When I take you to Roxil, the three of us will create a firestorm to stop the madness as we dragons did in the days of old. At that point, you will have to put aside doubt and trust me, for you will be sorely tempted to change your mind."

"I am sorely tempted now to reject your command." Thigocia flashed her eyebeams at him, bouncing them off his snout. "You have never explained how you survived the great flood. God declared through Noah that all flesh died except for those on the ark."

Arramos turned on his own eyebeams, intersecting hers. "Noah wanted it to appear as if he was the only righteous one on Earth. All of his progeny and all creatures great and small would then be indebted to him for eternity. The fact is that the flood washed away the Watchers and Nephilim who had attacked me, and Michael the archangel carried me here to the Bridgelands until it was time for me to return. He taught me how to open the barriers between the dimensions so I could explore every realm." Arramos moved his head directly in front of Thigocia's. His eyes flashed, and his beams brightened. "The truth is really quite simple. Noah lied."

65

Thigocia growled and spewed a line of fire between her and Arramos that charred the rocky sand at their feet. "I cannot accept that. Noah was a righteous man."

Arramos stepped across the line. "And on this shaky foundation you and I must do battle. Makaidos had great faith in humankind – in Noah's word and in the ideal of dragons serving men – but when man became corrupted, the ideal passed away. You have to admit that their behaviour does not shed a kind light on man's character. Even righteous Noah became drunk and exposed himself, so none of them can be trusted. I intend to invoke the Maker's wrath upon these vermin and prevent the destruction of the Bridgelands." He scraped his claws across the sand, obliterating the line. "I must protect my son at all costs!"

Thigocia turned away and gazed into the sky. "I am not ready to believe what you say about Noah, but I will help you destroy the tower. Earthbound man is not ready to ascend into Heaven. That much I know."

"That is enough for me. Come. We will conduct a brief search for Makaidos, then we must find Roxil."

She kept her gaze fixed above. "Please wait for me at the top of the ridge. I want to see the image of my mate one more time in private."

"It is a mere rainbow you see, but I understand. If, however, you want more time to search for him in reality, you must hurry." Arramos reared up on his haunches and rose into the air, skimming the river as he shot up the falls before disappearing.

Thigocia beat her wings and skittered across the shoals to the oracle's pool. After stepping into it, she said, "Makaidos." The image of her human husband again appeared in the spray. She studied it for a moment, trying to memorize every detail. Just before the portrait scattered, she noticed the rubellite ring on his finger. It carried a white gem.

After glancing at the ridge for a brief second, she turned back to the oracle and whispered so softly she could barely hear her own voice. "Arramos."

The seven coloured ribbons painted a new portrait, another human male standing in blackness without a walking stick. This middle-aged man was dressed like Enoch, the tunic and sandals identifying him as an ordinary citizen from the pre-flood days. She took a step closer and looked at the ring on his finger. A white gem graced the shiny gold band.

Thigocia floundered backwards. Flapping her wings again, she righted herself and made her way back to higher ground. What could it all mean? Why was Arramos a human in the oracle and a dragon on Earth? Something was wrong, very wrong.

She launched into the air and hurried to meet the dragon she still doubted, now even more than ever.

5

CHAPTER

THE OTHER SIDE
OF HEAVEN

Timothy opened his eyes and blinked at the odd light fixture hanging from the ceiling's wooden panels. It appeared to be a circle of miniature lanterns sitting on a disc supported by three thin chains. He glanced at the other strange surroundings. Varnished wood railings bordered his bed, and an IV tube ran from his arm up to a wooden rack that looked more like a hat tree than an IV stand. And the hanging dispenser wasn't the sterile plastic bag or glass bottle he expected. It was a small leathery pouch, rough and brown like a well-worn saddle pack, and the liquid in the tube seemed polluted by the dispenser, tinged with oatmeal-coloured strands within the clearer flow. He fingered the exposed needle penetrating the back of his hand. *What kind of hospital was this?*

Leaning over to peer through the open doorway, Timothy called out, "Nurse! Can you hear me?"

There was no response. He ran his fingers through his sheets but couldn't find a button to summon help. "Nurse!" he called again.

A few seconds later, a young black boy wearing a "Lions" sweatshirt ran in, his long dreadlocks bouncing in time with his stride. The moment he saw Timothy, his eyes widened. "You're awake!" With a big smile, he turned and dashed from the room, yelling, "Mother! He's awake. The stranger is awake!" His shouts faded with his retreating footsteps.

A little girl, no more than ten years old, peeked around the door. With thin hair dangling over the rough, patchy skin on her gaunt face, she smiled and offered a weak wave of her hand.

As a gush of sympathy washed over him, Timothy returned the smile. This girl was probably suffering from some terrible disease and searching for a new friend in the hospital. "Hello," he said. "What's your name?"

She jerked her head away, and the sound of pattering feet echoed from the hall.

Timothy squinted at an analogue clock on the wall, but its numbers went up to twenty-four instead of twelve. "I guess it's about fifteen-thirty," he said out loud. "This must be a military hospital."

Pushing the sheet down to his waist, he examined his body. Fortunately, they hadn't dressed him in one of those awful, draughty gowns with the tie strings in the back. Wearing a loose T-shirt and boxer shorts made a lot more sense. He pulled up his shirt, exposing his stomach and chest. No wounds. No surgical scars. Just flabbier than usual. That meant a pretty long stay. Could he have been in a coma? The boy's reaction indicated something like that.

He rubbed his chin. No beard. That meant a recent shave. He mentally checked the rest of his body. No pain anywhere except the slight sting where the needle pricked his skin. His toes moved fine, so no spinal injury to worry about. Since the coma was over, it made no sense just to lie around. Maybe he could carry his IV out to the hall and find out what was going on.

Drawing his knees up, he shifted his body toward the side of the bed, but a new voice interrupted his plan.

"Where are you going, Ichabod?"

Timothy jerked his head around, expecting to see a nurse with the same ebony skin he had seen on the boy, but a young white woman smiled at him from the door, her blonde tresses draped over green scrubs. With bright eyes and smooth, radiant skin, her joy dressed her face with beauty.

Timothy settled back in the bed, smiling. "You caught me trying to get up."

"*Caught* you?" She gave him a blank stare. "I think you are too big for catching."

He gazed at her expression. Was she joking, or did she really not understand? She was either a great actress or completely clueless. He massaged his thighs, trying to get his circulation going. "I guess a doctor has to make sure it's okay for me to stand."

"Your guess is correct." She strode to his bedside and pulled a multicoloured leaf from her pocket. Pinching the stem in her fingers, she dangled it over his face. The yellow near the bottom tip slowly changed to orange, while the red near the top changed to green. "Your energy flow is slightly below normal, Ichabod, but, other than that, your vital signs are perfect." She returned the leaf to her pocket. "We were never able to find your companion, so it's no wonder you were out for so long. Most of us thought you couldn't possibly survive without it."

"My companion? What are you talking about? And why do you call me Ichabod?"

"That's the name the Prophet gave you." She laid a cool hand on his forehead. "You must have amnesia. If you can't remember your companion, you must have taken a terrible blow to your brain."

"My first name is Timothy. But I don't remember a last name or much of anything else. I guess I must have banged my head pretty hard if I can't even remember that I had a ... a companion." He glanced at a ring on his finger, a gold band with an embedded

69

white gem. Could it be a wedding ring? Maybe. But it was on the wrong hand. "If I do have a companion, I don't know what happened to her."

"A companion is not a 'her'." She bracketed her hands in front of her chest as if holding an invisible grapefruit-sized ball. Her palms radiated a white glow that passed across the gap between her hands. A translucent egg appeared, slightly smaller than a hen's egg, almost ghost-like and floating in mid-air.

"An ovulum!" Timothy whispered.

She lowered her head and peered at him through the egg. "That's what the Prophet sometimes calls them. We just call them companions, because that's what they are."

" 'Ovulum' just popped into my mind. I don't know what it is."

She separated her hands, and the ovulum faded, but its outline remained, barely detectable and floating without any visible means of propulsion. "The Prophet has a special, stationary one he calls 'Enoch's Ghost' that he keeps on a table at his home, but ours are smaller and mobile." The companion zipped up to her shoulder and perched there, rocking back and forth. "Clearly you remember something about them, or you would not have known its name."

"I can still see it on your shoulder," Timothy said, pointing. "It was invisible before."

"It has always been visible." She glanced at the strange lamp hanging from the ceiling. "Sometimes the lighting makes it hard to see."

Timothy shut his eyes. There were just too many new and odd surroundings to figure out. Had he been abducted by aliens, or was this the most vivid nightmare in history? "I must be dreaming," he said. "Or else I'm losing my mind."

He felt her fingers comb through his hair, stopping at a spot near the top of his head. A slight twinge of pain blended in with the soothing sensation. "When we first found you, there was quite a lump right here, so it's no wonder your memory is impaired."

"How long have I been here? And where is *here*, anyway?"

She laughed gently. "The Prophet said that questions would fill your mind. He anxiously awaits your release so he can answer as many as possible."

"What does the doctor say?" he asked, his eyes still closed. "Can I leave soon?"

"She says that you may leave. In fact, she insists that you leave immediately. The Prophet's instructions were clear. Now that you have awakened, you must go to him."

Timothy opened his eyes and smiled. Her fingers felt heavenly. "I'm guessing that you're the doctor."

"You seem to enjoy guessing, and you are correct again." She pointed at a closet. "You will find your clothes in there. I will send my son in to assist you."

"I heard him call you 'Mother'. Is he adopted?"

Her blonde eyebrows scrunched toward her shining blue eyes. "Of course. Aren't we all?"

"Uh ... No. I don't think so."

She set her hands on her hips and tapped her foot. "Timothy, I think we'll have to work hard at understanding each other. I get the impression that some words have different meanings where you come from."

"And we obviously have different customs. Not that I minded, but I was surprised that a child is allowed to come and go as he pleases." He nodded toward the clock. "Especially in a military hospital."

She looked up at the clock. "Military? What do you mean?"

"Uh ... Army? Navy?"

"Ah!" she said, nodding dramatically. "We do have an army." She deftly removed the needle from his hand, but as she wound the tube over the IV hanger, a single drop of the grey liquid fell to the floor.

Timothy rubbed the wound on his skin, wondering what kind of alien medicine had been pushed into his veins.

She lowered the bed rail and waved toward the closet. "Take careful steps." As if demonstrating, she padded slowly toward the door. "We wouldn't want you to bump your head again."

Just as she reached the exit, the boy walked in, now wearing a blue "Lions" baseball cap that matched his sweatshirt. "Mother," he said. "When are we leaving?"

She laid a hand on his shoulder. "Very soon. I will take Listener home first so we'll have room to transport our guest. You can stay here and help him get ready."

The boy tilted his head and rubbed her hand with his cheek. "Will you leave Father's companion with me, too?"

"No, silly man," she said, pressing his cap down. "Now that we're going home to stay, I'm going to put it back on its shelf."

"May I see it again before you leave?" The boy extended his cupped hands. "Please?"

The doctor smiled at Timothy. "I hope you'll pardon this interruption."

"Of course," Timothy said. "Please take your time."

She reached into her pocket and withdrew a purple velvet-covered box, similar to, yet somewhat bigger than a ring box. After flipping open the hinged lid, she tipped out a glass egg into the boy's hands. His eyes widened, as did his brilliant smile. Transferring the egg to one hand, he petted the top with his fingers. The touch seemed to make it glow with a pale yellow hue.

The doctor lowered herself to one knee and stroked her son's back. "That means your father loves you, and he misses your touch." As she continued, her voice began to break. "Don't ever forget what a great man he was or how much he loved you."

"I won't, Mother." A tear passed from his eye to his cheek as he continued to stare at the glowing orb. "Every time I hold his companion, I feel him hugging me."

After a few more seconds, she held the open box under his hands. "That's enough for now. I have to take your sister home."

The boy petted the egg one more time before lovingly rolling it back into the box. His mother closed the lid and nodded solemnly to Timothy. "I will be back very soon." With that, she swept through the doorway.

The boy turned a dial on the wall near the door, and the flaming wicks above grew brighter. "Do you want me to get your clothes for you or help you walk to the closet?"

Timothy wiped a tear from his eye and sat up, dangling his legs. His bare toes brushed the rough, wooden floor. "Yes, please bring my clothes, if you don't mind."

While the boy gathered the clothing in his arms, Timothy glanced out the single, unadorned window. Clouds and filtered sunlight filled the view – no grass, no trees, no parking lot. This room was obviously on a high floor.

The boy dropped the clothing bundle on the bed. Two soft-soled walking shoes tumbled off the top but stayed on the sheet. He placed them side by side and smiled. "I think that's all."

"Thank you." Timothy pulled out his trousers, a freshly laundered and pressed pair of beige khakis. "What's your name, young man?"

"Candle," he replied, his grin revealing a lovely set of bright teeth.

"Candle?" Timothy slid his trousers over his legs, then lowered himself to the floor and pulled them the rest of the way up. "I've never heard of anyone named Candle before. Do other kids tease you?"

Candle's brow furrowed. "Uh ... No. I don't think so. I know two other boys and a girl named Candle. It just must not be a popular name where you come from." His brow smoothed back out as a new smile lit up his face. "My mother likes my name because she says I light up a room whenever I walk in."

Timothy patted Candle's shoulder. "Well, I certainly agree with that! Your mother chose well."

"She didn't choose it. She just likes it." Candle rubbed his cheek against Timothy's hand, just as he had done to his mother's.

"I see." Timothy slowly drew his hand away, wondering if he might be committing a social blunder by ending his show of affection, but since Candle's smile never dimmed, this brush of the cheek must have been similar to a quick pat on the back. Timothy pulled a polo shirt over his head and began tucking it in his trousers. "I didn't catch your mother's name."

"*Catch* her name?"

"Yes." Timothy zipped his trousers and tightened his belt. "She never mentioned it."

"Angel. Her name is Angel."

Timothy sat on the bed and picked up his socks. "How appropriate."

Candle smiled. "My father thought so, too. He said she's a gift from Heaven. And my sister is named Listener. She doesn't talk, but she listens to and remembers everything."

"Being a listener is a great character quality." He stretched a navy blue sweater over his head and pushed his arms through the sleeves. "Is she older or younger than you?"

"Younger." Candle helped him pull the sweater's hem down to his waist. "But not by a whole lot."

After quickly tying his shoes, Timothy reached for the final garment, a heavy collegiate jacket, blue with orange trim. "Is it cold outside?"

"Pretty cold, but no colder than it usually is up here." Candle flapped his sweatshirt's long sleeves. "I was comfortable in this."

Timothy dropped down to the floor again and lifted each leg in turn. They felt heavy, but not too bad. He put on his jacket and smiled at Candle. "Where to now?"

Candle slid his hand into Timothy's. "To the loading platform. We'll walk slowly so Mother has time to return before we get there."

"I would have liked to meet your sister while she was here."

"She came to your door." Candle nodded toward the exit. "Didn't you see her?"

In his mind, Timothy redrew the little girl's gaunt, scaly face peering around the door frame. "I did see a young girl, but I thought she was a patient here."

"Well, that was Listener. Mother likes for both of us to come whenever she's assigned hospital duty."

"She seems like a friendly girl." Timothy pressed his lips together. It was probably best not to keep asking about Listener, though her pitiful appearance raised plenty of questions.

As he guided Timothy out the door, Candle smiled and squeezed his hand more tightly. "I hope Valiant can meet you."

"Why is that?"

"He is my village's leader." Candle turned the dial by the door. The lanterns in the hanging fixture winked out. "Valiant was worried that someone without a companion might be altered."

Timothy looked for Candle's companion. He caught a glimpse of it floating near his shoulder. "Altered?"

"Yes." The boy's dark eyes seemed to dance. "But you're not one of them. I can tell."

As they walked down the hallway, Timothy marvelled at Candle's noble innocence, feeling free to walk in public hand-in-hand with an adult male. Was he twelve years old? Thirteen? A few boys his age might hold hands with a father, but probably not with a stranger.

75

The dim corridor was unlike any hospital he had ever seen – roughly hewn beams instead of tiles for floors, a single hardwood bench serving as a waiting area instead of sofas surrounding a television, no visitors carrying flowers or balloons, no nurses with trays of medicines, and no patients lying on trolleys awaiting transport to the next battery of tests. The place felt more like a rustic log cabin than a hospital.

Passing room after room, all with closed doors, Timothy gazed down the seemingly endless hall. "Where is everyone?" he asked, his voice echoing.

Candle pushed their clasped hands into a gentle swing. "Mother will meet us on the transport deck. We're almost there."

"No. I mean the patients. It feels like we're alone in here."

"We are. You're the only patient, and I'm glad. Now Mother and Listener and I can go back to our farm."

Timothy looked down the hall behind him. The end seemed at least a hundred yards away. "Such a huge hospital, and I'm the only patient?"

Candle turned into a short hallway that led to a double door. "The last war was almost three years ago, and nearly every room was filled. We even took care of some of the altered tribe." He pushed open the swinging door. "Here we are."

A frigid breeze swirled into the hall. The doorway led to a concrete platform that ended abruptly about fifty feet out, a dead end at the cloud-filled sky. There was no apparent driveway up to that level, and the platform was too small for a helicopter to land safely, especially in this wind. The thick overcast made it impossible to see any surrounding buildings, and even the ground below was hidden in a gloomy mist that enveloped everything.

Candle held the door. "Aren't you going through?"

Timothy zipped up his jacket and stepped out onto the ledge. His fingers immediately stiffened, and his lips dried out. As his teeth chattered, he buried his hands in his pockets and bounced on his toes. "It must be ... below zero ... out here."

Candle joined him, seemingly unaffected by the cold. Now his companion was easy to see as a stream of vapour formed around the egg and blew away with the wind. As his black dreadlocks flapped under his cap, he held the bill to keep it in place. "Here comes the transport," he shouted, pointing up.

Following Candle's finger, Timothy spotted a huge winged creature among the clouds, closing in as it disappeared and reappeared, passing from one cloud to the next. "A dragon?" he asked.

"What else is big enough?" Candle half closed one eye at him. "You don't ride on birds, do you? The altered tribe uses birds."

Timothy tried to smile, but it probably looked more like a frozen grimace. "I have ... never flown ... on a bird."

With a powerful beating of its wings, a huge dragon landed. The splendid creature flashed purplish scales and breathed a thick vapour that crystallized and rained to the landing platform in icy pellets.

77

Three seats had been tied in single file to the dragon's back, fastened with wide straps that wrapped under its belly. As the dragon lowered its head, the rider waved at them. "Hurry aboard! Ichabod looks cold!"

His teeth still chattering, Timothy nodded at the female rider, Angel, now wearing a black leather jacket and corduroy pantaloons instead of green scrubs.

"Ever since Father died," Candle explained, "Mother has had to fly our dragon herself." He stepped up the dragon's spiny stairway. "Come on," he called back, waving. "Grackle will warm you up."

Still burying his hands in his pockets, Timothy climbed the neck, trying to keep his balance in the stiff breeze. When he made it to the top, Candle and his mother reached out their hands. He finally had to expose his frigid fingers again as they guided him to the seat in the middle.

As soon as he sat down, Angel shouted. "Give us a bit more heat for our guest."

A soothing radiance rose from Grackle's scales, instantly thawing Timothy's fingers and toes. The dragon swung his head close to Angel and blew a series of high-pitched whistles.

Twisting her body, Angel reached for a belt attached to Timothy's seat. "Grackle wants to know if you're comfortable now," she said, fastening the belt over his waist.

Timothy unzipped his jacket halfway. "I'm fine. In fact, it's quite warm."

"I'll tell him to lower the heat a notch." Turning back to the dragon, Angel whistled a sweet, warbling tune. Flashing a set of eight sharp incisors, Grackle nodded and stretched out his wings.

Candle tapped Timothy on the shoulder. "Hang on! Grackle loves to give new riders a thrill!"

Timothy gripped the back of Angel's seat. "Thanks for the warning."

As Grackle lifted off, Timothy looked back at the hospital, expecting to see the usual high-rise building shooting up from a medical office complex. Instead, a narrow, single-storey, tube-like metal rod hovered in the sky.

"How does it float like that?" Timothy asked.

"It's not floating," Angel replied. "It's flying. We keep the hospital moving to protect it from the altered tribe. A circuit of magnets on the ground keeps it in motion."

"I don't remember anything this advanced. How long was I out?"

"Candle found you in the birthing garden about a month ago. We don't know how long you were there already."

Suddenly, Grackle plunged. With his stomach pressing into his throat, Timothy rose an inch from his seat, but the belt kept him from flying away. Still, he felt no fear, only a sense of exhilaration, even joy.

Candle lifted his hands and belted out an ecstatic cry. As the flight levelled, he called forward. "Good dive, Grackle! Maybe the best one yet!"

Releasing Angel's seat, Timothy laid a hand on his chest. "That was good," he said. "An excellent ride."

Grackle flew around a village, a group of low buildings nestled in a thick forest of tall evergreens. Thatched roofs of bright yellow covered the majority of the humble cottages, while a few carried dark reddish tiles on sharply angled decking. To Timothy the hamlet looked like a cross between an African tribal community and a low-income development in urban America.

They passed over a massive garden, a field of black soil and spots of greenery that lay just outside the village boundary. Several rows of tall, bushy spruce trees encircled the garden, like sentries protecting the harvest. As the dragon descended, a grassy meadow came into view beyond the village's opposite border. A fruit-filled orchard lay between the grass and the village, and a mountain ridge hemmed the meadow in on the far side.

The dragon settled into the lush field, spreading his wings gracefully and landing with hardly a bump. After unbuckling his belt, Timothy stood and stretched his arms. The air, though still crisp and cold, was far more tolerable than at the hospital, more like temperatures he remembered from somewhere in his past. Could he have lived in a village like this? It certainly didn't seem familiar.

After waiting for Angel to disembark, Timothy stepped down the dragon's neck, followed by Candle. As the boy skipped from one spine to the other, his egg-shaped companion bounced along with him, slightly more visible now.

While Angel reached under Grackle to loosen the buckles that held the seat straps in place, Timothy slid his hands into his pockets and watched her companion slowly orbiting her head. It

79

paused for a moment at her ear as if whispering a secret. She flashed a smile, then laughed gently.

"What did it say, Mother?" Candle asked.

Angel tweaked Candle's nose. "A privacy. A funny one, but still a privacy."

"Why doesn't my companion ever tell me a privacy?"

"Because you're too young." She gestured toward a path in the forest. "On our way down, I saw Whetstone climbing a tree. I'm sure you can find him."

Candle reached for one of the straps. "I'll help you with the seats first."

"No need." She nodded at Timothy. "Our new friend will likely offer his help."

Timothy jerked his hands out of his pockets. "Of course. Glad to."

"Thank you, Mother!" Candle dashed away, followed closely by his companion.

Timothy watched Angel guide the first seat down the dragon's flank and copied her motions, pulling on the strap attached to the middle seat. "Do your ovulums speak to you often?"

Angel set the front seat down and shook her hair out of her eyes. "Your words are a confusing blend to me, Ichabod—I mean, Timothy. You speak as one who has never known the joy of a companion, yet you continue to say their ancient name as if you knew them in the days of our genesis."

"I'm sorry." He laid the seat next to hers and kept his gaze fixed on it. "I'm just trying to communicate the best I can. I don't mean to be so ignorant."

"No fault of yours. Your brain is injured, but surely it will mend soon." She combed her fingers through his hair until she found the bump. "Does it still hurt?"

"Not much." He wanted to finish his job, but her gentle touch gave him reason to pause. "Does the bump feel smaller?" he asked.

She lowered her hand and smiled. "Much smaller."

Timothy pulled down the final seat and set it with the others. "Where do you store these?"

"Store them?" She withdrew a bottle from her pocket and poured thick goop on a cloth. Reaching under the dragon's belly, she massaged the spot where the buckle had rubbed against his body, smearing the goop and pushing it between the scales. Grackle responded with a deep-throated purr. "Why would we store them?" She looked up at him while continuing the dragon's treatment. "They are not affected by the wind."

He spread his arms over the seats as if covering them with a tarpaulin. "To keep them safe from rain and thieves."

She pushed the cloth and bottle back into her pocket. "I have heard of rain from the Prophet, but I have never seen it, and we have no thieves among our people." She rocked one of the seats back and forth. "They will be safe here."

Timothy searched a nearby ridge for any sign of a cave. "Where do you keep Grackle?"

"Keep Grackle?" She gave him a surprised look. "Do you mean as a captive?"

The dragon snorted, spewing ice crystals that scattered across Timothy's feet.

He jumped back and stumbled over one of the seats, landing on his backside. Angel rushed over and hoisted him easily, her strong arms almost lifting him right off his feet. "You must be careful," she said. "Grackle knows many words."

Brushing the grass from his trousers, Timothy glared at the dragon. "I think I'd better keep my distance until I get to know your ways better."

"At least from him," Angel said, shaking a finger at Grackle. "He enjoys humour at the expense of strangers."

Timothy bowed toward Grackle. "I apologize. I should have known that dragons aren't held against their will."

81

He bowed in return and whistled a cheery sounding note.

"Grackle is free," Angel said, "but you can always find him close to home, unless you come during mealtime. Then he will likely be hunting in the rabbit fields just over the ridge close to where my village lies."

Timothy eyed the ridge and imagined another village beyond it much like the one he had seen from the air, perhaps bordered by a field teeming with rabbits being chased by a purple dragon. A lone eagle crossed the ridge, flying rapidly toward them. Timothy pointed at it. "That's the first bird I've seen since I've been here."

"An eagle!" Angel clutched his forearm tightly. "Does it have a black underside?"

As it flew closer, the predator's details became clear – long brown wings, white head and tail feathers, and a coal-black breast. "Its underbelly *is* black. It looks kind of strange."

"Because it carries an altered one. Since he is out in the daylight, he must have come from a surprise attack somewhere."

"Should you warn anyone?" Timothy asked. "Can someone chase him?"

As Angel watched the eagle, her grip on his arm loosened. "It's too late. He is on his way to the basin of shadows." She lowered her chin. "We will likely hear bad news very soon."

A happy shout sounded from the forest. Candle and another boy clung to branches near the top of a tall spruce and waved down at them.

Angel waved back and yelled, "I will meet you here later!"

"I'll watch for you!" came the wind-blown reply.

The fresh breeze forced Timothy's hands back into his pockets. "Candle is a delightful young man," he said, trying not to shiver.

"Yes, I know. He learned a great deal from his father in a short amount of time."

82

"He mentioned that your husband died. May I ask what happened to him?"

Angel gave Timothy an inquisitive look. "My husband? I'm not familiar with that word."

"Uh ... Your mate? Your man?"

Her eyebrows lifted. "Oh! My Adam."

"*My* Adam? You mean his name was Adam?"

"His name was Dragon, because he was bold and fearless, but he was my Adam, and I was his Eve" – she interlocked her fingers – "man and woman joined together until death. But since he was killed in the last war and his spirit has passed beyond the Bridgelands, and since it is not wise to raise a son without the guidance of a father, our laws require me to seek another Adam, if possible, before three years have passed."

Timothy shrugged his shoulders. "Well, it shouldn't be hard for a beautiful woman like you to find one." As soon as those words spilled out, he regretted them. Obviously she hadn't remarried, and he was too ignorant about this place to know why.

She gazed at him. A hint of tears glistened in her eyes, and her face flushed pink. Turning quickly, she nodded toward the village. "The Prophet instructed me to bring you here as soon as you recovered your senses."

"I've committed enough social errors to prove my senses aren't quite up to snuff, but I'll do my best."

She repeated her inquisitive stare. "Snuff?"

"'Up to snuff' is an idiom. It means ... um ... 'working normally'."

"I understand," she said, nodding. "Perhaps the Prophet can help you reach snuff. He is a wise and powerful man."

Timothy stifled a laugh. "Then, please lead me to him."

She turned to the dragon and whistled a few low notes, then a melodic warble. Grackle gave a short whistle in reply.

"He will wait for us." Angel folded her hands at her waist and scanned Timothy from head to toe. "Your attire is suitable, but I perceive that your unfamiliarity with our customs will make people very curious."

Timothy straightened and copied her suddenly formal manner. "I think that is wise to assume."

"Then I will instruct you as the need arises." Angel pressed her palms together in front of her chest. "This is our prayer posture. We must walk this way or the people will stop us."

Timothy mimicked her position. "Like this?"

"Excellent." She pointed toward a well-worn path in the woods. "Walk in front of me, and I will tell you which way to turn."

Timothy headed toward the path, walking slowly to make sure Angel kept up. "Why would the people stop us?"

"They are friendly and will want to know all about you. Your pose is a polite request to allow you to proceed without distraction. They will smile and bow their heads as we pass, and we should do the same."

"That should be easy enough." Timothy followed the path through the increasingly dense forest until he came to a fork.

"To the right," Angel said.

Timothy veered right and maintained his slow pace. "Wouldn't it be easier for you to lead the way?"

"Easier? Yes. Proper? No."

He kept his eyes focused ahead and his mouth closed. It probably wasn't a good time to ask about gender roles. He would likely just stick his foot in his mouth again.

"We are coming into the village," Angel said. "When we clear the tree line, walk on the right boundary of the road and double your speed. We will avoid stares if people don't have a chance to notice your lack of a companion. After passing the centre circle, proceed along the street lined with wooden rails and look for a small house on the left, one with a dragon banner on each side of the door."

"Is that the Prophet's house?"

"It is."

Timothy reached the clearing and quickened his pace. "What is the Prophet's name?"

"Many call him 'Father' when addressing him, and the elders call him Abraham, but when we speak of him in conversation, it is always 'The Prophet'." She cleared her throat and whispered. "Let us be silent now."

Passing over the road's hardened beige-coloured clay, Timothy marched near a long rail to which three donkeys were tied, one on his side of the street, and two on the other. An occasional gap in the rail allowed for entry into a much narrower, parallel walkway that crossed in front of the doors of the humble homes.

Only a few people walked by, smiling and bowing as Angel had predicted, each one with a companion hovering somewhere over his or her shoulder, some more visible than others.

Timothy responded with smiles and head nods, hoping he wasn't committing any unintentional faux pas. A young lady coming out of a stacked-stone house stared at him, but when her companion orbited close to her ear, she quickly smiled and bowed, her face reddening.

As they neared the end of the street, the village's centre came into view. More people streamed into it from the eight identical roads that intersected at a central roundabout. Families walked in groups, a man and woman linking elbows, and one to four children tagging along in no apparent order. Two families stopped and congregated, laughing and chatting. One couple walked in the prayer posture, marching quickly without interruption. Another man led a young woman riding a donkey. They stopped and talked with another couple while three children petted the donkey.

"The woman on the donkey," Angel whispered, "is betrothed to the man leading her. Adams and Eves stay side by side. A woman leading a man indicates that the man is her suitor in a courtship arrangement."

"I am leading you," he whispered back. "Will people think we're betrothed?"

"I am not riding a donkey!"

Timothy shook his head and mumbled, "I have so much to learn!"

He circled the roundabout, staying to the right as he navigated through the intermixing streams of people. Companions hovered all around. Sometimes it was impossible to tell which ovulum belonged to whom, but as he passed close to one teenaged boy, he caught a glimpse of something inside the boy's companion, an almost imperceptible pair of eyes. As it passed around from ear to ear, the ovulum's gaze never wandered from its apparent owner.

Although the mix of adults, teenagers, and children seemed normal enough, no one appeared to be more than thirty years old. Not a grey hair or a wrinkle marred the head or face of man or woman.

When he reached the opposite side of the circle, he came upon another road lined with rails. Donkeys stood tied to them, waiting in front of various homes. He searched the houses on the left and spied the dragon banners on each side of an open door. The hut was no more than an adobe shack with a thatched straw roof, smaller than any other home on the street.

A man bowed at the doorway, apparently in homage to someone inside. Rising again, he walked to a donkey at the hitching rail and extended a hand to the woman who followed. As Timothy and Angel approached, the man smiled while helping the woman mount, then led her away.

Timothy paused at the low doorway, gazing at the colourful banners, red dragons on blue backgrounds, each breathing streams of fire through mouth and nostrils as if aiming at each other or at anyone passing into the house.

"Just walk in," Angel said, her voice rising above a whisper.

Timothy ducked his head and entered the dim one-room hut. Near the back, a man sat on a chair facing the door, gazing at an ovulum on a small table in front of him, larger than the hovering companions and much easier to see. A soft red aura surrounded the glassy egg, a glow that feathered out and disappeared a few inches from the shell.

The man looked up. Along with his reddish, neatly trimmed beard, a gentle smile decorated his ruddy face. "Angel," he said cheerily, "you have brought our stranger. I thank you for your labours."

Angel bowed low and pulled Timothy into a bow with her. "It is always an honour serving you, Father."

As they straightened, the Prophet tapped the surface of the ovulum. "Enoch tells me that your home has need of your presence, though I don't know the reason. You must hurry there immediately."

Angel's brow furrowed, but, as her hovering companion nuzzled her cheek, no other hint of concern broke through. She bowed again and walked backwards toward the door. "I am at your service, Father." Once she reached the threshold, she turned and ran.

The Prophet motioned toward a chair on the opposite side of the table. "Sit, friend, and we will talk. I have long awaited this opportunity."

Timothy slid into the chair. He fidgeted, pressing the toes of his shoes against the dirt floor. He fumbled with his hands before deciding to fold them on the table. A beam of light from a small hole in the roof struck an array of dangling crystalline beads on the adjacent wall, giving the entire room a rainbow-spattered glow and colouring his nervous fingers with dancing hues.

"There is no need to be anxious," the Prophet said, covering Timothy's hands with his own. "You will find no evil in my home."

"I detect none." Timothy took a deep breath and let it out slowly. "I am perplexed by mystery. I remember my name ... Timothy ... but little else." He quickly scanned the space around the Prophet's head, but the strange lighting must have kept his companion hidden in shadows.

"You may call me Abraham." The Prophet caressed the glass egg as its glow flooded his fingers in red light. "I think I might be able to help you learn more about yourself."

"Okay," Timothy said, flattening his hands on the table. "I'm all ears."

Abraham chuckled. "That is a fine idiom. I will remember to teach it to my people."

"I noticed that they use idioms I've heard before, but some of mine are foreign to them."

88

"That's because as I learn them, I pass some along and keep others to myself." Abraham pressed his finger on the glass. "But I learn much more than simple idioms. I taught my people several languages, finally settling on English as it became the language of a certain prophet on Earth I used to watch. Also, most of our technology comes from what I was able to copy by studying what you have in your world."

Timothy pointed at himself. "My world? I'm not from this planet?"

"I believe you come from another realm and dimension, one that I have watched for countless years." Abraham gazed into the red glass. "But the fact that another world exists should not shock you. Many authors in your realm have speculated such things, so the idea is not foreign to your people."

"Maybe not so foreign, but reading about a new realm feels a lot safer than suddenly showing up in one." Timothy leaned closer to the ovulum. "You can see my world in there?"

"And much more." With a curled finger, he signalled for Timothy to peer into the strange egg. "This orb is called Enoch's Ghost. It is the twin of one the great prophet Enoch possessed long ago, and he now often speaks through this very glass to give us a window to other worlds – to your world, to worlds of the afterlife, and to Heaven itself. It also replays the annals of times gone by."

Timothy looked inside. "I see a dark chamber and a girl with white hair and brilliant blue eyes."

"I have seen her many times," Abraham said, "almost always in that dark room. I don't know why Enoch shows her to me from time to time, but I perceive greatness in her. She has suffered cruel treatment over the years, but she has overcome every challenge."

Entranced by her sapphiric eyes, Timothy drew closer. "She is mesmerizing. Do you know her name?"

"Only through a brief song Enoch sings about her on occasion."

Timothy pointed at the glass. "The ovulum sings to you?"

"Oh, yes." Abraham laughed softly. "Before any rooster considers crowing, Enoch makes sure I arise bright and early with a song, and he grants me encore performances throughout the day."

The image of the girl faded, leaving only a swirling red fog within. Timothy settled back in his chair. "Can you sing the one about the girl?"

Abraham cleared his throat. "My voice is no match for Enoch's, but the song is short enough to keep you from seeking a rock to hide under." He took a breath and sang in a rough tenor.

> To see beyond the veil of men
> Demands a child of piercing sight.
> Sapphira Adi, born of earth,
> Is now a daughter of the light.

Timothy let the name roll quietly off his tongue. "Sapphira Adi."

"A lovely name, isn't it?"

"It *is* lovely ... and familiar." Timothy leaned forward and gazed at the chaotic swirl within Enoch's Ghost. "Sapphira Adi," he whispered, "For some reason, I think we have met before, and I believe we are destined to meet again."

6

CHAPTER

THE ENDLESS STAIRCASE

Holding Excalibur in front, Walter scampered down the uneven, rocky steps, occasionally skipping one or two as he hurried along.

Ashley hustled to keep up, but each echoing footfall brought new reminders of her recent upwelling of frightening recollections. The dark staircase felt like an old nightmare come to life, a deepening vision of vague, shadowy dreams that had haunted many troubled slumbers. The last thing she wanted here was to be alone. "Slow down!" she called, trying to catch her breath. "I can't see where I'm going!"

Walter stopped and looked back. "Sorry. I just want to get there as fast as possible." The light from the blade shone on each side wall. The stairway was so narrow they had to descend single file to keep from scraping their shoulders on the rough stones. "Besides, who wants to stick around this creepy corridor?"

"I know what you mean." She unzipped her jacket and flapped it to cool her body. "I'm getting kind of claustrophobic, but we can't hurtle into the unknown at ninety miles an hour. Who knows what might be down there?"

He pointed the sword at the stairs below. "If it's something dangerous, then we should go even faster. Karen needs us."

"But we'll be exhausted when we get there." She leaned against the wall. "Don't forget. Going down is a lot easier than coming back up. If Karen can't climb, it might take all day to get back."

"Good point." Walter exhaled loudly and rested his back on the opposite wall. After a few seconds his eyebrows lifted. "Have you wondered how a dragon can make a hole like this open up? I mean, is that a weird dragon power we haven't heard of yet? Can some of them make things move with their minds?"

Ashley pushed a shock of wet hair out of her eyes and wiped the perspiration on her jeans. "I've been thinking about it ever since we started down this hole. I doubt that dragons can defy the laws of physics. They're limited to using their natural traits, just like humans are, and creating a hole and a staircase like this out of the blue isn't anywhere close to natural."

Walter's eyes gleamed in Excalibur's weak glow. "So, what's your conclusion, Miss Mighty Mind?"

A twinge of pain pinched Ashley's heart. She expected Larry to zing her with barbed nicknames, but not Walter. She tried to hide the sting with a laugh. "Didn't I ask you to stop joking about me?"

"But it wasn't a joke."

"Then what was it?"

"Uh ..." His eyes averted, finally fixing their gaze on the stone wall. "A term of endearment?" Even in the low light, the redness in his cheeks was obvious.

She smiled and sighed. "Okay. Fair enough."

Walter's gaze stayed locked on the wall. "That's kind of weird."

"What's kind of weird?" Ashley followed his line of sight and searched the bare stone. "What are you staring at?"

"You can't see it at first," he replied, rubbing his finger along a darker spot, "but if you concentrate, you can make out a design."

She leaned closer. "What kind of design?"

"Kind of like letters, but it's pretty ragged." He brought Excalibur near the wall. Its glow poured into the crags, revealing a series of odd shapes that ran head high and parallel to the sloping staircase, staying within a hand's-breadth range. "You can see it pretty easily now."

Ashley ran a finger along the stone. "It's too broken to make out, but it's definitely a string of words of some kind." She tapped her jaw and spoke into the air. "Larry, are you still listening in?"

"Your signal is weak, O Anthrozilic Angel, so I will boost my power and extend the auxiliary antenna."

"Yeah, right. And increase the volume on your annoying alliterations." She reached into her duffle bag and pulled out her handheld computer. "I have my tracker turned on. Are you monitoring us?"

"You are still at your former residence in Montana, but your elevation has changed. You are now at only one hundred and twelve feet above sea level, four thousand and six feet lower than before."

"I hope we don't hit water," Walter said. "I didn't bring my swim fins."

She set the computer close to the wall. "I'm sending a scan. It'll be pretty rough, but see if you can clean it up and read it to me."

"Ready for transmission."

Holding down a button on the side, Ashley guided the computer along the etching and stopped after a few feet. "That should be enough of a sample."

Several seconds later, Larry's voice buzzed through again. "I compared the phrase to several dictionaries and calculated the most likely rendering. It says, 'Lasciate ogne speranza, voi ch'intrate'."

93

Ashley slid the computer back into her pocket. "Sounds like Italian."

"Affirmative. It repeated a few words before the transmission ended, so I considered the extra verbiage dispensable."

"Yeah, it looks like the same message over and over." Ashley laid her hand on the letters again. "What does it mean?"

"I found the exact rendering in my electronic library, so I will provide the version in that translation. It means, 'Abandon hope, all ye who enter here.'"

She jerked her hand down. "What did you say?"

"Abandon hope, all ye who enter here. Shall I adjust my volume again?"

"No. ... No, that's not the problem." Ashley grabbed one hand with the other, trying to keep from trembling. "It's from Dante's *Inferno*," she said, "the first part of his *Divine Comedy*."

"A comedy?" Walter shook his head. "Someone needs a better joke writer."

"'Comedy,' Ashley explained, "just means it's supposed to have a happy ending. In Dante's book that phrase is inscribed at the gates of Hell."

"Not exactly a welcome mat," Walter said, "but it's not going to stop me from barging in. I've been there before." He turned and descended. "Let's get moving."

Ashley took in a deep breath and followed. Since Walter had slowed down, she was able to count the steps, announcing the number at each hundred. Larry added to the bulletins, providing a report of their elevation every five minutes.

All along the way, she kept glancing at the writing on the wall. The same morbid letters repeated themselves again and again while Larry's voice echoed in her mind, *Abandon hope, all ye who enter here.* As the echoes grew louder, her heart raced, and sweat streamed

94

down her cheeks. Her childhood nightmares were coming true. How many times had she descended these stairs during her fitful dreams? Once at the bottom would she find tormented souls? Since she had never truly believed in her grandfather's God, would she become one of them, lost forever in Hell? Finally, her heart pounding, she leaned against the wall again, breathless. "We have to rest!"

Walter retreated to one step below her level and leaned against the wall. "We're almost to ten thousand." His chest heaved as he spoke. "The air's stuffy, it's getting hot, and my ears are about to implode."

"Because," Larry interjected, "your elevation is eight thousand three hundred and sixty-three feet below sea level, give or take an inch."

"Eight thousand feet!" Walter let out a low whistle. "That's more than a mile!"

Ashley closed her eyes. "One point five, eight, three, nine miles, to be exact."

Walter wiped his brow with his sleeve. "It doesn't take a computer brain to figure out that getting back to the top is looking more impossible with every step down."

Slowing her breathing, she gazed into the dark descent. "But we can't just leave Karen."

"I know, but what if the dragon was lying? What if she's not there at all, and we're just going down an endless spiral staircase? Maybe he just wanted to get rid of us."

"It can't be endless," Ashley said, closing her eyes again. "There are no actual infinites in the physical cosmos. It's impossible."

"Perhaps there are actual infinites you do not yet understand, dear child."

"Dear child?" Ashley opened her eyes and squinted at Walter. "I don't mind terms of endearment, but ... 'dear child'?"

"I didn't say that." Walter set his feet and raised Excalibur. "I thought it was Larry, but it sounded too clear."

95

Ashley angled her head upward. "Larry? Did you just call me 'dear child'?"

"Negative. My terms of endearment of late are draconic in nature and usually alliterative."

"I noticed." Ashley looked up the dark stairwell and listened. Nothing. She then padded softly down two steps and halted, listening again as she stared into the deep, spiral void. Still nothing.

Walter whispered into her ear. "Do you believe in ghosts?"

His question chilled her heart, but she quickly shook it off. Wrinkling her nose, she sharpened her voice. "Of course not. Do you?"

"After all I saw in the Circles of Seven, I'm not sure what to believe." Walter looked up the dark stairway. "I was thinking that someone who calls you a dear child wouldn't mind being seen. So the voice either came from a sociable ghost or a very shy friend."

Ashley tugged on his sleeve. "You're scaring me, Walter."

"Sorry. I guess talking about ghosts is—"

"It's not that," she interrupted, shaking her head. "You're using logic. That's scaring me."

Walter's eyebrows knitted. "So much for terms of endearment." He spun and headed down the stairs again, pointing the sword's light into the depths. "Ghost or no ghost, we have to keep going."

"Walter, wait!" She skipped down the steps. "I didn't mean it that way!"

He halted and faced her, Excalibur's light reflecting in his fiery eyes. "What way did you mean it?"

Ashley stopped in midstep and bit her tongue. Why did she say something so stupid? Walter was such a good, brave friend. He didn't deserve that slap even as a joke. And why did such a condescending put-down even enter her mind anyway?

"Walter," Larry said, buzzing through Ashley's teeth, "it seems that the fire-breathing femme has lost her flaming tongue."

As she let out a long breath, her shoulders sagged. "I'm sorry, Walter. Really I am. It was a stupid thing to say."

He glared at her long and hard. Finally, his expression softened. "It's okay, but I'd like to trust every word you say, too."

Sliding her backside down the wall, Ashley sat on the step. She blew hair from her eyes and sighed. "We need to talk."

Walter sat against the other wall and laid the sword on his lap. "What about?"

She pointed at him and herself in turn. "You and me."

"Uh ... Okay." He clenched his hands together and cleared his throat. "I guess."

Ashley held back a groan, not wanting to hurt his feelings again. She tried to keep her voice calm, but fear rattled her words. "I don't mean" – she made quotation marks in the air with her fingers – "'you and me' as in 'having a relationship'. I mean why are we so different? You're charging down this staircase to Hell like it's ... like it's just the stairs from your bedroom to the living room. You act like it's all a video game, while I'm ..." Her voice pitched higher, but she couldn't help it. "While I'm so scared I'm about to ..." Tears filling her eyes, she held out a trembling hand.

Walter took her hand in both of his. "About to lose your cool?"

She nodded, shaking a tear loose from her cheek. When it fell to her sleeve, she steadied her voice and continued. "I'm supposed to be older and more mature, Miss Independent who practically raised herself, the smartest girl in the world, a guaranteed success in whatever field she chooses." A new surge of emotion tightened her throat. She closed her eyes and squeaked, "But I'm such a fraud!"

"No, you're not," Walter said, gently compressing her hand. "You're the most confident person I know."

She pressed a clenched fist against her chest. "Sure, I'm tough on the outside. I had to be tough or I'd have fallen to pieces. Everyone in school thought I was a freak. Legally, I'm an adult,

97

and no guy has ever given me a second look." Raising her eyebrows, she waved her hand at him. "Not that I need that, but a girl likes to know she's not an ugly troll."

"I know what you mean," Walter said, nodding. "My dad used to call Shelly his little princess all the time, even when she was in high school. No matter how many times I called her ugly, she would stick out her tongue at me and say, 'Daddy says I'm pretty'."

As she gazed toward the dark ceiling, Ashley lowered her voice to a dreamy whisper. "I was too young to remember my father. Did he ever pick me up and tell me I'm pretty? Did he ever call me his little princess? Did he sing me songs and tuck me in at night? That's what I really needed, a daddy who made me feel like a lady." She licked her lips and met Walter's gaze again, her chin quivering. "I guess I never really had a daddy."

His brow knitted sympathetically. "Didn't your grandfather ever do those things for you? From what you told me, he sounds like he was a really cool guy."

"He was great, and he called me sweet names, but he got sick pretty early on. I mean, I was changing his bedpan before I was eleven. He loved me, but he wasn't strong enough to be the support I needed. I dreamed of a powerful king who could pick me up and call me princess, not someone I had to reach down to and wipe the dribble from his chin." She looked up at Walter. "Is that too harsh? I mean, was I asking too much?"

He shook his head. "I don't think so. You were hiding a lot of pain."

"And fear. I mean, how do you do it? Are you just holding it in? Are you scared and pretending not to be? Or am I the only fraud?"

She began to withdraw her hand, but Walter held it fast. "I said you're not a fraud, and I meant it. You're just carrying too much weight. You've always been taking care of people – as a healer, as a genius lab assistant, and now you've put everything on your shoulders – finding your father, your brother, your dragon sister, and Karen." He caressed her knuckles tenderly. "It's not all up to you. You have to let it go."

"How can I let it go? We still have so much to do."

"Hey, I know what you mean." He pressed his thumb against his chest. "I'm the one carrying the sword, remember? And I'm not half the swordsman Billy is. But I just do what I can. I can't worry about anything else."

"So ..." Her voice trembled again. "Are you scared?"

He shrugged. "Sure. I guess so. Who wouldn't be?"

"But you never show it. You're always so confident."

Walter leaned his head back against the wall and sighed. "Look, I make jokes and talk big sometimes, but that's to remind me of what I've already been through." He pointed at himself again. "You have to remember, I've been to Hades before. I saw stuff that would make Superman hide under his cape, but everything still worked out okay."

Ashley tried not to laugh, but Walter's mischievous grin made it impossible to hold it back. "Okay. You win. You do have more experience than I do."

"Yep. The more I remember walking alone in the seventh circle of Hades, staring down a dragon that wanted to fry me for supper, and fighting Morgan while she possessed Bonnie's body, the easier it is to keep going. I mean, I trusted God through all of that. Why should I think he's not around now?" He leaned forward and slid his hand back into hers, gripping it firmly. "You're a strong, beautiful woman, Ashley Stalworth. I'm proud to be your partner, either on Earth or in Hades. I trust you with all my heart."

Tears welled in her eyes again. She tried to swallow back the surge of emotion, but it leaked out through her trembling voice. "Walter ... you know what I said about you and me?" She rubbed her thumb along his finger. "Maybe someday. ... I mean, when we're older." Her cheeks flushed hot, and she shook her head. "I guess I'd better shut up. I'm getting all sappy."

Setting Excalibur on the steps, Walter rose to his feet and pulled Ashley to hers, keeping their hands locked together as he gazed into her eyes. "Listen carefully. We're going to find your brother, your sister, and even your father, and put your family back together. Then, someday when I'm old enough to learn to be at least half the man your father must have been, I might come knocking at his door and speak to him about a lovely princess I'd like to have a lot more adventures with."

Her tears now flowing, Ashley laid a hand on his cheek. It was hot and damp. "Walter, I ... I don't know what to say."

"Then don't say anything. We have at least a few years between now and then." He picked up Excalibur and hurried down the stairs. "We'd better get going."

She followed, trying to keep pace. It seemed that Walter's emotions had fired up his energy. How could he take off like that after such a catharsis? Her own energy had drained away. His stunning confidence in her, the constant written reminders of their apparent descent into Hell, and the strange feeling that some unknown entity was lurking had worked together to weaken her legs and churn her stomach.

Finally, after almost a thousand more steps, they came to a wall, a dead end of solid stone. Walter pounded the wall with the heel of his fist. "You gotta be kidding me! All this way for nothing?"

Sniffing the air as she turned a slow circle, Ashley laid a hand on his arm. "You notice something?"

Walter took in a deep breath. "Fresh air?"

She moved his arm downward, casting Excalibur's glow on the floor. Several dime-sized holes pierced the rock around their feet. "Air vents?" she asked.

He bent over and inserted the tip of the sword into one of the holes. "Think anything down there is organic?"

"Could be," she said, rubbing her shoe on the floor. "There are likely to be carbon molecules, maybe some microorganisms." She looked back at him. "Why?"

He tightened his grip on the hilt. "Stand back. Let's see what happens with a little burst."

"Just a little one!" she warned. "We don't want to get zapped ourselves."

"Just enough to widen it so I can see what's down there." The beam's energy trickled into the hole. Veins of light crawled along the rocky floor like cracks in ice, zigzagging under their feet.

After a few seconds, he turned off the beam, leaving only the blade's glow to light the chamber. He knelt and peered through the hole, now the size of a golf ball. "It's too dark down there."

Ashley stooped and listened. "Can you hear anything?"

"Just a crunching sound, like someone chewing on rocks."

When she laid her palm on the floor, a tingling sensation ran along her skin. "That's not chewing!" She grabbed his arm and pulled. "Quick! Up the stairs!"

The floor crumbled, and they plummeted into the void, but their plunge lasted only a fraction of a second. Their shoes hit solid rock again just several feet below. Fresh air breezed upward, drying their perspiration. The air swept past the original floor level, now just out of reach above their heads.

"That was a gut-buster!" Walter said.

Ashley, her hair flying around her eyes as the air breezed past, laid a hand on her abdomen. "I think my gut turned a flip."

Still holding the sword, he directed the light downward. "There's a trapdoor here with lots of holes in it, like a wooden grating."

"That's where the air's coming from. It must be a vent for something underneath."

Walter poked his fingers into the gap around the door and lifted. With a quiet creak, the wood panel swung upward, and he let it fall to the other side. "I see a light down there."

"Point the sword over here," Ashley said. "There's some kind of line at my feet."

He moved the energy field, illuminating an old rope that began in a coil near the door, passed under Ashley's tennis shoes,

101

and wound around a thick stalagmite behind her. "Someone's climbed down this way before," he noted.

She stooped and rubbed her hand along the frayed rope. "Not recently is my guess, but it might hold."

"I'm going in." He slid Excalibur into his back scabbard, dimming the air vent chamber, and tossed the coil into the opening. "Keep your hand on the rope. I'll give it three tugs when I get to the bottom."

She looked into the hole. "Going down should be easy, but have you ever climbed up a rope? It looks pretty far."

"Lots of times in gym class. Billy and I had this cranky Phys Ed teacher. He screamed so loud, it sounded like a pit bull barking at us. We shinnied that rope in a heartbeat." Walter looped the line around his waist. "How about you?"

She shook her head. "I'm not very good at going up, but I think I could if I had to."

Taking up the rope's slack, Walter pulled his sleeves over his palms, then, bracing his feet against the edge of the open hatch, he leaned backwards over the hole and pushed away, spending the rope through his protected hands as he dropped.

While hanging on to the taut rope, Ashley peered through the hole again. A dim light from somewhere underneath kept Walter illuminated as he reeled downward into the nebulous world below. After a few seconds, he disappeared in the shadows. The rope wiggled a few times, but it stayed tight, like a fishing line trolling in deep water.

She drummed her fingers on the floor. What could be taking so long? That rope couldn't have been longer than forty feet or so.

"Worried about him, dear child?"

Ashley gulped and swung her head from side to side. She ducked low and whispered, "Who are you? Where are you?"

"Just regard me as a friend, a very old friend."

She peeked behind the stalagmite. "Why can't I see you?"

"Because it is too dark."

"If you were here, I'd see you." She strained her eyes but saw nothing. "It's not that dark."

"There is more than one kind of darkness."

The rope suddenly went slack. Three emphatic tugs followed.

Hoisting her bag over her shoulder, Ashley stood and pulled her sleeves over her hands. "I have to go," she whispered. "Are you coming, too, whoever you are?"

"I will stay close until your journey is complete."

She pulled the rope tight and balanced over the opening. "My journey? You mean finding Gabriel?"

"Locating your brother is one facet of your journey, but you will learn that your road is much longer. I cannot stay with you to the end, but I will accompany you through these dark hours."

Three more tugs came from below. She glanced around the chamber one more time. "Will you at least tell me who you are?"

Ashley waited, but the voice didn't return. Again, three much more aggressive tugs jerked on the line. She sighed and began sliding down into the empty expanse. With mysteries both above and below, the darkness felt like a vice, adding to the crushing atmospheric pressure of the tremendous depths. She glanced up at the hole as it disappeared in the dimness. The only way of escape lay thousands of feet straight up, and who could tell how much farther down they would have to go?

Elam awoke. As the glow of dawn cast its rays of yellow light over the field, a breeze wafted across the grass, brushing the blades against his cheek. He sat up and stared at the delicate white flower in his hands.

He lifted it close to his eyes. "It was red," he said out loud.

Scrambling to his feet, he gazed out over the field. A wide path of white flowers stretched in the direction he had come as far as the eye could see. He raised the blossom to his nose and took a long sniff. He recognized the delicate aroma – earthy, yet sweet.

"It smells like Sapphira," he said, sighing. "I hope she made it out okay."

103

He tucked it carefully into his pocket, allowing the petals to stick out. After scanning the field for anything else new, he pulled on his cloak, lowered his head, and skulked toward the edge of the forest. There was no sign of the malevolent creatures that stalked the woods the night before, but he found the strange lump, a crumpled half-naked body, lacerated with long, bloody gashes on its hairy back.

Giving it a shove with his foot, Elam turned it face up. With skeleton-thin bare arms and legs, it looked more like an emaciated man than a monster, but two sharp fangs overlapping its lips gave the corpse a beastly aspect. It seemed half human and half ... something else.

Elam wrinkled his nose. This thing smelled worse than Nabal, even on a bad day. After glancing around, he pulled out the spyglass and peered into the forest. Nothing but trees and more trees.

He collapsed the tube and dropped it in his bag. "No time like the present," he said as he strode in.

The leafy canopy darkened the tree-filled landscape, reminding him about possibly stumbling over the transparent man he was looking for. He slowed his pace and extended an arm, waving it from side to side as he shuffled forward, but after several minutes, his arm ached, so he let it fall to his side.

He stopped and raised the spyglass again, adjusting it to its maximum magnification. Turning slowly, and listening for the slightest pop or rustle, he studied every detail – gnarled elbows in the lower limbs, fungus-infested knots in most of the trunks, and multicoloured toadstools peeking through the fallen leaves. But, other than organisms of decay, there was no sign of life – not a bug or a bird in sight.

Something moved. Elam froze the spyglass on the spot and waited, breathless. It moved again, a short, spindly form that seemed to flow like thick clear liquid.

"The gatekeeper," he whispered.

104

THE GATEKEEPER

When Ashley's toes touched the floor, Walter reached for her and pulled her to a crouch, whispering, "There's a girl over by the wall. She's saying something, but I didn't get close enough to make out the words."

Ashley peered through the darkness, picking up the image of a girl standing in a dim light about thirty feet away. She kept her voice low as well. "How old do you think she is?"

Walter shrugged his shoulders. "Maybe fourteen? She's kind of small for fourteen, but her face looks older."

"If you got close enough to see her face, why didn't you talk to her?"

"There's a bunch of men lined up against the wall. At least I think that's what they are. I only got a good look at one of them, a big guy with an ugly mug even a mother couldn't love. He didn't move a muscle, so I thought they might all be statues, but it looked like she was talking to them, so I wasn't sure."

Ashley strained her eyes. Multicoloured lights mingled within dark depressions in the walls, illuminating vague forms, but the light was too dim to discern any details. "You have Excalibur," she said, "so if the statues get aggressive, you can discourage them."

"Sounds like a plan." He stood and withdrew his sword. "I'd better keep it ready."

She pushed the blade, making it rest on his shoulder. "Carry it like that and maybe you won't scare her half to death."

"Got it." He strolled casually toward the girl.

Ashley followed, clutching the back of Walter's jacket to stay close. As they drew near, the girl's details came into focus. She was slender, maybe five feet tall, and her most obvious feature, her stark white hair, dressed her head and shoulders in snowy raiment. The flame from the lantern she carried made her eyes shine an unearthly blue.

Standing on a low stone platform, she spoke to someone inside a cleft in the wall, but it was still too dark to see whom she addressed. A huge body lay on the platform near her feet, apparently a giant of a man, but he, too, was shrouded in shadows.

Walter stopped and stared. Ashley leaned close and whispered in his ear. "She's beautiful!"

"I noticed." He quietly cleared his throat and began edging forward. "Uh … I guess I'll just introduce myself."

The girl's pale lips trembled. "I'll get you out of here. I'll get us all out of here, so help me God!"

Walter paused. "Is she talking to us?"

"Only one way to find out." Ashley brushed the wrinkles from her jacket and marched ahead. "Excuse me," she said as she hopped up to the platform. "Can you tell me where we are?"

The girl's eyes shone with radiance, but her thin smile seemed less than joyful. "Ashley? What are you doing here?"

Ashley shuffled backwards and stepped down, pointing at herself. "How do you know who I am?"

Walter quickly joined her. He put the sword away and bowed his head. "Hi. My name is—"

"Walter," the girl finished. "I saw both of you from inside the Great Key when the dragons came through."

"You did?" Walter combed his fingers through his hair. "Cool! I'm more famous than I thought."

The girl stepped off the platform and extended her hand. "I'm Sapphira Adi. Pleased to meet you."

"Pleased to meet you, too," Walter replied, taking her hand.

Sapphira gave Ashley a formal curtsy, though it looked strange coming from a girl in old jeans and a tattered sweater. "I am honoured to meet a princess, a daughter of the dragon king."

"A princess?" Ashley glanced at Walter as she gestured for Sapphira to rise. "How do you know so much about us, and what is this place?"

Sapphira's smile widened, but her eyes still gave away a sombre mood. "I know about you, because I saw you on the day you were born. I watched you through your brother Gabriel's eyes." She spread out her arms, turning slowly in a half circle. "And this place is the mobility room, once used for training an army of giants that were genetically engineered from a blend of plant material and fallen angels." She halted her spin and focused on Ashley again, her eyes wide and serious. "I think the son of King Nimrod wants to use them to take over the world, but first he has to get them out of this dimension. We're thousands of feet underground in the third circle of Hades."

107

Ashley's stomach ached. The word *Hades* felt like a dagger in her gut. She pulled Walter's sleeve and whispered, "The inscription in the stairwell."

"I was thinking the same thing." Walter replied, not bothering to whisper. He nodded at the dark forms lined up in the wall. "What are those?"

Setting down her lantern, Sapphira stepped back up on the platform and took the hand of one of the huge men. Although several beams of light cast various colours across his indistinct body, only his hand and hairy wrist could be seen clearly. "These are the Nephilim, the giants I was telling you about." She pointed at the body lying on the floor. "That one is named Yereq. I took him when he was just a seedling and weaned him from the soil by feeding him ground worm guts until he was ready for mobility, but he fell out of his chamber today and died."

"He's enormous!" Walter said. "Must be a lot of vitamins and minerals in the worms around here."

"Walter!" Ashley hissed. "This is no time for joking!" She lowered her voice to a whisper again. "We're in Hell, for crying out loud. And I think she's upset about the dead giant."

Walter scuffed his shoe on the floor. "Sorry," he said to Sapphira. "I guess if you raised him from a seedling you must have been close to him."

Sapphira smiled weakly. "I was, before they transferred him to mobility. I hoped I could talk to him after he woke up and before he could get to the living world, but ..." Her brow suddenly wrinkled. "How did you get into my dimension from there, I mean, from the living world?"

Walter pointed up. "A dragon opened a hole in the ground, making a friend of ours fall in, so we followed a million-step staircase to find her, and that led us here."

"A dragon made her fall down here? What dragon would do a terrible thing like that?"

"Arramos," Ashley said abruptly. "But that's a long story." She swivelled her head, but darkness in the gloomy chamber kept her from seeing beyond ten feet or so. "Have you seen a girl wandering around here?"

"Does she have red hair and freckles?" Sapphira asked.

Ashley jumped, nearly losing her balance. "Where is she?"

"Right over here." Sapphira picked up the lantern and lifted it close to the next cleft in the wall. A red-headed girl hovered

108

inside, the beams painting her arms and legs with every colour of the rainbow.

"It's Karen!" Ashley leaped up to the platform and latched on to her hand. "Is she okay? Can I pull her out?"

"Don't!" Sapphira withdrew a small, rectangular object from her pocket and showed it to Ashley. "It's a digital counter. As soon as it drops one more tick, I think everyone will wake up. And it won't be long. I've been watching it for years, so I know it's almost ready to hit zero." She put the counter back in her pocket. "We have to wait. Yereq died because I tried to wake him up too soon."

Ashley grabbed Sapphira's wrist. "Did you put her in there?"

Sapphira winced. "No. I can build growth chambers, but I've never put someone inside one."

Slowly loosening her fingers, Ashley sighed. "Sorry. It's just that she's my adoptive sister."

"It's okay." Sapphira set the lantern down and rubbed her wrist. "I just came here today for the first time in quite a while, and after Yereq died, I went out to get a cloth to wash his face, and when I got back, Karen was in Yereq's chamber. I have no idea how she got there."

Ashley followed one of the coloured lights back to its source and touched the edge of a brick that emitted a yellow laser beam. "Do these bricks have some kind of magnetic field generator that keep her and the giants suspended?"

Sapphira touched a brick on the opposite side that shone a blue beam on Karen's hand. "I think so. They create a field inside the chamber that counters gravity, and the colours feed the photoreceptors inside the giants. We don't have sunlight down here, so Mardon had to invent something to simulate it."

"Who's Mardon?" Walter asked.

Sapphira picked up the lantern and hopped down to the main floor. "He's the son of King Nimrod I told you about, the scientist who came up with these inventions. He's been gone for years and years, but I know he's up to something. I just don't know what it is."

Ashley pushed on a brick in Karen's wall cavity. "Have you thought about taking one of these out to see what happens?"

Sapphira looked up at Ashley. "A thousand times, but I decided I didn't want to deal with a giant if it woke up in a foul mood. Since Mardon trained them, I don't think they're going to be friendly."

Walter edged closer to Sapphira. "So why are you here? Can't you find a way out?"

"I'm pretty sure I can leave," Sapphira replied, "but I need to figure out how to take Ashley's brother Gabriel and her sister Roxil with me."

Ashley spun away from Karen. "My brother and sister are here?"

"Roxil's behind me," Sapphira said, pointing over her shoulder with her thumb, "and Gabriel's standing right next to you giving you a hug."

Ashley swivelled her head. For a brief second, she thought she saw a young man extending an arm around her shoulder, but the vision quickly faded. "There's no one next to me."

"Oh, he's there, all right." Sapphira covered a grin with her fingers. "You just can't see him."

"Another ghost?" Walter asked.

"Don't get me thinking about ghosts again," Ashley snapped. "This place is already creepy enough."

Walter raised his hands in a surrender pose. "I didn't mean to ruffle your feathers, but I've seen lots of stuff weirder than ghosts lately."

Blowing out a loud sigh, Ashley shook her head. "You're right. … I'm sorry. I'm wound up so tight, I'm about to pop a spring." She shuffled toward Sapphira and Walter. With every step, she imagined a ghost following her, raising a shiver. Perching on the edge of the platform, she looked down at Sapphira. "There's so much weird stuff going on, I don't know what to believe."

Sapphira reached up and laid a gentle hand on Ashley's forearm. "Let me see if I can show him to you. That should ease your mind."

"Fair enough." Ashley firmed her jaw and nodded. "Seeing is believing."

Sapphira addressed the space next to Ashley. "Gabriel, can you shrink enough to fit in my hands?" She waited a second and cupped her hands together. "Good. Just float up here and let's see if I can make you glow." She blinked at Ashley and Walter. "You might want to stand back. I'm not sure how this is going to work."

Walter scooted behind Sapphira while Ashley stepped close to Karen and the wall of giants. A tiny flame sprouted from Sapphira's hands, then three tongues of fire that rose several inches, like a blazing flower with flaming leaflets. A radiant silhouette formed in the centre, a boy with dragon wings on his back. He glowed orange, his eyes trained on Ashley as he reached for her and pretended to pull her close in a loving embrace. Finally, he seemed to let out a sigh, bowing his head with his hands folded at his waist.

"He can't speak," Sapphira explained, her blue eyes brighter than ever. "But at least you can see him now."

Ashley felt her mouth drop open. "That's ... that's my brother?"

Walter leaned over Sapphira's shoulder from behind. "He's an anthrozil! Cool!"

With a breathy blow from her lips, Sapphira extinguished the flames. As Gabriel faded away, she let her hands fall to her sides. "Like I told you, your dragon sister is here, too. Roxil was born to Makaidos and Thigocia long before they became your human parents, but she's also in an energy state, so you can't see her either."

"This is just too much!" Ashley laid her palms on her head and closed her eyes. "I think my brain is choking!"

Walter covered Ashley's hands with his own. "How do you give a brain a Heimlich manoeuvre?"

Ashley jerked her arms down and spun toward him. "Walter!" she shouted. "This is serious! If Roxil's really here, then Arramos lied, and my mother's in big trouble."

"Sorry." Walter raised his hands again and backed away. "I was just trying to lighten the mood."

Turning to Sapphira, Ashley softened her tone. "I apologize for my outburst, but I need to get everything straight in my head." She took a deep breath and tried to smile, but it felt like a queasy grin. "Maybe I should start with these giants. If they're programmed to wake up at any minute, things could get ugly around here."

"That's probably true," Sapphira said. "Mardon isn't around to give them orders, but he did train them to fight, and Morgan taught them to hate. If you know anything about Morgan, then you know what that could mean."

"Know about her?" Walter wrinkled his nose as though smelling a foul stench. "She wanted to poison the whole Earth with some kind of weird gas, so she probably didn't spend her time teaching the giants table manners." He glanced toward the spot where they climbed down the rope. "Getting out of here as fast as possible makes a lot of sense to me."

Ashley walked up to the wall cavity again and took Karen's limp hand into hers. "But we have to stay here for Karen, whether she wakes up or not."

"I didn't mean me." Walter nodded at Ashley. "You two go. It's a long way up, so you'd better get moving."

"Uh-uh!" Ashley shook her finger. "No way I'm leaving you alone to face a bunch of giants."

Walter reached back and tapped Excalibur's hilt. "I have an ugly giant skewer. I'll be fine."

"But someone has to help you get Karen up the stairs."

"We'll take it easy. We'll get there eventually."

Ashley wagged her head. "There has to be another way." Tapping her finger on her chin, she scanned the wall of giants. "No scientist would create such an elaborate system with a timed shutdown and not include a manual override, so there has to be a way to do it. Then we could all leave with Karen and not worry about these gorillas."

Sapphira raised a finger. "There *is* a way." She hustled to the end of the line of wall cavities, disappearing for a moment in the darkness. A few seconds later, she returned with a scroll. "Mardon documented everything he did," she said, unrolling one of the dowels. "I think he left a code that describes the shutdown procedure. I tried for years to figure it out, but I gave up on it and stuck the scroll in the corner."

Ashley took the other dowel while Sapphira continued unrolling. "It's near the end." She set her finger on the yellowed parchment. "Here it is. It's seven lines of numbers. I tried matching them to letters a thousand different ways, but nothing made any sense."

Leaning over their shoulders, Walter let out a whistle. "That looks like a job for Larry."

"Maybe." Ashley frowned at the scribbled entry. "I can't pick up any obvious pattern. Even the number count in each row isn't consistent."

Sapphira touched Ashley's shoulder. "Mardon used the combination six, nine, and thirteen to unlock a door and a gate. Does that help at all?"

"It might. It could be an encryption key." Ashley tapped on her jaw. "Larry? Are you there?"

A garbled reply buzzed through her tooth.

"I guess we're too deep now. There's no way we can verbally communicate all these numbers through that static."

"How about scanning it?" Walter asked. "It worked great with that writing on the wall."

Ashley shook her head. "The wall script was a lot neater. Larry would spend too much time just reading these numbers accurately. If he got even one wrong, the code would be unusable."

Walter nodded toward the ceiling exit. "Then I guess I'll have to wait for Karen while you and Sapphira start climbing out of here."

"No," Ashley said, tightening her grip on the dowel. "I can figure it out. I've cracked lots of codes tougher than this one."

"How do you know how tough it is? You haven't cracked it yet."

Ashley took the other dowel from Sapphira and spread the scroll out on the floor next to the lantern. She knelt in front of it and, pulling her hair back, studied the code. "Walter, this Mardon guy was just trying to hide a secret from any ordinary Joe who might be lurking in his laboratory. He's not going to stump me with a bunch of numbers he chicken-scratched on a roll of parchment."

114

Walter pointed at Sapphira. "She's been trying for years, and she hasn't figured it out. Are you going to do it in a few minutes?"

Ashley spoke through her teeth, barely moving her lips. "Walter, I'm not Sapphira."

Sapphira stared at Ashley, without a blink or a twitch of her lip. Her hands and cheeks began to glow, and tendrils of fire rippled over her skin, like flaming grass in the wind. Her eyes sparkled, and twin beams of iridescent blue poured forth, expanding as they crossed Ashley and covered her body.

Ashley shot to her feet and back-pedalled, swatting at the beams. "What are you doing to me?"

Sapphira clenched her eyes shut, extinguishing the blue light. "I'm sorry." She rubbed her eyelids with her knuckles. "Something came over me. It's only happened once before." She opened her eyes again and took a step closer, but Ashley backed farther away.

A tear trickled down Sapphira's pale cheek. "I ... I saw this strange, dark shadow inside you. It looked like a dragon."

Ashley's chin trembled. "You ... you saw a dragon inside me?"

"It was sort of like a phantom, a shadow that filled your body."

"I guess that makes sense," Walter said. "She's the daughter of a dragon."

Sapphira shook her head slowly. "That couldn't be the reason. Bonnie is also the daughter of a dragon, and when I saw her shivering in the snowstorm back when the slayer killed her mother, the same thing came over me. I looked inside her and saw an angel of light."

Ashley's cheeks flamed. "Exactly what are you trying to say? Are you mad at me for dissing you about cracking the code?"

Just as Sapphira opened her mouth to reply, a loud click echoed in the chamber, followed by a low hum.

Walter yanked out Excalibur. "What was that?"

"It's the timer!" Sapphira showed him her digital counter. "It hit zero!"

Elam lowered the spyglass and scanned the field of crooked trees, but the gatekeeper was now nowhere in sight.

"Glewlwyd?" he called.

Leaves crunched. Elam jerked around toward the noise. Could the Caitiff be lurking somewhere? Keeping his eyes focused in the direction he had seen the gatekeeper, he called again. "Glewlwyd, I am Elam, son of Shem, grandson of Noah the ark builder. Merlin has commissioned me to go to the altar of martyrs and find Enoch and two worthy young ladies for an important mission."

A high-pitched male voice replied, scratching its way through its words. "So you say, young man." The voice drew closer. "I would know Merlin by sight, but how am I to believe who you are?"

Elam squinted at the source, a barely visible, stooped old man, now standing two arm lengths away. His transparent image seemed to undulate, like ripples on a pond.

"I don't know how to prove who I am," Elam said. "Merlin just told me to answer your questions."

"He did, did he?" Glewlwyd rubbed his hands together. "Well, what shall I ask this wanderer who looks sixteen but would have me believe he is Elam, a boy born thousands of years ago but kidnapped and thought dead?"

"You seem to know a lot about me," Elam replied.

A low howl drifted through the trees. As the skinny needles on a nearby fir tree trembled, Elam tensed his jaw. The old man, however, seemed to pay no attention to the howl. His voice stayed calm. "I am Glewlwyd the Guileless, the oracle of integrity and candour. I see through to the soul, and I speak all matters plainly. Since we commune at the altars of Heaven, I am well acquainted with Noah and his family, but I have never met this son of Shem."

116

"That's because you couldn't have seen me in Heaven. I ate fruit from the tree of life, so I never died."

"I have heard the old tree-of-life story before." Glewlwyd raised a barely visible finger. "But there is another possible reason for someone's absence from Heaven. The real Elam could be an unbeliever wandering in Hades, a lost soul who will someday suffer eternally in the Lake of Fire. You, on the other hand, are obviously one of the faithful, for I perceive not a single dark spot in your soul."

Elam tapped himself on the chest. "Then you must know I'm telling the truth. If I'm spotless, then I couldn't be a liar!"

"But you could be deceived," the old man replied, half closing one eye. "You might truly believe you are Elam, and you would be making that claim with all integrity. But I must doubt your claim. The light in your eyes indicates that you are among the living, not one of Hades' prisoners. If Elam were alive, he would be more bent and ugly than I am, and that is a considerable statement."

Another howl sang out from the opposite side, closer. The first call answered, closer still. Elam shifted his eyes from left to right. The Caitiff were coming.

The old man smiled. "It seems that we will soon have some very dangerous visitors. Perhaps I should ask you a question that will test your claim so you can either escape through the gate or run for the grasslands."

Elam nodded. "Go ahead, but we'd better make it fast."

"This should be easy." Glewlwyd's liquid fingers stroked his equally liquid chin. "Name all of your brothers."

"Okay." Elam tucked his spyglass under his arm and began counting on his fingers. "Asshur and Arpachshad were the only ones born when I was kidnapped, but I memorized the rest of them from the Bible, so there's also Lud, Aram, Uz, Hul, Gether, and ..." He paused, glancing for a moment into the tree canopy overhead. "Meshech," he said, looking down again at the old man.

"That is correct, but as you indicated, anyone could learn that answer, especially someone who is trying to impersonate Elam. So the value of that question is now void."

Elam heaved a loud sigh. "Then can you ask another?"

"Certainly. I thought of another while you were counting."

A new sound trickled into Elam's ears, soft footsteps crackling leaves – in front, to each side, and from behind.

Glewlwyd raised a finger again. "How many souls lived in the uppermost level of the ark?"

"Ten," Elam replied quickly. "Eight humans – Noah and his wife, Noah's three sons and their wives, and two dragons, Makai-dos and Thigocia." He pointed at Glewlwyd. "You can't find those two names in the Bible."

"An excellent attempt, whoever you are, but you are wrong. The correct answer is eleven, because Canaan, son of Ham, was there, born on the ark during the flood."

117

Elam spread out his arms. "That's a trick question!"

"Not a trick, young man. It was designed to be answered only by a true grandson of Noah, for the time of Canaan's birth is not recorded in the Bible but is still well known by his family."

"But I knew the dragons' names!"

"True enough. Very impressive. Yet even their names have been repeated through the centuries in songs, so I cannot give you full credit." The old man smiled. "Still, I am a fair-minded gentleman, so I will ask a third question, but this is your last chance."

"Okay." As the crunching footsteps grew louder, Elam swallowed and licked his lips. "I'm ready, but please hurry."

Glewlwyd rested his chin in his palm and tapped a finger on his cheek. "I must conjure something that only the true Elam could answer, one that cannot be found in book or rhyme."

Elam caught a glimpse of a grotesque face peering around a knotted tree trunk. Its red eyes flashed, and its fangs slipped over its bottom lip before it pulled back again.

118

"I have it!" The old man drew close and looked Elam in the eye. "What was your mother's favourite colour?"

"Her favourite colour?" Elam's jaw tensed so hard, his teeth ground together. Could he possibly remember such a detail? It had been thousands of years since he had seen her!

More ugly faces peered around trees, then arms and torsos emerged. With only dirty grey cloths wrapping the loins of their hairy bodies, they formed a wide circle and began a slow march toward him, each one baring its long, pointed fangs.

Elam froze in place, his eyes darting from one beast to the other. They seemed jittery, perhaps wondering if he might raise a weapon, but with each second, they stepped closer with more resolve.

"You had better answer quickly," Glewlwyd said. "If you really are Elam, I will rescue you. If not, then I have no choice but to leave you to your own devices, for now that these monsters have surrounded you, the gate is the only way to elude them."

Closing his eyes, Elam tried to lock the danger out of his thoughts. He had to concentrate and take his mind back in time. After a few seconds, images from millennia past drifted in, some he had recalled hundreds of times before – the cave he and his family had to live in during King Nimrod's despotic reign, the tower that scourged the distant skyline in the midst of smoke rising from tar pits, and dragons who patrolled the skies from dusk until dawn.

A cascade of hues rained over his mind, the dull beige in his mother's dress, the purple in the apron she wore to keep charcoal from drawing grey streaks on her clothes, and the scarlet blush in the flower she often wore in her hair. But one colour kept breaking through over and over – the vines she draped around the doorway, the garlands she would make from fresh cuttings and arrange on the table, and the single emerald his father had given her that she always wore in a ring that never left her finger.

119

Elam took a deep breath and looked Glewlwyd in the eye. "Green." He exhaled and smiled. "Green was her favourite colour."

CHAPTER

THE AWAKENING

The hum reverberated, growing louder by the second as vibrations rippled under the feet of Ashley, Walter, and Sapphira. Dust and pebbles drizzled from the ceiling and pecked the floor with loud taps. A white light poured from each of the giants' alcoves, illuminating the cavern. With a deafening crack, a jagged fault line fractured the chamber wall. One of the giants toppled forward and sprawled on the floor, groaning.

Walter slid Excalibur into its scabbard and leaped up to Karen's growth chamber. "You two get out of here!" he yelled.

As she stared at the cracking walls, Ashley backed up, grabbing the air behind her in search of the rope. "But we have to—"

A stalactite crashed next to her feet, splashing fragments over her legs. Another crack ripped through two alcoves as a second giant tipped out. The first one rose to his knees and looked around. Red beams shot from his eyes and scanned the room like twin neon flashlights.

"For once, don't argue with me!" Walter shouted. "And get up there now!"

Ashley finally caught the rope and called to Sapphira. "You go first. I'll be here to catch you if—"

The growth chamber wall exploded, spitting out Karen and the remaining giants in a hail of debris. Walter caught her and rolled on top, using his back to shield her from the storm of spewing rocks.

"Walter!" Ashley screamed. She ran through the cloud of dust and knelt at his side, brushing dirt and pebbles from his shoulders and back. "Walter! Say something! Are you okay?"

"I'm okay." Walter rose to all fours, still shielding Karen, who was lying face down, motionless. "But Hades is giving me a headache."

Ashley laid a hand on Karen's back. "Is she alive?"

"She's alive." He hoisted her limp body into his arms. "I could feel her breathing."

Ashley passed a trembling hand over Karen's dirty red locks. "She's so pale!"

With light still emanating from the blown-out wall cavities, Walter scanned the room. "Where's Sapphira?"

"I'm here!" Just a few feet away, Sapphira pushed up from under a mound of debris and shook the dust from her hair. She crawled over and crouched next to Karen.

"We'd better get going," Ashley said. "It looks like they're waking up." She nodded toward a series of rock piles, each representing one of the giants. Three mounds began to move, revealing massive bodies arising from under the rubble.

Karen blinked and moaned. "Where am I?"

Ashley slid her arm under Karen's back. "No time to lose." She clutched Walter's sleeve with her free hand. "You'd better fire up that sword."

One of the giants stood upright, his entire body glowing and his red eyes flashing. With a grunt, Ashley lifted Karen and carried her to the rope, then set her down and supported her back. "Can you sit up by yourself?"

Karen rubbed her eyes. "I think so."

Sapphira marched up to the waking giant and stood with her hands on her hips, her head angled sharply upward. "Chazaq!" She continued speaking to him, but now in an odd language.

As other giants rose to their feet, Chazaq's beams tipped down and fell upon her. "It has been many years," he said with a deep voice and perfect English, "but I recognize you, Mara."

"So, Mardon taught you English." Sapphira shook her head, laughing. "I should have expected that. He wasn't one to ignore the details."

"He taught us many languages, including modern dialects that came about after we began our sleep. Even as we slumbered, he spoke to our minds through a communications device he imbedded at the base of our skulls, enabling us to be completely prepared to carry out his plan."

Twelve other giants gathered behind Chazaq, each one with his own set of ruby lasers slicing the dusty air.

Walter lit up Excalibur's glow but kept the destructive beam turned off as he edged toward them.

Sapphira kept her hands on her hips and took another step toward Chazaq. "Do you remember how you used to pull me up and down in the elevator shaft?"

"I remember. You were one of the intelligent ones. I admired that."

"If you admire intelligence, then why have you allowed yourself to fall prey to Mardon's trickery? He put you all to sleep, and now it looks like he left you here to die."

The giant laughed, and those behind him smirked. "I have not fallen prey to trickery. Mardon told us to expect to awaken without him. It is all part of the plan."

123

While Ashley shuttled rocks to the rope, piling them in a pyramid next to Karen, Walter skulked toward the giants. Just a few more steps and he would be close enough to strike with either beam or blade.

"Is that why he poisoned the other giants?" Sapphira continued. "Was that part of the plan, too?"

Chazaq reached down and picked up two grapefruit-sized rocks. "Morgan taught me the cold facts of our cruel existence. Nothing matters but power and control." He smashed the rocks together, pulverizing them over Sapphira's head. "Getting rid of excess giants was simply a necessary chore."

Sapphira ran her fingers through her hair, scattering the gravel as she coughed through her words. "And where is Morgan now? Do you know?"

"Because you are obviously baiting me with that question, I assume that she has reaped the hatred she has sown through the years." Chazaq brushed his hands together, raining more grit on Sapphira. "But her fate is inconsequential. It is Mardon who now guides our destiny, and we are to ascend to Earth's surface and carry out his orders."

Sapphira stepped out of Chazaq's spiteful dust shower. "Mardon might be able to guide you in this realm, but he's dead, so he can't go to the land of the living."

"He told us that we would already be in the living world when we awoke, just thousands of feet below the surface." Chazaq cast his beams on her again. "Perhaps you noticed a dimensional shift."

Sapphira stared at him but said nothing. Walter crept closer, also remaining silent. Ashley continued piling rocks, keeping her eye on the giants.

"Your silence proves that you did notice." Chazaq's eyebeams swung to Ashley, then to the rope and trapdoor above. "I believe I have found the way out that Mardon promised."

124

Sapphira raised her arms. Flames erupted from both hands. She began swirling the fire into a flaming cyclone that expanded toward the Nephilim.

Chazaq wrapped Sapphira around the waist with one arm and pulled her against his chest, binding her and extinguishing the flames. "Travelling to another dimension is not in our plans, Mara."

Sapphira's face turned red as she gasped for breath. She looked like a struggling toddler in his massive grip.

"Let her go!" Walter marched toward Chazaq, Excalibur's beam blazing.

Chazaq laughed. "Here comes another David, thinking he can slay Goliath, but he comes with a shining blade to replace sling and stones."

"Maybe you need a demonstration of what this sword can do." Walter angled the beam toward one of the other Nephilim. "I can't use it on you while you're holding Sapphira, but I'll fry your toadies one by one until you let her go."

Chazaq squeezed Sapphira, making her eyes bulge. "Go ahead and test your feeble blade. This should be entertaining."

"Then laugh at this!" Walter swiped the beam at the closest Naphil. The light surged into the giant's body, but instead of disintegrating him, it seemed to infuse him with energy. His skin glowed, and he sent out twin beams in a more vibrant scarlet than ever.

"Walter!" Ashley called. "Sapphira said they have plant genes, so they must be phototrophic. Light gives them energy."

"Yeah," Walter said, dousing Excalibur's beam, "I guessed that."

Chazaq loosened his hold on Sapphira, allowing her to breathe. "The inhabitants of Earth will learn of our skills soon enough. In the meantime, we will take Mara with us. A little insurance might be beneficial."

125

Sapphira slipped an arm free and desperately gulped air. "He can't ... kill me. ... If he does ... he will die."

"Is that so?" Walter drew back the sword. "You plant creatures might be immune to the beam, but I haven't heard of one yet that can withstand an axe." He charged at the Naphil he had energized and sliced through his leg, cutting it off just above the knee. The giant toppled over and crashed to the ground. As his life fluids poured out, he roared, writhing in pain.

Drawing back the gleaming sword again, Walter scowled at Chazaq. "Want to be next?"

Three of the Nephilim lunged at Walter, but he leaped out of the way, slicing a finger off one giant as he breezed by. The others made a circle around him and closed in slowly. Walter swung Excalibur frantically in every direction, lunging whenever one of the giants came within range.

"Stop!" Chazaq commanded. "We cannot afford any more casualties."

126

As the Nephilim backed away, Walter let out a huge sigh, sweat dripping from his chin. The fallen Naphil now lay still in a pool of dark blood, his face ashen.

"Begin the ascent," Chazaq ordered. "When we are fully energized on the surface, that little sword will not be so effective." He stomped over to the rope and picked up Karen with his free arm, releasing Sapphira at the same time. As his arm locked Karen close to his body, she gasped and her head lolled forward. "Here is our new insurance. When we are safely out of this hole, I will let her go."

Lifting his sword once again, Walter charged.

Chazaq squeezed Karen's throat. "One more step, and she's dead!"

As Karen gagged, Walter halted, letting the sword's tip rest on the floor, his face flaming red. "Coward! Hiding behind the skirt of a little girl!"

"Not cowardice. Expediency." Chazaq released her throat and waited while the other giants made a human ladder to the trapdoor high above. When the fourth giant's hands reached the door, the others climbed up the bodies. Once the seventh Naphil began his climb, Chazaq transferred Karen to him. "Take her to the top. When we're all safely away, we will return her."

Seconds later, only Chazaq and the four giants forming the ladder remained in sight. The top one pulled himself into the air shaft, then reached down for the others. The three remaining linked themselves hand-to-ankle while the giants above hoisted them upward. As the bottom giant rose, Chazaq wrapped an arm around his feet and rode upward with the chain of Nephilim. "Farewell, valiant warrior. I must admit that you have great courage. It's a shame you're on the losing side."

As Chazaq's feet disappeared through the door, Sapphira stepped underneath and called upward. "How are you going to lower Karen down safely from way up there?"

Walter dropped the sword and rushed to her side, whispering, "Don't give him any ideas."

In a flurry of red hair and flailing limbs, Karen dropped from the ceiling. Walter held out his arms, and she crashed into his chest, crumpling his body. Karen rolled to the side and groaned.

Ashley knelt next to them and laid a hand on each of their heads. "Are you two all right?"

Walter blinked at her. "Not exactly a gentleman, is he?" Just then, the rope slid down, collecting in a pile on his leg, and the trapdoor slammed shut.

Laying a hand on her stomach, Karen wheezed. "I ... can barely ... breathe."

Sapphira stooped at their feet. "I think Chazaq collapsed her lungs! We have to get her out of here!"

"I was working on building a pile of rocks," Ashley said, "but those creeps knocked it down. We'll have to start over."

Sapphira raced through her words. "There might be an easier way back at the museum room. The portal is gone, but if the
dimensional barrier is still thin, I should be able to get us
through. Even if we go to an unexpected dimension, at least we'll
be out of this place, and maybe I can figure out what to do from
there. But there's no way Karen can get very far in this state."

"Sapphira's right," Walter said, struggling to his feet. "Ashley,
you'd better try to heal Karen right now."

Ashley pointed at him. "I was just thinking that." She sat down
and pulled Karen up into her arms. "Better stand clear, Sapphira."

Sapphira backed away a few steps. "I think I've seen you do
this before. How does it work?"

Walter picked up Excalibur. "Ashley is a healer," he explained.
"When I shoot the sword's beam through the ground and into
her, somehow she uses the energy to heal people. Since I'm an
heir to King Arthur, I can make the sword do some pretty cool
stuff." He raised the blade and summoned the beam. "Watch."

128

The shaft of light burned into the ceiling above. Walter slowly lowered it to the ground, making it sizzle across the scattered
debris as it sent up grey puffs of smoke. Then, guiding it toward
Ashley, he called out, "Ready?"

Ashley hugged Karen's heaving body close. "Ready!"

The streak of energy surged into Ashley, lighting up her
whole body. White beams poured from her eyes and into Karen's
chest. As arcs of energy danced around both girls, Karen cried out
with a loud moan.

"That's enough!" Ashley shouted.

Walter jerked the beam to the side and shut it down. The light
from Ashley's eyes blinked off with a tiny popping noise. Then,
like a heated coil cooling down, her radiance faded. "Whew!" she
said, rubbing her eyes, "I don't think I'll ever get used to that."

Karen, her face gaunt and dirty, shook her head slowly. "I
hope someone wakes me up soon. I don't like this dream at all."

Walter put the sword away and hurried over to the two girls, extending a hand to each of them. "I think this nightmare is far from over."

"Can she walk?" Sapphira asked. "With those Nephilim heading to the surface, we should get going. There's no telling what they're planning to do."

Karen stood and tested her legs. "Yeah. I'm okay." She squinted at Sapphira. "Who are you?"

"I'll explain later." Sapphira marched toward a door at the far end of the room, tongues of white fire emanating from her hands. "Everyone follow me. That includes Gabriel and Roxil. I'll be our lantern."

"Wait." Ashley limped to a pile of rubble and tossed fragments to the side. She pulled out a finely polished, rectangular block and held it up. "Is this one of the gravitational field bricks?"

Sapphira looked back. "Yes, but it's only one of seven different kinds."

Ashley spotted the strap from her duffle bag and yanked it out of a pile, then stuffed the brick inside. As she unearthed another brick, a miniature landslide from the top of the pile exposed an enormous bare foot. "Hey!" she called. "One of the giants is still here, and it looks like both legs are intact, so I don't think it's the one Walter killed." She leaned closer. "He has six toes on his foot!"

"They all do. Six fingers on each hand, too." Sapphira continued her march toward the door. "That giant is Yereq, the one Karen replaced in the growth chamber. I'll have to figure a way to get his body out of here, but that can wait."

Walter wrapped his arm around Karen's back and followed Sapphira. "I wouldn't bring too many bricks in your bag," he called back to Ashley. "We might have to haul it pretty far."

"True." Ashley dropped the second brick on the floor. "They're probably all pretty much the same." She hustled to catch up with Walter and took Karen's hand.

129

After following Sapphira for about a minute, Walter looked over at Ashley. "What do you think?" he asked. "Does she know what she's doing?"

Ashley blinked at the strange girl who left a fiery aura in her wake, literally blazing the path ahead of them. "I don't know what she's all about, but when she looks at me, I feel like she sees right through me, like I'm standing naked in front of God himself."

"I think I know what you mean." Walter laid a palm on his chest. "Whenever I see those bright blue eyes, my heart beats like a bongo on steroids and tries to jump up into my throat."

Ashley felt a pang deep inside and swallowed back a sigh. "I guess if I were a guy, I'd feel the same way. She really is pretty."

"Yeah. She is. But that's not what causes it. I've been around pretty girls ever since we left West Virginia, so I'm used to it."

A surge of warmth flooded Ashley's soul. She glanced at Walter, but he kept his eyes focused straight ahead. She opened her mouth to reply, but Karen squeezed her hand, making her pause. Ashley squeezed hers back and kept silent. Walter had given them an honest compliment, and they both basked in its soothing tenderness. Nothing more needed to be said.

With only Sapphira's bodily glow lighting the wide tunnel, they had to pick up their pace to stay in the oracle's trailing halo. Karen stumbled, but Ashley caught her and braced her back.

"You going to make it?" Ashley asked.

Karen winced and continued her hobbling steps. "Depends on how far it is. I guess I needed a little more healing."

"Almost there!" Sapphira called. Her sweet voice echoed, rolling past their ears like a lilting melody.

"I guess she heard you," Ashley whispered. "We have to be quieter if we want to keep any secrets from her."

"Secrets?" Karen whispered back. "Don't you trust her?"

"I'm not sure yet, but it's best to keep our own counsel for now – you and Walter and me."

Karen focused on the circle of light surrounding their guide. "Maybe, but like you and Walter said before, there's something really cool about her. She has so much confidence and life, I want to believe her. She reminds me of Bonnie."

"Bonnie? Why?"

"Even without all that fire, she just kind of ... you know ... glows."

Ashley watched Sapphira's white hair bouncing in the midst of her full-body halo. As they passed through a darker part of the corridor, the aura strengthened, making the tunnel seem like a moonlit path. "I think I know what you mean," Ashley said. "I'm trying to be cautious, but it feels wrong not to trust her."

After a few minutes, Sapphira stopped under an archway at the end of the tunnel and pointed into the darkness ahead. "Ignite," she called. As if in response, a light flickered somewhere in front of her. Still pointing, she called out, "Ignite," several more times until the chamber beyond the archway filled with an orange glow.

131

She waited there, her blue eyes shining to match her radiant smile. When Walter, Ashley, and Karen joined her, they entered a huge cavern.

"I called this the museum room." Sapphira extended her arm toward an enormous building. "And here is the museum, the ground floor of the Tower of Babel."

Ashley gazed at the magnificent structure, following its ancient architecture upward until it disappeared in the dim upper recesses. Tapering slightly as it rose, the curving wall revealed etchings of human shapes and archaic words, carved deeply into sun-baked bricks. Recessed arches framed tiny windows at precise vertical intervals, perhaps lookout points for guardians of the ancient city or maybe air vents for the tower's inhabitants to help them find a cooling breeze. Old-fashioned lanterns lined the exterior perimeter, their flames painting the walls with an orange tint.

"It used to be filled with thousands of scrolls," Sapphira continued, "but I could only keep the most important ones. I needed fuel for heating during the years I couldn't get out. I usually keep the lanterns off to save oil, but I thought you might like to see the museum."

Ashley walked slowly toward the massive doorway, still gawking at the amazing sight – one of the oldest artifices in all recorded history, once holding the greatest library the world at that time had ever known and now housing ancient documents of incalculable value.

Although she longed to browse the remains and drink in its educational bounty, her eye caught something of more immediate and practical value. Scattered around the walls she found a few scrolls; piles of old books, magazines, and newspapers; and a glass gallon-sized jug filled with clear liquid. She touched the glass and turned toward Sapphira. "Is this drinking water?"

"Please, help yourself! I collected that stuff during my visits to the land of the living, and the water is from our springs."

Ashley withdrew her empty water bottle from her bag and filled it from the jug. After taking a long drink, she recapped it and tossed it to Walter, who shared it with Karen. Ashley picked up the jug and raised her eyebrows at Sapphira. "Want some?"

"No, thank you. I need very little to survive."

"Really? Why is that?"

Sapphira lowered herself to the floor and sat cross-legged. "Maybe this is a good time to tell you the whole story. Now that I think about it, even if I can make a portal, it might take us to the exact spot where the giants will come out, and that probably wouldn't be a good idea. Let's give them some time to move out of the area."

Walter, Ashley, and Karen joined her on the floor. With the museum looming like a tall haunted house and Sapphira's unearthly blue eyes shining, a midnight hush fell over the chamber. Sapphira told her story from her first memory of her slavish life under Morgan's tyrannical rule, through her adventures with the dragons, all the way to her role in rescuing the great creatures from Dragons' Rest. When she finally finished, she let out a long sigh. "And now, we, that is, Gabriel and Roxil and I, are hoping to find Makaidos."

"But now he's called Timothy," Walter said, pointing at her. "How in the universe do you find a guy who blew up in a house but didn't show up in Kingdom Come?"

Ashley tapped his knee. "Walter! This is my father we're talking about. Get a clue."

"Sorry." Walter shrugged his shoulders. "It just seems too weird to be for real."

Ashley locked her gaze on Sapphira's blazing eyes. "Like everything else going on around here."

"So," Karen said, leaning close to Sapphira, "all the dragons had to do was say Jehovah-Yasha, and they could go through the veil?"

"Yes." Sapphira took Karen's hand, and her glow covered the younger girl's arm. "But for dragons, a confession is much more than just words. To penetrate the veil they had to believe in Jehovah's Messiah in order to pass on to eternal life, just like humans do."

Karen nodded slowly, eyeing their clasped hands as the glow spread up to her shoulder. "That makes sense."

Ashley took a sip from her water bottle and recapped it. "So now that you've eaten from the tree of life, do you think you might live forever?"

Sapphira pulled her hand, but Karen hung on, covering it with her other hand. As the glow washed over Karen's face, Sapphira smiled at her. "I don't think I would die a natural death, but maybe I could be killed."

"But if anyone tries to kill you ..." Walter slapped his hands together. "Smack! He gets the hammer." He pushed against the floor and rose to his feet. "That was a cool story, but I'm ready to get out of this creepy place."

Sapphira drew the clutch of hands to her face and kissed Karen's ring finger, her lips passing across the rubellite and turning the gem white for a brief moment. Releasing Karen, she got up and walked past a pair of matching sleep mats, stopping at a clear spot on the floor. "The portal used to be right here," she said, spreading out her arms, "so gather around, and I'll try to get everyone into the fire."

Ashley followed her to the open area. "Into the fire?"

"It's the only way." Sapphira brushed a hand across the air. The lanterns surrounding the museum winked out one by one until only two remained lit. "Trust me. You won't feel anything except a tingly sensation."

Her eyes adjusting to the dimmer room, Ashley edged closer, a new anxiety weakening her legs. "How about Gabriel and Roxil? Will they come with us?"

Sapphira laid her arm around an invisible bystander. "Gabriel's already right next to me, and Roxil's behind him, so I think they'll come along. If not, I'll try to come back and get whoever is left."

Bright plumes of fire erupted from Sapphira's palms. As she waved her arms in a wide circle over her head, a cyclone of flames swirled above, growing in diameter. Walter, Ashley, and Karen huddled underneath, and a fiery wall lowered around them, a cylindrical curtain of dancing orange tendrils.

In spite of the warmth, Ashley shivered. The yellow tongues licked the air as they created a stream of hot, dry wind that slurped the moisture from her eyes. She shut them tightly. A tingle crawled along her skin, like a swarm of centipedes creeping up her back. Then, with a loud whoosh, the hot air swept upward, and damp coolness returned.

"Well, that wasn't so bad," she said, opening her eyes. "In fact, it was kind of—"

Ashley gulped. The museum was still there! The old books, dirty scrolls, and sleeping mats were all still there! She swung her head from side to side. Walter, Karen, and Sapphira were gone! Now shivering harder, she hugged herself, rubbing her upper arms. "Walter?" she called, her voice quaking. "Karen?"

No answer.

She took a timid step backwards, but her elbow struck something solid. She wheeled around and came face to face with a dragon!

"Aaaugh!" She fell backwards and landed on her behind. "Who are you?" she shouted, pedalling her feet to scoot away.

The dragon, sitting on its haunches, cast twin eyebeams on the floor between them. "I am your sister. At least that is what I am told."

Ashley eyed the red dots on the floor and followed the beams to the scaly beast. "Roxil?"

"Yes," the dragon replied, taking a step toward her, "and since you can see me now, we obviously have a problem."

"Problem?" Ashley slid farther back. "You'd better believe there's a problem. Sapphira and the others are gone, and we're trapped here."

"That is exactly my point." Roxil swept her tail across the empty space between her and Ashley. "Sapphira is gone and has left us in Hell, so to speak. When I first came out of Dragons' Rest, Gabriel and I were physically solid. Then, we became merely energy for a short time until the giants and Sapphira departed. Now I am physical again."

The dragon's non-threatening, matter-of-fact tone set Ashley at ease, at least about being trapped with a dragon. The talk about Hell, on the other hand, racked her nerves. She rose slowly to her feet and brushed dirt from her hands. "What do you make of it?"

"This is merely a guess, but it fits all the circumstances. For a short time, this place was transported to the world of the living,

135

so you were able to descend into it, and the giants were able to climb out. During that period, Gabriel and I lost our physical forms. Just now, Sapphira created a new portal that took her and your friends out but sent us back to the land of the dead. Since I actually died in the living world, it makes sense that I would be physical here and something of a ghost there."

Ashley pointed at herself. "What about me? Does that mean that I'm—"

"Dead?" Roxil opened her claws and looked at their sharp points. "Not necessarily. Other living humans have been abandoned here before."

Ashley tried to hide her tight-throated swallow. "Abandoned?"

"Desolate. Deserted. Forsaken. Choose your own synonym."

"But why? What did I ever do to Sapphira?"

"Who can tell? She is an odd one to say the least. She destroyed Dragons' Rest, a perfectly reasonable place for dragons to spend eternity." Roxil's eyes glowed with a brighter red. "Long ago, a young man named Elam tagged along with her to Dragons' Rest. On her most recent visit, she brought Gabriel along to help her demolish our home, and now she has taken your Walter to do who-knows-what. She seems to enjoy collecting young men as she blazes a destructive path."

Trying not to shake, Ashley glanced at her wristwatch. "Maybe we should give her time. She said she would come back if she left anyone behind. It's only been a few minutes."

Roxil snorted. "Put your faith in humans if you wish. But you shouldn't hold your breath" – the dragon smiled scornfully – "unless you really want to be dead."

The dragon's last word sliced into Ashley's mind. Dead. The very last word she wanted to think about, a state she didn't want to consider.

Lowering her chin to her chest, she closed her eyes. There had to be an answer. There had to be a way out. Taking a deep breath, she finally settled down and concentrated on the events of the last hour, going backwards in time – Sapphira's story, the journey to the museum chamber, the giants climbing out of the mobility room.

She snapped her fingers. "The mobility room! I can still get up to the staircase and climb out."

"But the rope is on the floor," Roxil said. "How do you expect to get up to the ceiling?"

"Can you give me a boost?" Ashley started toward the corridor and called back. "You can get there, can't you? The corridors between here and there looked big enough."

Roxil let out a sparks-laden sigh. "I suppose I can, but if you leave, what will I do?"

Ashley halted. "If I find Sapphira, maybe she can come back for you. Maybe it was all a mistake, and she's trying to figure out how to find us right now."

Roxil twitched her ears and raised her scaly brow. "Considering that she has played the temptress, usurped your position with your young man, and left you here to rot, I am surprised at your trust in her."

"Temptress? What are you talking about? Sapphira's too sweet to do anything like that."

"Perhaps you didn't notice the attraction, but my experienced eyes tell me far more than your human vision can detect." Roxil flicked her tongue out and in. "The evidence is quite convincing. She and your young man are together, and you are here. Why should you trust such a deceiver?"

Averting her eyes, Ashley kicked aside a pebble. Something about this dragon was definitely strange. Why was she so filled with distrust? She couldn't be right about Sapphira, could she? "If you have a better idea," Ashley said, "then let's hear it. Otherwise, Sapphira or no Sapphira, I'm getting out of here, and I'll do whatever I can to rescue you."

Roxil lumbered toward the exit. "I still think we are in Hades, so I have my doubts whether or not the staircase remains, but I suppose it is worth a try."

As cold drizzle pelted his head, Mardon stood at the edge of a highway next to one of his giants. The road to his left climbed a slope and curved around a low grassy rise, disappearing about half a mile away. To his right, the highway descended into a more forested area where tall spruces reached into an elevated fog bank.

Mardon tapped the giant's hip and pointed at a white Ford Explorer cruising toward them on the rain-slicked road. "That one will do nicely, Bagowd."

The giant stepped onto the road and waved his arms over his head. As the Explorer's wheels locked, the female driver screamed. Sliding while it decelerated, the SUV came to a halt with a not-so-gentle bump into Bagowd's legs. The young woman flung open the door and leaped out, but the giant, in three limping strides, snatched her by the coat collar, hauled her back to the Explorer, and threw her behind the steering wheel.

"You will drive," he bellowed.

Mardon opened the door on the other side and slid into the passenger's seat. "I apologize for frightening you, Madam, but my need for a vehicle is urgent. When my giant carries me, our progress is much too slow."

Her arms shaking violently, the short-haired brunette reached for the gear stick on the steering column and shifted to drive. "Where ... where do you want to go?"

He nodded at Bagowd, who had bent over to rub his injured legs. "Follow him."

She settled into her seat, straightening her coat around her. After taking a deep breath, she raised her hands to her temples and said, "Okay, Kaitlyn, you can handle this. Remember your boot camp training." Now wearing a forced smile, she turned to Mardon. "If your friend's going on foot, why did you need a ride?"

Mardon raised his eyebrows. "I'm sure you will see very soon."

The giant loped down the road, increasing his speed with every stride. Kaitlyn stepped on the gas and followed. After a few seconds, she looked down at the speedometer. "Wow! He's doing forty already! I guess our little collision didn't bother him at all."

"Apparently not. This happy outcome is good for both of us."

She squinted at Mardon. "Is he some kind of circus freak or something?"

"I suggest that you address him by his name, which is Bagowd. Calling him a freak to his face would endanger your health."

Kaitlyn laughed. "You're pretty funny, Mister ... uh ... What did you say your name was?"

"I didn't." Mardon kept his gaze locked on the giant.

"I'm Kaitlyn Peabody." She extended a hand, but Mardon just glanced at her and refocused straight ahead. "Are you two actors or something?" she asked. "I mean, your sandals and tunics are great costumes, but I'll bet you're cold in them."

Mardon replied in a firm monotone. "Miss Peabody, I would appreciate silence. I am concentrating on my giant's form. If he tires too quickly, I will have reason for concern."

"He could ride on top." Kaitlyn covered her lips. "Sorry. I'll be quiet."

Mardon let out an exasperated sigh. "I appreciate your concern, but I want him to exercise. I must know if he is strong enough for the task ahead."

Kaitlyn drove on, keeping at least three car lengths behind the sprinting giant. After a few minutes of silence, Bagowd slowed down as he neared a gravel service road on the right.

"Drive in here," Mardon said.

139

As the Explorer's wheels rolled over the popping gravel, a uniformed man walked out of a small gatehouse near a fenced entryway. When he spotted Bagowd, his jaw dropped open.

The giant stalked toward him. With a frantic spin, the guard hustled back to his one-room station and slammed the door.

When Kaitlyn parked, Mardon got out and, turning back to her, bowed low. "I thank you for your service. I am gladdened that my giant didn't have to kill you."

She stared back at him through the open door, barely moving her lips. "No problem."

Bagowd marched to the gatehouse and glared through the door's window. "Unlock the gate," he shouted.

The guard pulled a gun from his holster and aimed it shakily. "Get back!"

Bagowd punched through the glass, knocking the gun away with his meaty hand. Then, wrapping his fingers around the man's throat, he lifted him off the ground.

Mardon turned to Kaitlyn and bowed again. "I'm sorry you had to see this."

Jerking forward, she shifted into drive. "I didn't see anything!" With a mad spinning of tyres and slinging of gravel, the SUV roared away, its passenger door still hanging open and wagging on its hinges.

Mardon turned back to the gatehouse. The guard now lay face down, his midsection resting over the broken window as his arms dangled limply.

"Such a shame," Mardon said as he rejoined Bagowd. "But sacrifice is necessary along the road to Heaven's gate." He nodded at the fenced entryway. "Let us proceed."

Bagowd pushed his fingers through the chain links and ripped the gate from its moorings. With a mighty heave, he tossed it to the side. The gate spun on a corner and landed against a power company truck.

140

Mardon and the giant marched toward the power plant side by side, the sound of rushing water rising from somewhere in the distance. "I fear," Mardon said, "that we will encounter more resistance inside, so you must be prepared to offer more sacrifices."

"What of the driver?" Bagowd asked. "Will she alert the authorities?"

Mardon laughed. "They will be too busy with a greater crisis. Our friend Chazaq will soon make sure of that."

141

THE BRIDGE

Green is correct." Glewlwyd touched Elam on the chest. Just as the Caitiff pounced, the world around him suddenly fractured into puzzle pieces and scattered in the wind. A new world took shape, a beautiful forest glade with vibrant green leaves waving from statuesque trees and lush grass as soft as a kitten's coat. Flowers sprinkled the landscape with dazzling colours – reds that would shame rubies and blues more brilliant than sapphires.

"This place is amazing!" Elam turned in a slow circle. "Where are we?"

Glewlwyd, now opaque, stood straighter and rubbed his hand across his scant white hair. "Many call it the Bridgelands, but I like to call it Heaven's Gauntlet, a front porch, if you will, that leads to Heaven. To enter the final shield you must have the scarlet key in your hand."

"A scarlet key? How do I get that?"

"You will get it when you pass the tests of character that correct my mistakes."

143

"You mean the people who you thought were worthy but really weren't?"

The old gatekeeper laid a wrinkled hand on his leathery forehead. "Alas! Although I see into a man's soul, I do not always catch the dark areas if he has learned to hide them well."

Elam opened his cloak and let the gentle breeze blow through. "What kind of unworthy people would venture into Molech's Forest? They'd have to be willing to risk a lot."

"Very true, for if the Caitiff kill them in their wandering bodies, their souls go directly to the Lake of Fire where they will suffer for all eternity. At least in Hades they can delay the inevitable for as long as possible, but they are still desperate wretches who are convinced they don't belong there, so they go to great lengths to escape."

"Who would be so desperate? I mean, I understand why anyone would want to get out of Hades, but facing those monsters takes a lot of courage."

"They have courage, to be sure," Glewlwyd said, "but courage is not always accompanied by purity. Many are preachers or theologians who loudly quote their confessions and institutes to prove their piety, but the darkness in their hearts screams obscenities that drown out their oratory."

"There are theologians in Hades?"

"Certainly. Not all go there, of course, for I am a theologian myself. Yet many fail to understand that it's not studying God that gains his favour; it is obeying him."

"Well spoken." Elam hiked up his shoulder bag. "So what do I do now?"

Glewlwyd waved his robed arm across the expansive scenery. "Go forth, and seek so that you may find ... but beware. There are great trials in this place, either from evil wanderers who could not complete the gauntlet, or in the form of tests that will assess your character."

"That's no surprise. Merlin told me one of Enoch's prophecies. He said there's a dangerous enemy who wants to drink my life, something about taking my fruit that burns within, a flame that melts a subtle knife. Any idea what that means?"

"I do, indeed." A sparkle gleamed in Glewlwyd's eye. "Fruit and life have twofold meanings. You have consumed Eden's eternal fruit, giving you extraordinary length of life. Someone longs for this gift, craves for it with lustful passion, and would, if you do not act with wisdom, drink it straight from your blood. If you are wise enough, however, perhaps you will conquer your enemy with the second meaning. Your fruit and life are the harvest of your faith. If your enemy feeds on these, a different outcome is assured, one that will bring you great blessing."

Giving the old man a smile, Elam shook his head. "Your explanation is almost as cryptic as the prophecy."

Glewlwyd replied with a friendly cackle. "I intended for it to be cryptic. How could wisdom be tested if every step is given in advance?" He patted Elam on his chest. "If your heart is pure, you have nothing to fear. If, however, you have hidden any darkness in those secret places I could not see, your enemy will find it, and I cannot bear to tell you what would happen in that case."

Elam took a deep breath. "I don't have any choice. I have to find Acacia and Paili."

"You are right." Glewlwyd moved his hand to Elam's upper arm and squeezed his bicep. "Loyalty and confidence in your character will get you far, but those two alone will not be enough. You will need clear vision and spiritual foresight."

"Speaking of foresight ..." Elam pulled the spyglass from his bag and searched the horizon. "I see some kind of trench with a bridge across it."

"Considerably more than a trench, as you will see. It is Zeno's Chasm, much wider and deeper than it appears, and the bridge

145

is old and very dangerous, yet you must cross the chasm to get to Heaven's altar."

Elam collapsed the spyglass. "Is there a way around? A safer bridge, maybe?"

"I have heard tales of such a passage." Glewlwyd pointed to his right. "They say if you go in one direction, the chasm becomes narrow and shallow enough to cross, but you will not be able to see the passage from the bridge, even with your spyglass." He shifted his finger to the left. "If you go the other way, the chasm just gets deeper."

Elam looked in the direction the gatekeeper pointed. "So that way is the wrong way, right?"

Glewlwyd shrugged. "I am not sure, and you should not care. The bridge provides the key to entering Heaven's altar, so it would be foolish to go any other way. It is a fearsome path, to be sure, and only those with a perfected heart are able to cross, but it is the only path that guarantees the destination."

"What happens to travellers who try to find the safer passage?"

The old man shook his head. "I have heard of travellers who search and never find their way back to the bridge. A wrong choice could lead to an eternity of wandering."

"That doesn't make sense. All they would have to do is turn around and follow the edge of the chasm back to the bridge."

Glewlwyd pointed at him and winked. "In your world, yes, but here you must get accustomed to many new realities ... and new dangers."

"I hope the dangers aren't any worse than the Caitiff." Elam laid the spyglass in the bag and patted the side. "I don't have any weapons."

"I suggest preparing your mind for obstacles far more deadly." The old man's body began to disappear, becoming transparent again as his voice faded. "You already have the greatest of weapons."

The moment Glewlwyd vanished, Elam shifted his bag higher on his shoulder and marched straight toward the chasm. As he whisked past the flowers, a new fragrance buoyed his senses, a fresh, lively aroma the wildflowers in Hades could only dream of creating.

Light seemed to emanate from somewhere over a forested hill beyond the chasm. The top of that rise would be a good place to get a view of the entire area and plan the rest of his journey.

As he drew closer to the chasm, it seemed to grow wider and wider, so wide that when he finally reached it, he felt like a mouse at the edge of the Grand Canyon. The span was nothing more than a simple rope bridge with parallel ropes on top and bottom and loose or broken boards tied between the lower pair, barely wide enough for walking. A stiff breeze blew through the chasm, swinging the bridge as its arch dangled over the massive gap.

Elam peered down the sheer drop. No bottom was in sight. Even though the opposite cliff was far away, the two sheer walls seemed to meet in the nebulous distance below. The odd perspective dizzied his brain. He had to lurch backwards just to keep from falling in.

Pulling out his spyglass again, Elam searched both directions, but, just as the gatekeeper had warned, there was no shallow passage in sight.

He tapped the spyglass on his head. According to Glewlwyd the bridge guaranteed his destination, something about providing a key to the altar, but he didn't say going the safer route made it impossible to get there. Should he chance a guess and look for the passage? Choosing right would give him a safer road, but choosing wrong could mean being lost forever.

Elam sighed. It would be a foolish risk to go any other way. If the bridge provided the key to the altar, he had to go out and get it, no matter how impossible it seemed.

147

A soft voice drifted into his ears. "Take care, young man. The bridge is dangerous."

Elam spun around. A woman wearing a hooded red cloak stood before him. Her velvet sleeves covered all but the ends of her fingers, and only her bare toes were visible at the bottom of her cape. As she pulled back her hood, wavy brown hair spilled over her shoulders and framed a lovely young face.

"Thank you for the warning," Elam said, bowing, "but this is the only way I've seen to get across."

She extended her hand toward the bridge, exposing a slender arm. "I have watched hundreds fall into the chasm, but there is a safer passage. I have led many travellers such as yourself across."

Elam looked back at the bridge. "I think I'll take my chances this way."

Her voice stayed soft and smooth. "Only those with a perfected heart are able to cross the bridge. Do you judge yourself more capable than the great men who have attempted passage and fallen?"

"I'm not comparing myself to anyone. Since I haven't seen any of these men you're talking about, I have no basis on which to judge."

"Then you doubt my word, though I have watched this bridge for centuries. You must think me a deceiver when I warn you of the danger."

Elam glanced back at the swinging bridge again. "I believe it's dangerous. I can see that for myself."

She extended her hand toward Elam. "Then come with me. Join the others who have made an honest evaluation of their imperfect hearts and followed the path of realism. Is it not folly to stand alone in a dangerous place when you can walk safely in numbers?"

"Numbers mean nothing to me." Elam tapped himself on his chest. "I've been alone most of my life. I have learned to follow the people I already trust, namely Enoch and Merlin. Merlin told me to find Glewlwyd, and Glewlwyd said I should cross the bridge, so that's what I'm going to do."

"You are listening to empty promises – mere words." She reached for his hand. "I offer you reality. No one can really make this impossible passage. It is far too difficult."

Elam pushed her hand down. "I think you've delayed me long enough. I'm going to cross."

A sad smile thinned out her lips. "Very well." She raised the hood over her head and lowered herself to her knees at the foot of the bridge. "I will pray for your crossing, though you will surely fall with the others. Only do not curse me as you plummet to your death, for I gave you fair warning."

"That you did." Turning abruptly, he stuffed the spyglass back in the bag. While gripping the ropes on each side of the bridge, he slid his foot out onto the first plank. Testing the next step with his other foot, he shifted his weight forward, hoping he could hang on if the plank broke. It held firm. The next plank, however, was already split, though not completely broken. Taking a longer step, he bypassed it and landed on the next plank. It snapped, and his leg plunged through, pulling his other leg with it. With one hand clinging to each of the upper ropes, he dangled, his chest at the level of the planks and his arms spread painfully wide.

"Oh, the folly!" The woman in red sang out. "The folly of those who think themselves holier and wiser than the sages who went before them!"

A new gust of wind jerked the bridge. One hand slipped off, and his shoulder bag slid down his arm. As he tried to grab the strap, his other hand slipped, but just before he could fall through the bridge, he slung his arms over the lower rope and hung on. His bag plunged into the depths, tossed about by the wind as it shrank in the distance of the apparently bottomless chasm.

The woman spread out her arms, making her cloak look like a pair of red wings. "Pride goeth before a fall, young man, and since your pride was so great, your fall will be great as well. The reality of the chasm will swallow you and prove the vanity of your imagined moral character."

Elam gasped for breath, his heart pounding in his ears. The wind tossed the bridge, throwing his dangling legs into a swinging frenzy. Pulling up with all his might, he pushed his elbow over a plank and muscled his body higher until he could reach the next plank and pull again. With every two inches of progress, the bucking bridge shoved him back an inch and a half. Finally, grabbing plank after plank, he crept over the walkway and sprawled over the wooden steps, hanging on to each side rope as the bridge continued to sway.

"Do you still believe you will make it to the other side?" The woman's voice rode the wind. "You survived only the first of many false steps, and the mishaps will only become more treacherous as you learn the true nature of this bridge. If you come back, I will hold no grudges and lead you to the safer way."

Elam looked ahead. The other side of the chasm was still far in the distance. Twisting his neck, he looked back at the woman. She rose to her feet and held out her arms as if ready to carry him away. She wasn't far at all. Just a short leap or two, and he'd be back to solid ground and safe in her grasp.

He clenched his fist. No! He couldn't give up now! That would prove Merlin wrong and destroy everything he believed in! Pushing up to hands and knees, he crawled forward inch by inch, grasping each plank so tightly the ragged edges cut into his hands. Every gust halted his progress, making him steel his arms to keep from toppling over the side as the bridge swung to a precarious angle. Each time it settled, he forged ahead, more confident that the planks would hold now that his weight was distributed over four points of pressure rather than two.

After what seemed like an hour, Elam reached the lowest part of the sagging bridge. He looked back again. The woman in red stood there, much farther away than before, but his destination seemed no closer at all. And now that he was at the lowest point, the bridge swung more wildly than ever.

His hands now aching, he pushed on, gripping the crossbars ever tighter as he crawled up the swaying incline. Another hour passed, and another. Still, the other side seemed far away, not an inch closer than when he started. But it had to be closer. It didn't make any sense to move toward something and not make any progress.

He pressed forward, closing his eyes to shut out the bottomless canyon and the seemingly unreachable goal at the end of the bridge. Plank by plank, they would eventually all pass under his hands and knees. There couldn't be an infinite number. That would be impossible.

Glewlwyd's words came back to his mind. *"In your world, yes, but here you must get accustomed to many new realities."* Then the taunts from the woman in red echoed. *"The mishaps will only become more treacherous as you learn the true nature of this bridge."*

Elam looked ahead again and sighed. Still no closer. How could that be? Since he had been crawling upward for hours, he had to be way past the midpoint. Was that the bridge's true nature, that it really was endless?

Sprawling once again, he rested and let the bridge swing his body in a peaceful sway, like a baby in a wind-blown cradle. He was too tired to go on. The other side was just too far away. The infinite was simply beyond his grasp.

A voice whispered in his ear. "Have you given up the quest, Elam?"

He jerked his head up. No one was in sight. "Who said that?"

"I am an old friend. Close your eyes and ease your mind, for only rest will prepare you for the long journey ahead."

"Your voice *is* familiar." Laying his head back down, Elam closed his eyes and yawned. "Where have we met?"

The voice was soft and soothing. "Many times in many places, but that is not important. For now, you must sleep."

"But if I sleep, I might roll off the bridge."

"No one who trusts in the bridge will ever fall off."

"But I almost did, way back at the beginning. The steps broke."

"True enough, but after you lost your bag and crawled, how many steps gave way?"

Elam brought the sight of thousands of stepping planks into his mind. "None gave way. But the wind made it almost impossible to crawl, and I just can't seem to get to the end. It never gets any closer."

"Storms blow on us all, and the goal seems unattainable to the mortal mind, to those who believe in their inability to take hold of what is freely given."

"So what do I do?"

The voice blended in with the whistling wind. "Reflect on these signs. Rely on the bridge. Rest in your faith. Only then can you do the impossible."

As the breeze rocked him back and forth, Elam relaxed his grip and rode with the swing. He let his mind drift, recalling all the years of suffering at Morgan's hands, the months of hunger, back-breaking work, flea-infested dosshouses in Glasgow, and worst of all, the endless days of separation from Sapphira Adi, the only girl he could ever imagine as his wife. Even after thousands of years of knowing her, the time for their union was still far in the future, years that seemed as numerous as the planks on the bridge. There was too much to do – journeys that couldn't wait.

Soon, he was asleep, dreaming of the trials of yesterday. In his dream, he put Morgan and Naamah into his shoulder bag, then the coal-stained cap he always wore at the Glasgow shipyards, and finally, a gold band, a wedding ring, pausing to gaze at it for a moment before he let it drop inside.

Standing at the centre point of the bridge, he slung the bag into the chasm, then, not bothering to watch it fall, he ran across the bridge toward the destination side, closing his eyes and leaping for the brink. He tumbled into the soft grass and lay there, taking in the delightful aroma of the surrounding flowers.

Elam fluttered his eyelids open. Blades of grass veiled his view. The aroma of fresh flowers graced his senses as the yellow and white head of a daisy bowed toward his nose, giving way to the breeze.

Leaping to his feet, he spun toward the yawning canyon. It was behind him, the impassable gulf now a mere crack in the sidewalk. The woman in red was gone.

He lifted his feet up and down in turn. The solid ground never felt so good. He held up his stinging, aching hands, gashed across the palms from thumb to little finger and oozing blood. He smiled in spite of the pain. Although every muscle ached, he never felt better in his life. There was no greater feeling than to conquer the impossible, even when given help by the infinite.

153

Turning his back to the chasm, he strode ahead toward the rise in the distance, the vista he had hoped to use as an overlook to get the lay of the land. When he crested the hill, he gazed out over the lower elevations all around, but trees blocked his view in every direction.

He set his hands on his hips. That spyglass sure would come in handy now, but it wouldn't do any good to wish for something he had lost and couldn't get back.

As he scanned the scene, his own vision seemed enhanced. Every detail was sharp and magnified, similar to how Sapphira had described her vision whenever she came near a portal location. The colours were breathtaking – dazzling blue ponds, flowers that seemed so saturated with reds, oranges, and yellows they were ready to drip, and trees so green, his mother's emerald paled in comparison.

He jerked his gaze back to a small pond in a stand of massive trees. Something moved near its edge. Leaping forward, he galloped down the hill. The spongy grass cushioned every step, and when he arrived at the pond, he didn't feel winded at all. Sweeping the area with his gaze, he searched for the source of movement, but not a leaf stirred. Near the border of the pond, however, hoofprints marred the rich earth.

He stooped at the prints and looked out over the crystal pool, a perfect circle no wider than he could leap if he had a running start. With the water so clear, he could see the tiniest details in the smooth stones at the bottom, yet its depth seemed a mystery. Could it be five feet? Fifty feet? The clarity made it difficult to tell.

"Drink, stranger. The water is free."

Elam shot to his feet and swung around. A beautiful white horse stood a few paces away, its tail swishing, though there wasn't a fly to be seen.

154

"Did you speak?" Elam asked.

The horse turned its head one way, then the other before looking at Elam again. "Since there is no one else here," it replied in a bass tone, "I assume your deductive reasoning is sorely lacking. But it is no sin to be without sense, so ..." He bowed his head low. "My name is Dikaios."

Elam bowed with him. "And I am Elam."

Dikaios turned his head to look Elam in the eye. "You are an interesting specimen."

Patting his torso, Elam checked for changes in his body. "Why? Don't I look human?"

"Indeed, you are human in form, but we are not concerned with shape or skin here. Yet I must say that you have already behaved unlike most humans I have ever seen."

Elam stooped and stirred the water with his finger. "I hope you weren't offended that I didn't drink from the pool even after you offered."

"Not at all. Many humans are careful about what they drink in strange lands. Your inaction is merely prudence."

"The water looks safe. I just wasn't thirsty."

"You will not become thirsty here, but this water is a delicious gift that you are free to take at any time."

"Thank you," Elam said, rising to his feet. "I appreciate it."

The horse shook its head. "Do not thank me. Thank the one who provides it."

"I will be sure to do that." Elam scanned the area on the other side of the pool. "I need to get to Heaven's altar to find some friends. Could you tell me how to get there?"

Dikaios eyed him again. "Stranger and stranger."

Elam squinted at the horse. Why wouldn't he answer a simple question? Would every creature in this place be so oblique? He cleared his throat. "It was a pleasure meeting you, Dikaios, but I must move on now." He bowed again and began walking around the pond.

With a swift gallop, Dikaios blocked his way. "You may ride me," he said in a gruff tone.

Elam halted. "I didn't ask to ride you."

"But you want to." Dikaios lowered his head. "All humans want a ride."

"Is that so?" Elam chuckled. "If I were tired or in need of a swift transport, I might have asked for a ride. But since I don't even know where I'm going ..." Patting the horse's neck, Elam passed him by. "I won't be a burden to you."

As he strolled, Elam heard the sound of hoof steps behind him, soft and slow. Soon, the bobbing head of a horse appeared at his side. "I am coming with you," Dikaios said, "because you have piqued my curiosity."

Elam smiled. "You are certainly welcome to join me, but if you know the way, perhaps you would like to lead."

"Do not think of Heaven's altar as a physical destination," Dikaios said. "Although it exists in a real place in this dimension, it is better to perceive it as a spiritual objective, gained by inner purity. Once your character is proven, you will find it."

A shadow glided over the grassy carpet, causing Elam to look skyward. A golden-brown eagle soared overhead, its wings in full sail, riding the wind with hardly a flutter. "So," Elam said, sliding a hand into his pocket, "maybe I'll just keep looking around this place until something happens. It's hard to have a plan when there's no road map to follow."

Dikaios gently nudged Elam with his nose. "You must not be casual about this journey. It is too dangerous."

"Casual?" Elam halted and crossed his arms. "My good horse, there's a big difference between casual and confident. I'm aware of the danger, but ..." As he searched his mind for the right words, Merlin's warnings flowed through his lips. "I want to maintain a confident mind-set in full assurance of faith, otherwise my heart might melt within me."

156

"Ah! An excellent speech! No doubt you have rehearsed it, but it is a good, wise saying, so there is no harm in reciting it." Dikaios shook his head hard, scattering his mane into disarray. "But it will take more than words to pass the tests you are about to face. I have yet to see a human make it through the shield of Heaven without special concourse, but you are quite unusual, so I will watch with interest." The horse's eyes seemed to grow larger as he drew closer. "Take care that your confidence does not swell into arrogance, for that is the downfall of every man of pride."

CHAPTER

THE ALTERED TRIBE

Timothy pulled back from the ovulum. "Sapphira's face is so familiar, it's like I'm seeing a fleeting image from my past, and other images fly through my mind, too, but nothing's staying put long enough to set in a time or place." He folded his hands on the table and leaned forward again. "Maybe if you tell me how I got here, I can start putting together the pieces."

"All I know," Abraham said, "is that Candle found you in the birthing garden, where our younglings are tended."

"Birthing garden?" Timothy laughed and leaned back in his chair. "You'd better treat me like an ignorant alien. I don't know what you're talking about."

"First-hand experience is the best teacher, even for an alien." Assuming the village's prayer posture, Abraham stood up and walked toward the door. "Come with me. I will show you the new Garden of Eden."

Timothy followed, also pressing his hands together. Heading away from the centre of the village, they passed only a few of the citizens, but the ones they met stopped and bowed low as the

157

Prophet walked by. Abraham smiled and nodded at their votive gestures, but he seemed uncomfortable with the attention.

One family, after bowing low, stared at him as if awestruck, a muscular dark-skinned man, his shorter, equally dark wife, and their pale, freckled daughter, who seemed no more than twelve or thirteen.

After they passed, the mother chided the girl. "Don't ask such questions. The Prophet's interests lie elsewhere, and you're too young to be anyone's Eve."

Abraham chuckled, but he didn't look back. When they reached the end of the road, they walked down a gentle slope, through a sparse stand of trees, and into a low-lying field. Stretching out across at least a hundred acres, the field boasted rows and rows of plants sprouting in the damp soil. From each plant two huge leaves grew vertically out of a thick stem, the edges touching each other, much like a pair of hands propped in the village's prayer posture. Still, the "palms" of the leaves left enough of a gap to create a pocket in between them, as if they were hiding something sacred within their dark-green grasp.

158

The Prophet strode into the garden and stooped at the first plant, an especially large one that shifted back and forth in the cold wind. He caressed one of the leaves and gazed at Timothy. "This one is almost ready. It quickened long ago and will soon open to reveal its fruit."

"What's inside?" Timothy asked.

Abraham looked out over the field. "Ah!" He pointed at a group of four gardeners surrounding one of the plants. "You are about to see for yourself."

With Timothy following, Abraham marched to the spot where a man and a woman stooped, each with a hand on a leaf, while another couple stood over them. Their four egg-shaped companions buzzed around so quickly, it was impossible to spot the eyes to see which companion belonged to whom.

"Watch," Abraham whispered, "and listen."

The man who stood laid a palm on the stooping man's shoulder and spoke with oratory fervour. "It is time to bring forth what was once cast away. Let us redeem that which was considered inconvenient and make it precious. The chaff of another world is now the harvest of this realm."

The lower couple joined hands, and each pulled on a leaf, while the other woman leaned the plant toward them. As the leaves parted, a large white seedpod tipped out into the stooping couple's cradled arms. With trembling fingers, the woman tore its velvety coat open, revealing a female infant, pink and wiggling, yet not making a sound.

Timothy stepped closer. The baby clutched something in its tiny fingers, a glass bauble. After gently prying the orb from the child's grip, the man set it on her forehead. The egg-shaped glass rocked back and forth, then rose an inch or two from her skin, its tiny eyes blinking.

"An ovulum," Timothy whispered.

Abraham nodded. "Her companion. Watch what it does."

The companion moved slowly over the baby's body from head to toe, as if examining its newborn charge. After almost a minute, it returned to her head and nuzzled her cheek, making the little girl smile.

All four gardeners laughed, and their companions zipped around their heads as if joining their gaiety. The woman took the baby into her arms and bundled her in a thick shawl, while the other three helped her to her feet.

Abraham stepped forward. "Congratulations, my friends."

While the mother smiled and dipped her knee, the other three bowed low. Rising again, the father set his hands in the praying posture. "We are blessed by your presence, Father."

"The blessing is mine and your daughter's." Laying two fingers on the baby's forehead, he gazed at the new parents. "Have you chosen a first-year name?"

"Sunrise," the mother replied. "Her arrival fulfils the promise of a new day."

Abraham looked up into the sky, his hair tossed by the cold wind. "May Sunrise bring light and warmth to all. She will dry widows' tears and set ablaze the hearts of the despondent." Tucking the shawl under the baby's chin, he nudged the newborn companion playfully. "Remember these words when you choose her next name." After swirling around the baby's tiny nose, the companion sat on the tip, appearing to nod in the affirmative.

"The companion chooses her name?" Timothy asked.

"It suggests an appropriate name based on the child's personality, and her parents will likely agree. A companion is so familiar with its charge, the name is always suitable."

"I see."

Abraham turned to the new mother. "You need not stay on my account. Your milk is likely to come in at any moment, and Sunrise will soon be hungry."

As the four strolled through the garden, Timothy pushed his hands into his pockets and gazed at the field in new wonder. Every plant carried a developing child! And the villagers watched over them, anxiously awaiting a precious harvest! But how did the babies get there? Who could plant a child's seed in the earth? How did they decide which couple would receive the next newborn?

"Timothy." Abraham stopped and waved his hand across the field. "This is where Candle found you, sitting and shivering where one of the recently harvested plants had been. He helped you stagger to the village where you passed out in the street. Angel volunteered to take care of you in the sky ward, and, of course, Candle had to go along. After all, he felt as though he harvested you."

Timothy shook his head in wonder. "I guess you know this manner of childbirth is new to me."

"You guess correctly." Abraham smiled at him. "This guessing is an idiom I should add to my people's language."

Walking toward the village, Abraham stepped into a parallel row to avoid another foursome of harvesters. "As you heard, these children are cast-offs from a different world. Their lives were terminated by cruel or ignorant people, so here they are given an opportunity to finally be born and live. Yet, they have a better existence here. Even after they mature, they are so pure and innocent, if not for the cold winds, they would likely wear no clothes and no one would care. They also never age beyond their prime years. Some of the youthful adults are three times their apparent age, according to the norms of your world. They have no disease, only the occasional injury associated with work and play and ..." Abraham paused and furrowed his brow. After a few seconds it seemed that he had decided not to continue.

"So that's the reason for the sky ward," Timothy concluded. "But it seemed like such a large hospital. I think I was the only patient."

"You were. We have ground-based infirmaries for most injuries. The hospital in the sky is for times of war. Our enemy is unable to reach it, so it is a safe refuge for our wounded."

"Candle mentioned times of war." Timothy searched the sky for any sign of a bird. "Who is your enemy? The altered tribe?"

"That is the name my people gave them, but to you it probably makes them sound like mutant American Indians on the warpath." Abraham smiled at his own attempt at humour. "Actually, I prefer to call the closest altered tribe the shadow people."

"That conjures even stranger images. What's a shadow person?"

"Again, it is better for you to see than for me to explain."

Timothy nodded toward the village. "Through Enoch's Ghost?"

"I will bring it with us. Where we are going, we will need the protection it offers. They live in a dark region filled with mysteries, one of which I would like for you to help me solve. Perhaps when I show it to you, we will also see the shadow people."

161

They returned to the village and, after collecting the ovulum, travelled back to where Timothy had left Grackle. Abraham blew a shrill whistle into the air. Another whistle echoed his, and then, in the distance, a third barely audible response returned on the breeze.

"Albatross will be here soon," Abraham said. "I assume Angel and Grackle have given you a dragon-flying lesson."

"Oh, yes. It was quite a ride!"

Abraham revealed a hint of a smile. "Perhaps more than you hoped for?"

Timothy shook his head. "It felt good to soar through the air. I'm ready to go again."

"Albatross will not be so gentle," Abraham said with a frown. "The white dragons lack both cleverness and courtesy."

A huge shadow blocked out the sun. Albatross approached, a dragon even bigger than Grackle, two seats already strapped to his back. As he landed, his spiny white tail swiped toward Timothy.

"Jump!" Abraham ordered.

Timothy leaped over the tail just in time. When the dragon settled, he spewed a frosty spray of blue ice crystals at Timothy's feet.

"Albatross!" Abraham shook his finger. "Do you want to go back where I found you?"

The dragon shook his head and trumpeted a loud, mournful wail.

"Then you had better give us a smooth ride to Shadow's Basin."

Albatross shook his head again, this time trembling.

"There is nothing to fear." Abraham nodded toward the descending sun. "As long as we have light, we will be safe."

After spewing another spray of ice on the ground, Albatross lowered his snout, creating the stairway. A few seconds later, Abraham and Timothy were on board. Abraham stowed Enoch's

Ghost in a bag attached to his seat, and, as soon as the dragon heated his scales, they took off into the chilly breeze.

Abraham shouted above the sound of wings and wind. "It is quite late to be travelling to the basin, but we will not tarry long. We just have to be back in the air before sunset."

"Is it more dangerous there at night?" Timothy shouted back.

"Much more so, but I also neglected to bring heavier cloaks. If we have to fly after sundown, we will be very uncomfortable, even with heated scales."

After several exhilarating minutes, with gorgeous views of rivers meandering through dense forests and green meadows, the great white dragon carried them over a ridge, and the land descended sharply into a deep bowl-shaped valley. Mountains encircled the entire depression, making the circular dale look like a fortress. A waterfall on one side sent foaming water and chunks of ice plunging into the valley, and on the other, the river churned through a narrow gap in the cliff.

163

Abraham pointed at the river's exit. "For most of the shadow people, the river is the only way to leave, and we guard its outflow. And there is another reason they hesitate to go near that gateway, which I hope to show you soon."

With the dragon's wing blocking his view, Timothy had to lean forward to get a better look. "Then how do the wars begin if they can't get out?"

"They have trained some of the winged creatures to carry them, though few birds are smart or deft enough to make the journey, and, of course, dragons are too wise to be coerced into their schemes. Over time, however, even with just a few eagles and owls helping them, they can amass enough troops to attack."

"I saw one of them earlier," Timothy said. "A dark-breasted eagle flying near your village. Angel seemed concerned about it."

"She was wise to be concerned. That dark spot on the eagle's breast was a shadow person riding underneath so he could avoid the sunlight. Although my people are now aware of these warning signs, for a long time, they were too naive to suspect danger, and they tended to be unprepared, so we suffered great losses. In recent times, however, I have managed to convince them to be more vigilant. The altered tribes still perpetrate small raids, but our men have learned to fight them off. That is likely the reason we have not had a large war in three years. Still, the occasional ambush can catch our people off guard."

As the dragon banked to one side, Timothy leaned into the turn. "What do they want? Your land? Your birthing field?"

"Something far more valuable, which I will explain when we arrive."

A shrill whistle sounded from behind them. Grackle, his wings beating furiously, closed in. Angel waved a red flag as she pulled her dragon alongside Albatross. "Father!" she shouted. "An altered one has taken my Adam's companion! He escaped under an eagle!"

164

Abraham's face blazed red. "The murderer has returned for his spoils, has he?"

"Yes!" she cried, tucking the flag under her seat. "I must have it back!"

Abraham dug his heels into the white dragon's side. "Albatross! Take me to the falls glade. I will confront them myself!"

As the white dragon swerved downward, Angel caught up again. "I'm coming with you!"

Abraham pointed back toward the village. "Candle and Listener need you. Would you leave them without consolation?"

She drew a club from behind her seat. "Candle and Listener need their father's memory. I have to retrieve it at all costs."

Abraham sighed. "Very well. You may follow." He slapped his dragon's scales. "Make haste, Albatross! Time is of the essence!"

The dragon dove toward the waterfall side of the valley, descending so quickly, Timothy lifted off his seat. Tightening his belt with cold, stiff fingers, he breathed in the smoke-tinged air. Something below was burning, wood mixed with an oily fuel.

Albatross followed the river toward the waterfall and landed near the shore, bumping his undersides in the sand as his legs scrambled to find good footing. When he finally came to a stop, Abraham slid off his flank and waved for Angel and Grackle to join him. Since the falls spilled into the river only paces away, the roar of tumbling water filled the air, accentuated by random splashes as ice boulders tumbled from the ridge, masking every other sound.

Timothy copied Abraham's quick dismount, and, seconds later, Grackle landed abreast of the white dragon. Wielding her club, Angel hopped to the sand and rushed into Abraham's embrace. "Father! I cannot bear it! Without my Adam's companion, we will lose his memory forever!"

While Angel's little companion caressed her tear-streaked face, Abraham hugged her close. "Dragon was a great man," he said. "He surely lived up to the courage behind his name. We will find the murderer and restore your Adam's presence to your children. It is our only hope to bring Dragon back to the living."

"But will it ever happen?" Angel pulled back and gazed into Abraham's eyes. "The others in my village fear to raise their laments above a whisper, but you know the separated companions have been little more than painful reminders. I have hung on to this hope for almost three years, but no one has yet returned from the dead, at least none that I can remember."

Abraham clasped her shoulders. "We await the prophecy. I cannot promise that even that will bring back our fallen warriors, but until then, you have the reminder of your Adam's love."

Closing her eyes, Angel shook her head. "A reminder will not teach Candle how to sharpen an axe or build a home, nor will it provide Listener the peace and joy of a masculine presence." Opening her eyes again, she continued, her voice breaking. "In the evenings, it will not play sparkles during twin moons ... or sing hymns in the firelight. On the coldest nights it will not wrap me in strong arms and keep me warm." She laid her cheek on his shoulder and wept bitterly.

Abraham patted her on the back and glanced at Timothy. "My people know so little heartache, when it comes, it devastates them. The loss of a beloved mate she slept beside every night for over one hundred years nearly killed her, and now the loss of his symbolic presence will likely tear her apart as well."

Wiping a tear from his own eye, Timothy nodded. "I don't know why, but I share her pain. It's like I've lost someone close, too, but I have no idea who it is."

"Perhaps we can soon find the answers you seek, but for now—" Abraham jerked his head toward the trees on the other side of the river. "I saw something."

Timothy pointed. "There! Something dark. A moving shadow."

Angel wrung the club with her fingers and tromped into the flowing water. "An altered one!"

Just as Timothy jumped in the shallows to stop her, the companion zoomed in front of her eyes and flashed red.

Angel halted. As she stood knee-deep in the icy water, she sagged her shoulders. "You're right. It is foolish to take the lead when the Prophet is here."

Abraham waded in and took her club. "We will go together." As he scanned the churning river, an ice boulder tumbled through the current and smashed into an underwater stone, cleaving it in two. The broken halves rushed downstream, spinning in separate eddies.

"We had better ride the dragons across," Abraham said.

They waded back and remounted the dragons. With his wings beating the misty air, Albatross bounded to a large stone protruding from the river, then leaped again to the opposite shore. Grackle flew gracefully across, spanning the hundred-foot-wide river without a break. Abraham leaped down, pulled Enoch's Ghost from the bag, and strode into the woods, followed by Timothy and Angel.

With the sun well behind the ridge and the tree canopy blocking ambient light, the landscape grew darker as they penetrated the forest's boundary. After handing Timothy the club, Abraham cradled the ovulum in his hands. As it began to glow scarlet, he peered into the glass. "We have company," he said. "Four ... no ... five of the shadow people."

"Will they attack?" Timothy asked.

"Only by stealth or if they perceive they have a strong advantage. They are cowards by nature, and few will come out of hiding unless their numbers are far greater than those of their enemies." He pulled the ovulum closer. "Aha! Our search has been blessed. I see the murderer!"

"How can you tell?" Timothy tried to look into the ovulum. "I don't see anything."

"He carries the evidence. It shines against his blackness."

Timothy raised the club. "What do we do?"

"Here. Take the ovulum." Abraham handed it to Timothy, then charged ahead and dove on the ground, his arms grasping at the forest's failing shadows. Rising to his knees, he wrestled a dark form and dashed it against the leafy floor.

"Help!" Angel fell to the ground. Two black hands latched on to her ankle and dragged her toward a thicket. She grasped a loose root and kicked against the arms, but her tightened fingers slid down the bark, stripping it bare.

Setting down the ovulum, Timothy lunged head first into the fray and slid into Angel's attackers. He yanked their arms away from her while beating their heads with the club. The two assailants seemed rubbery in his hands. They slipped from his grasp, squeaking and moaning as they melded into the darkest shadows and disappeared.

167

Timothy pulled Angel to her knees and gently brushed leaves from her jacket and hair. "Are you all right?"

She spat out a leaf and nodded. "I think so."

After picking up Enoch's Ghost, Timothy combed his fingers through her tangled hair, loosening a clump of dirt. "Good. I'd hate to see anything happen—"

"Well done!" Abraham called.

Timothy smiled and looked his way. The Prophet stood upright with his foot pinning a human-shaped shadow. He turned toward his captive and reached out his hand. "Now give it to me!"

The shadow, trembling under Abraham's grinding foot, stretched out a long, spindly arm, jet black and flat as a ribbon. In its blunt hand it displayed an ovulum, much smaller than Enoch's Ghost, but slightly larger than Angel's companion.

Abraham snatched it away. "Did you slay one of my people?"

A low clicking sound rose from the dark form's head.

"You just found it lying on the ground?" Abraham pointed at the larger ovulum in Timothy's hand. "If Enoch judges you guilty, I will cast you into the light tunnel."

The shadow stiffened. More clicks sounded from his imperceptible mouth, higher pitched and faster.

"Bring me Enoch's Ghost," Abraham said, extending his hand.

Timothy rushed over and set the ovulum in Abraham's palm, while the shadow thrashed under his crushing foot. "Settle down," Abraham ordered, "or I will plant my foot in your face!"

When his prisoner quieted, Abraham leaned over and set Enoch's Ghost on its chest. As the ovulum began to glow with white light, a flood of clicks erupted. The light covered the shadow, melting away its black shroud. A white skeleton appeared in its place, a two-dimensional X-ray without depth or contrast, exposing thin strands that looked more like paper than bone.

At the centre of its spidery ribcage, a red light, the size of a toddler's fist, pulsed in an even rhythm.

168

Abraham grabbed the ovulum, and the prisoner returned to its shadowy state. He shook his fist at the dark form. "You have human life energy. You must have killed Dragon."

New clicks rose, this time with a questioning inflection.

"Because you came back for his companion. That's how I know." Abraham glanced around. "He's stalling for time. The others must have gone for help." Grabbing the shadow's foot, he stomped toward the river, dragging the struggling creature behind him. "Hurry. Evening is upon us. Until Pegasus appears over the ridge, we are vulnerable."

Timothy and Angel followed. "Pegasus?" Timothy asked. "The winged horse?"

"Pegasus is First Moon tonight," Angel replied, jogging to keep up. "Where have you seen a winged horse?"

"I haven't seen one." As they neared the river, Timothy gazed at Angel. Tears gleamed in her eyes – searching, forlorn, desperate. He wanted to say more … offer comfort, set her free from the pain that ripped through her heart. Yet, seeing her suffering again aroused his own submerged pain. Could it be the absence of a long-time mate, his Eve?

When they arrived at the waiting dragons, Abraham climbed Albatross's neck, still dragging the shadow creature. "Ride with Angel," he said to Timothy. "I must tie this scoundrel to my other seat."

"Father!" Angel rose up on tiptoes, shouting over the waterfall's roar. "Do you still have the companion?"

"One moment!" Abraham twisted the strap and fastened the shadow to the rear seat. Reaching into a pocket, he retrieved the smaller ovulum and handed it down to her.

A radiant smile lit up her face. She pressed the little egg against her chest before tucking it away under her jacket.

Abraham jumped into his pilot's chair and waved his hand. "Hurry! The shadow people are massing at the forest edge!" He glanced up at the purple sky just over the ridge. "We have only seconds!"

Timothy and Angel scrambled up Grackle's long neck and threw themselves into their seats. "Good thing you brought two!" he shouted, his arms flying as he buckled himself in.

"Candle strapped them on." She tightened her belt with a quick jerk. "He wanted to come with me."

A flood of darkness swarmed along the sand, like oil streaming on water, filling the gap between the forest and the dragons.

Angel slapped Grackle's neck. "Fly! Now!"

Just as the black flood reached the dragon's claws, Grackle launched into the sky. Serpent-like fingers jumped from the sand, but too late to catch the purple dragon.

Albatross beat his wings, but only rose a foot or two. Three dark limbs stretched between him and the beach as tight bands snaked around his back leg.

"Angel!" Timothy called, pointing down. "Look!"

Angel swung around and kicked Grackle's left flank. "Dive!" she ordered. Grackle banked hard and swooped. Angel whistled and pointed at the struggling dragon's leg. "Ice those vermin!"

As Abraham swatted Albatross's side, the dragon's wings faltered. His huge body edged closer and closer to the mass of outstretched arms. Grackle spewed a thin beam of blue light. The beam solidified into a streak of ice that pierced the bands holding the white dragon and spread a frosty coat over the dismembered bodies.

Albatross shot away. Grackle pulled up hard, narrowly avoiding the grasping black arms. After a few seconds, both dragons soared above the wiggling sea of shadows.

Now safe in the sky, Timothy bundled his jacket close and shivered. It was no wonder. With the wind once again assaulting his face, even colder now with the loss of sunshine, anyone would shiver. Yet, the tremors penetrated far more deeply than a mere chill could reach. Could it be fear?

As he gazed at Angel's back, her long hair beat with the wind, too dark now to see its Nordic highlights, but as they rose above the ridge, Pegasus coated her frame in its creamy glow and painted her locks in gold.

He shivered again. This wasn't fear. It was thrill – the thrill of danger and rescue, the exhilaration of saving a life and restoring a slender slice of comfort to a bereaved widow. An even deeper passion had awakened, and it stirred his heart. The beautiful woman sitting only a few inches away, bobbing up and down as she guided Grackle close to Albatross, flashed an image in his mind, another light-haired lady whose absence brought the coldest chill yet. But who was she? Who was this fleeting image, one of the many haunting portraits that streamed chaotically through his mind?

Someone was definitely missing. His heart and soul had been torn away. As the two dragons flew side by side in the frosty heavens, the scene looked all too familiar. But why? Now, soaring far above danger and safe from its grasp, the thrill of rescue streamed away, and the sense of loss replaced it as grief flooded his heart.

171

A sudden drop shook him back to reality. Grackle descended, following Abraham and Albatross as they headed toward the river's outlet, now barely visible in the moon's glow. Down in the valley, a bright light filtered through a dense clump of trees, interrupting evening's dark curtain.

Abraham guided Albatross toward the light, and Angel followed, both dragons circling once before landing near the river's edge just outside of the light-emitting woods.

"The shadow people should not trouble us here," Abraham said, untying his prisoner. With his hand around the altered one's throat, the Prophet seemed to be dragging along an animated cardboard cutout as it thrashed in his grip, clicking and squeaking.

After Angel dismounted, Timothy scrambled down Grackle's outstretched neck. "What is this place?" he asked.

"The entrance to the light tunnel." Abraham nodded toward the forest. "I mentioned that I wanted to show you a mystery, and now that we have this murderer to take care of, I can demonstrate its unusual properties."

"Is this an execution?" Timothy asked.

"In a manner of speaking." Abraham raised his eyebrows. "Why?"

Timothy spread out his hands. "Don't you have trials here? Witnesses? Testimony?"

"I am the judge in this world, and this creature has borne witness against himself." Abraham lifted the shadow person off the ground, letting his feet thrash as he clicked madly. "We are shooting a rabid dog. We are clubbing a viper. There is no prison that can hold him, and once he escaped, he would kill again. Should I allow this murderer to continue to threaten my people?"

Timothy dug his hands into his pockets. "I suppose you're right. But what about his soul? Does he have an eternity?"

"He sold his soul. They all sold their souls at another time and place when they taught their followers the ways of the hypocrites. They were the blind leading the blind, and they have fallen into this pit. Now, they believe if they possess a companion, they will regain what they forfeited, but they have to drain a life force to snatch it away."

Albatross whistled a mournful tune, and Grackle joined in. Angel rubbed the purple dragon's scales and looked at Abraham. "The dragons fear this place, Father. Shall I command them to fly and return later?"

He shook his head. "They will be safe here. The shadows fear the light."

Angel stroked each dragon's neck and whistled a few short bursts. They nodded and huddled close together.

Still dragging the condemned shadow, Abraham strode away from the river's edge, sweeping aside branches as he plunged into the light-flooded woods.

Timothy walked a pace or two ahead of Angel. Even when he slowed to allow her to walk abreast, she slowed, too, and stayed at his heels. He reached back and took her hand. "Let me help you."

She pulled her hand away. "You are not my Adam."

"We are not in the village," he said, reaching again. "No one will be offended."

Sliding her hand into his, she allowed him to pull her to his side, but she kept her gaze straight ahead as they forged on through the woods.

Well inside the forest, a brilliant shaft of light poured into a clearing from a hole in a cliff, the high ridge that circumvented the home of the shadow people. Keeping the prisoner behind him, Abraham approached the tunnel from one side and stood near the entrance. "Enoch's Ghost awakens me every dawn with a hymn," he said to Timothy, "and he speaks of this place. Perhaps after I sing it, you will be able to help me understand its meaning." Pursing his lips, he sang, this time in a lower, smoother voice than before.

When souls are lost on darkest paths,
When fathers weep and mothers wail,
No salve can cool the fevered wound,
No solace calms the tossed travail.

A tale of hearts I tell in twos,
By inward scales their souls are weighed,
For one is brazen, shameless, proud,
The other gentle, wandering, strayed.

The rebel's heart is veiled within,
With stubborn pride rejecting sight.
Her calloused eyes perceive no flaws,
For darkness blends them with the night.

The wayward heart will seek the light,
But finds a counterfeit instead,
And celebrates the knowledge found
In human wisdom's lofty head.

O who can rescue scarlet souls
Who shake the fist or wander blind?
The souls they forfeit, gems so rare,
Are broken glass to darkened minds.

174

A stranger comes, a man who weeps
A father's tears for loved ones lost.
He hearkens from a land unknown
In search of restoration's cost.

In desperation's hope he calls,
"A soul to trade, a soul to sell,"
For better one to suffer flames
Than daughters loved to burn in Hell.

A path of light within the rock
Will purge all falsehood from within
And bring to light the hidden truths,
The love ignited once again.

The tunnel leads a warrior chief,
A youth with mystery in his eyes,
With flames he walks to burn the chaff.
A child he leads to silence lies.

And once the hearts of gold he trains
Are drawn to lights of holy depth,
Then wielding swords they journey where
Corruption's harvest draws its breath.

As he lengthened the final word and faded the tune, Abraham closed his eyes, exhaling dramatically. Everyone stayed silent. Even the dark prisoner had stopped jerking. Finally, Abraham opened his eyes again and looked at Timothy expectantly. "Any thoughts?"

"Many." Timothy laid a hand on his head. "So many, I think my brain is about to explode."

Angel pushed her hand into Timothy's hair and pressed down on his scalp.

"It's just an idiom," Timothy explained. "My brain isn't going to explode."

"I know," she said, smiling. "I guess I'm getting up to snuff with your idioms."

175

Abraham lifted his prisoner higher. "Let me take care of this viper, and we'll talk." He nodded toward Angel. "May I have the companion?"

Angel unzipped her jacket a few inches, reached underneath, and withdrew the glassy egg. Gazing at it as she handed it to the Prophet, she said, "Its light and eyes are gone." Tears tracked down her cheeks as she strained to finish. "I have never seen a companion restored from this state."

"We shall see." Abraham took the companion and pushed it against the prisoner's chest. As he walked into the shaft of light at the mouth of the tunnel, the shadow figure in his grip thrashed once again. He raised the creature high and let the rays of light bathe its shadowy form. With a crackling sound, the edges of its frame sizzled and slowly disintegrated. Sparks ate toward its midsection and grew brighter while Abraham kept the companion pressed against its pulsing red heart. As its body disappeared, its flat white bones dangled from its frame, some breaking and dropping to the ground.

Finally, when the popping sparks converged on the heart, a tiny explosion erupted, sending a pulse of energy into the companion. As the prisoner's remaining bones broke apart and fell from Abraham's grip, an aura expanded from the ovulum. He stepped out of the light and extended the glowing egg in his open palm. "The companion is restored, precious Angel. It is not the same as having your Adam, but its presence will keep his memory alive."

When Angel reached for the companion, it lifted off Abraham's palm and floated toward Timothy. As it hovered a few inches in front of his face, its eyes gazed at him, unblinking. Then, after making three orbits around his head, it settled just above his shoulder and stayed there.

Abraham stared at Timothy, then at Angel. Timothy cocked his head, trying to see the companion, but could only get a glimpse of the semi-transparent egg as it floated back and forth with his every movement.

"Remarkable!" Abraham set his hands on his hips. "I have never seen a companion take on a new charge. This is surely unexpected."

Angel drew close to Timothy and watched the ovulum. "But it's not unreasonable. Besides you, good prophet, we have never known anyone of our race who lacked a companion, so this opportunity has never arisen."

"What is it doing?" Timothy asked. "It feels like its tickling the inside of my head."

Angel laughed gently. "It is petting your soul with its soft fingers."

"That is how it probes your mind," Abraham explained. "It makes a spiritual attachment with you so it can be a helper in times of need."

"Father!" Angel cried, lifting a hand to her mouth. "Could it be?"

Abraham squinted at her. "What is it, my child?"

Lowering her hand slowly, she gazed at the reborn companion. "Since Timothy is now attached to Dragon's companion, could he be my new Adam?"

CHAPTER

THE LAKE OF FIRE

Walter kept his eyes open, hoping to see the switch from one world to the next. Hades had been an exciting place to visit, but he definitely didn't want to live there. The column of fire spun violently, whipping hot air across his cheeks. Within seconds, it faded, then vanished, leaving a dim, dreary sky with a blanket of clouds hanging overhead.

"Whoa!"

Walter spun toward the cry. Flailing her arms, Karen teetered backwards over the stairwell hole. He snatched her waistband and yanked her away, shouting, "Not again, you don't!"

When she regained her balance, he helped her stand upright. "You okay?"

"Whew!" Karen laid a hand on her forehead. "That was the worst déjà vu I've ever had! I don't want to fall down any more bottomless pits!"

Gabriel flew to her other side. He fanned out his wings and stretched one around her. "This is cooler than iced cucumbers," he said. "I'm solid again!"

Karen leaned away, startled. "Oh! Hi! I'm Karen."

"I know." As Gabriel patted her shoulder with a wing he extended a hand toward Walter. "Glad to meet you."

"Same here." Walter shook his hand but glanced around, counting the dimensional travellers. "Where's Ashley?"

Gabriel took his turn surveying their crew. "And Roxil."

Sapphira leaned over the hole, placing her bare foot in one of several huge footprints leading away from the edge. A cold drizzle added to the shallow puddle forming inside the print. "I don't see them anywhere. Could they have materialized right over the hole and fallen in?"

"Oh, no!" Karen leaned over the opening and shouted, "Ashley! Can you hear me? Roxil?"

Walter dropped to his knees and peered down, his hands clutching the muddy edge of the hole. "I see some stairs, but they're receding. I think I can jump to them if I hurry."

"No!" Karen shouted. "You won't be able to get back up!"

Grabbing the edge of the hole, he lowered himself into it. "I'll figure out that part later." He let go of the rim and plummeted. Bending his knees, he landed on the stairwell and tumbled down the steps, bumping his knees and elbows until he could brace his body against the curving wall and slow his momentum.

When he finally came to a stop, he sat up in the darkened spiral corridor, every part of his body throbbing. "Okay, that wasn't cool," he mumbled.

A loud crunching noise sounded from above, getting closer by the second. Jumping to his feet, he whipped Excalibur from its scabbard and flashed on its beam. The stairway was collapsing!

He spun around and dashed down the stairs, skipping three at a time. With each slap of his shoes against stone, the sound of crashing steps followed only inches behind, like a growling lion nipping at his heels. Finally, the step he landed on gave way, and he plummeted into blackness.

Still clinging to Excalibur, he jerked his head back and forth, searching for something to grab, but only chunks of debris fell within the sword's glow. For some reason, he felt no fear. He had gone through dimensional portals before, and this vertical plunge gave him the same tingly sensation, though this episode seemed to stretch out much longer than any of the others.

Picking up speed with every second, he fell on and on, much farther than he and Ashley had descended down the stairwell. Wherever the bottom was, it would be deeper than the level of Hades they had visited ... if there was a bottom at all.

After another minute or so, a strong breeze, hot, dry, and stale, buoyed his body, slowing his descent. He pointed Excalibur downward, trying to find the source of the wind. A dark red light mixed with the sword's glow to reveal a huge man standing underneath him. As he drifted closer, the breeze steadily weakened until it finally shut off. With the loss of the support, he plummeted once again, falling right into the giant's outstretched arms.

Although the man grunted, he absorbed the impact with only a slight sag of his cradling arms.

"Let me go!" Walter shouted, thrashing his body, but the giant held firm, gripping Walter's wrist in his enormous hand and immobilizing Excalibur.

The giant shushed him with a commanding whisper. "Be quiet, son of man!"

Walter immediately calmed his body. Something about this man's voice forced instant obedience, like a father's urgent appeal that would save the life of a child.

The giant lowered Walter to the ground and, softening his tone, released Walter's wrist. "We must maintain silence. There are dangerous creatures here, and I do not wish to alert them to our presence."

"Sounds good to me," Walter whispered, moving the sword closer to get a better view of this huge man who was easily as tall

179

as the Nephilim in the mobility room. The maroon-tinted light seemed to adorn his head in a scarlet hood, making his features indistinct. "I'm looking for a teenaged girl, a little older than me, about my height. I think she fell down the same hole, maybe a minute before I did. Have you seen her?" He considered mentioning Roxil, as well, but thought better of it for the moment.

The man shook his head. "I have only been here a few hours. I saw the shining sword as you descended, so I created your air cushion. I hope that I sufficiently eased your landing. I fear that my breath was exhausted a little too soon."

"Thank you. It was enough. I've had worse landings." Now sweating, Walter unzipped his jacket and searched for the source of heat. Hanging low in the rusty sky, a dark-red sun shot out snaking tongues of fire from its perimeter and coated the blackness in a dim, bloody wash. Still, it was enough to illuminate a huge black ocean perhaps a hundred yards away. Far out in the surf, red spots of light floated, bobbing and weaving like ships' beacons on a rough sea.

The giant leaned down and laid a hand on Walter's shoulder. "I am very glad to see you, son of man, though you are not quite what I expected."

Walter had to push up to keep from sagging under the weight of the heavy hand. As he guided Excalibur closer to the man's head again, the glow washed over his collar-length hair and scraggly beard, but most of his face was still veiled by scarlet shadows. "Well," Walter replied, keeping his voice low, "I'm not sure what you expected, but you're not exactly who I was hoping to find, either."

The man set a hand on his bushy brow, shielding his eyes. "I apologize for my rudeness. Since you are so young, I assumed you were not skilful with your sword, but I was probably assuming too much."

"I'm okay with it." Walter ran a finger along the blade's engraved design. "Do you need me to do something?"

"I am searching for a way of escape, but there are unfriendly forces here, so it is too dangerous to roam freely. With you and your sword, we can travel more boldly. I am big and strong, but I do not think I can fight more than two of them at once."

"Them?"

The man curled his finger. "Come. I will show you."

"Wait." Walter stretched his fingers tightly around Excalibur's hilt. "First I need to know who I'm dealing with. Are you one of the Nephilim?"

"I have been called that." The man raised his chin a notch. "I am one of the giants of old, but I prefer not to be associated with those who wear the Nephilim name too proudly."

Walter pointed the sword at the giant's feet. "So you're not one of Mardon's plant creatures? You weren't suspended in a growth chamber for years?"

The giant scrunched his brow. "How do you know about Mardon and growth chambers?"

"Let's just say a little blue-eyed girl told me."

Crouching to Walter's level, the giant drooped his shoulders. "I see. ... You know Mara." He let out a blustery sigh that whisked through Walter's hair like a stormy breeze. "If she informed you," he continued, "then you are likely acquainted with many details about Nephilim."

"Her name is Sapphira now, and she did tell me quite a bit. I met some of the other Nephilim, and they looked almost exactly like you, but they had red eyebeams, kind of like lasers."

"I have them as well." The giant flicked his beams on and then back off. "But in this place of scarlet light they only serve to give away my location. It is better if I keep them off and stay in hiding."

"So are you like the others? Are you one of Mardon's hybrids?"

"Only in that I developed from a hybrid seedling in a growth chamber. I acquiesced to Mardon's plan, because I learned that obeying him was the only way to survive. He and Morgan had no patience with even the slightest hint of insubordination. Many of us suffered death by poisoning."

Walter scratched the pebbly soil with Excalibur's point. "Any idea how you ended up here?"

"We were running low on food, so Mardon told us his plan to make us sleep until he could figure out how to get us into the upper lands. After we dug out new growth chambers, he implanted a device in the strongest of us that would wake us up when the time came. He then gave us a potion that would make us sleep, and I stepped into my chamber. After that, I woke up in this dark place. How I came here is a mystery."

Walter propped Excalibur on his shoulder again, whispering to himself. "Maybe you're the one Karen replaced."

"If you are addressing me," the giant said, "I cannot hear you."

Walter shook his head. "I'm just thinking out loud."

182

"Thinking is good, but we would be better served now by acting. If, however, you keep waving that glowing blade around, you will likely not survive long. Your presence will soon be noticed by the devils."

The word echoed shakily from Walter's lips. "Devils?"

The giant rose to his full height. "If you are a valiant man, then please follow." He marched into the darkness.

Walter let the sword's glow diminish to a bare minimum and trudged through the mixture of gravel and sand. No sense in not following. Even though this giant looked just as dangerous as Chazaq and his buddies, his story about trying to fool Morgan was convincing enough. Besides, flying back up to the surface wasn't exactly a reasonable option.

Now that his eyes had adjusted to the dim red light, Walter darkened Excalibur and scanned the coastline. With its areas of beach and rocky promontories, it reminded him of the coastline he visited in Oregon, though this one lacked any hint of the Pacific breezes that had chilled his skin in the North West.

As the giant headed toward the floating red lights, a sulphur smell drifted into Walter's nose, growing stronger and stronger as they neared the black ocean. When they reached the water, a wave washed over the ground near the giant's bare feet. He jumped back to avoid it. As the wave receded, it left strings of dark vapour rising over the stone.

Walter guided the blade near the edge. The glow fell over the black waves, a restless ocean seemingly coated with thick oil. Although the lapping of gentle surf masked all other sounds, Walter kept his voice quiet. "Is the water too hot for dipping your toes?"

The giant whispered in return. "It is hot, indeed." He lowered himself to one knee and shot his beams into Walter's eyes. "May I address you by your name, swordsman?"

Squinting at the red light, Walter fumbled with his words. "Uh … My name's Walter."

183

The giant shut off the beams. "Walter, please pardon my visual intrusion. My beams are harmless. When I look into someone's eyes, I can often judge his character, and since we will be passing by an area where I have seen the devils before, we might soon have to go to battle together. I want to be sure I can trust you."

"I'm cool with that, but I don't have eyebeams. How can I be sure I can trust you?"

The giant lowered his head. "I could tell you more about my life's story. Perhaps then you will be able to judge my character."

"Fair enough, as long as the devils stay away."

"We can only hope." The giant took in a deep breath and spoke slowly. "I suppose I should begin with my name. Mara gave it to me many, many years ago when I was a mere seedling. I still remember how her voice chirped like a songbird when she said, 'How about Yereq? It means green'."

Walter pointed at him and blurted out, "You *are* the one Karen replaced."

Yereq clapped his hand over Walter's mouth and jerked him close, whispering into his ear. "Walter, you must keep your voice down. If you wish to summon the devils, then, by all means, do so, but please give me fair warning so that I may watch from the shadows while they pierce your lungs with knives and cast you into the Lake of Fire."

Walter squeezed out a barely audible, "Lake of Fire?"

Pointing at the dark ocean, Yereq slowly released his grip. "The second death."

Walter squinted at the rising and falling waves. "That doesn't look like fire."

"It is black fire. Flames that emit no light. I heard some strange creatures talking about it. They seemed great and powerful, so I was hoping they might be able to get us out of this place, but they are so fearsome, I have not decided if they will be friendly to us." He hunched over and whispered even more softly. "If you have decided to trust me, come, and I will show them to you as well as the tragic end of the faithless." With the black fire on his left, he walked slowly along the beach.

184

Walter followed Yereq's huge footprints, glancing from side to side as he tromped, imagining shadows of pitchfork-carrying devils lurking behind the head-high boulders scattered along the beach. The sun, now close to the bloody horizon, provided just enough light to help him stay out of the fire, but too much to allow him to feel safe from the dozens of eyes that were probably staring at him this very moment. The feeling of dread shivered his bones. Night was approaching. The devils could probably see better in the dark than he could, and it would be impossible to find his way back to the portal that brought him to this dismal place.

After a few minutes, a white light shone from around a rocky promontory that jutted into the lake. The cape looked like a huge foot with its toes in the flames and the rest of the foot sloping up and out until it rose sharply into the "leg", a vertical wall that reached into the darkness above.

With his hands on the promontory's "ankle", Yereq peered around the edge, while Walter, holding on to the crannies in the wall, scrambled up to get a look. A two-foot-high jetty ran at least a hundred feet into the lake. Three dazzling angels stood at the beach end of the jetty with their backs to the sulphurous flames. From the darkness to the right, a line of ten or so slumped-over figures shuffled toward the angels. Fettered with manacles and dragging long chains that linked ankles from prisoner to prisoner, they cowered as they drew near.

Walter wiped sweat from his brow. These angels were only about twenty feet away from their hiding place! Did they know he was watching? Would they mind?

Yereq pressed his mouth close to Walter's ear. "Some new arrivals," he whispered. "Listen to the shining creatures, and you will learn what is happening here."

185

One of the angels spread out his four wings and stepped closer to the line of shadowy figures. He seemed to shine with a light of his own. The white radiance washed over the prisoners, giving detail to their bodies and faces.

Walter stifled a gasp. One of the chained arrivals looked familiar ... too familiar. There was no mistaking the silky gown, the slender figure, the angular face, and the long black tresses. Unable even to whisper, he mouthed the name. Morgan!

He glanced up at Yereq. The giant's slack jaw proved that he, too, had recognized her.

A low, hissing voice rose from behind them. "What have we here, Grindle? A lost boy and a wandering Naphil?"

Walter jumped back from the promontory and pointed Excalibur toward the sound. The sword shone brightly, sending a ghostly glow over four reddish-black figures nearly as tall as Yereq. One raised a notched dagger. With dark wings his only adornment, he flexed his muscular arm as he cackled. "Look at the boy's eyes, Grindle. He is definitely alive."

One of the other devils flapped his jagged wings. "Excellent. We shall have his blood in our goblets tonight."

"Not if I can help it!" With a quick downward swipe, Walter lopped off the first devil's hand, then, swinging the sword back up, narrowly missed his face. The other three flew at Walter and Yereq, each waving long stilettos and clawing with pointed fingernails.

Yereq grabbed a devil by the arm and dashed him against the wall. Walter dropped to the ground, allowing the second one to zip over his head. Thrusting Excalibur upward, he pierced the attacker's belly as he flew over and rammed the blade completely through. Then, ripping it out again and leaping to his feet, he wheeled around and sliced through the third devil's waist, cutting him in half.

With the devil he skewered writhing on one side, and the one he cleaved wiggling in two halves on the other, Walter lowered Excalibur and gasped for breath. Strangely enough, there seemed to be no blood flowing from his victims, nor from the smashed body of the one Yereq was now dragging back from the wall.

The devil Walter first attacked leaned over and picked up his severed hand. "It will take years for it to heal," he muttered as he turned and slunk away. The second devil rose from the ground and spread open his belly wound as if checking for missing innards. He then picked up his stiletto and scuttled into the darkness.

Yereq tossed his pummelled victim down. Crawling on its belly, it slithered away inch by inch. The fourth devil pushed against the ground with his hands and slid his upper half toward his hips and legs. "One dark night, we will catch you off guard," he snarled. "No one has ever escaped this realm, and you cannot hide from us forever."

A new light poured onto the scene. Walter spun around. One of the bright angels was watching them from the other side of the promontory. His booming voice echoed. "Walter and Yereq, Jehovah has commanded that you come and see the execution of justice upon his enemies."

"Yessir!" Walter slid his sword into its scabbard and hustled to the wall. The angel reached over with one arm and, grabbing Walter by his coat, pulled him across. Grappling the rock with his long limbs, Yereq climbed over the promontory and joined them.

The angel led Walter and Yereq across the gravelly beach toward the jetty and its long wooden ramp that led out over the lake. As they approached the ten chained prisoners waiting near the beginning of the ramp, Walter kept his head angled away from Morgan, but as he walked by, a shiver crawled along his skin, no doubt a result of the icy stare he was trying to avoid.

As they tromped down the narrow ramp, black foam gathered along the edges of the supporting rocks, raising a noxious stench – sulphur mixed with burning flesh. Walter gagged. How could he possibly breathe in this place? Just a few more seconds and he would heave everything in his gut!

187

Fortunately, when they neared the end of the jetty, the fumes dissipated. The ramp widened out into an octagonal platform, maybe fifteen by fifteen feet. As he stepped onto the flat stone, Walter scuffed his foot across an etched design. It looked like a compass with a multi-pointed star in the centre and narrow spires tapering in the direction of the octagon's sides.

The angel brushed a wing across a wooden bench at the very edge of the platform. "The witness seat," he said in his resonant voice. "Please sit in silence until you are called upon to speak."

Walter set his hand on the waist-high bench. Since it had no back, he could choose to sit facing toward the lake or away from it, but facing the lake would mean that his feet would dangle over the black fire.

His legs shaking, he eased onto the bench with his back to the lake. When Yereq sat at his side, the bench's wooden frame groaned under his weight. The giant clenched his hands together, but his face showed no signs of fear.

The other two angels led their prisoners to the centre of the platform, stopping them over the star on the floor. Trying to keep his gaze focused away from Morgan, Walter looked over at the lake, just a few feet to his side. The glow from the angels illuminated the surface. Black tongues of flame leaped and fell like waves on a storm-tossed ocean. Finally, those bobbing red lights came into focus – the heads of flailing people, their faces and hair afire in crimson flames and their mouths open in silent screams.

Walter clutched his chest. It felt like his heart was ripping in two. Hot prickles ran across his skin. Such awful pain! Who could stand a minute in that fire, much less an eternity? As he imagined himself in the lake, fear rifled through his body – a dagger that peeled away the lining of his stomach and shredded his bravado. He felt like a cowering pup. If he had had a tail, he would have tucked it between his legs and whined. This is what Ashley must have felt in the stairwell to Hades, the gut-wrenching nausea of naked exposure while trapped deep within an inescapable pit.

"Let the first condemned soul approach!" the lead angel boomed.

Walter jerked his head back to the prisoners. Morgan stepped forward. Her stare, red and flashing, locked on his. An evil smirk dressed her face with insolence, but she said nothing.

Unable to pry his gaze from Morgan's wicked glare, Walter intertwined his fingers and twisted them painfully. She had never looked so evil, so hate-filled.

The angel's glow brightened. The light seemed to ooze into Walter's body, soothing his stomach and quelling his shakes. That helped, but Morgan's stare kept the shivers running up and down his arms.

Opening a book that spread over his palms, the angel looked at Morgan. "Your name is not written in the Book of Life, so the

188

Lamb has sent you here from his judgment seat where he condemned you to the eternal fires. Justice does not demand that I explain the Lamb's sentence, so I do this for the sake of the two witnesses who can testify against you if called upon. They will bear this witness to the race of humans and hybrids, not for the purpose of proving your guilt, for your sins against dozens of generations are already well known. Their witness will serve to give the waking world hope and renewed confidence that, even though there is much evil and suffering in their realm, justice will ultimately prevail."

Morgan spat at his feet. "Jehovah is pure cruelty! Any so-called god who would condemn someone for all eternity is worse than cruel. He is a hateful monster. If all of you angels had joined my lord Lucifer in his quest to unseat that tyrant, we would be enjoying wisdom, freedom, and the pleasure of our bodies. You would—"

"Silence!" The angel closed the book and pointed at Morgan. Her lips melted together, and her face withered. Within seconds she looked like a hairy prune – dark, warped, and wrinkled.

189

The angel's eyes blazed with white fire. "I need not defend Jehovah-Sabaoth to you, but for these witnesses I will proclaim the truth. Every man, every woman, every ancient witch who suffers in the second death is a faithless rebel. They are liars. They are murderers. They are idolaters. They are stumbling blocks to those who seek the truth." He pointed at Morgan again. "And you, Lilith, are the symbol that represents all of these sins. A day will come when Hades will give up its dead, and all of your kind will join you in the Lake of Fire, but you and these other nine must go now."

The other two angels grabbed her arms and dragged her to the edge of the platform. As they passed by the bench, Morgan's dress swept across Walter's arm, boiling his stomach once again. Then, picking her up, the angels threw her into the lake.

Walter grimaced, expecting to hear the sounds of horrible agony – a blood-curdling scream or a lamenting wail, but not even the tiniest splash erupted from the lake, only a strong sulphur odour that quickly diffused. Morgan's wrinkled head bobbed to the surface, her face in red flames as she joined the other crimson beacons in the eternal black void.

The lead angel's voice boomed again. "The rest of you come forth!"

The other nine shuffled forward. Most seemed well dressed and groomed, making them look like respected professionals who might be gladdened by the company of angels, but their terrified faces and shaking bodies revealed the horrible truth – they feared the torture that lay ahead.

Nodding at his colleagues, the lead angel said, "Bring the millstones." The two angels flew away, returning only seconds later with ropes and nine stone discs. They tied a wheel-like disc to the neck of each of the nine, leaving just enough rope between stone and neck to allow both the wheel and the prisoner to stand upright.

The lead angel reopened his book. "You are of the liars Yeshua decried when he said, 'But whoso shall offend one of these little ones which believe in me, it were better for him that a millstone were hanged about his neck, and that he were drowned in the depth of the sea.'"

As the angel closed the book, his glow brightened again and arched over the trembling prisoners. "You have caused many little ones to stumble. You are entering Perdition in this manner so that these true witnesses may testify that all who bring such offence will earn a place in the Lake of Fire."

The two angels began pulling the nine and their millstones to the edge of the platform, some kicking and flailing their arms.

His throat constricting tightly, Walter watched each condemned prisoner's feet drag across the star's spire that pointed toward the lake. The six men and three women poured out anguished wails but no words – no protests of innocence, no pleas for mercy, no curses. One by one, the angel picked up the millstone and pressed it against the prisoner's chest before throwing both in.

When the last of the nine plunged into the lake and disappeared into its depths, Walter covered his face with his hands and wept. Shaking so hard his ribs ached, he peeked between his fingers at Yereq. The giant just sat and stared at the setting sun, wide-eyed, a single tear tracking into his beard.

The lead angel sat next to Walter. "Many questions are in your mind. Do you care to raise them?"

Walter licked his dry lips and tried to stop shaking. It was just too awful! Those poor souls would suffer in those flames forever and ever and ever! They could never get out, not in a million, billion years.

Looking out over the black turmoil, he spotted Morgan's face, her mouth agape in anguish. Was she right? Was God really a cruel tyrant?

He shook his head hard. No! It couldn't be! If God sent those people here, then it had to be the right thing to do, no matter how pitiful they looked, no matter how horrific an eternity of punishment would be.

As the sulphur fumes again assaulted his nose, the nausea rekindled and his shakes worsened. The angel spread a wing over him, immediately calming his nerves. Sniffing, he gazed into the angel's radiant face and squeaked out his words. "I guess ... I guess they had a trial, didn't they?"

The angel's wide brow lifted. "Indeed, they did. They went before the judgment seat, and their deeds were exposed. They knew their guilt, so, as you witnessed, all but one had no words of protest. There is coming a great judgment day when all will come to the judgment seat in like manner, and even the thoughts and intentions of the heart will be laid bare."

Walter swiped his sleeve under his nose. "What about Morg—I mean, Lilith? Can you answer all that stuff she said?"

The angel's eyes blazed again. "She is Lucifer's personal min-ion, one who willingly worships him. She is like a rebel angel her-self, so she was well versed in attacking the light of truth. Like the serpent of old, she twists the minds of those who are foolish enough to listen." As the fire in his pupils settled, his voice eased into a gentler tone. "Eternal punishment is not cruel; it is deserved. Every condemned soul has resisted the call of God and rejected the light he was given. As a created mortal, you cannot understand the severity of lifelong rebellion against the immortal Creator. Living without surrendering honour to the Life-giver is the very heart of rebellion. It is the worship of self, the sin that leads to all others and establishes the heart of pride."

Walter again gazed at the flaming heads in the lake, reading the agony in the screaming faces that represented horribly tortured minds. As a new wave of nausea boiled inside, he pushed his palm against his stomach and bent over. "I think I'm going to be sick."

The angel stroked his back. "As all men of compassion become when they consider the destiny of the unrighteous. We angels cel-ebrate the judgment, for we see what you do not see, yet cannot feel what you must feel when you sympathize with their pain."

Walter swallowed back an eruption of acidic bile. The burn-ing sensation refreshed the pain he felt for those in the black fire. Their burning was far worse, a scalding torture that enveloped their entire bodies, but they couldn't swallow it away.

He glanced again at the silent screamers, the angel's words echoing, *the heart of pride, the heart of pride*. As one of the women floated closer, in his mind, a new face covered hers – Ashley's.

The thought of her in that horrible lake stung his heart. He wanted to ask the angel, but should he? Could he bear to hear the answer he dreaded? He closed his eyes tightly, trying to shake away the image, but he couldn't. He had to know! He just had to!

Clearing his throat, he looked down and twisted the toe of his shoe against the platform. "I have a friend ... Ashley Stalworth.

She has nightmares about going to Hell, so ... I was wondering ..." He looked up at the angel, trying to keep his voice from squeaking. "Is she in your book anywhere?"

The angel nodded sympathetically. "You are concerned about her destiny."

"Uh-huh. She doesn't really have much faith, because she's kind of ... I don't know how to say it ..." He twisted his shoe even harder. "Maybe it's like you were saying before ... I guess she has a heart of pride."

The angel reopened his book, flipped through a few pages, and ran his finger along an entry. "She has not yet made her final decision, so her destiny is yet to be determined." He looked again at Walter. "Your prayers and the prayers of others have ascended on high, and Yeshua is calling Ashley to himself. Whether she responds to his call is ultimately up to her."

Walter caught a glimpse of the book, but the angel didn't seem to mind. The page was filled with beautiful but unrecognizable characters. He clenched his fist and set his hand on Yereq's knee. "But we can help, right? We can tell her about this place and warn her!"

Yereq shook himself out of his trance and turned toward Walter and the angel. "I am ready to serve in any way I can."

The angel stood and drew a flaming sword from his robe. Its dazzling blade dwarfed Excalibur's both in size and in brilliance. Walter trembled, and he could feel Yereq shaking the bench.

"What emotion do you feel?" the angel asked.

"Scared." Walter edged farther back in his seat. "So scared I'm getting sick again."

The angel swiped the point of the blade within an inch of Walter's nose, so close he felt the scorching heat. He lurched back, nearly losing his balance, but Yereq caught him before he could fall.

Giving Walter a stern look, the angel's voice boomed. "Does the sight of this blade cause you to love me?"

193

Walter could barely breathe, but managed a weak shake of his head.

The angel's sword continued to blaze. "Fear rarely creates a heart of devotion. It is love that begets love. Since Ashley is a sceptic and already lives in fear, telling her of this place could drive her even further from the heart of God." He put the sword back into his robe. "If, however, the faithful show her the love of a perfected heart, her sceptic's heart of stone will more easily be made into one of flesh."

As if cued by the vanishing sword, Walter's throat loosened, and his nausea eased. "How do I show her that kind of love?"

"Sacrifice. Since you are one of Yeshua's lambs, sacrifice is the one and only word you need to know and perform. She will see his face in you."

Walter pushed himself to a standing position, but his legs still shook badly. "So how do we" – he nodded at Yereq – "get back to the world above?"

The angel produced another sword, just as large but without flames, and gave it to Yereq. "God still has a purpose for this Naphil, but he must remain here battling the wandering devils until a later time when I will restore him to his proper place. Those devils will eventually be swept into the Lake of Fire, but for now they are well suited for preparing Yereq's heart, mind, and body for his upcoming task."

Feeling much stronger, Walter smiled at Yereq. "Is it all right if I tell Sapphira that he's okay?"

"You may, if you wish, but for Ashley's sake, I advise against it. It would be better to avoid all mention of the Lake of Fire if you hope to replace her fear with love and hope."

Walter sighed. "She has a lot of fear. That's for sure."

The angel spread out his wings. "And that is why you were brought here."

Walter didn't bother to ask what he meant. He already knew. He could finally feel Ashley's greatest terror, the darkness of the abyss, and now fear and love combined to stoke a raging fire in his soul. He had to show Ashley what love was all about – the sacrifice of a devoted heart. He had to make sure she would never have to fear this place again.

"Come," the angel said, reaching out his hand. "I will take you back to your friends."

CHAPTER

NO ESCAPE

Twisting around on the witness bench, Walter hugged Yereq's bicep. "Take care of yourself. I hope I'll see you again soon."

Yereq patted him on the back. "You are the warrior I had hoped for. It will be an honour to fight with you again someday."

Walter stood and touched the angel's hand. Darkness immediately surrounded him. Wind rushed through his hair and clothes. Before two seconds passed, a light appeared over his head, a bright hole in the sky. As his body rose toward it, cold drizzle fell on his hair. "That's the pit I jumped into," he said out loud. When he neared the surface, he slowed down, finally stopping near the top.

Two hands reached down, both slender and feminine. When he grabbed them, he surged upward and lunged into daylight, toppling over Sapphira and Karen before rolling along the wet grass. When he came to a stop, cool fingers swept across his cheek. He looked up to see Sapphira's sparkling blue eyes.

Karen joined her, kneeling at his side. "Are you all right?"

"I am now." He sat up and glanced around. "Still no sign of Ashley or Roxil?"

Karen shook her head. "You were gone so long, Gabriel flew down to check things out, but he hasn't come back yet."

"How did you fly up the hole?" Sapphira asked.

"I don't think I'm supposed to tell. Let's just say I got a lift from an out-of-this-world driver." Walter climbed to his feet and helped Karen and Sapphira to theirs, but his legs still felt so wobbly he could barely stand.

"I'm not sure anyone fell in," Sapphira said, blinking away droplets on her eyelashes. "Roxil is too big for the hole, so if she didn't transport through the portal, maybe Ashley didn't either. Maybe it's because they have dragon essence."

Walter straightened his scabbard belt and adjusted Excalibur. "Gabriel has dragon essence, and he came through. Why wouldn't they?"

198

Sapphira stroked her chin. "I've been thinking about that, but I haven't figured it out. Ashley and Roxil were as close to me as anyone, and I'm sure I made the fire column big enough to envelop all of us."

Walter focused on Sapphira's stunning blue eyes, hypnotizing and tranquil. Both of his hands trembled. Was it her enchanting beauty that made him shiver, or was his heart still stirred by the tortured faces in the Lake of Fire? He clenched his hands into fists to calm them. "We both saw a bunch of dragons enter this dimension," he said, "so we know it's possible."

"Yes," Sapphira said. "I don't think I told you that I helped create the covenant veil so they could pass—" Her face suddenly turned almost as white as her hair. She spoke slowly, in monotone. "Roxil couldn't leave the land of the dead, because she never affirmed the covenant."

"Affirmed the covenant?" Walter repeated. "What are you talking about?"

"Jehovah-Yasha. The Lord is my Saviour. She has to believe that to pass through. Maybe we have to make another veil and get her to agree to the covenant. Maybe the threat of staying in Hades forever will convince her to try."

Walter shook his head. "I remember that part of your story, but I don't think trying to scare her is the right way to go about it."

"But we have to give her a chance." She drew close to Walter and Karen. "Will you both go with me? It will take two to make a veil."

"I guess so." Walter stood near the edge of the hole. "But Roxil can cool her heels for a while. I want to wait for Gabriel to come back with a report. I can't tell you what I saw at the bottom, but I hope he doesn't try to go all the way down."

"I'll watch for him." Sapphira nodded at the trail of giant tracks leading into the woods. "I wonder what we should do about them."

Walter scooped a beetle out of a footprint's puddle and set it free on the grass. "If they start causing trouble, Larry will hear about it. He monitors all the media outlets."

"But we can't contact Larry without Ashley," Karen said.

Walter grimaced. "Right. No communications except for ... Wait!" He fished in his pocket for his cell phone and flipped it open. "It's showing a signal, but just barely."

Karen peeked at the display. "Give it a try."

"I'll call Billy. He can check with Larry for me." Walter punched a speed dial and held the phone to his ear. "Billy! It's Walter."

"Talk louder," Billy said. "It's really fuzzy."

"Yeah, I know. Listen. I need you to monitor Larry's media input. Find out if there's anything going on with the giants. They might be causing trouble."

"The San Francisco Giants are causing trouble?"

"No, not the baseball team, or the football team, either. Real giants. Here's what happened. We had an argument with a dragon that was born at the beginning of time, so Karen fell into a hole that went all the way to Hades, but the hole turned into a spiral staircase, so Ashley and I climbed down a zillion steps to Hades looking for her, at least that's what the Italian words on the wall said, something from a bad comedy. When we got to the bottom, we found a bunch of giants who grew from the ground like plants and ate worms three times a day, and they were hanging inside antigravity walls for centuries, but this old-as-Methuselah teenaged girl came along and showed us this guy with dragon wings by sprouting fire from her hands, then the giants woke up, and I sliced a leg off one of them, making his boss really ticked, so they climbed out of Hades and went stalking off to make trouble somewhere. In the meantime, this Methuselah girl wrapped us all in a flaming cocoon and shot us out of the ground, but now Ashley's missing."

Walter paused and waited.

After a couple of seconds of silence, Billy replied. "Same old stuff, huh?"

"Yeah, pretty much, but I couldn't call you earlier. No cell towers in Hell, you know. So, anyway, if Larry hears anything important, give me a call."

"I'll call Bonnie, too. We'll keep our ears open."

The connection died, leaving only static buzzing in Walter's ear. He slapped the phone closed and stepped back to the edge of the hole where Sapphira and Karen stood peering in. "Any sign of Gabriel?" he asked.

Sapphira pointed into the hole. "I think I see something." A few seconds later, Gabriel's head appeared, then his wings, flapping hard and scraping against the sides of the pit as he rose. Walter grabbed his arm and pulled him to solid ground.

As he righted himself, Gabriel folded in his wings. "Flying straight up is for the birds!"

"Did you see Ashley?" Sapphira asked.

Gabriel shook his head. "It was too dark to see anything, but since my wings brushed against the walls all the way down, I would've noticed if I passed anyone. It's just a sheer cylinder with rocky sides until you get to a dead end way down below."

"But how is that possible?" Walter asked. "I was just down there, and there wasn't any dead end." He winced. Now they would drill him with questions.

Sapphira pointed at the giants' footprints. "When the Nephilim climbed the stairs they probably made the shaft really fragile. I guess it collapsed right after you got back and blocked the passageway."

"That might be it." Walter finally noticed the chilly air and zipped his jacket. "I guess we'd better try to go back and see if we left Roxil and Ashley behind. We don't have much choice."

The cell phone chimed. Walter snatched it up. "Hello?"

"Walter. Billy here."

"Yeah, Billy. What's up?"

"Larry says the power grid's failing in the West, and it's spreading across the country. Lots of other weird stuff is happening in the big cities, strange creatures stalking the streets, and with no power, there's panic everywhere."

"Yikes! That's not cool!" Walter turned toward the others. "Power grid's failing. Everyone's losing electricity."

Karen stepped close and shouted into the phone. "Tell Larry to switch to emergency power immediately. The solar batteries should hold him for a while."

Walter pulled away from Karen. "Did you get that?"

"Got it," Billy replied, "but there's a lot of static."

"It's getting worse. Cellular service might die when all the power goes out."

"I'll try to call you again if I find out anything new."

"You can try, but I have to go back to Hades now. See ya."
Walter closed the phone and put it back in his pocket.

"We might not be going back to Hades," Sapphira said.
"I think you and Karen might have stayed in this dimension the
entire time. Since Roxil and Gabriel were in an energy state while
you were there, I think the underground realm got shifted to this
dimension somehow. But now that Gabriel is solid here in the
land of the living, I'm not sure what to think."

Walter set his hands in front of her, as if bracketing his words.
"Look, I don't care if it's Hades or Harlem. All I want to know is
if you can get us back to wherever Ashley is. The giants are obviously up to no good, so the world needs Ashley and her brains
more than ever."

As Sapphira lifted a hand, a new splash of fire arose from her
palm. "I'll give it a try, but I don't know where we'll end up. I
thought I'd be able to travel wherever I wanted to, but it feels like
the dimensions are playing musical chairs."

Hanging on to a flickering lantern with one hand, Ashley
reached for the trapdoor with the other, just inches away
from her fingertips. Her duffle bag dangled precariously from a
strap over her shoulder. "A little higher," she called to Roxil as she
stood on tiptoes.

"I cannot stretch any farther," Roxil said, "and your shoe is
pressing against my eye."

"Sorry." Ashley moved her foot. "Can you jump?"

"Dragons do not jump well. I can beat my wings to give you
a boost, but it will be unsteady."

Ashley braced herself, keeping her eyes on the door above.
"Go for it!"

With a sudden shake, Ashley lurched upward. She raised her
free hand and pushed the trapdoor open, and her momentum
threw her into the vent tunnel. After rolling and skidding, she

jumped to her feet, keeping the lantern upright throughout her landing. "I made it!" she called down.

Roxil's eyes flashed from below. "Good. I will wait here while—"

Ashley leaned into the trapdoor opening, poking her head into the mobility room. "Roxil? Were you going to say something else?"

She waited for a reply, but none came. Leaning down as far as she could, she listened, but the room below was quiet, and shadows obscured the floor. "Roxil?"

Again, no reply. The glowing eyes had disappeared. Ashley sat up and fiddled with the zipper on her bag. Was Roxil okay? Why wouldn't she answer?

Pushing her hair out of her eyes, she scanned the area. The rope was gone, and there didn't seem to be any other way to get down. She couldn't check on the moody dragon even if she wanted to.

She stood and set her hands on her hips. What was she worried about anyway? Roxil was a dragon. She could take care of herself. Besides, she was probably just pouting.

After tossing the bag up onto the stairs above, Ashley leaped and set the lantern on the edge of the staircase landing, then leaped again and caught the edge with both hands. The crumbling rock made it hard to get a good hold, but, inching her fingers to the side, she finally found a solid place to grab. With a swing and a lunge, she propped her elbow on the ledge, then, grabbing another handhold on the first step, she wrestled her way up, swinging a knee to the landing, then a foot. Finally, she managed to get her whole body up to the stairs and sat heavily on the third step.

Wiping sweat and grime from her forehead, she laughed to herself. That was the easy part. Now several thousand steps into the mountain overhead awaited her already weary legs. She opened

203

her bag and felt for the contents – the gravity brick, a water bottle, her photometer, and her handheld computer – all safely swaddled in her change of clothes. They would probably feel like anchors after a while, but they were too important to leave behind.

Picking up the lantern, she stood and began a slow, methodical climb, counting each step as she went. Based on the approximate average height of the steps and Larry's earlier elevation reports, she could guesstimate the total number, maybe fifteen thousand or so. It might take all day, but at least she would know when she was getting close to the top.

After a hundred steps, she stopped and leaned against the wall. Maybe it would be a good idea to rest after every hundred and catch her breath. No sense hurrying and getting dehydrated.

Continuing her upward march, she noticed the writing on the wall, the morbid warning about her recent descent into the dark realm. The more she climbed, the clearer the lettering became, etched deeper, each line blackened by shadows cast by the lantern's flickering glow.

She murmured the words, *"Lasciate ogne speranza, voi ch'intrate,"* then translated the phrase, speaking it into the dim, upward spiral as she trudged on. "Abandon hope, all ye who enter here." It was so quiet, even her whisper echoed, repeating the gloomy words in a phantom voice – her own voice twisted and deepened as it reverberated off the spiralling walls.

The lantern felt heavier, her legs weaker. The shoulder bag seemed to grow in weight, dragging at her like a stubborn child who refused to follow. Even after a scheduled rest, she didn't feel any better, but she had to go on. Six hundred steps. Seven hundred.

The phrase continued to haunt her mind. *Abandon hope, all ye who enter here.*

Eight hundred. Nine hundred.

Abandon hope, all ye who enter here.

One thousand.

Ashley stopped and sat on a rocky stair. A longer rest. That's all she needed. Every thousand steps, take a longer rest and a small drink. She set the lantern down and withdrew the water bottle from her bag. After taking two sips, she returned it and rested her elbows on her knees, cradling her chin in her hands. As the tiny fire flickered, its light undulated on both walls and the ceiling, perhaps seven feet above the stairs.

She imagined the troop of giants passing through, ducking their heads as they tromped upward, their broad shoulders barely fitting through the narrow tunnel. As she rested, she listened to the sounds of silence – the thrumming of her heart, the rush of blood through her ears, the sizzle of the wick, but now, thankfully, no ghostly echoes.

A soft clump sounded from far below. Ashley sucked in a breath and shot to her feet. Another clump. Louder. Who could it be? No one else was supposed to be there.

It didn't sound like footsteps, just single thumps, like someone beating a drum every few seconds. But they were definitely getting closer.

She swallowed, but the lump in her tight throat wouldn't go away. Should she call out? Might it be Sapphira coming back to find her? Why would she make such a strange noise?

She licked her lips and tried to speak, but only a rasping whisper came out. "Hello?" She cleared her throat and tried again. "Hello down there." Her stronger voice echoed, calling back to her three times before fading away.

"Is somebody down there?"

Clump ... clump.

Ashley picked up her lantern and bag and took a step back, rising one stair.

Clump ... clump.

She took two more steps, then turned around and tiptoed up as fast as she could. A friend would have answered. A friend would have cried out with joy. This was no friend. She could feel it – a stalker, a hound of hell coming to drag her back to the realm of abandoned hope.

She tripped and banged her knee. The lantern clattered against the stone, breaking the glass, but the wick stayed lit.

Jerking up the lantern, she ran as fast as she could, not caring how loudly her shoes slapped the stone or how desperately her laboured breaths echoed down to whoever or whatever followed her. But how long could she run? Her legs ached. Her heart thumped in her throat. Her lungs were about to explode. And she still had thousands of steps to go!

HEART OF A HARLOT

Elam crested a bare hill and turned in a slow circle. Nothing but gorgeous greenery and dazzling flowers as far as the eye could see. He glanced at Dikaios, who was munching a mouthful of grass.

"There doesn't seem to be anywhere to go," Elam said. "Should I just stay here and wait for something to happen?"

Dikaios swallowed. "Why do you ask me? I am no authority on what humans who seek Heaven's altar should do."

"But you have seen others. Maybe a white-haired girl and a smaller girl who was probably being carried?"

The horse shuddered his mane. "Carried by Joseph the grail-keeper?"

"You did see them! How did they get to the altar?"

Dikaios lowered his head and gathered another mouthful of grass. He took his time chewing, glancing up at Elam every few seconds. He grabbed another bite, and chewed, still peering up.

Elam scanned every horizon with his enhanced vision before turning back to Dikaios. He watched the horse's eyes dart between him and the ground. Would this strange animal ever answer his question?

Finally, Dikaios raised his head again. "You are indeed unusual. That is certain."

Elam averted his eyes. "I'm sorry. I hope my staring didn't offend you."

"There is no need to apologize. I was not speaking about your ocular focus."

Elam sighed and spread out his hands. "The two girls are very precious to me, so I'm hoping to find them and bring them back to the world of the living. Merlin the prophet gave me this task, so I have to succeed."

"Is that so?" the horse asked with a casual air. "Why?"

"Which are you asking about – why they are precious, or why I have to succeed?"

"Either one. It matters little." Dikaios reached for another mouthful of grass.

Elam raised two fingers. "I will answer the second, because the first needs no answer. Merlin gave me this mission, and his word is good enough for me, even if I don't understand the purpose. If it's important to him, it's important, full stop."

Dikaios nodded. When his mouth cleared of grass, he replied. "Then I suppose you will learn the purpose when you finish your journey."

"I'm not sure of that, either. I just need to listen and obey."

Dikaios drew close and sniffed Elam's face. "Most unusual," he said, drawing back again. "Most, most unusual."

Elam again stared at the horse. Obviously he wasn't going to get a straight answer. He strolled down the slope, heading toward another stand of trees in the distance. As the sound of soft hoof steps followed, he smiled. "Still coming with me?" he called back.

"You intrigue me. I must learn more."

Elam slowed to let the plodding horse catch up. "I get the impression that you have already learned a lot about humans,

208

otherwise you wouldn't find me so unusual. There would be no one to compare me to."

"A wise deduction." Dikaios now walked at his side. "I have seen many humans tread the fine grasses of the Bridgelands. Some still wander here searching for the altar and its scarlet key, even after centuries of futility."

Elam's gaze darted from side to side. "Are any close by?"

"I do not keep track of their comings and goings. I merely see them in passing as they peer under the same stone for the tenth time, or come out of a cave they searched the day before and the day before that."

"What are they looking for?"

"A clue, perhaps a riddle or a poem that will allow them to deduce the way to the everlasting. They analyse, they pick apart, some even speak the Scriptures, quoting every verse from memory as they sermonize from one end of this sanctuary to the other, yet they never seem to learn the heart of the very words they chant."

Elam slowed and walked closer to the horse. "And what is that heart?"

Dikaios halted. "Why do you ask this question? You have already given me its answer."

"I did?" Elam stopped at the horse's side and looked around. Something felt different ... very different. It wasn't a physical change, more like a spiritual shift. Everything had felt peaceful and at rest, but now a sense of anxiety crept into his mind. A shadow approached, a shadow of mind and soul. He scanned the trees, now only a dozen or so paces away.

Dikaios's voice became low and serious. "You are troubled, Elam."

"I sense something ... something familiar that brings back bad memories. I hear a voice, a song ... sad and forlorn."

"Does it frighten you?"

"I'm not sure." Elam stood as quietly as he could. "I think tension is a better word ... a curious tension."

209

The gentle sound of weeping drifted from the trees, a whimpering sort of humming, soft and feminine, yet filled with the lyrics of poetic verse.

Elam tiptoed toward the woods. As he drew close, the words became clear – a melancholy song warbled in a lovely contralto.

My heart is ice, my prayers are cold,
I've lived too long, I'm tired and old.
My sins, their scarlet threads I've weaved,
A gown of mourning I've received.

O who will wash the stains I bear
The harlot's mark of sin I wear?
Exposed and shorn of all I prized,
And now I beg for mercy's eyes.

210

As the last sighing note carried across the stillness, Elam took another step closer to the woods and whispered to Dikaios. "I recognize that voice."

"Interesting," Dikaios said. "I have grazed this area a thousand times and not heard it before."

Elam's tone grew cold. "I have heard it too many times. She was one of my torturers centuries ago. She used to come to the brick kilns and tempt me to go to her chamber with her, but when I refused, she would have me stretched out and beaten with thorn bushes. She would laugh at my torment, but whenever Morgan, her mistress, came by, she would sneak away and avoid her wrath. I saw her and Morgan together many years after her tortures, but she pretended she didn't know who I was."

"Such a wicked seductress!" Dikaios said. "Certainly this sadistic harlot deserves death, does she not?"

"No doubt she does." Elam listened to the words again as the singer repeated each line. He stepped back toward Dikaios. "Why would a seductress be here? Glewlwyd told me there was evil here, but I didn't expect to see her."

"You will learn to expect the unexpected." Dikaios pawed the ground. "This is a bridge between two everlasting lands, Hades and Heaven, a courtyard where special concourse takes place. Even Lucifer himself once traversed this field when he and the sons of God were summoned to present themselves before the Lord. It could be that she has been brought here for a purpose that you know nothing about."

The song repeated, piercing Elam's heart. Every phrase was so sad and lovely, filled with remorse and dampened with bitter tears. Yet, could this be the prophesied enemy? Surely she could easily be the one who would lust after his fruit, a bat in voluptuous disguise ready to drink his life's blood.

"I'm going to find out for sure." Elam called into the woods. "Who is there?"

At first, a soft gasp drifted from the trees, then a timid voice. "I am called Naamah."

Elam took yet another step closer. "Naamah, the seducer of men and minion of Morgan Le Faye?"

The voice drifted again from the dark woods, wounded and forlorn. "I am no longer in her service. If you know of my past harlotries, please have mercy on me."

Setting his feet, Elam cleared his throat. "Come out, Naamah. If you have any weapons, drop them first."

"I cannot come out. Not only do I have no weapons, my clothing is shredded and does little to cover me, so it would be shameful for me to show myself."

Elam squinted at the tree line. A young woman peeked out from behind a trunk, her hair draping a bare shoulder. Her face suddenly turned pale, and she hid herself again. "Elam!" she cried. "Go away from me! I am a sinful woman who deserves nothing from you but death."

Elam's heart melted. The fear in her eyes was more real than any he had ever seen. Switching to the most soothing tone he could muster, he called again. "Come out, Naamah. You have nothing to be afraid of." He took off his cloak and held it in front as he walked toward her tree, watching the ground at his feet. "Let me know when I'm close enough. Then, please cover yourself with my cloak."

After a few more steps, her soft voice came to his ears. "You are close enough."

Elam turned his head and locked his gaze on Dikaios. The horse eyed him back, as if probing his mind for a thought.

As the cloak pulled away from his hands, Elam kept his eyes on Dikaios and spoke in the same soothing tone. "Let me know when you're covered so we can talk face to face."

After several seconds, she spoke quietly. "I am covered."

Turning back toward her, Elam saw the familiar face from the magnetite mines, the place of his childhood slavery. Still petite and beautiful, yet with streaming tears marring her lovely face, Naamah stood before him, her arms crossed in front of her as she shivered. She had gathered the cloak's long cape, passed it between her legs, and tied it at her hip. Her legs showed from the knee down along with a dangling black shred from her dress underneath.

Seeing her, Elam's bitter memories of her cruelty quickly fled from his mind. "Why are you here?" he asked.

Backing away a step, Naamah replied, her words punctuated with sobs. "It ... It is all such a mystery. I remember ... getting stabbed in my guise as Constance in Dragons' Rest. I remember bleeding ... bleeding all over the street. ... Everything went dark, and someone picked me up off the ground."

She sniffed hard, and her voice settled. "Then I was clothed in my old black dress, and I walked through a dark tunnel for hours and hours, maybe even more than a day. A voice kept echoing in the tunnel. It said, 'Abandon hope, all ye who enter here' over and over again. That's when I knew I must have died. After a while, I saw Morgan walking next to me, but she couldn't hear me no matter how loud I cried out to her. I screamed, 'You lied to me! You promised me eternal life! You lied to me!' But she just kept walking. I wanted to grab her throat and strangle her, but for some reason, I couldn't reach out at all. I just had to walk on and on.

"Finally, we came to the end of the tunnel where an angel sat at a huge table. He had four faces and four wings, and when he stared at me, it felt like his gaze burned into my mind and read every thought inside. He spoke to Morgan first. He said, 'You cannot go to Hades, for you have become the mistress of that place and have the power to conquer and subdue it once again. You will go directly to the great judgment seat where your sentence will be delivered and the manner of your final death revealed.'

"Morgan never even flinched. She didn't cry or beg for mercy. She just stared defiantly without a word. Then, another angel wrapped a heavy chain around her and dragged her away."

213

Naamah lowered herself to the ground and sat cross-legged on the grass, tucking the cloak around her legs. While Dikaios grazed nearby, Elam sat at her side, leaning close. "So, what happened to you?"

"The angel pointed at a page in a huge book that sat on a table and said, 'You have followed an unusual path and arrived here without dying.'

"Of course, I was shocked. 'I died twice,' I told him, 'at least it seemed that way. The first time, Morgan pushed me out of the ark and made me a wraith, then someone stabbed me with a staurolite blade, which can even kill a wraith, and that's how I came to be here.'

"He stared at his book long and hard, as if he were reading my life's history. 'No,' he finally said, 'you were merely translated without dying. The staurolite blade can, indeed, kill a wraith, but Lilith never had the power to raise a soul from the dead or transform you

into a wraith. Her master, the father of lies, deceived her and did
not tell her that God is the one who transformed you, but into a
being of a higher order than a wraith. Lilith was jealous of your
lack of need of regeneration and invented the lie that her contin-
ual deterioration was due to her union with a Watcher, when the
truth is that you retained a real, living human spirit that kept you
whole.'

"Again, I was shocked. I could only blurt out, 'But why?'

"He said, 'It seems that God has another purpose for you. You
have, however, used your God-given gifts of beauty and song for
wanton pleasure and seduction, so God has pronounced his judgment, as he did against Israel by the mouth of Ezekiel. Therefore,
O harlot, hear the word of the Lord. Because your lewdness was
poured out and your nakedness uncovered through your harlotries
with your lovers and with all your detestable idols, behold, I shall
gather all your lovers with whom you took pleasure, even all those
whom you loved and all those whom you hated and expose you
to them. They will strip you of your clothing and will leave you
naked and bare. Behold, I will bring your conduct down on your
own head, so that you will not again commit this lewdness on top
of all your other abominations.'

 214

"I wept bitterly and cried out, 'Is there no mercy? It is true; I have
been deceived by Lilith, the ancient witch. And, yes, I willingly
accepted her offer of eternal life and beauty, but I was a foolish sheep
led to slaughter. Will God have mercy on this wretched soul?'

"Then the angel's face began to glow, and he said, 'The Lord
has heard your cry, and like Israel, he will establish a covenant
with you, and you shall know that he is the Lord, in order that you
may remember and be ashamed, and never open your mouth in
perverted song because of your humiliation, when he has forgiven
you for all that you have done. You will wander in the Bridgelands
until someone comes who takes pity on you and covers your
nakedness. He will have the fruit of righteousness within him, and

the blood of eternal life runs through his veins. If you want to prove your repentance, then serve him in righteousness for as long as he has need of your wisdom, and he will offer you the life you seek.'

"'But I have no wisdom,' I said to him. 'I am a harlot, as you have rightfully proclaimed, so what good would I be to such a man?'

"Then he said, 'I will teach you what you need to know.'

"After his teaching, the angel took me to this forest and left me here alone. I have since spent many nights waiting for deliverance, yet the men who have come by have only offered to expose me further, attacking me and tearing my clothes, but they were struck blind and wandered away before they could do me more harm."

Naamah sighed and lowered her head. "And now here I am."

"I'm the one who covered you," Elam said, "so I guess you're supposed to tell me what you learned."

"But it is such a mystery! The angel showed me the face of a mountain, like a tall slab of marble, that drew pictures on itself as he sang. He told me that I should lead my new master to the cliff and that the words of a new song would alter the scenes and explain what my master needed to know. I didn't understand the drawing or the angel's song, so how can I explain them to you? And I don't even know where the cliff is. How can I possibly lead you to it?" Naamah spread out her hands and sighed. "Since I didn't have a chance to ask the angel before he left, these thoughts have tortured me ever since. And now that I have found my new master, how can I ever gain the eternal life that flows in his blood, since I'm unable to do this task?"

"I know of a cliff that holds drawings," Dikaios said. "It is far, but I think we can reach it before we tire."

Elam stood and brushed off his trousers. "Then, if you would be so kind, good horse, please lead the way."

Dikaios snorted and gazed at Elam. "Most unusual, indeed."
He turned toward a high ridge in the distance and loped away.

Elam reached for Naamah. "Shall we follow?"

"If it pleases you," she replied, taking his hand. "But I fear
that I will disappoint you greatly."

After a few minutes of walking, they came to a grassy field
striated with bands of knee-high red flowers. More stones than
usual littered the grass, most smaller than hens' eggs, but a few
would have taken both hands to lift. Dikaios picked up the pace,
avoiding the random stripes of nodding blossoms, and pulled
ahead by about forty feet.

Elam quickened his gait to match the horse's, but Naamah
slipped away and waded into one of the flower beds.

"We'd better get going," Elam said, waving his hand. "He's
leaving us behind."

"Wait!" Naamah bent over and picked three red flowers.
"The aroma is so sweet!" She ran up to him and pressed the petals
up to his nose. "You see?"

Elam sniffed. The smell was sweet ... dizzying. He backed
away, feeling confused. "Dikaios!" he shouted. "Wait a minute!"

Hoofbeats sounded. "Get rid of those flowers!" the horse
yelled.

Naamah threw them to the ground. Dikaios grabbed Elam's
sleeve with his teeth and pulled him away from the garden while
Naamah followed, her head bowed.

When they were in a clear, grassy area, Dikaios let go. "Those
flowers are for weary travellers," he said. "The scent helps them
get to sleep quickly."

Naamah yawned and laid a hand on her brow. "They work
very well." Lowering herself to the ground, she yawned again and
stretched her body across a soft bed of grass. "I'm sorry. I just can't
help it. I have to rest." The moment her head touched the
ground, she fell asleep.

Elam rubbed his eyes. "It's got me, too." Yawning, he looked at Dikaios. "How long does it last?"

"It depends on how deep a draught you took and how tired you are. When did you last sleep?"

Elam shook his head, barely able to see through the fog building in his vision. "I had a pretty bad night's sleep in the second circle of Hades, but I don't know how long ago that was. Time passes so strangely. And I slept for a little while when I first got here, but that wasn't exactly a normal nap."

"Since you are both still among the living, you require sleep." Dikaios nudged his ribs. "It might be better if we all take a rest. The journey is difficult."

Elam yawned again. "Just a short nap." He knelt close to Naamah and was about to lie down, but he quickly rose again. "I'd better put some space between us." As he walked about twenty paces away, putting Dikaios between himself and Naamah, the horse just watched, saying nothing.

Interlacing his fingers behind his head, Elam lay back and closed his eyes. Within seconds, he was asleep. At first, he knew a dream had begun, but the scenes absorbed his mind, making them come alive.

He was back in the brick kilns with Raphah, his fellow slave in the days before Nabal, the giant taskmaster, cruelly whipped him to death. They had just finished a day's work and were washing their hands and faces in the underground spring. They scrubbed away kiln residue that had coated their bare arms, exposed by short-sleeved tunics necessary for the hot labours of brick making.

Nabal entered, Naamah at his side. "Nabal," she said, pointing at Raphah, "take him to the antechamber."

Jerking Raphah's arm, the giant led the boy away. Raphah looked back at Elam and pressed his hands together in a prayer posture.

Naamah, wearing a silky black gown, slinked up to Elam and gazed into his eyes. Her lips pursed as she pressed close. "Elam," she said, caressing the muscles rippling across his bare arm, "you have been strong. You have honoured your father's rules, and I'm sure he would be proud of you. He wouldn't expect you to suffer." She glanced briefly at a pair of shadows projected onto a rocky wall, two forms standing behind a partition, the larger one raising a whip. "Or your friends to suffer."

Elam averted his eyes, keeping them trained on his day's work, a tall stack of bricks still radiating heat and smelling of smoke. He tried to slide his arm away from Naamah's fingertips, but the sight of Raphah's imminent beating paralysed him.

"You have something I want, Elam. This is my third visit, and it is not often that I can come here without Morgan's knowledge. You won't disappoint me again, will you?"

Crack! The whip's cruel bark echoed from wall to wall, but no human cry followed.

Elam sucked in a breath. Raphah was holding his tongue. Brave, brave Raphah.

"There is no need for anyone to suffer," Naamah continued, her fingers creeping toward his shoulder, "when pleasure is so close at hand."

Elam's cheeks burned. Prickles crawled across his skin from head to toe. He had to escape. Just run away. But where?

Crack! This time a muffled grunt blended with the whip's sadistic echo. Raphah's shadow collapsed, and Nabal's silhouette began to raise the whip yet again.

"So, Elam ..." She pinched his tunic and pulled him away from the wash basin. He shuffled his feet, following her tractive gait, still watching the shadows out of the corner of his eye. Naamah stopped next to his bed. She laid both hands on his chest and nestled her head between them. A subtle aroma from Naamah's hair sweetened his rapid breaths. She sighed, sending warmth through his tunic. "What is your answer?" she asked, her voice cooing like a dove. "Will you give me what I desire?"

"No!" Elam shook his head violently and snapped open his eyes. A blue sky? Grass and flowers? He exhaled loudly. It was just a dream. He was back in the Bridgelands. But the familiar scent hovered in his nostrils. Naamah's hair. The same gentle touch.

He glanced down at his body. She was there! One hand was on his chest, and her face was close to his neck but pulling away slowly. Were those fangs over her lip? He lurched to his feet and scuffled back, shouting, "What do you think you're doing?"

Lying in the grass, Dikaios thrashed his body and lunged upright. "What? What did she do?"

Naamah rose slowly to her knees and stared at them, her cheeks awash in red. "I ... I was trying to get close to you. I woke up all alone, and I was scared, so I wanted ..." She covered her face with her hands and wept.

"She was after your life's blood!" Dikaios yelled. "She was using her harlotries to seduce you so she could steal your eternal life for herself!"

Elam's stomach felt like daggers were piercing it through. "Naamah? Is that true?" As he waited for an answer, the prophetic rhyme swam through his brain.

> But still there lurks a dangerous foe
> Who seeks to drink of Elam's life,
> To take the fruit that burns within
> The flame that melts a subtle knife.

Staying on her knees, she scuffled toward Elam, her hands folded. "No, Elam," she cried, "Please believe me. I just wanted to be close to you. You're the only one who ever showed me any mercy." Grasping his ankles, she bowed low and dripped tears on his sandalled feet. "I confess that I thought about stealing your

219

life while you slept, but I didn't do it. Even as my lips drew near to your throat, I changed my mind and decided just to rest at your side." She wiped the exposed part of his feet with her hair, and her cries became a long wail. "Please forgive me!"

As her head bobbed up and down, Elam glanced at Dikaios. The horse wagged his head hard. "The only reason she didn't steal your life is because you awakened before she could strike! She has used your goodness against you, Elam. She gained your trust only to get close enough to drain your life. She is the worst of harlots! She is a deceiver! A betrayer!"

Elam stepped back, pulling free of Naamah's grasp. "What should I do?"

"The harlot must die. If you let her live, she will only seek your life again. She is insatiable and can never change." Dikaios kicked a stone next to Elam's foot. "You must do away with her. Stone the wretch and cast her into the eternal fire."

Elam bent down and picked up the fist-sized stone. Tightening his grip around it, he lifted it to his shoulder and glared at Naamah. "You have been a deceiver all your life. You tortured both Sapphira and me and many other labourers in your slave pit. Give me one good reason why I shouldn't do what Dikaios says!"

"No, Elam!" Naamah raised her folded hands. "You must believe me! The angel said a man would cover me and offer me life. Other men came by, but they did the opposite. They talked of Jesus, but it wasn't the Jesus I knew. It wasn't the Jesus I met in Palestine. He offered me freedom from Morgan's spell, but I refused. He was kind and gentle, not like those fools. They mistreated me and counted me as nothing but a harlot, a worthless harlot."

She paused and took a gasping breath, her eyes growing wider. "But you ... you covered me, so I knew you were the one who had life. All I had to do was somehow get it, but I thought when I came to the mountain face I would be unable to make the drawing change, and you would send me away. So, in my vain imaginings, I wondered if I could take the blessing before you learned of my inability to serve you. But I didn't do it, I ..." Again she paused. Lowering her hands, she gazed at him. As new tears dripped down her chin, she bent her body low and curled up into a trembling ball. "I *am* still a foolish harlot," she said quietly. "Do to me what you must. Even for thinking about betraying you, I deserve worse than stoning."

Dikaios nudged Elam's arm. "She has finally spoken the truth. Take back your cloak, which she has defiled with her filthy body, and cast her into the Lake of Fire. One stone well-aimed will take care of this witch once and for all!"

As Naamah's body continued to shake, a tremulous melody poured from her lips – lamenting, forlorn, and plaintive.

O who will wash the stains I bear
The harlot's mark of sin I wear?
Exposed and shorn of all I prized,
And now I beg for mercy's eyes.

O Jesus, look upon my strife
And spare this foolish harlot's life.
I bow, surrender, pour my tears;
Forgive my sins and draw me near.

Finishing with a sigh, Naamah covered her head with her hands.

Dikaios snorted scornfully. "Her words have proven vain, Elam! She cannot be trusted. Take your vengeance now!"

Elam gazed at the shivering woman on the ground, still wearing his cloak, the very covering he offered in love and acceptance, even after all she had done to him. He glanced at the stone in his clenched hand. Would Raphah have forgiven her? She ended up

221

causing his death when she accused him in front of Morgan. And now, if not for a startling dream, would she have taken his life, the one who offered her help when no one else would? Could she ever be trusted?

He turned to Dikaios, but the horse said no more. His big eyes drilled an icy stare.

Finally, as Naamah's quaking grew, Elam dropped the stone and laid a hand on her back. "You asked me to forgive you, Naamah. Who am I to refuse?"

She looked up at him. Wet strands of hair stuck to her dirty face. As her eyes widened once again, she could barely whisper, "Do you mean, you ..."

He lowered his hand to her. "I forgive you. That's really the only life I have to offer ... yours."

Reaching out her trembling fingers, she took his hand and rose to her feet. When he released her, she just stared at her palm, as if he had left something there. Her mouth opened to speak again, but no words came out.

Elam kicked the stone far away. "You don't have to say anything. You don't have to do anything at all." He nodded at Dikaios. "If you will lead the way, good horse, I will follow. What Naamah does is up to her."

Without a word, Dikaios turned and loped in the direction they had been travelling before.

Elam marched behind him, glancing back at Naamah every few seconds. With her hand still in front of her face, she continued staring, and as the distance grew between them, her petite form seemed to shrink even further.

Turning to the front, Elam strode up a gently sloping rise, and when he reached the top, he halted. Dikaios stopped and turned around. Saying nothing, he lowered his head and sniffed the grass.

Elam raised a fist and stared at his hardened knuckles. Naamah really was a deceiver, the worst kind of harlot, but she

222

chose not to follow. Why would that be? If her new repentance was another deception, wouldn't she just tag along again and continue her pretence, waiting for another chance to take his life's blood?

Not wanting to turn to look, Elam pictured Naamah behind him, standing pitifully in the distance, watching her hand, waiting. But waiting for what? Elam opened his own hand and stared at his palm. Blistered and bloodied from hanging on to the bridge, dirty and grass-smeared from lying in the fields, his hand was no more majestic than any other. It was human – strong, real, the ultimate symbol of reaching out from one wanderer to another. Finally, it all made sense.

Slowly turning, Elam stretched out his arm and extended his open hand toward Naamah. She leaped forward and sprinted toward him, her bare legs and feet kicking up the hem of his cloak. When she reached the hill, she dashed up the slope and dropped to her knees. She grabbed his hand and kissed his palm, crying, "You won't regret this, Elam. I promise, you won't regret your mercy."

He raised her to her feet and looked into her teary eyes, speaking softly. "To be wanted and not lusted for. To be loved and not pitied. To be asked and not commanded." After passing a hand over her bedraggled hair, he slipped it into hers, touching their palms together. "Is that right?"

As her cheeks flushed, a shy smile emerged. In contrast to her red face, her white teeth dazzled, but now her fangs were gone. "And to be believed, even after all my lies."

CHAPTER

CHASING THE LIGHT

Candle held a torch high over his head, searching the skies. Still no sign of Grackle or Mother. It was getting so late. Pegasus had already risen, and the spider frogs had begun their nightly chants. Soon, the village guard would chase him away from the rabbit fields and back inside with a warning about owls and shadow people, but he had to stay out and watch. He couldn't bear to look at that empty shelf where his father's companion once sat in a bed of velvet.

Pulling up the hood on his ankle-length cloak, he strained his eyes, trying to find any sign of Grackle's purple glint, but the moon-washed canopy returned just a few white glimmers. With Pegasus ruling the nightscape, only the three brightest stars twinkled in the cold breeze – Shachar and the twin stars, Makaidos and Thigocia.

Something tugged at his sleeve. He jumped away and swung the torch, barely missing Listener's face. The little girl flinched but stayed put.

"Listener!" he scolded. "You scared me! I could've—"

His companion whispered into his mind. *Your sister has no voice to signal her approach. She did not know you would be so ready to lash out at her touch.*

Candle sagged his shoulders and sighed. "I'm sorry. Next time, please clap your hands or whistle when you come up behind me like that." Laying a hand on her shoulder, he nodded toward the torch-lit village. "Go on back. I'll be home soon."

She shook her head and lifted something in her hand, a bag with a strap.

"Where did you find this?" He took the bag and rubbed his hand along the smooth exterior. "It looks like a fruit harvest bag, but it's softer, like clothing."

Listener made signs with her fingers and pointed at the forest.

"In the trees? You were climbing a tree?"

She nodded.

He dangled the bag from its strap. "Was it hanging from a branch like this?"

She nodded again.

After pushing the end of the torch into the ground, Candle opened the bag and rummaged inside. "There's something in here." He pulled out a metallic cylinder about the length of his forearm. As he examined the tube, it expanded in his hands and slipped from his grasp.

Listener picked it up and stared through one end. Her mouth dropped open, and her eyes widened.

"What do you see?" Candle stooped beside her and looked up the tube's line of sight. "Not many stars are out."

She handed it back to him and made more signs with her fingers.

"The stranger? Do you mean Timothy?"

She nodded excitedly.

Candle pointed the tube at the sky and looked through it. "I don't see anything but Makaidos and Thigocia." He guided it across the sky until it swept over the moon. "Amazing! Pegasus looks as big as a house!" Lowering the tube, he rose to his full height. "This is like the Prophet's magnifying glass, only bigger and stronger, but I didn't see Timothy."

Listener pointed at herself and nodded. Picking up the torch, Candle cast its glow across his sister's scaly face. With her gleaming eyes and furrowed brow, she never looked more sincere.

Candle laid a hand on her shoulder. "You're not playing a game, are you?"

She shook her head and pointed at the sky, her arm trembling.

Raising the tube again, Candle searched the region she indicated but found only three stars he wasn't able to see with his naked eye, two white and one red. He sighed and took Listener's hand. "Let's get you to bed. Maybe Mother will figure out what's going on when she returns."

227

A shley's legs buckled. She collapsed and tumbled down the stairs. When her body smashed into the curved wall, she slid three more steps before finally stopping.

Pain stabbed her limbs. Both elbows and knees ached. Hot spikes drilled into her back, and white spots swirled in her vision, then slowly melted away.

She blinked at the darkness. Had she gone blind, or had the fall extinguished the lantern? Groping for something to hang on to, she braced her hand on the edge of a stair and pushed herself to a sitting position. Every inch of movement sent tingles up and down her spine.

Now panting for breath, she groped for her bag. There it was, right next to her. She grabbed it and hugged it close. Any other time, she would have stayed put and waited for help, not wanting to risk further injury, but what could she do? She couldn't stay put. Who could tell how close her stalker was now?

Again, she blinked at the total blackness surrounding her, listening. So far, nothing. She tapped her jaw and whispered breathlessly, "Larry! Larry, can you hear me?"

No response.

She ventured a slightly louder call. "Larry? Are you there?"

No Larry. Just a hint of static.

She pulled her photometer from the bag and turned it on. The red LED digits flashed a bright row of zeroes. Whew! At least she hadn't gone blind, and the reading proved what her surroundings already indicated. It was totally dark.

She stuffed the photometer into her jacket pocket, and, sliding the bag's strap over her shoulder, she gripped the crags in the wall and pulled herself to her feet. Trying to slow her breaths, she took a single step up. A trickling sensation crawled down her cheek and ran to her chin. Was it sweat or blood? She wiped it away with her finger and tried to look at it, but the veil of darkness still blinded her eyes.

She took another step, then another. Each one stretched her cramped legs, shooting more pain into her back, but the progress warmed her muscles and her confidence. Maybe, just maybe, she could make it.

Clump!

Ashley spun her head toward the sound. Oh, no! It's coming again!

Trying not to grunt, she pushed through the pain and hurried up the stairs, frantically limping through one step after another. What was the count? Twelve hundred? But she lost some falling down. Eleven ninety?

Clump!

Ten more steps. More pain. Twenty steps. Nausea swilled in her stomach. Thirty steps. Throbs hammered her head. Her skull had to be cracking! Fifty steps!

228

A tinkling sound rose from the stairs. Something had shattered at her feet. She halted and bent over, feeling for the object she had kicked. She found it. Something metal.

Picking it up, she moved on, letting her fingers crawl over the surface, smooth and quite warm. Her thumb brushed along something soft and hot, very hot. A wick! It was a lantern! A recently used lantern! One of the giants must have left it behind, dropping it and shattering its glass shield as they marched up the stairs.

But what good would it do her? With no lighter or matches, it would just slow her down. She stopped and sniffed the oil. Maybe she could slow down her pursuer. It wasn't much of a chance, but at least it was something.

She poured the oil over the steps and, after setting the lantern in the middle of the pool, hobbled up the stairway. Maybe the stalker would slip and fall. In this darkness, anything could happen.

Feeling stronger, she increased her pace and quickly covered another forty steps, but as she slowed again, a strange odour filled her nostrils.

Suddenly, her foot slipped, and she fell forward, smacking her hands on the stairs but catching herself before her knees struck the stone. As she rose again, her hand brushed against something. She snatched it up and felt its familiar metal surface. *The lantern! I slipped on the oil! The oil that I poured out!*

But how could that be? I climbed dozens of steps! It's impossible!

Ashley's head pounded again. She sat down, panting heavily. Clamping her oily hands over her ears, she tried to concentrate. What could she do? The laws of physics and logic didn't work in this place. What good was it to have super smarts in a world where two plus two equals ... She grabbed a fistful of hair and pulled ...

Five, a three-eyed Bigfoot, a flying saucer, anything but four!

Clump!

229

She drooped her shoulders. Not again! She struggled to her feet but could only lean against the wall. What good would running away do? If she was going in an insane circle, she would just wear herself out and still not get away.

Sliding down, she huddled against the wall, pressing as close to the stone as she could. Maybe her pursuer would just pass her by ... not even notice her. After all, only bats could see in total darkness, right? And this was no bat.

Sighing, she closed her eyes and listened, but the telltale clumps had silenced, at least for the moment. As she concentrated, a recent image played back in her mind, her descent in this very same stairwell with Walter as they read the etchings on the wall. *Abandon hope, all ye who enter here.* The words drifted through her mind and seemed to echo once again in the darkness, somehow audible, though she couldn't be sure. *Abandon hope, all ye who ...*

The air grew cold. Hugging her knees, Ashley shivered, trying not to make a sound.

"Are you frightened, dear child?"

Ashley held her breath. The voice! It was back!

"You are shaking. What troubles you?"

She whispered as softly as she could. "Something's chasing me, and I keep going in circles."

Laughter blended with the voice. "A spiral staircase is bound to lead you in circles."

"Shhhh! It will hear you!"

"What will hear me?"

"The thing that's chasing me!"

He chuckled, quietly this time. "Let me show you something."

A light flickered, and a glow illumined the stairway. An old man wearing blue jeans and a white sweatshirt held a lantern. A cracked shield encased the wick. "It took some doing to mend it, but it still works."

She reached out and touched the base. "My lantern?"

"The very same." The man set the lantern on the stair and sat down. When he looked at Ashley, he winced. "You're hurt." He pulled a handkerchief from his pocket and dabbed a spot just above her cheek. "Don't worry. It's clean."

Too weak to protest, Ashley let him nurse her wound. As she gazed into his grey eyes, another old image flashed across her mind. "You look familiar," she said dreamily.

"I'm glad you noticed." He gave her the handkerchief and set his palms on his knees. "We had a nice time discussing quantum physics on a flight to London. I was most interested in your invention ... Apollo, I think you called it."

"The smelly old man on the plane!" Ashley slapped her hand over her mouth. "I'm sorry. I didn't mean it."

"Of course you meant it, but I take no offence."

"But why are you here now? How did you get in this staircase?"

"First things first." The man extended his hand, palm up. "May I see the dime and two pennies?"

Ashley narrowed her eyes. "Dime and two pennies?"

"The coins your mother asked you to keep, the ones from the box she hid under the hearth."

She dug into her jeans pocket and withdrew the coins. "How did you know about these?"

"As you might have guessed by now, I am far more than the smelly old man I appeared to be. I have been watching you for quite some time, and I said I would be with you throughout this part of your journey."

She laid the coins in his palm. "Why are they so important?"

The man picked up the dime and eyed it closely. "I gave your father these coins when you were born. They were freshly mint-ed then, so they bear the year of your birth." He held one of the pennies in his fingertips so she could see the date. "Your mother already told you that the two pennies symbolize the two faithful witnesses, so rare in their faith, they are similar to the widow's mites, the old woman's precious gift to the temple treasury. In like fashion, the pennies represent your two greatest gifts, so the next time you exercise one of your gifts, be sure to hold one of these pennies in your hand to signify your willingness to use your gift sacrificially. Your faith in the Gift Giver will lead to your deliverance, and all things will be made whole."

"You were the street vendor? A street vendor with a doctorate in physics?"

He dropped the coins into her jacket pocket and extended his hand. "Doctor Dan Allen. I have other names, but that one will do for now."

Ashley took his hand. "I guess you already know my name. I—"

Clump!

She jerked away and stiffened. "It's coming!"

"Yes, I know. He is the Naphil whose leg fell prey to Walter's sword. Though he walks now with the help of a staff he fashioned, he is quite dangerous."

"But he was dead!"

"*Is* dead, you mean."

Clump!

"What does he want?"

"To escape, but since he is quite stupid, he hasn't figured out that he's walking in an infinite loop. He will never be allowed to leave, because, as I told you, he is dead, and this is his home until the final judgment. But he is resting again, so we have some time to talk."

Ashley wagged her head back and forth. "This doesn't make sense. Nothing here makes sense. I need to get out of here."

"How do you plan to do that?"

"I'll keep climbing." She pushed her hand against the step and rose to a crouch. "This can't be an infinite loop. The stairs have to lead somewhere."

"They do lead somewhere." Dr Allen pointed at the stairs. "Back to this spot."

She flopped back down and leaned against the wall, her head throbbing. "But that's nonsense!"

"The concept of infinity seems to elude you, dear child. Perhaps believing in something truly infinite makes your brain choke." He added a gentle laugh.

"I don't find that amusing!" she barked, scowling.

"Yet you have used the same phrase many times to harvest smiles from your friends."

Ashley pushed her hair out of her eyes and exhaled heavily. This guy had her nailed. It was almost like he had seen her life's history in a movie. Softening her tone, she traced her finger along the Italian phrase etched in the wall. "Maybe, but you can't have an infinite in a finite space. It's impossible."

"Isn't the universe infinite?" he asked.

"No. It can't be. Having something that goes on and on forever just isn't conceivable."

"What are the other options? If you could fly to the edge of the universe, would you run into a wall, a two-dimensional barrier with nothing on the other side, not even space? Or does the universe somehow loop back on itself like a strange spiral stairwell?"

Ashley laid a hand on her head. "Stop it! You're making my head hurt!"

"But the universe must be either infinite or finite, mustn't it?"

"Yes, of course!"

Dr Allen slid closer and gently brushed a hand across her hair. "Ashley, not all truths can be conceptually or analytically grasped, but that doesn't make them impossible, so we must accept some truths by faith. The Infinite One has pierced the veil of the finite and has dwelt among us, and the only way to know him is to merge your intellect with faith as you try to grasp what you cannot understand. Only then can you find true wisdom."

"How can I do that?" she asked, gazing into his peaceful eyes. "I'm not like some of my friends. They seem to be able to put their

233

brains in the garbage disposal and believe whatever someone tells them, a dream that there's a super daddy in Heaven who reached down to save us with a sacrifice too good to be true. No one has that much love, so people made up a god who supposedly does. It's just so irrational."

"I see." He looked down for a moment, pursing his lips. "Is that the way you feel about Bonnie Silver? Is her faith irrational?"

Ashley bit her tongue. The very idea that Bonnie's faith would ever be in question stung her heart. She thought back to when she first met Bonnie. She had admired her glow, her seemingly unquenchable faith that led her to dive into the candlestone prison in search of her mother.

Leaning her head back again, she sighed deeply. She would never forget a note she had found in Bonnie's journal, a message signed to her.

234

You may think no one understands you, but God knows everything about you. He knows who you really are.

"Come now, and let us reason together, saith the LORD: though your sins be as scarlet, they shall be as white as snow; though they be red like crimson, they shall be as wool."

Red will be made white
Darkness shall become light
Faith will be made sight
Squire shall become knight

As the sweet phrases sang in her mind, Ashley shook her head. Bonnie's irreproachable wisdom had conquered her once again. "No," Ashley replied. "She's not irrational. I just don't understand her."

Dr Allen raised a finger. "Exactly. Never dismiss as folly that which you simply do not understand."

"So what do I do now?" Ashley pointed at the floor. "I mean, right here, right now?"

The kind gentleman smiled and touched her palm. "Remember David and Goliath, and you will do well." The lantern faded, and Dr Allen's voice faded with it. "Combine your intellect with faith, and always follow the light."

The corridor darkened again to complete blackness. Ashley felt for Dr Allen but found only the lantern, still warm. She slid it toward her and listened once again to the void.

Clump!

The sound was closer than ever. Ashley squeezed against the wall and froze, holding her breath. She closed her eyes and waited. Sheer terror chilled her heart.

Clump!

Vibrations in the steps buzzed through her body. The giant had to be just a few feet away now.

Clump!

It stopped next to her. A sniffing sound pierced the dark silence, then a deep voice. "Your own stench has betrayed you, but I will let you live if you help me escape this place."

Ashley swallowed quietly. What should she do? Did he really know where she was in this darkness?

Thin scarlet shafts of light sliced the black void, slowly scanning the stairs. Inch by inch they edged toward her hiding place. She squeezed even closer to the wall, but the infrared eyebeams would be on her in seconds.

She tossed the lantern down the stairwell. It clattered over the steps, its noise diminishing as it rounded the spiral.

The giant lumbered toward the sound. His heavy footsteps masked Ashley's escape as she snatched up her shoulder bag and scrambled to her feet. Trying to silence her breaths, she stormed up the stairs, but with her body still aching, she wouldn't last long at this pace.

As she hurried, frantic thoughts raced through her mind. Dr Allen said to follow the light, but there was no light. He said to have faith, but there was nothing around to believe in, except that murder-minded monster, and she already believed every word he said. But she couldn't help him escape. Dr Allen said he would never be allowed to leave.

A jingling sound interrupted her thoughts. She reached into her jacket pocket to silence the coins Dr Allen had dropped there, and her fingers slid around her photometer. Slowing to a halt, she leaned against the wall, trying not to pant too loudly. Maybe she should wait. If this was really a loop and she kept going, she might run into the giant from behind.

She pulled out the photometer and ran her fingers over the familiar switches. *Not all light is visible,* she thought, *so maybe there is a light to follow after all.* Finding the power switch, she turned it on. The LED digits on the tiny display screen flashed to life again. Turning the dial through its spectrum settings, she read the numbers in her mind. *Ultraviolet is zero, Infrared is zero. Gamma is zero. What's this? Visible spectrum is positive now! How can that be? With this illuminance, I should be able to see where I'm going!*

Still watching the photometer, she moved up a step. The intensity went up. Another step. Higher intensity. She continued ascending until she reached the sixth step and began leaning toward the seventh. The intensity ebbed. So the sixth step marked the highest reading.

As she listened for the giant, she started down, expecting the intensity to drop, but instead, it began to increase again. Each step down brought a higher number, until she passed where she began and reached the third step below it. Finally, it dropped once more.

She looked up into the darkness, mentally sketching the stairway. Six steps up to the brightest light going upward, but then nine steps down to an even brighter light. It just didn't make any sense.

236

Clump!

The giant was pretty far below her, but there wasn't much time. She ascended again, still watching the meter, and once again, the intensity heightened. Three steps. Still higher. The ninth step, where it was highest during her previous climb, showed still higher, and now ... Ashley continued climbing. The intensity rose again. Finally, on the fourteenth step, the intensity dropped. The thirteenth step represented the highest peak yet. Would going down again show another rise?

Clump!

But going down would take her closer to the approaching giant. Still, she had to try. She descended one step. The reading plummeted to almost zero. She jumped back up. The intensity recovered.

This had to be it. This had to be the highest peak. Scanning the area with the photometer, she searched for any hint of a source point, but the apparently invisible light seemed to come from all around. She had followed the light, just like Dr Allen had said, but what now? The giant would be there in a heartbeat!

The strange sound thumped closer, rounding the spiral steps until the giant had to be only a dozen or so away. Still watching the photometer, Ashley shivered, and with each tremble, the light reading dropped.

She steeled herself, firming her jaw as she spoke into the darkness. "Halt! Come no closer!"

The thumping stopped. The light reading steadied. Then, a low laugh rumbled from several steps below. "I thought I detected a sweaty female. Your voice resembles Morgan's, and you smell like Naamah after a night of prowling in the upper lands."

Ashley gripped the photometer tightly, ready to bash him in the head, though she knew it would be a feeble defence. She felt for the brick in her bag. She didn't want to lose it, but it might be her only chance. "If you come any closer, I will be forced to use

237

my weapon." She glanced at the reading. The lumens count almost doubled.

"A woman against a Naphil?" The voice was closer now, maybe five steps away. His eyebeams flicked on, hitting the step just below her. "Even Morgan shuddered as she watched us train for battle. Are you a more powerful sorceress than she?"

"I am not a sorceress. I am the daughter of Thigocia, the warrior queen of all dragons."

"You do not sound like a dragon, certainly not like the one I met in the mobility room before I began climbing these cursed stairs."

Ashley forced a steady voice. "That was Roxil, my sister. How did you get past her?"

The awful "clump" sounded again. "I am sure you have heard my staff as I ascended the stairs. I used it against your sister and now rely on it as a walking stick. She was a formidable combatant, especially since I lack a leg, but she is no longer in any condition to fight." The eyebeams rose a step and scanned up her body slowly. "I see you now, and you are no dragon."

Ashley gulped. New shivers raced across her skin. She glanced at the photometer again. The reading slowly diminished.

Swallowing hard, she squared her shoulders. "If you think my sister was a fighter, then come to me, and I will show you what battle is all about. All you have is a brutish little staff, and you will be fighting blind. You'll be worse off than Goliath when he lost his head to a shepherd boy."

The meter reading soared, the digits changing so rapidly she could barely read them. She set her feet firmly and allowed a smile to break through. "I am standing in the light. That will be enough to defeat the likes of you."

Suddenly a brilliant flash burst into the stairwell. The Naphil looked up, terror in his eyes as he tumbled back. Ashley jerked her gaze upward. The central stairway support, along with the stairs, collapsed and vanished as a swirling storm of fire plummeted toward her.

Sapphira swirled her hands above her head, once again creating a fiery cyclone. "Okay," she called, "I need to concentrate on finding Ashley. I pray that Jehovah will guide us to her."

Karen scooted close to Sapphira on one side, while Walter pushed between Sapphira's other side and the hole, his foot just inches from the edge. Gabriel stood behind Sapphira and stretched his wings around everyone.

The swirling wall descended its flaming envelope, creating a loud swooshing sound as its orbit accelerated. When the orange tongues swiped against the grass, the ground beneath one of Walter's feet suddenly crumbled. "Not again!" He flailed his arms, trying to lunge back to the edge.

Gabriel grabbed Walter's shoulder with his hand. "I've got you!"

More earth gave way, and the entire company toppled into the hole. The column of fire came along, surrounding them like a flaming tornado and widening the pit as they fell. Gabriel fought the downward plunge, hanging on to Walter with one hand and Sapphira with the other while beating his wings, but he could only slow their fall. As Karen passed by, Walter grabbed her belt, and they all dropped together. Gabriel finally gave in to the overpowering force and folded in his wings.

Walter looked through the funnel's downspout several feet below. With flames lighting the way, the hole brightened, still widening, as though the fiery cyclone were drilling a massive quarry, but instead of throwing dirt and rocks upward, the orange tornado disintegrated the debris. Soon, another person came into view, a body spinning in the wind as the cyclone approached it from above. "Someone's down there!" he called into the swirling heat. "I think we're gaining on them!"

239

A few seconds later, the funnel pulled the body into its grasp, slurping it into the swirl. As it floated upward, Walter grabbed the feminine arm with his free hand and turned her face toward him. With wide, terrified eyes, she stared at him.

"It's Ashley!" Walter hugged her close. "Don't worry! I've got you! We'll be all right!" He angled his head upward. "Sapphira! What's going on? Can't you stop this runaway train?"

With Gabriel hanging on to her jacket collar, Sapphira kept her hands churning. "As long as we're falling," she yelled, "I have to keep the flames going. Otherwise, we'll crash at the bottom of this hole. The portal fire is the only thing keeping us safe."

"How do you know?" Karen cried out.

"You just have to trust me. I've done this before."

"She's right," Gabriel shouted. "This is kids' stuff compared to what she and I fell through at Dragons' Rest!"

The fiery cyclone finally touched ground, sweeping away huge boulders and thousands of stones as it polished the floor beneath and created a cushion of air that slowed their plunge. Walter landed first. His feet touched gently as the others floated down next to him. When all were safely standing, Sapphira lowered her arms, and the flames died away.

Walter kept his arm under Ashley's elbow, helping her stand. As she shivered violently, a shoulder bag slipped down and fell to the floor. He wrapped her up with both arms, hoping to give her warmth. Something was wrong with her. The air was cold, but not that cold. Light from above illuminated her pale face, and when their glances met, she smiled, her teeth chattering. "Hello, Walter. ... I hope ... I hope I'm not dreaming."

"You're not," he said, grinning, "but logically, if you were dreaming, you shouldn't trust what I'm saying."

"Forget logic!" She embraced him tightly. "You're here, and you're warm. That's all I need to know."

240

Walter looked up. They stood at the bottom of a deep, massive crater that opened to the drizzling sky. Daylight. Cloud-obscured, to be sure, but it was still daylight. He turned to Sapphira and nodded upward. "Is that the top level of Hades, or are we still in the real world?"

"Hard to say. Since Gabriel is solid, my guess is Hades, but maybe he can fly up there and—" Sapphira's eyes shot wide open. "Roxil!"

Walter spun in the direction of her stare. A huge dragon lay sprawled on the ground about twenty feet away.

Sapphira ran to Roxil and knelt at her side. "Roxil! Can you hear me?"

Flapping his wings, Gabriel glided across the ground, landing near Roxil's face. He laid a hand gently on her brow. "Her scales are cool. I don't think that's a good sign." He passed his finger in front of Roxil's snout. "But I feel warm breath. She must be alive."

Walter, Ashley, and Karen joined them, Ashley still shivering. "Is it time for another healing?" Walter asked.

"I can try." Ashley rubbed her hands up and down her arms. "But I feel weak, like everything's drained out of me. I climbed over a thousand steps and faced the giant that clubbed Roxil. I guess the adrenaline rush wore me out."

"Let's give her a few minutes to rest," Gabriel said. "In the meantime, I'll see what's going on up top. It won't take long to figure out if we're in Hades or not."

"I know a faster way." Ashley tapped her jaw. "Larry, can you hear me?"

A static-filled reply buzzed from Ashley's mouth. "Your signal is weak, O loquacious leviathan. I am on generator power, so my reception and transmission capabilities are diminished."

"We must be in the real world." Ashley's gaze drifted from Walter to Gabriel to Sapphira. "Larry, any news reports that would indicate very strange phenomena?"

"Strange, indeed! Because of a widespread power outage, my access to the Internet is malfunctioning, but I have been scanning a variety of radio frequencies. It seems that electricity is being drained from several strategic locations, thereby disrupting the power grid. Authorities suspect terrorism, and they are working to pinpoint the drainage spots. Many cities are in a panic with widespread looting and out-of-control fires. A very recent report indicates that unruly hairy men are swarming in the streets and committing acts of unspeakable violence, especially against children. To put it in layman's terms—all hell has broken loose. This, of course, is exactly what a terrorist would want."

242

"It's not terrorism," Ashley replied, her shivers returning. "I think you nailed it when you said, 'All hell has broken loose'."

"Your words are cryptic. If you know the cause, then perhaps I should notify the authorities. I can send an anonymous shortwave message to—"

"No. They can't help us." Ashley knelt close to Roxil and caressed her dull tawny scales. "We need a special kind of firepower."

Thigocia sniffed a footprint in the mud at the edge of a narrow bubbling stream. "It is the same man we spoke with," she said, lifting her eyes toward Arramos. "Zane's odour is unmistakable."

Sitting on his haunches in the surrounding grass, Arramos tapped the end of his tail on the ground. "He is the only wanderer we have found in all these hours. Are you satisfied?"

Thigocia let out a low growl. "For now."

"Good." He rose to all fours and unfurled his wings. "We must meet with Roxil as soon as possible. We have a very long journey ahead, and our delay has compromised our schedule. Great haste is now a necessity."

"Do not worry about me." Thigocia stretched out her wings, but her span, though wide and impressive for a female, was no match for his. "Fly quickly," she said. "I will keep up."

"As you wish." With a great flap of his wings, Arramos shot into the sky and ascended at a dizzying rate.

Thigocia followed, beating her own wings furiously. After several minutes of exhausting flight, she caught up and flew to the right of and slightly behind Arramos, decelerating to keep to his new, slower pace. With every downbeat of his powerful reddish wings, his profile came into view. He didn't look back at her, but she detected a cynical smile. Of course he had slowed down to allow her to catch up, but not out of mercy. His was a condescending leniency, not a loving act of grace.

243

As she continued watching his face, she heaved a sigh. Had she made a mistake going with him? What would happen when she finally had to trust him in battle? And would they ever really find Roxil?

She edged away to avoid brushing her wing with his. Again, she sighed. With Ashley, Walter, and Karen risking their lives, the stakes had risen too high to make a blunder now.

CHAPTER

THE PROPHETIC WALL

After guiding Elam and Naamah across a marshy field populated by wood ducks and hefty bullfrogs, Dikaios led them
up to a drier plane and stopped at the edge of a forest. "This is
the Skotos Woods," he said. "Since it is dense and quite dark,
some of the wanderers in these lands hide or sleep here after they
have wearied themselves trying to find the altar."

Elam stepped over an oak's low-hanging limb and set his
hand on the trunk. "Have they ever shown any signs of violence?"

"I believe violence is possible. They are desperate, so their
behaviour is unpredictable. We would be wise not to alert them
to our presence."

Wearing a wreath she had fashioned with marsh reeds and
white flowers, Naamah scanned the long line of trees. "Is going
around an option?"

"It is an option," Dikaios replied, "but Skotos is very wide at
this point, so going around would take at least three additional
hours."

"Lead the way, Dikaios." Elam nodded toward the woods. "We'll just have to be as quiet as possible until we come back out into the light."

As they navigated between massive tree trunks on a meandering path of trodden leaves, the canopy thickened, and the woods grew darker. Ducking under vines that formed sagging bridges between the trees, Elam pushed away branches that invaded their path, holding them until Naamah could pass by unhindered.

Soon, the forest began to thin out. The smell of burning wood hung in the motionless air, but no crackling logs or fireside chatter gave any audible hints to the source of the odour. Dikaios stopped at a hedge that bordered a glade. The bushes rose high enough to prevent someone from peering over the top, but there were several gaps that allowed for easy passage.

When Elam and Naamah caught up, he plodded into the clearing, glancing back and forth as he high-stepped over leaves that had blown on the path. In the centre of the oval glade they found the remains of a campfire and several places where the leaves had been swept together into bedding.

Elam bent down and picked up a long stick with a charred end. He touched the black ashes. Still warm, but just barely. Quietly setting it down again, he nodded to Dikaios, and the horse continued on the path.

Just as they reached the other end of the clearing, a timid voice called out. "Excuse me?"

Turning in the direction of the voice, Elam gestured for Naamah to move behind a wide tree. A bespectacled, middle-aged man emerged from the forest and tripped over a root. He stumbled into the clearing and fell on his face.

Elam hustled to his side and helped him to his feet. As Dikaios and Naamah joined them, the man brushed off his clothes, a button-down white formal shirt and a pair of ragged black trousers. With dirty smears and fingertip-sized holes covering his garments from top to bottom, he seemed well acquainted with stumbling.

His hands trembling, he bowed his head to Elam, then to Dikaios and Naamah. His voice matched the tremors in his hands. "I am lost and in need of help. Have you come to take me to Heaven's altar?"

"Have you found the key?" Elam asked.

The man shook his head sadly. "I have searched everywhere. I was hoping that if I found the door to the altar, I might see what kind of key is needed. Then, once I knew its size, I could continue my search with a better knowledge of what I'm looking for."

Dikaios stepped forward. "What is your name, and how did you get here?"

"I was called Zane on Earth, and my friends here call me Maestro, because I often lead them in song. My coming to this place is the result of a harsh journey. You see, when I knew death was approaching, I went to sleep expecting to awaken in Heaven, but I found myself in a strange land. After asking countless people where I was supposed to go, I wandered into a forest where I had to fend off a hairy beast, but a barely visible man rescued me. After asking me countless questions, he allowed me to enter this place. While it is lovelier than the previous land, it still seemed somewhat of a disappointment compared to the glorious splendour I expected to see in Heaven."

"This is not Heaven," Elam explained. "These are the Bridgelands, the approach to Heaven."

"Yes. Yes, I learned that from the transparent fellow who brought me here from the other land. I also learned that I need to find the final gateway, Heaven's altar, but that destination has eluded me for years."

Elam glanced around. "You said you have friends. Where are they?"

"They are out on their daily search." Zane pushed one of the leaf beds with his foot. "We are ten in all, and we regularly congregate here. We warm ourselves around a fire and discuss our journeys, and we find it beneficial to compare notes about what we discover."

"Did they all get here the same way you did?" Elam asked.

"We arrived at different times, but we all followed the same course. First, I met the transparent gentleman in the forest, and, after arriving here, I came upon a deep chasm. A rickety bridge spanned the gap, and it seemed much too dangerous to cross. Thanks be to God, a lady in a red cloak guided me to a much safer passage. Ever since that time, I have been searching for the altar."

"Did the other nine mention the lady in red?"

"Yes." Zane slid his glasses higher on his nose. "She was a grand topic of conversation. Since the ten of us have similar backgrounds in theology, we are able to converse using the language of our discipline, so we debated her symbolic meaning in our journeys. Since she came to us at the moment we had to cross the bridge, we decided to call her Providence, the symbol of divine intervention."

Dikaios slapped his tail against Zane's backside. "The camaraderie of similar scholarship helps isthmian thinking flourish."

Zane glared at the horse. "Excuse me? I don't grasp your meaning."

"'*Cannot* grasp' would be a better phrase," Dikaios grumbled.

"Never mind him." Elam brushed the remaining leaves from Zane's shirt. "We are also in search of the altar. When we find it, I hope to do as you mentioned – learn more about the key and what is needed to enter. Then, if we are allowed to return and tell others how to follow, I will."

"That would be excellent!" Zane pressed his hands together and looked at Elam hopefully. "May I come with you?"

Elam glanced at Dikaios, but the horse merely blinked at him.

"Would you leave without your friends?"

"Oh, they will return soon, I'm sure. Very soon. You will wait, won't you?"

"Let's do this," Elam said. "When your friends come back, build another fire and stay together. If I don't return by the time it becomes ashes, then you can assume that I'm not coming back."

Zane began breathing hard, almost hyperventilating. "How tall should I make the pyre? How much wood do I use?"

"How big is your faith?" Elam smiled and walked away, stealthily glancing behind him to catch Zane's confused expression.

Finally, Zane lifted a thin branch and waved it. "I see! The larger my fire, the more willing I am to wait!"

Elam took Naamah's hand and patted Dikaios on the neck. "Let's go."

When they travelled out of earshot, Dikaios muttered, "Have you given this man false hope? How do you know you will return?"

"I only told him I hoped to return, and I assume his hope should be built upon the faith he has." Elam pushed aside a branch as they passed through the bordering hedge. "If there's one thing I learned from Merlin, it's this. When we aren't sure where we're going, faith and hope are the most solid stepping-stones we have."

"I see. You must have chosen to cross the bridge rather than follow the woman in red." Dikaios said nothing more, and the three walked through the remainder of the forest in silence.

After another half hour, the woods opened up into a wide, grassy plain, dressed from one end to the other with brilliant wildflowers. In the distance, low hills gradually gave way to rocky ridges and mountains with a path leading upward through the lower elevations.

Their walk through the scented grass proved easy and pleasant, and when they arrived at the upward path, Elam felt refreshed and ready to climb. After about an hour, the path grew steeper, though it remained grassy and wide, comfortable for feet, shoes, and hooves.

Rocky banks rose sharply on the right, and a sheer drop into a river valley threatened on the left. Tropical trees lined the river far below, sporting branches alive with activity as small animals resembling monkeys swung from vine to vine.

When they reached a point where the rising shoulder to the right sloped more gradually, Dikaios stopped and bobbed his head at a sheer mountain face about a hundred feet away, a massive marble wall that jutted straight up for about a thousand feet.

"The Cliff of Promise," Dikaios said. "It reveals truths that cannot be seen with the eye – truths from the past, present, and expected future."

"Expected future?" Elam asked.

The horse nodded. "A wise man once told me that God's promises of future tidings always come true, but many events about which God remains silent lie in the realm of the merely possible."

"Okay," Elam said, stretching out the word, "that's a little too deep to go into right now." He gazed at the drawing on the white cliff. In the centre, a globe of the Earth displayed the western hemisphere in the foreground. To the left, seven black discs hovered, one on top of the other, with white spacers in between that matched the thickness of an individual disc. The height of the entire stack equalled the north-to-south diameter of the Earth. To the right of the Earth, a stone prayer bench sat beneath an altar of gold. Two girls knelt at the bench, while an old man stood next to the altar wearing a long robe.

As he took in all the amazing detail, the drawing moved. The Earth slowly rotated, while the discs spun almost imperceptibly. The man at the altar bent over and laid a hand on one of the girls, apparently speaking to her.

"If it's a drawing," Elam said, "how does it move?"

Dikaios set a foreleg on the slope. "Look closely. Every line is made up of living dots. They are insects of some kind, though I am not aware of the name of the species."

With Naamah following close behind, Elam walked up the gradual slope until he was within reach of the cliff. "They look like big grasshoppers," he said.

"Locusts." Naamah bent over and eyed one closely. "They are of the same variety God used to smite Egypt."

"So," Elam said, backing toward Dikaios, "what's this wall supposed to tell us?"

"Did not the angel say that a new song would change the drawing?" Dikaios asked.

Elam crossed his arms over his chest. "So I guess one of us has to sing."

"Not I," Dikaios said. "My voice would frighten the insects away."

"Well, I'm no singer." Elam looked at Naamah expectantly. "But I know someone who is."

Her eyes darkened as she stared back at him. "I am a songstress, Elam, but I have no words to sing in such a holy place. Who am I to command a prophetic image to appear on this sacred wall?"

"The angel said you were supposed to explain it." Elam spread out his hands. "So who else can do it?"

Naamah gave a quick curtsy, then, scooting in close to Elam, clutched his tunic and whispered. "Master Elam, you put me in a quandary. I wish to obey and sing, but I haven't the words. The songs I know are vulgar and dark."

"Maybe if you just close your eyes and hum one of your tunes, new words will pop into your mind."

Naamah released his tunic and backed away. She stared at him again for a moment, then slowly bowed her head. "I will do as you say, but I cannot promise a sensible song."

"Just do the best you can." Elam turned and walked away from the mountain face. "Let's move to where we can see the drawing better."

When they arrived at the original path, Naamah lowered herself to her knees, folding her hands and closing her eyes. With the garland of reeds and tiny white flowers resting on her jet black hair, she looked like a fairy princess ready for bedtime prayers. At first, she just moved her lips silently, as if praying, then, a beautiful melody arose, like the morning psalm of a heavenly nightingale.

Dikaios and Elam moved closer to Naamah. Elam knelt next to her, listening intently while gazing at the slowly spinning Earth on the cliff. Soon, words began to blend in with the melody, and phrases seemed to take physical shape, like doves made out of pure light, flying from Naamah's lips toward the massive drawing. The song flowed on the breeze as the feathered words made flight and blended in with the dark insects on the wall.

252

Created holy, man has died
And reaped the evil seed he sowed,
So now he ploughs in futile sand,
The ox who kicks the prodding goad.

As the song proceeded, the locusts formed images to match the words, rapidly changing each scene. They showed a man and woman with a fruit, then a man pushing a plough and shaking a fist in the air.

To God he builds a tower of stone,
His pride, an arrow to the sky,
Believing clay and flesh and blood
Can reach the holy seat on high.

The drawing shifted to a tall ziggurat that pierced the clouds, but dragons flew around the tower and toppled it with a cyclone of fire.

Alas! The tower begins anew,
A threat that now has breached the wall
That separates the men of Earth
From souls who live in Hades' hall.

The image of the Earth and the seven stacked discs reappeared. The two worlds drifted closer and closer together until they collided. The discs transformed into locusts that flew into the Earth, and the image seemed to magnify, as if the one viewing the scene were flying in for a landing somewhere in the United States. Suddenly, hairy men with fangs appeared. They prowled a city street, chasing small humans into dark alleys.

253

A giant reaching to the sky,
With bolts of lightning twisting 'round,
Is seeking not to climb to God,
But strives to bring the heavens down.

The altar with the praying girls reappeared on the face of the mountain. To the left, a giant lifted his hands, and jagged streaks shot out from his fingers. The streaks wrapped up in a vortex and reached for the altar like twisted strands of spider webbing shooting at a victim. The streaks grabbed the altar and drew it closer and closer until ...

The image suddenly vanished, but Naamah's song continued.

Protect the Earth, my chosen one,
By standing fast at Heaven's shield,

For Mardon's plan will come to pass
If Elam's faith should bend and yield.

Turning pale, Naamah exhaled loudly and toppled to the side. Her cheek thumped heavily on the path.

Elam pulled her upright and whispered, "Naamah, are you okay?"

Her head swayed back and forth for a moment, but it finally steadied, and she opened her eyes. A gentle smile graced her lips. "I did it, didn't I?"

Elam brushed specks of grass and sand from her face. "You were amazing!" Rising to his feet, he pulled Naamah up.

"So do you understand the song?" she asked. "The words came through my mind, so I sang them, but they were a mystery to me."

Elam gazed at the massive wall. "I understood everything except what I'm supposed to do. I have to stand fast at Heaven's shield, whatever that means, and that's supposed to stop Mardon's plan to bring Heaven down to Earth."

Dikaios nudged Elam with his nose. "Heaven's shield is a gate that leads to the altar of God. This is the very place you have been searching for since you arrived."

"Do you know how to get there?"

The horse turned his head, avoiding Elam's stare. "You have asked me this question before."

Elam stepped back into Dikaios's line of sight. "And you didn't answer."

"I had to wait until you passed the tests, and you have done so."

"I did? What tests?"

"Your tests of character." Dikaios gave a snorting laugh. "You passed them, and you were not even aware you were being examined."

Elam extended an arm toward the path. "So can you tell me now? How do I find the shield?"

"I will show you, but you must ride. We have a long journey to the shield, too long considering the task that lies ahead after we find it."

Naamah pulled together her borrowed cloak and clutched it tightly against her waist. Leaning her head against Elam's chest, she pleaded, "I beg you to take me with you. I know that my usefulness has already been spent, but I can do manual labour. You have seen me work, Elam. I am not a lazy woman."

Elam hovered his hand over her circlet, wondering if he should comfort her. With her enchanting voice vibrating his skin, it seemed that his own heart vibrated in response. But was this from sympathy, or was it a warning? Could she still be the enemy who wanted to drink the life within? Or did her tears really signify contriteness in her soul?

Heat and wetness from Naamah's tears penetrated Elam's tunic and dampened his skin. He gently caressed her hair and said, "Of course you're not lazy." He looked at Dikaios. "Can you take two?"

255

The horse turned toward the wall. The image of the Earth had reappeared, but this time, the discs lay superimposed on the globe, and twisting webs were shooting toward the altar on the right. He lifted his eyes toward the sky. Dark clouds boiled on the horizon behind them, churning and racing in their direction.

Dikaios bobbed his head. "Very well. The lady may ride behind you." He lowered himself to the ground and looked up to the sky. "Climb on quickly. The storm to end all storms is fast approaching, and it will take all my speed to stay ahead of it."

Ashley pulled one of the pennies from her pocket and clutched it tightly in her hand. Stretching her arms and legs as far as she could reach, she spread her body over Roxil and aimed her eyes at her dragon-sister's chest. "Let's go for it, Walter!" she called. "She's huge, so give it all you've got!"

Walter charged up Excalibur's beam and pointed it at the ground. Energy sizzled across the rocky floor and surged into Ashley once again. She lurched but hung on. White light streamed from every part of her body, radiating into the scales, while two narrow beams shot from her eyes and drilled into Roxil's chest. "More!" Ashley called. "We need more!"

Tightening his grip, Walter threw all his energy into the sword. A new flash of light burst forth and charged into Ashley. She lurched again and cried out with a blood-curdling scream, her limbs locking around her sister.

Walter's hands shook so hard he could barely hang on. His shout vibrated with his tremors. "Should I stop?"

Ashley's body quaked violently as she formed words with her screams. "Not ... until ... her eyes ... open!"

Sapphira dropped to her knees in front of Roxil's face. "I'm watching her eyes! I'll let you know!"

His arms locking in place, Walter continued blasting Excalibur's beam into Ashley. Her body bucked so violently, she had to latch onto Roxil's foreleg and one of her spines to keep from falling off. She bit her lip so hard, blood oozed down to her chin.

"I see her eyes!" Sapphira yelled. "She's awake!"

Walter shut the beam off and hustled to Ashley, resheathing Excalibur as he ran. She lay motionless on the dragon's flank, face down and arms splayed. He laid a hand on her back but withdrew it quickly. "She feels like she's on fire!"

Roxil lifted her head and swung it back to where Ashley lay. "Why is this human lying on me?" Her tail came forward and began pushing Ashley's body down her flank.

"No!" Walter shoved Roxil's tail away. "For your information, that's your sister Ashley, and she just healed you." He cradled Ashley and carried her away from the dragon, ignoring the stinging heat radiating from her body. "We have to cool her down somehow!"

256

Sapphira held out her hand. "The rain's getting heavier, and it's ice cold."

"That should help." Walter laid her gently on the floor. "But will it be enough?"

As she pulled off Ashley's shoes, Sapphira nodded at Gabriel. "Take Walter to the top and see if you can get any news. Karen and I will sponge her down."

Still on his knees at Ashley's side, Walter caressed her hand. "But I can't leave her until I know she's going to be—"

"Go!" Sapphira ordered. She and Karen hurriedly stripped off Ashley's jacket, rocking her body to the side to pull it free. "Roxil will get us out of here when we're ready."

Turning his head, Walter shuffled away, kicking through the debris the fiery cyclone hadn't spun into oblivion.

Gabriel ran up and patted him on the back. "You ready for a ride?"

"Sure." Walter shrugged his shoulders. "Let's see what's going on up there."

Gabriel unstrapped Walter's scabbard, sword and all, and handed it to him. Then, wrapping his arms around Walter's chest from behind, he lifted off.

When Gabriel turned into the breeze, Walter resisted the urge to look back, choosing instead to gaze up into the weeping sky and concentrate on breathing slowly through Gabriel's tight squeeze. Needle-like ice mixed in with the rain, stinging his cheeks. But that was good – the colder, the better. Cold was now a gift from above, something that could undo the terrible damage he might have done.

Walter gnashed his teeth. That stupid dragon wasn't worth saving, not if it meant losing Ashley! Sister or no sister, Roxil was a pest. She seemed callous and cold. He mocked the dragon's words in a high, exaggerated tone. "Why is this human lying on me?"

"Did you say something?" Gabriel asked.

257

"Yeah, but I'd better not repeat it."

Gabriel laughed. "Suit yourself. We're almost there."

A few seconds later, Walter felt his weight press down on his feet again. Wind gusts from Gabriel's wings bounced off the ground and breezed into his face as the pressure around his chest loosened.

Tucking the scabbard under one arm, Walter dug out his cell phone and flipped it open. No signal at all. He drooped his head and walked far enough from the pit to avoid a view of the bottom.

"Don't worry," Gabriel said. "She's thousands of feet down. You wouldn't be able to tell skin from scales from this distance."

Walter shoved the cell phone back into his pocket. "Aren't you worried about your sister?"

"Worried sick." Gabriel clenched Walter's shoulder. "But we have to do what we have to do."

"And what would that be?" Walter turned in a slow circle, eyeing the surrounding trees for any sign of movement. "There's nothing to do around here."

Gabriel zipped his lightweight jacket all the way up and pointed at the grass. "These should give us a clue." He pressed his foot into one of the giants' tracks. "The ground's probably wet for miles, so we should be able to follow their trail, at least for a while."

Walter smirked. "On the ground or in the air?"

"I'm not about to carry you all over the countryside. You take the ground, and I'll patrol from the air. With all the crazy stuff going on, I don't think anyone's going to think twice about a winged teenager flying around."

"Sounds cool." Walter slung the scabbard back on and jerked the strap tight. "Tangling with massive, laser-eyed giants who laugh at Excalibur's beam is a great way to pass the time. That's my kind of party."

Gabriel pumped his fist. "Now you're talking!"

Walter glanced back at the enormous pit but could see only a dozen or so feet of the sheer wall on the opposite side. He turned in the direction the tracks led and pumped his own fist. "Let's get going."

With three wing beats, Gabriel lifted off the ground, and, a few seconds later, he was circling from about a hundred feet overhead. "Can you hear me?" he called.

"Yeah! Loud and clear!" Walter marched alongside the huge tracks, glancing up at Gabriel every few seconds. When the path led into the surrounding forest, he grabbed a thick walking stick. Every several yards, he plunged it into the ground and gouged out a fist-sized ball of earth. "Hansel and Gretel have nothing on me," he mumbled.

The tracks became harder to find, but scattered leaves mixed with mud usually led him in the right direction, and Gabriel frequently swooped closer and pointed out muddy patches farther ahead that gave away the giants' distinctive prints.

With rain and sleet pelting his hair, Walter pulled his jacket tightly closed and began to trot, pausing every twenty steps to gouge the earth again. He hoped the effort would keep him warm, but after three or four miles, he had to slow to a walk. "You have to keep going, you lazy bum," he chided himself while puffing heavy plumes of white vapour. "You can't stop now."

He glanced up and caught sight of Gabriel getting buffeted by the worsening weather. His verbal self-urging felt good, so he continued. "If Gabriel can keep going, I can, too. He's old enough to be my grandfather, and he's doing fine." He slid down a grassy slope, then resumed a quick trot. "I gotta find the creep that's causing all this. I owe it to Ashley to stop him. If she dies, I'll ..." He swallowed a lump in his throat and stayed quiet.

Finally, Gabriel landed in a clearing about fifty feet ahead. He stooped low and examined the path.

Walter hustled to join him. "What did you find?" he asked, trying to slow his breathing.

259

"They split up here." Gabriel waved his finger across the muddied leaves. "It looks like they're all going in different directions now."

"Look for the biggest footprints. That should be Chazaq. If we follow him, maybe he'll lead us to that Mardon guy." Walter pointed his walking stick at one of the trails. "There's the biggest one. You agree?"

Gabriel nodded. "Looks like Bigfoot's heading toward the highway. I saw a road from the air. It's about a mile away."

Walter tapped his walking stick on the print. "If he walked on tarmac, we won't be able to follow him."

"True, but there's a huge power plant down the road at a waterfall. I'll bet I know where he was heading."

Walter grinned, in spite of his gloomy mood. "To find the biggest outlet and plug himself in?"

"That's my guess."

Walter pointed his stick again. "Then let's go."

"I'll stay on the ground for a while," Gabriel said. "I think our path is pretty much set."

Walter leaned into the swirling breeze and followed the prints, Gabriel at his side. Now that he was soaked, the bitter wind chilled him to the bone, so he started jogging again, still pausing to scar the ground with his stick.

Gabriel nodded at the ground. "I've been wondering why you're doing that."

"A trick I learned from Ashley. Always leave a trail."

"Good thinking. It sounds like you and she make a great team."

As he jogged, Walter glanced at Gabriel. His thin jacket was plastered to his chest, and his lips had turned blue. "You must be freezing."

"Yeah," Gabriel replied through chattering teeth. "I'm pretty cold."

"Now would be a good time for a Sahara treatment. Know what that is?"

"Sure do. I saw you get one after Ashley healed you during the flood."

Walter squinted at him. "You were there?"

"Yep. I followed Bonnie around for years. I was sort of like her guardian angel, but I couldn't do much to help her. I guess I was more like a ghost than an angel."

Walter shivered harder than ever. "That creeps me out. I wonder if any ghosts are following me around."

"You never know." Gabriel raised his eyebrows. "I've seen stuff so weird, you'd never believe it."

Walter grinned. "Try me." He quickly shook his head. "Never mind. It's not smart to trade creep-out stories with a guy who has dragon wings."

Gabriel and Walter laughed together as they jogged on and on. After a few minutes, they arrived at the highway. As expected, the tracks disappeared, so they followed the road toward the power plant. Not a single car or truck came in sight as they hustled, making the going easier, but the bitter cold kept biting through their wet layers. Walter continued plunging the stick into the ground just beyond the edge of the road.

A half hour later, the entrance road to the plant came into sight. The remains of a fence gate, bent and torn, leaned against a power company pickup truck. Slowing his pace as he approached the guard's gatehouse, Walter dropped the stick. The upper half of a man's body protruded through the station's broken window, hanging limply with his arms dangling near the ground.

Gabriel ran to him and felt his neck for a pulse. After a few seconds, he looked up at Walter, pain in his eyes. "He's dead. Probably strangled. His throat looks like it's been flattened."

Walter lifted the guard's limp hand and rubbed his thumb across his wedding ring. "I wonder if he had any kids," he said sadly. He put his shoulder under the lanky man's body and gently pushed him back inside the tiny room, careful to avoid the blood and jagged glass. As he seated the corpse on a stool and leaned him against the back wall, he spotted a coat and an umbrella within reach. Grabbing both, he pulled back out and showed them to Gabriel. "Are you thinking what I'm thinking?"

"Dress as guards?" Gabriel asked. "Go into the plant in disguise?"

"That was my first thought, but I've seen too many bad movies where the good guy tried it. The script always made the bad guys too stupid to notice." As he tapped the umbrella on the road, the faint sound of an alarm siren floated across the breeze. "I don't think real life works that way."

"You might as well wear it. At least it'll keep you warm. I'd never be able to fit my wings inside."

As cold rain continued to fall, Walter gazed down the service road leading to another broken gate. "You say the plant's at a dam?"

"At the base of it, yeah."

"It must be hydroelectric." Walter pointed the umbrella at the gate. "If it's like the one Professor Hamilton took our home-school group to see, it'll be pretty much automated – not many people around."

Gabriel nodded. "A perfect choice for an energy-hungry giant who doesn't want media attention."

"Right." Walter stripped off his wet jacket and slid his damp arms into the guard's coat sleeves. The thick lining felt heavenly, and the bottom hem fell close to his knees, providing more warmth.

Gabriel touched the sword protruding from Walter's coat. "I think this might make someone suspicious."

"Yeah, but I might need it. At least the blade works on the giants, even if the beam doesn't."

"Try to hide it, then." Gabriel pulled up Walter's collar. "I'll see if I can create a distraction from above. If Chazaq spots

me, the better it'll be for you." After flapping a spray of droplets
from his wings, he took to the air.

Walter popped open the umbrella and hustled down the serv-
ice road, following the roar of water and the faint alarm horn.
Soon, the main elevator came into view. Two more bodies lay
near its door. As he stared at the wet corpses, his knees weakened.
He drew Excalibur from its scabbard and strangled the hilt.
Somehow he had to stop that murdering fiend, no matter what.

Finding a stairwell, he stepped over a broken door that had
been torn from its hinges – obviously the path the Naphil took,
since he was likely too big to fit into the elevator.

He closed the umbrella and left it near the door, then hustled
down the metal stairs on tiptoes as the path wrapped around the
central elevator shaft. The brick corridor walls blocked out the
cloud-veiled sunlight, while battery-powered emergency lamps
hanging at each landing provided only the barest illumination.
The stairwell grew darker and darker as he descended, giving him
the same doomed feeling he had while climbing down to Hades
with Ashley.

Finally, he reached the bottom level and exited onto a dimly
lit concrete floor at the base of the dam. With the alarm still blar-
ing, he padded toward a bright glow in the distance, sidestepping
to avoid three more dead bodies along the way. A sign near the
top of a mammoth steel door warned of danger ahead in the turbine room, but a gaping hole in the metal proved that Chazaq
hadn't bothered to yield.

As the glow poured through the hole, Walter skulked through,
stooping low and shielding his eyes. With light rain drizzling on
his head, he quickly scanned his surroundings. The ceiling and
roof had been torn away, exposing the workings of the electricity-
producing core of the plant. His scan followed the turbine's massive outer casing up to the generator. Chazaq stood at the very top
where the transformer should have been, his arms extended and

his fingers spread. Although his two thumbs stayed inactive, his ten fingers poured out white streaks of light in every direction, piercing the clouds above. Twin red lasers shot from his eyes and blended in with the electrical array.

Keeping a watch for Gabriel, Walter tiptoed ahead. With all the racket from the waterfall and the alarm, maybe Chazaq wouldn't notice him. He spied a ladder leading toward the generator just below the giant's level. All he had to do was climb it, breach the fence that guarded the top of the turbines, and scale the higher generator access ladder while avoiding all the electrical hazards. Once up there, he could slice through Chazaq's legs and short circuit that demonic dynamo.

"Piece of cake," he whispered to himself.

After throwing off his coat, he slid Excalibur back into its scabbard, hoisted his foot to the first rung, and boosted himself up. It only took a few seconds to get to the top of the turbine, then a few seconds more to climb the fence, but when he grabbed the rung of the final ladder, red beams fell across his body. He froze and looked up at the giant. Chazaq glared at him while keeping his hands pointed skyward.

"Where are you going, little boy?" the giant bellowed.

"I'm touring the power plant," Walter replied, shouting over the din. "I thought I'd come and get a closer look." He scrambled up the rungs and stood less than ten yards from the giant's massive feet. The monster had swelled in size, so much so that Walter's head barely reached past the giant's thigh. As the electrical field pulsed, Walter's hair stood on end, and his skin tingled.

The giant's eyebrows arched. "I see who you are now, the warrior from the lands below. I thought you learned that your sword's beam was useless against us."

"But the blade works fine." Walter pulled Excalibur from its sheath. "Ask your suddenly shorter friend about that."

"If you dare to attack, you would be electrocuted before you could get in range. You are already endangering your life where you stand."

Walter squinted at the giant's brilliant glow. Was he telling the truth? Was it worth risking an attack? What was this power plant takeover all about anyway?

Trying to avoid suspicion, he let his eyes dart quickly to the skies. Gabriel was nowhere in sight. He cleared his throat and yelled up to the giant again. "Tell you what. Let's say for the moment that I believe you – it's too dangerous for me to attack. But it looks like you're too busy to swat me like a fly. Why don't you tell me what you're doing, and I'll be on my way?"

"You are such a fool! It is not because I cannot move that I have spared your life." His glow suddenly brightened, creating an electric shock wave that blasted Walter off the generator and sent him flying. Gabriel swooped down and grabbed him right out of the air. Beating his wings madly, he settled both of them into a soft landing on the turbine room floor.

265

Walter stood on wobbly legs and picked up the guard's coat. "Thanks. That was close."

"Sorry I took so long." Gabriel pushed Walter toward the exit. "Come on. I think I figured out what they're up to."

CHAPTER

HEAVEN'S SHIELD

Angel spun away from Timothy and Abraham. Stiffening her body, she spoke into the air, directing her speech to no one in particular. "The law is clear about this, is it not?"

Abraham glanced at Timothy before focusing on Angel again. "When two companions show affinity, we know the man and woman are to join as one, but I don't know if that union between companions survives your Adam's death. It seems clear that both of you are eligible, but I will have to give it some thought."

With a drop of sweat trickling down his back, Timothy looked at Abraham. "Uh ... Father, I think we are straying from our purpose, aren't we?"

"It depends on which purpose you're referring to." Abraham held out his hand for Angel. "My dear lady, your desire to follow our statutes is laudable, but this man is not yet comfortable with them."

Angel turned toward him, her head drooping slightly and her hands folded at her waist. "I understand. I assumed too much. Perhaps I do not please his eyes."

"No!" Timothy said, lifting a hand. "That's not it! You do please my eyes. I mean ..." He stared at her. What did he mean? She was definitely beautiful, but her straightforward manner seemed so odd. And how could he even consider a marriage arrangement when he wasn't completely sure of his own marital status? He let out a sigh and shook his head. "I don't know what to say."

A soft voice whispered in his mind. *Wait for the light. Then you will understand.*

Timothy winced and stared at Abraham. "Wait for the light? What do you mean?"

"Wait for the light?" Abraham raised a finger. "Ah! Your companion must have spoken to you."

Tilting his head to the side, Timothy rubbed his ear. "I think you're right. This is going to be hard to get used to."

Abraham walked into the shaft of radiance. "I hoped to see if the tunnel would restore your memory, and your companion has confirmed my thinking. Not only that, this gives us the opportunity to defer this rather awkward legal matter to another time." He waved toward the mouth of the tunnel. "Come. There will be pain, but it is the pain of relief, the massaging of inflamed memories."

Timothy leaned toward the light. "That sounds bad enough."

Taking Timothy's wrist, Abraham guided him closer. "It is frightening, to be sure, but you will come out refreshed and renewed, and if you go a second time, there will be no discomfort at all. All of my people have bathed in its cleansing flow; it is a rite of passage of sorts for our young people when they come of age."

Glancing down at the murderer's bones, Timothy edged into the tunnel's beam, his companion hovering near his chin. The light tingled at first, raising an ocean of goose bumps. Then, the tingles seemed to seep into his mind. Every thought, every inkling of brain activity, raised a tiny jolt, like touching a low-voltage fence. Trying to ease the pain, he relaxed his thoughts, and it seemed that the fingers probed deeper, reaching far within and grasping for long-lost memories. One of the fingers pulled back, as if dragging something up to the forefront of his mind.

A memory streamed into his inner vision – alive, vivid – a movie that enveloped his thoughts and swept away all else. Voices accompanied the images, and he felt himself melding into the body of one of the players on the screen.

With the tyres popping against gravel on the sloped mountain road, Timothy raised his voice as he swung the car into the final bend. "Are you sure of the number? I stopped counting after about four thousand years."

"You're such a romantic!" Hannah scooted close and snuggled. "We passed through our covenant veil exactly—" She paused, her brow furrowing deeply. "Something's wrong."

Timothy pressed the brake and slowed to a crawl, looking for any sign of trouble in the trees that lined the road on both sides. "What do you mean?"

"It's so strange." She clutched his arm tightly. "I … I sense danger. I have never felt this way in human form, but it's so strong. I'm sure of it."

He stopped the car. "Then we will trust what you feel." Opening the door quietly and getting out, he whispered, "Let's walk through the woods and come up from the back." His gentle breath raised puffs of white in the cold night air.

She slid out through the driver's side. Leaving the door open, they padded through the sparse forest between the road and their home. When the dark house came into view, they stopped. "No lights," Timothy said, his voice barely a whisper.

"Whose car is that?" Hannah asked.

"Where?"

269

She pointed. "Behind the rear window. Next to the propane tank."

"I see it now. Not a normal place to park, is it?"

"We wouldn't have seen it if we had come in from the front."

As they sneaked around the side, Hannah's grip tightened around Timothy's arm, but she said nothing. Shadows moved about within the house, a profile sweeping past the window, then another. Timothy bent down and removed his shoes. Hannah followed suit.

"Stay here," he whispered.

Her steely eyes gleamed in the moonlight. "Would you leave a warrior behind when going to battle?"

He sighed and gestured with his head. "Come on."

Since the chilly breeze masked their barefooted steps, they hurried to the front door and stooped, one at each side. Timothy sniffed and raised his brow. Gasoline fumes tinged the air. Hannah inhaled, then pinched her nose and nodded.

Rising slowly with his back to the wall, Timothy twisted his body and peeked in the living room window. Two hunched figures stared out, apparently unaware of his presence. He gazed past them, searching for any sign of Ashley. Nothing stirred.

He slid back down and showed her two fingers, then punched them with his fist. She nodded, biting her lip. Next, he kissed his fingers, pressed his hands together, and leaned his head against them, symbolizing his assumption that Ashley was asleep. She nodded again, but this time fear widened her eyes.

Taking a deep breath, he reached for the knob and turned it slowly. Giving Hannah a three count with his fingers, he threw the door open and charged inside. As he rushed for the prowlers, he grabbed an aluminium bat he kept in a corner. With a mighty swing, he lunged toward one of the dark forms, and Hannah leaped for the other, but after a metal-on-metal clang, his bat suddenly felt light as it swept through empty air. Somehow it had been cut off near the handle.

While Hannah scratched and clawed at her victim, a sharp blow to the chin knocked Timothy backwards. He rolled and jumped to his feet, ducking under a swinging object just in time. The moonlight reflected on a metal blade as it swept past. Staying low, he landed a punch that sent the attacking shadow crashing into a table. Breaking glass joined the cacophony of gasps and grunts. When his victim lay motionless on the floor, he grabbed the other prowler's hair and pulled as hard as he could, dragging him away from his wife.

Hannah rose to her knees. Something small lay limp over her fingers. "A doll!" she cried out. "What did you do with my daughter?"

His clothes reeking with the odour of gasoline, Timothy jerked the man to his feet and slapped at a light switch, but the lamps stayed dark. He slammed the man's head against the wall, and as he crumpled to the floor, he grabbed Hannah's hand. Yanking open a bureau drawer, he snatched up a flashlight and flicked it on. They hustled together to a room down the hall where a toddler's crib sat empty near the back window. He threw open the closet door and guided the flashlight's beam inside. Nothing but hanging clothes and three pairs of shoes.

They dashed to an adjacent room and found another empty bed. An open window poured cold air through flapping curtains.

Still holding Hannah's hand, Timothy stomped back toward the living room. "Where is my daughter?" he shouted.

A car engine roared to life. Tyres spun away, shooting gravel that pecked against the back window.

The odour of gas again assaulted his nose. He pointed the beam at the front door. "Run!"

A flash of light blinded him, and a rush of heat flooded his skin, burning torture that ripped through his limbs, torso, and face. A sensation of melting collapsed his legs, and he dropped to his knees. All he could see was his fiery hand clutching Hannah's and her pleading, pain-struck eyes. As flames leaped all around, he pulled her close, and they melded into a single human torch.

Timothy stepped out of the shaft of light and toppled over, gasping for breath as he scratched the ground with both hands. "Hannah!" he wailed. "Oh, my darling Hannah! Why couldn't I stop those murderers?"

Weep, a gentle voice whispered in his mind. *Cry out to your heavenly Father, and he will soothe your soul.*

Timothy sobbed, clutching dirt. He threw it to the side and clutched more handfuls. "I failed you! I couldn't keep you or Ashley safe!"

A hand rested on each of his shoulders, one a strong grasp and the other a light touch.

"He has lost his Eve?" a tender voice asked.

"No doubt Hannah was as dear to his heart as Dragon was to yours."

"Who is Ashley?"

"A daughter, perhaps. ... Yes, that would make sense, if he is here to fulfil the prophecy."

Timothy spread out his palms and pushed away from the ground. The two hands helped him sit upright. Angel stood and, after unzipping her jacket, mopped his brow and cheeks with the tail of her shirt.

He sniffed and cleared his throat. His voice cracked with every word. "I apologize ... for my outburst."

Angel knelt again at his side. "No need for apologies. Your love is a beautiful gift to behold. I know your passion and loss all too well."

"The tunnel of light," Abraham explained, "enflames the passions of your heart. Since you grieve, your laments have become cries that make the angels in Heaven weep. If you feel love, then it becomes so overwhelming, even the shadow people are beautiful in your sight, and those you already loved are the greatest treasures in all Eden."

Timothy nodded. "I know what you mean. My heart hurts so much, I just want to die." He took Angel's hand and pulled her close, then put an arm around Abraham. "But my love for both of you is so strong, I want to stay here forever."

Abraham patted him on the chest. "It seems that our heavenly Father has brought you here to live a new life, perhaps better than the one you had before, much like the children who sojourn here."

Angel nuzzled his arm. "We have each risen from the dead. Though the longing for your Eve may never pass, I will do my best to ease your pain."

Abraham reached over Timothy's shoulder and gently caressed Angel's cheek. "While emotions are running rampant, there is danger in making hasty decisions." He rose and extended a hand to each of them. "Let us finish what we have come to do, and we will discuss your potential union tomorrow."

273

"As you wish, Father." Angel bowed her head and edged away from Timothy, smiling.

"What is left here to do?" Timothy asked.

Abraham tapped a finger on his head. "Do you think that your memories are fully restored?"

"It's hard to know for certain." Timothy laid a hand on his head. "My memories are so many, it might take time to sort them all out and piece them back together."

"If you are the prophetic stranger who weeps, then it appears that you have two daughters, one who is rebellious and one who is lost in some sense, a wanderer."

Timothy angled his head upward. "My memory of my daughter Ashley is clear. If she and her grandfather escaped the slayers, she might still be alive."

Abraham's brow arched. "Slayers, you say?"

"Dragon slayers. They were trying to kill Hannah and me, because we were once dragons."

Angel gasped but quickly stifled it.

Abraham stroked his chin. "Go on, Timothy. This is very interesting. What was your dragon name?"

"Makaidos. My mate's name was Thigocia, before she became Hannah."

"Makaidos and Thigocia?" Angel repeated. "You were named after stars?"

Abraham raised his finger, silencing her. She folded her hands in front of her waist and lowered her head.

"Stars?" Timothy glanced back and forth between Abraham and Angel. "What does she mean?"

"I will explain at another time. Did you have any dragon daughters who might be part of the prophecy?"

274

"My firstborn daughter, Roxil, was rebellious, but she was killed by the same slayers centuries ago. Before I died, I heard that Hartanna, another dragon daughter of mine, was still alive, but she was devoted to me in every way. I also had a son, Gabriel, who has been missing for many years, but I don't see how I could have another living daughter who would be considered rebellious."

"I see," Abraham said slowly. "You were dead, but now you live. Perhaps Roxil has found the grace to live again as well." He leaned close and whispered softly, "And let us remember that Hannah is not exempt from such a miracle."

Timothy nodded. "I understand. As you said, it is unwise to be hasty."

Clapping his hands, Abraham continued. "So, tell us more about your untimely death."

"This might sound crazy, but after I died the first time ..." Timothy paused and smiled, waiting for a response to his odd statement.

"How many times have you died?" Angel asked.

He held up two fingers. "After the first time, Roxil and I built a village called Dragons' Rest, an afterlife haven, of sorts, for slain dragons. I left that place and was restored to Earth as a human. I never learned what happened to her or to Dragons' Rest."

Angel clutched Abraham's sleeve. "Father, would Enoch's Ghost know?"

"Perhaps." Abraham leaned into the shaft of light. "But the tunnel might very well tell us now."

Timothy leaned in with him. "How so?"

"I have ventured inside. The light is so brilliant, even when I close my eyes, it blinds me. I had to stagger out and feel my way to Albatross. I couldn't see for hours. So I came back wearing a thick, dark garment wrapped around my eyes. Even then, the light was blinding, but I came to a wall that felt as smooth as a crystalline face. When I touched it, I heard a quiet female voice that said, 'What do you seek, dear Abraham?'

"I didn't know what to ask, so I just blurted out, 'Who are you?'

"Gentle laughter filled her voice. She said, 'I am an Oracle of Fire. I reside at Heaven's altar.'

"'If you are an oracle,' I said, 'Can you tell me the meaning of Enoch's hymn?'

"'The one he sings at dawn?' she asked.

"Of course, I was thrilled that she knew the hymn. 'Yes! Yes!' I shouted.

"Her gentle laugh filled the tunnel again and echoed all around. 'The meaning is reserved for the two men who will come to fulfil it.'

"I bowed and backed away, longing to look upon her, knowing that her radiant beauty must have been beyond compare. I assumed that gazing upon her would likely burn holes in my eyes forever, but the memory of her glory would be worth the pain."

"But you can see," Timothy said. "What happened?"

Abraham sighed. "As I was taking the garment off, I stumbled and hit my head on the wall. That blow knocked some sense into me, so I bade farewell to the oracle and hurried out."

Timothy pointed at himself. "So you want me to go in there and see if she'll tell me the meaning of the hymn."

"Exactly. The very reason I brought you here."

Timothy unzipped his jacket, raised it above his head and over his companion, and rezipped it. "Will that be enough?"

"You will soon find out."

Timothy felt a hand taking his, and he followed its lead. "I will guide you to the entrance," Abraham said, his voice muffled as it passed through the jacket, "then you will have to feel for the walls. The way is straight, and the path is narrow. You shouldn't find any obstacles."

Another hand rested on his elbow – Angel's now-familiar touch. "I will stay at your side as long as I can and meet you on your way out."

276

Ashley sat up and zipped her jacket. "Thank you," she said, nodding at Sapphira and Karen. She swivelled her head toward Roxil. "And thank you for the dry clothes."

"It was the least I could do." Roxil bowed her head low. "I was most impressed by your sacrificial act, and I apologize for my initial harsh reaction."

Ashley reached for Sapphira. "Maybe my sister will offer us a ride out of here."

"What's that on your hand?" Sapphira pulled Ashley to her feet and turned her palm up. "Look!"

Ashley touched the edge of a wound on her palm, a rough hole with a copper coloured stain encircling it. Blood oozed from the exposed muscle under the punctured skin. "My penny!" she whispered.

Karen caressed the heel of Ashley's hand. "That looks awful! Does it hurt?"

"Yeah. A lot."

"We don't have any antiseptic," Karen said, "but maybe we can make a bandage."

"I don't want a bandage." Ashley dug into her pocket, withdrew the remaining dime and penny, and displayed them in her other palm. "I feel like I'm supposed to keep the wound in the light, but I'm not sure why."

Sapphira rolled Ashley's fingers over the coins. "Jehovah reveals mysteries only at the proper time and in the proper place. For now, we should go to see if Walter and Gabriel need help."

Ashley gazed at the petite hands that clasped her fingers, then let her eyes connect with Sapphira's sparkling blue orbs. Something deep within this amazing woman poured forth – compassionate honesty, uncompromising virtue, steadfast purpose. Nearly as old as the Earth itself, yet somehow brimming with tender youthfulness, she could be trusted without reservation.

277

Ashley sighed. *So what did she mean when she said she saw a dragon inside me?*

"Is something wrong?" Sapphira asked, laying a tender hand on Ashley's brow. "Your mind seems so far away."

"Nothing's wrong." Ashley shook her head and pulled back. "I need to contact Larry and see where the guys are." She tapped her jaw and looked up at the grey sky above the top of the pit. "Larry, can you hear me?"

Only a buzz of static responded.

"Larry?"

Again, only static.

Ashley probed for the tooth transmitter with her tongue. "Either that blast from Excalibur fried my transmitter, or Larry's run out of power."

"Maybe we can get a better signal up top," Karen said.

"Possibly." Ashley scanned the area. "It looks like we're back in the mobility room. Let's get some of the gravity bricks, at least one of each colour besides the one I already picked up. I have an idea."

"There should be a manual override switch on the end of the bricks," Sapphira said. "That will turn on the light."

After finding Ashley's shoulder bag, Sapphira and Karen rummaged through the scattered debris until they located the remaining six types of bricks and piled them in the bag.

Ashley set a hand on Karen's shoulder. "Help me climb on Roxil, please."

Roxil lowered her head to the ground, making her neck a stairway to her back. "I have never flown with human passengers, and our ascent will have to be almost vertical, so be prepared for a rough ride."

Sapphira, carrying the bag of bricks, leaned down and kissed Roxil's cheek. "I trust you completely."

A plume of sparks flew from the dragon's nostrils. "Neither your trust nor your kiss will make me fly any better."

Sapphira smiled, and her voice lilted like a song. "On the contrary, I think they will."

Roxil huffed another stream of sparks. "You humans are such a mystery."

With Ashley holding onto Sapphira's shoulders and Karen supporting Ashley from behind, the three walked up Roxil's neck and seated themselves on her back, Karen at the front and Sapphira at the rear holding the bag in her lap.

As Roxil rose to her haunches, Ashley leaned back toward Sapphira. "Ever flown before?"

"Not on a dragon. I flew pretty high over a snake-infested swamp one time, but I'll have to tell you that story later."

Ashley looped her arms over the spine in front of her and held on tightly. "Then hang on to me. Dragon riding is pretty rough even without a vertical climb."

Roxil beat her wings and lifted off the ground, pointing almost straight up to avoid the mobility room walls. Flying in an upward spiral, she rose faster and faster, as if scaling the old stairway.

Ashley's stomach churned, and Sapphira's tight grip on her abdomen made it worse. If this vertical climb didn't end soon, she would heave her guts for sure.

After almost three minutes, Roxil levelled off and skidded to the grass on the mountaintop.

Karen began to rise, but Ashley pushed down on her shoulders. "No use getting off. We'll have to leave in a minute anyway." She tapped her jaw once again. "Larry, can you hear me now?"

This time a voice seemed to break through the static, but the words were too garbled to understand.

"Larry," she said, raising her voice, "go ahead and boost your signal even if power is low. We have to find Walter. If you've been in touch with him, let us know where to look."

The static reply seemed more garbled than ever.

"Voice transmission takes too much power." She twisted around, reached into the bag in Sapphira's lap, and pulled out her handheld computer. She spoke again into the air as she turned it on. "Don't bother with voice digitization. Just send ASCII characters to my handheld."

She stared at the computer screen. At first, the LCD just stared back at her, but after a few seconds, letters began to appear, slowly at first, then faster.

Ashley read them out loud. "I have not heard from Walter, but since the media reports indicate a power grid failure, I suggest that you find a nearby power plant. Even if Walter has not gone there, perhaps you can learn what is causing the crisis." She scanned the horizon for smokestacks. "Can you tell us where the closest one is?"

More letters lined up across the screen. "I do not have that data stored locally, and my Internet access is down. May I suggest following the power lines to their source?"

Ashley groaned. "They might lead to a transfer station, not a power plant. It could take hours to trace the source."

"How about the tracks?" Karen said, pointing at the ground. "They might not go very far, but at least we'll get started in the right direction."

"True, but then what? We'll be back to searching for power lines."

Roxil swung her head toward her riders. "Your discussion is becoming tedious. Shall we follow the tracks or not?"

Ashley nodded. "Let's go. It's worth a try."

With a gust of wind and a spray of water droplets, Roxil launched into the air again, this time with a more gentle angle. Following the footprints, they soon crossed the line of trees, and the trail was quickly obscured.

Roxil turned on her eyebeams and scanned the leaf-strewn slope. "I see only an odd imprint every once in a while, as if someone has intentionally scarred the ground."

"Follow it, Roxil!" Ashley yelled.

Fanning out her wings, she descended to a lower flight level, staying just above the treetops. "Easily done. The marks are quite consistent."

Ashley clenched her fist. "Good ol' Walter," she said with a sigh. "He remembered."

Roxil huffed a blast of flames. "It is time to fry some giants!"

With Naamah grasping Elam's shoulders, Dikaios galloped along the path, his stride so fast and smooth, they seemed to glide. Only a few bumps and the horse's heavy breathing reminded them that a powerful animal carried them across the Bridgelands. The storm clouds racing behind them lost ground as the amazing creature tore across grassy meadows, leaped over small ponds, and scaled steep hogbacks as if they were tapered hillocks.

As they reached the top of a rocky ridge, Dikaios slowed to a trot, allowing his riders a moment to take in the scene before them. Pristine grasslands stretched out for miles with lush trees surrounding dozens of pools that dotted the verdant canvas, like sparkling sapphires inlaid on green velvet.

Elam whistled. "If this is just Heaven's front porch, I wonder what it looks like inside!"

Naamah gave his shoulder a gentle squeeze and whispered, "This is what Eden must have been like before the fall."

"Words are inadequate to describe the inner beauty," Dikaios said. "I am but a servant of the groom and have been invited inside but once. My single visit was enough to keep the vision of perfection forever imprinted in my mind. My one desire in life is for the promised day to come when I will take my master back to the Earth to do battle against the wicked. After his conquest, I will carry him inside the gate of pearls where the grass is far greener and more delicious, the air is never polluted by the odour of death, and my master shines a light that never sets or is veiled by clouds." Dikaios turned back to Elam, blinking away tears. "Then I will stay with my master forever."

"I can't wait to see it," Elam said, patting the horse's neck. "How much farther to the shield?"

"Do you see the horizon ahead, where the blue touches the grass like a curtain draped across a stage? It stretches from the plunging cliff on the left to the matching cliff on the right."

Elam shaded his eyes with his hand. "I see it."

"The blue backdrop is not sky. That is the door to the altar, Heaven's shield."

"The sky is actually the shield?"

"And the eastern horizon is the passage." Dikaios looked back at the gaining storm clouds. "Let us go. We will be there very soon."

Dikaios began with a trot, then accelerated into a full gallop. As he ran, the sky in the distance seemed to get bigger and bigger, as if it had become a painting that someone carried closer and closer every second. Finally, he stopped at a point where the grass ended at a line of blue, appearing as a cliff that plunged into nothingness.

"We have arrived," Dikaios announced.

Elam leaned toward the barrier. "So, how do we get in? I never found the scarlet key the gatekeeper told me I needed."

"Look at your hand. The key is already in your grasp."

Elam opened his fingers and stared at his palm. "What do you mean? I'm not carrying anything."

"Oh, but you are. You bear the marks of righteousness."

Elam flexed his fingers. His hand ached, still oozing blood from the cuts and scrapes he earned on the bridge. "I think I see what you mean."

Naamah reached forward and showed him her palm. "Mine is bloodstained, but the blood is not my own."

"Nor does the blood on Elam's palm belong to him." Dikaios bobbed his head at the horizon. "Touch the shield, both of you. The righteous may enter immediately, and the contrite may plead for a new heart."

Elam slid off and helped Naamah dismount. He edged close to the blue boundary, reaching out with his hand. As his fingers neared the expanse, he felt a tingling sensation and drew back.

"Go ahead," Dikaios said. "It will not harm you. You have the key."

Elam touched the border and flattened his palm against it. A hand-shaped set of tiny waves rode away from his skin, like ripples on a pond, yet they looked more like wrinkles of light – sparkling, multiple shades of blue. The sensation tickled, sending a warm flow up his arm and into his chest. His heart felt ablaze, a good, soothing heat that emanated into his brain and ignited a surge of emotion – intense, passionate feeling that couldn't be suppressed.

"Dikaios," Elam said loudly, "you are magnificent. You are a worthy servant to your master, and he will be pleased to have you at his side forever."

Dikaios bowed his head but said nothing.

Elam turned to Naamah and smiled. Words poured forth unbidden as the surge of passion continued. "Your harlotries are forgiven, O daughter of the ancient days. Touch the shield of Heaven, sing a psalm to your blessed Saviour, and fear not to shed your cloak, for you will be clothed with righteousness."

Reaching out a petite, trembling hand, Naamah leaned toward the shield. As soon as her fingers touched the blue light, a radiant white halo enveloped her body. Her skin glowed, and her face shone like that of an angel. A glorious smile spread across her face, and she began jumping up and down on her toes, a beautiful song trilling from her lips.

283

The fruit of Eden's ancient tree,
The seeds I plucked so long ago,
To plant and harvest scarlet sins
Are now forgiven, white as snow.

Forgiven! Shout the joyful truth!
This harlot's wanton flesh is slain.
Forever bound unto my Lord,
I cast aside the devil's chains!

Pulling back from the shield, Naamah stripped off the cloak, revealing a dazzling gown – a dress as white as the brightest stars. The flowers in her garland multiplied, the blossoms doubling in size, whiter than ever. She lifted her hands to the sky and twirled in a slow pirouette, but this time no song came out as tears of joy streamed down her cheeks. She just laughed and laughed.

Elam lowered his hand and looked down at his own clothes. He, too, now wore white – a radiant tunic lapping over equally radiant breeches that were tied at the waist by a golden cord. He rubbed one of the tunic's elbow-length sleeves. "It's soft as silk!"

A low, wispy buzz, like a breeze chasing leaves on a path, sounded from the shield. The blue canvas parted in the centre. A light split the two partitions, too bright to gaze upon.

Elam shielded his eyes and looked at Dikaios.

"You may enter," the horse said. "You have been found true and thus dressed according to your character. I will watch from here for the storm and stand ready in case you need me."

Elam bowed. "Thank you, noble horse." He reached for Naamah's hand. "For both of us."

"Yes. Thank you." Naamah curtsied. "I hope to see your master someday, face to face." Rising again, she took Elam's hand, and the two passed through the shining divide.

CHAPTER

A TALE OF TWO DAUGHTERS

Gabriel led Walter into a huge room inside the power plant's office building. Light from a row of windows illuminated several rectangular control panels that stood on the floor, their tops reaching head-high. Lit up with flat-panel monitors and covered with dozens of switches and dials, the place looked like a computer geek's dream come true.

"I saw someone come in here," Gabriel said, "so I followed him."

"An employee?"

"I don't think so. He wore sandals and a calf-length tunic tied with a leather belt."

Walter spotted a broom in one corner. "Head hippie in charge of maintenance?"

"Not likely." Gabriel pointed at a widescreen display. "He looked at this one for quite a while, then he left through the other door. It has to be Mardon."

Walter studied the screen. "Looks like some kind of map. It's got an X–Y grid and lots of points."

"That's what I was thinking." Gabriel moved his finger along the grid. "There are ten bright points from here all the way around to here. I think the eleventh point, the middle one, represents this station, and the ten other stations kind of make a ring around it."

Walter nodded toward the turbine room. "I saw energy beams shooting out from Chazaq's fingers, so that accounts for ten stations, like he's somehow connecting them all together. Think they're making some kind of power grid of their own?"

"I'd bet on it."

Walter pointed at a lever on the wall. "There's an alarm shut off."

"I wonder why Mardon lets it blare like that."

"Probably to keep people away. Who wants to go into a gazillion-megawatt power plant when something's gone wrong?"

"Good point." Gabriel grabbed the lever with both hands and pushed it down. The alarm died away.

Walter massaged one of his ears. "That's better. It was about to drive me—"

A new voice barged in. "Are you gentlemen interested in my project?"

Walter and Gabriel spun around. An oval-faced man wearing a long tunic stood at a waist-high control panel at the centre of the room, his hands behind his back.

"Uh, yeah," Walter said, edging away from the monitor. "I wanted to find out what was causing the blackouts, and when I found dead employees here, I decided to look around. Stumbling over dead bodies is kind of unusual, you know."

"So you came here with a winged friend." The man pushed his hand through his short white hair and walked toward them, arching his thin eyebrows. "That is also unusual, I think."

"Yeah." Walter laughed nervously. "Weird, isn't it?" He pulled out Excalibur and held it in front of his body. "And this is a really weird sword. It disintegrates anyone I touch with it."

The man halted. His eyes widened briefly, but his voice stayed calm. "Where did you get my father's sword?"

"Your father's?" Walter squinted at him. "This is Excalibur, King Arthur's sword."

"On the contrary, that is Chereb, the sword of Eden. Arthur obtained it from Morgan Le Faye, who took it from King Nimrod, my father. Since my father is dead and I am his heir, the sword rightfully belongs to me."

Walter tightened his grip. "Well, unless it has your name on it or you have your father's last will and testament to prove it, I think I'll hang on to it for a while."

"So, you're Mardon," Gabriel said. "You're the master of the Nephilim."

"You two are certainly knowledgeable for random curiosity seekers." Mardon leaned toward him and narrowed his eyes. "I take it that you're one of the anthrozils. I heard about their existence, but you are the first I have seen. Who are your parents?"

Gabriel crossed his arms over his chest. "I think I'll keep that to myself, if you don't mind."

"Oh, I don't mind," Mardon said, waving his hand. "It was just small talk, really. I was hoping to pass the time while I wait for my tower to be completed."

"Your tower?" Walter asked. "What tower?"

Mardon folded his hands behind his back again and began a slow pace in front of Walter and Gabriel. "To quote your winged friend, I think I'll keep that to myself. Tooting my own horn about my accomplishments would be entertaining, to be sure, but letting you know what my plans are would be foolhardy. Although it is not the two of you I fear, I see no reason for me to crow about what my giants are doing."

"No fear, huh?" Walter waved the sword from side to side. "Have you ever seen Excalibur operate?"

"Long before you were born, young man." Mardon backed away several steps and withdrew a dagger from underneath his tunic. "If you try to attack me with the blade from Excalibur, as you call it, I will merely run and hide in one of the many hallways in this edifice, which will put you at great risk should you seek me in dark places where I can ambush you."

He nodded toward the computer displays. "If you smash my equipment, the destruction will only serve to ruin data output. It will do nothing to the actual power infrastructure my giants are creating. If you were to use the beam, which might not even work in this current hybrid dimension, you would learn that you are at the centre of a vortex created by intense electromagnetic waves. The beam would be instantly absorbed by my friend up there atop the generator. You would merely be adding to my energy grid." He put his dagger away and waved his hand at Walter. "Try it, if you wish. I will wait."

Walter squeezed Excalibur's hilt and summoned the beam, but the blade merely reflected the light from the windows. "Nothing's happening," Walter said, lowering the sword. "It looks like I'll have to stop Chazaq the old-fashioned way."

"Chazaq?" Mardon glanced out the window. "Oh, that's not Chazaq. But I suppose they all look alike to you, don't they? My little power grid is fairly local, not enough to collapse the national grid, so Chazaq travelled to a larger facility, and, in concert with a few of Morgan's surviving accomplices in other cities, he made sure power would fail throughout the country. You see, widespread panic keeps the authorities too busy to find my tower, and he is the only one intelligent enough for that mission."

"Well, it was an enlightening experience talking to you," Gabriel said with a slight bow, "but we really have to go."

"I understand. You have to warn your friends and bring them here to try to stop me." Mardon wiggled his fingers at them. "Run along, then."

Walter shot a sideways glance at Gabriel. "That was too easy."

"Yeah. Something's not right."

"Gentlemen," Mardon said, "I have no power to keep you here. You have a sword, and my giant is occupied for a while. If you wish to wait for Chazaq's return, by all means, do so. Then, I will be able to dispose of you at will."

"No, thanks." Gabriel laid a hand on Walter's back, and the two hustled to the turbine room, then up the elevator to the service road entrance, staying quiet while the roar of river water drowned out every other sound.

When they arrived at the guard station, Walter looked in on the dead guard, still propped against the wall. He eyed a radio hanging loosely on the man's belt. Reaching into the broken window, he pushed the call button. "Can anyone hear me?"

He released the button and waited. Nothing. Not even static. Sighing, he backed away from the window. "We're getting nowhere fast."

Gabriel fanned out his wings and leaned against the guardhouse. "Well, we got some information out of Mardon. We know he's creating some kind of tower from the electromagnetic vortex, Chazaq's doing something sinister to keep the rest of the country in chaos, and someone or something has the power to stop Mardon's plans."

"Because he said we weren't the ones he feared, meaning that he probably feared someone else."

Gabriel pointed at Walter. "Bingo!"

Walter turned to the highway and scanned the wet, vacant road. "There's only one person I know who's smart enough to figure it all out."

Gabriel nodded. "Sapphira."

"Ashley," Walter said at exactly the same time.

Timothy felt Angel's gentle tug on his elbow pulling him into the brilliant light. Even within his shielding jacket, it seemed to be as bright as day. As he ventured farther in, his companion brushed against his ear. *Always follow the light,* it whispered directly into his mind. *Darkness is the way of death and the shelter of those who fear the light.*

Timothy didn't really know how to speak to the companion, so he tried directing a thought toward it. *Am I giving in to darkness by covering my head?*

Indeed not. A time will come when you will see all glories unveiled. For now, you must behold heavenly glory with shielded eyes.

The hand lifted from his elbow and guided his fingers to the side wall. "I have to go back a little ways," Angel said. "I will wait for you there."

He imagined her walking away, her head bowed and her airy pantaloons swaying as she escaped the blinding blast. The light was still working its magic. His love for her – a pure, holy love – overflowed, bringing tears to his eyes.

The light blazed brighter and brighter. Even with his eyes clenched shut, they tingled and burned. He turned around and walked backwards, dragging his fingertips along the wall. Even then, the light overwhelmed his senses. How could he go on? It would only get worse.

As he continued to back into the tunnel, the overwhelming sense of love seemed to transform. Love was still abundant, but something else was added – a presence of grandeur, a bigness that towered over him ... no, that enveloped him, embracing arms so huge their owner had to be ten times the size of the Nephilim of old. What was it? Pure otherness? A being incomparable? Now barely able to move, Timothy pulled off his shoes and socks and laid them on the ground. This was the answer to the mystery. This path to Heaven was surely holy ground.

Finally, he bumped into something, a flexible wall of some kind that gave a little, then pushed back. He halted and felt the barrier, smooth and tactile, like a rubber membrane.

Gritting his teeth, he turned to face it and called out, "Is the Oracle of Fire here?"

"I am here," a female voice replied. The voice seemed light and happy, like a songbird in springtime.

"I have come at the bidding of Abraham to ask about Enoch's hymn, the prophecy concerning this land."

"You have done well to come. I have been waiting for you."

Timothy pointed at himself. "Does that mean I am the man in the prophecy?"

"You are," came the gentle reply.

"What must I do?"

"Gaze into the oracle. I will reveal the truths you will need in order to bring about what God has planned for this world."

Timothy grimaced. How could he possibly remove the shield and open his eyes? The light would burn the eyeballs right out of their sockets!

His companion nestled closer to his ear. *You have come this far. Will you turn back now? Will you return to Abraham and Angel without an answer?*

He shook his head. *You're right. I'd feel like a fool for the rest of my life.* Slowly unzipping his jacket, he slid it down to his shoulders. Fresh, sweet-smelling air wafted across his skin. Then, bracing himself, he opened his eyes.

Instead of scorching pain, the glorious light bathed his eyes with comfort. The wall ahead of him looked like pure crystal, a flexible diamond that undulated as though a breeze played across its surface. Just beyond it, a girl stood in a hooded cloak of royal blue, opened at the front to reveal a brilliant white gown. She lowered her hood, allowing her long snowy hair to flow in the heavenly wind.

Timothy's jaw slackened. Those eyes! Such sparkling blue eyes! The most perfect pair of sapphires in the entire world, gleaming in the radiance of her abode, appearing to laugh as she smiled.

291

"You seem surprised, Timothy Autarkeia."

"I ... uh ..." He forced his jaw closed and licked his lips. "I am surprised. I did not expect to see an angel, especially one who knows my name."

"And your former name, Makaidos, king of the dragons. Our heavenly father knows all your names, and he loves you whether you are in dragon or human form."

The wind that played on her hair pushed toward him, kissing his cheeks and warming his body from head to toe. Heat rushed into his ears. Tears flooded his eyes. Swallowing hard, he tried to speak, but his breath seemed sucked away. "I'm ... not worthy. I'm only ..." He couldn't go on. He just dropped to his knees and wept. As his body heaved, his companion caressed his cheek, whispering, *God is love ... God is love.*

After a moment or two, he gazed at the lovely girl again. Staying on his knees and taking in a deep draught of the gentle wind, his throat loosened and strength flowed through every muscle. "I have been anointed by your holy breath, and the touch has invigorated me."

"It is not my breath," she said. "It is God's breath, his empowering inspiration. Our father has endowed you with the ability to carry out a task that would otherwise be impossible. He finds pleasure in using mortal vessels to bring about eternal purposes."

Timothy wrung his hands together, trembling. "What must I do now?"

"The prophecy mentions two hearts – your two daughters." She spread her arm toward a scene behind her. "Gaze upon them now and restore your memory."

The wind stiffened, ruffling his hair and warping the crystal barrier. Thinning out like a diffusing mist, the lovely oracle faded away. Grey skies replaced the darker backdrop, framing the head and neck of a tawny dragon in mid-flight.

"I see only an odd imprint every once in a while," the dragon said, "as if someone has intentionally scarred the ground."

A voice called out from somewhere unseen. "Follow it, Roxil!" Timothy snatched a gulp of air. "Roxil!"

The dragon extended its wings and flew just above the treetops. "Easily done. The marks are quite consistent."

Timothy's heart pounded. "My daughter," he said, now louder than a whisper.

Flames shot toward Timothy, splashing against the inside of the barrier. The edges of the scene caught on fire and burned toward the middle, revealing another scene behind it, a close-up of a pale and haggard young lady. A strong breeze whipped her hair, and she held on to a red-headed girl seated in front of her.

As before, a voice called from offscreen. "Ashley! I see them! I see Walter and Gabriel!"

Once again, Timothy's heart raced. "Ashley?" Tears formed as his voice crumbled. "Is that my little girl?"

Ashley looked straight into the screen, as if staring right at Timothy. Pale and weak, she nodded. "Thank God!"

293

Again, a fireball splashed against the screen, setting it ablaze. As it burned away, the cloaked oracle filled the undulating curtain.

"My daughters!" Timothy cried, his entire body quaking. "Are they really alive? Where are those places I saw?"

Her smile seemed to massage away his tremors. "Roxil and Ashley are living, though the lives of both hang by a thread. Ashley will give her life energy to the fallen until she breathes her last breath. Roxil lives on the Earth now only because the tomb of the dead has merged with the land of the living. Unknowingly, she and Ashley do battle against the evil force that has merged the two worlds, and if they succeed, Roxil will once again plunge into that nether land."

His throat cramped, pitching his voice higher. "So, if my two daughters do what they are called to do, they will perish."

"Yes, if not for the costliest solution of all." The oracle tilted her head upward and began to sing, her voice more beautiful than ever.

In desperation's hope he calls,
"A soul to trade, a soul to sell,"
For better one to suffer flames,
Than daughters loved to burn in Hell.

She looked at him again, her eyes blazing blue. "A sacrificial lamb could provide the soul to trade, but only if it comes willingly. The lamb has no obligation to make this trade, so you cannot use any coercion." She took a step closer to the crystal curtain, magnifying her lovely face. "Do you understand?"

"I think so," he said, his voice still cracking. He cleared his throat and lifted his head. "What must I do?"

"Your task is simple in concept, yet tragically difficult to carry out. The lamb has already been prepared, pure and innocent. Once you bring this sacrifice, you will complete your journey and prepare this world for yet another journey to come."

He tilted his head to the side. "Another journey?"

"The coming of the warrior chief. You see, a tare has been planted among the wheat, a deceiver who will attempt to bring about Eden's fall. If the corrupter succeeds, then corruption will spread like cancer and destroy this world as well as the one your daughters live in. But that journey is far beyond your horizon."

"This lamb I'm supposed to find – how is the sacrifice to be made? I can't bear the thought of killing someone pure and innocent. That seems impossible."

The oracle pointed at the tunnel's floor. "Just bring the lamb here, and that is where my counsel ends. You have many decisions to make, and wisdom comes from seeking the light as you take each step in your journey. Otherwise, you would never arrive at your ultimate goal. You will learn, however, that although our heavenly father's ultimate purpose is more firm than the foundations of the Earth, his plans on how to accomplish them can change according to the actions of those who serve him." The oracle backed away from the barrier, and the light began to fade. "Go now. When you have completed your task, come back to this place and receive the blessing you seek, the blessing of spiritual deliverance for your daughters."

As the glow continued to diminish, her voice dwindled to a faint whisper. "Remember, this journey is your choice, not a command."

The light blinked out, leaving Timothy in darkness. Still on his knees, he groped for the floor, his eyes emblazoned with the radiant images – the oracle, Roxil, Ashley – all flashing in a photo-negative collage.

Crawling back toward the entrance, he found his shoes and socks and picked them up. While rising to his feet, he lurched sideways and had to brace himself against the wall to keep from falling. A hand touched his, then a quiet voice whispered, "I am here, Timothy. Let me lead you."

Angel looped her arm around his and guided him to the outside. Now in the light, he could see Abraham and the surrounding trees, though they were blurry and superimposed on the image of the white-robed girl.

295

"Sit," Angel said, "and I will help you with your shoes."

A pair of stronger hands guided him to the ground. As he leaned back on the stony cliff, small, delicate fingers massaged his cold feet, then pushed socks over his toes and stretched them up to his calves. "I sense a change in you," she said, her voice sympathetic and warm. "Even your face glows. The light of the oracle has pierced your soul and enflamed a new passion."

Timothy blinked rapidly, trying to clear his vision. "It has, but I am unsure whom I should tell."

"Tell no one," Abraham said, "at least for now. Let wisdom guide you, and listen to your companion."

After slipping on his shoes, Angel fumbled with the strings. "I have not fastened shoes like these before. Shall I just tie a knot?"

Timothy reached for them. "Thank you. I'll do it."

With the help of four hands, he got up and brushed off his clothes. He looked around at the tunnel's threshold, his eyes still adjusting. Bones of shadow people littered the ground in various shades of grey. The newest victim's remains, still bright white, lay near Timothy's feet.

He sidestepped the debris and hobbled toward the sound of the river. "Are we finished here, Abraham?"

"We are."

Abraham was now walking at his side, and he assumed Angel followed as they exited the woods and came in sight of the dragons. "Good. I need to rest and think for a while. It's been a very long day."

"Indeed." Abraham guided him to Albatross. "You may have my bed tonight, and we will talk in the morning."

Timothy glanced at Angel. She shuffled toward Grackle, her head hanging low. "Abraham," he said, "will I see Angel again tomorrow?"

Angel turned toward them, a smile brightening her face.

"Is that your wish?" Abraham asked.

"I would like to speak to Candle and Listener, if I may."

"Ah!" Abraham stroked his short beard. "You wish to learn through the eyes of our young ones."

"That's true enough, but it's also a good excuse to get their wise mother at my side."

Angel averted her eyes, grinning. She scrambled up Grackle's neck and let out a series of whistles. "Let us fly!" she called, beaming as she looked back at Timothy. "Dawn will bring us a day of joy!" The purple dragon reared and took off into the moonlit sky.

CHAPTER

THE NEW TOWER

Ashley groaned and held on tightly to Karen. Compared to riding Thigocia, flying aboard Roxil was like careening around the hairpin turns on a malfunctioning roller coaster. The younger dragon's inexperience promised a meal-losing adventure. With every gust of wind, she corrected her angle without regard for her passengers, giving them hair-raising dips and swings through the misty skies. The three riders could barely speak during their ordeal, choosing instead to pray for calmer winds and settled stomachs.

After a half hour of low swoops to check for Walter's marks and quick upswings to search on a wider plane, Sapphira pointed at the road far in the distance. "Ashley! I see them! I see Walter and Gabriel!"

Ashley glanced at the two young men. Even though they looked tiny from so far away, the sight brought a surge of joy. "Thank God!"

Karen spoke through two fingers pressed over her lips. "Thank God is right!"

"I'll let them know we're coming!" Roxil spewed a blast of fire and zoomed to the ground, pulling up sharply to land between Walter and Gabriel. Not bothering to wait for Roxil to make a neck stairway, Karen slid down the dragon's side, deftly avoiding her wing. She staggered toward the guardhouse and leaned against the wall, her fingers still pressed against her lips. Suddenly, her eyes bulged, and she jumped back, pointing at the broken window, "Who's that man? He looks dead!"

"He *is* dead." Walter reached up to help Sapphira and Ashley as they negotiated Roxil's sloping neck. "He's a power company guard, and I'm wearing his coat. I think a Naphil strangled him."

"Is the Naphil here?" Sapphira asked. "Is it Chazaq?"

Walter took the shoulder bag from Sapphira and pointed past a mangled fence. "The Naphil's in there. It's not Chazaq, but you'll never guess who else we saw."

Sapphira's eyes brightened. "Mardon?"

"Well ... yeah. I guess it wasn't so hard to figure out."

Walter and Gabriel took turns as they told the story of what they saw inside the power plant. Gabriel provided a glowing account of Walter's bravery as he climbed up to the generator and tried to play the role of lumberjack, but Walter elbowed Gabriel's ribs and said he was exaggerating. When Walter concluded with a description of Mardon's power grid and his mention of the tower, Sapphira turned pale.

"What's wrong?" Gabriel asked.

"He's really doing it." Sapphira cupped her hands as if moulding clay and formed a miniature tower of fire between her palms. "He's building a tower to Heaven just like his father tried to do."

"But it didn't work." Ashley gazed at Sapphira's tower. Her eyes followed the fiery spin. "How could anyone believe in building any kind of structure that could reach Heaven? It's impossible."

"But since that time," Sapphira countered, "Mardon has learned about inter-dimensional travel. He knows that an energy vortex can break through the barriers. Maybe he thinks this power grid will create a cross-dimensional tower that can actually reach to Heaven."

Gabriel twirled his finger. "But doesn't it have to spin?"

"True," Sapphira said. "I'm not sure how he's planning to do that."

Ashley leaned against Walter and stroked her chin. "Since these giants have already been, in essence, magnetized in an anti-gravity environment, given enough electromotive force, he could use them as a giant magneto, but he already has all the current he needs, so he could also be making an enormous electromagnet."

"What good would that do him?" Walter asked.

"I couldn't explain it unless you're familiar with quantum mechanics and gravity theory." Ashley straightened and moved her hands in a wide circle as if she were rubbing a huge ball. "He could be creating a massive gravitational black hole that wouldn't just break through the dimensional barrier; it would eliminate it and draw the two dimensions into one." She finished with a clap of her hands.

299

"That explains a lot," Sapphira said. "If Roxil, Gabriel, and Mardon all have their bodies back, the same bodies they had while in Hades …"

"More than a lot." Ashley pointed at Sapphira. "It explains everything! The giants have already combined Hades and our world! The first step was to bring Mardon back, and that worked, so now …" She tilted her head upward. "Heaven's next."

Walter pulled out his sword. "So that's why Excalibur doesn't work. Billy told me it gave him trouble while he was in Hades. I'd try again with the blade, but after you stick a screwdriver into an electrical outlet and fry your fingers, it's pretty stupid to stick it right back in."

"Dragons have knocked the tower down before," Sapphira said, "maybe they can do it again."

"I was there." Roxil shuffled closer. "We did it with a firestorm."

Sapphira let a brief plume of flames rise from her palm and spun it around. "Could you do it again? Could you make another firestorm?"

"By myself?" Roxil shook her head. "I could torch a giant if he lets me get close enough, but I could never duplicate what we did at Shinar. We had more than a dozen dragons there."

"But would it work?" Walter asked. "Do we want to risk stirring the pot?"

"Good thinking." Ashley tapped her finger on her chin. "It might create just the vortex Mardon needs, but I can't know for sure unless I have data. I need to know the electrical output at every site and the distances between them."

Walter nodded toward the power plant. "I think the panel displays in the control room show all that."

300

"Okay," she said, looking down the service road, "lead me to it."

He pulled the handheld computer from the bag and showed it to her. "Would this help?"

"I won't have time to program it to do the necessary transforms." She took a deep breath and let it out slowly. "I really need Larry, but I'm not sure I can get hold of him, so I might have to do all the calculations in my head."

"What shall I do?" Roxil asked. "I will likely not be able to follow you."

Walter put the computer back in the bag. "Give us five minutes, and we'll be inside. Then fly over the dam and start closing in on the giant. If he sees you and doesn't do anything about your approach, that might mean he actually wants you to shoot fire and create the vortex."

"I see," Roxil said. "Bait the Naphil and hope for a revealing of his purpose."

Walter opened the front of his coat and tightened his scabbard belt. "If he does fight, I'll try to give you ground support, maybe distract him somehow."

"I hope I have not lost my reflexes," Roxil said as she unfurled her wings. "It has been many centuries since I last went to battle." She lifted up on her haunches and, beating her leathery canopy against the moist breeze, rose into the air.

Walter and Gabriel led the way to the power plant, while Ashley walked between Sapphira and Karen, still weak and dizzy. She refrained from talking, trying to recall her studies on quantum physics and the set of formulae she used for the electromagnets she built for the transluminators in the underground lab.

She shuffled her feet, kicking pebbles along the way. Could she do it? The calculations were so intensive, she had relied on computers to sort it out, though she did have to write the programs in the first place. Obviously she had the knowledge, but was that all she needed? Could her intelligence be the second widow's mite, the latter of the two gifts she should blend with faith and offer to God? She pulled the other penny from her pocket and held it tightly in her hand, her uninjured hand. There was only one way to find out.

Walter led them down to the spillway level and through a wide corridor. "If we go in there," he said, pointing at the hole the giant had ripped in the wall, "we'll find Mister Ugly in the turbine room perched on top of the generator, but this hall to the right should keep him from seeing us."

They walked down a dim corridor and entered a large office where flashing monitors greeted their eyes. Walter pointed at a display on one of the head-high rectangular boxes. "That's the power grid readout." He turned and touched the shorter desk-like control panel that faced the monitors. "I think Mardon used these gizmos to control it."

Ashley gazed at the panel, then, alternately looking at the controls and the display, began making slight adjustments to the dials.

"I can change the categories of data and the scales," she said, "but I don't see anything that actually controls the power."

"Yeah," Walter said, "that's what Mardon told us."

"But the different screens could give me all the data I need to figure out what's going on." Ashley nodded at the bag on Walter's shoulder. "Could you dig out the bricks and the photometer? I want to see what kind of energy they produce. Mardon's older technology might give me clues about his new stuff."

"Sure thing." He placed the seven bricks at Ashley's feet and set the photometer on the control desk. "Anything else?"

"Sapphira," Ashley said, "can you set them in a line and turn them on when I need them?"

"Glad to." Sapphira picked one up and depressed a button on its side. The brick let out a low hum, and a diode on one end emitted a thin blue light.

Ashley read the beam with her photometer. "Hmmm. Visible seems normal, but there are other frequencies to check." She did the same for the second brick and memorized its photometer readout.

"Want me to find a pencil and paper?" Gabriel asked.

Ashley raised a finger to her lips. "Shhh! I have to do it all in my head."

Walter leaned close to Gabriel and whispered. "You stay with Ashley. I'm going to peek outside and see if Roxil's out there yet. It's been almost five minutes."

"Sounds cool. Sapphira and I can handle Mardon if he shows up."

Karen grabbed Walter's arm. "Can I come with you?"

Walter glanced over his back at Excalibur's hilt. "Give me a minute to make sure the coast is clear."

When he left the room, Sapphira picked up the next brick in line and pressed its power switch. "This one's ready."

"Thanks." Ashley managed a weak smile. "Can you hold them up while I analyse the beams? I'm feeling kind of puny right now."

Ashley read the data, then looked up at the ceiling. "Okay, the gamma readout makes sense, but when I plug it into the formula ..." She grabbed a fistful of hair with her wounded hand and pulled it hard. "There's a constant missing in the formula. What is it?"

Sapphira held the brick with the red diode close to the photometer. "You can't do this alone, Ashley."

She released her hair, leaving a bloody smear. "I couldn't reach Larry. I already tried."

"I don't mean Larry." Sapphira's eyes once again blazed. "I think you know exactly what I mean."

Ashley looked up at her and stared. "If you mean have faith, that's what I'm trying to do."

"I know you're trying." Sapphira laid a hand on Ashley's cheek. A ripple of fire rode along Sapphira's forearm and crept into her hand. "You have been trying all your life."

303

Ashley closed her eyes. Heavenly warmth radiated into her cheek and flowed throughout her body, loosening her muscles and draining her tension.

"Relax, Ashley, and let Jehovah work through you. Faith asks that you let his power flow, not your anxiety, not your fears, and not your sweat. His power."

Ashley took a deep breath and opened her eyes. "Thank you. I think I understand."

"Psst!" Gabriel waved at Sapphira. "We have company!"

Ashley and Sapphira swung around. A man wearing an old tunic walked into the control room, his hands behind him. "Well, well," he said, smiling, "this is a surprise indeed!" He bowed toward Sapphira. "I never thought I'd see you again, Mara, but I must say, I am truly delighted. Your extremely long life is a grand tribute to our success in genetic technology." He drew near and extended his hand toward her head. "If I may, I would like to see if—"

Sapphira swatted his hand away. "You may not see anything, Mardon."

Gabriel stepped in front of Sapphira and pushed Mardon away.

Mardon's sandals slipped on the tiled floor, but he back-pedalled quickly and regained his balance. As he bent over to adjust his sandal, he laughed nervously. "The winged boy is chivalrous, Mara, but I only meant to check your scalp for deterioration. Our quest for knowledge is never over."

Sapphira's voice sharpened. "I am Sapphira Adi, a daughter of Jehovah. I am not your science experiment anymore."

Mardon held up his hands. "Very well. I meant no harm. But if you are a daughter of Jehovah, as you call him, you should welcome my pursuits. We will see your father face to face very soon."

"We figured out what you're up to," Sapphira said, "and it's crazy. Do you think Jehovah can't stop you?"

"Stop me?" Mardon chuckled. "God has long wanted fellowship with man, but my father and I failed to bring God and man together in Shinar because we insulted him by assuming that a physical tower could reach to his glory. Now that I have identified the dimensional barrier separating us, I am eliminating it. Far from stopping me, this is exactly what he wants."

Ashley read the photometer as she scanned the final brick. "If God wanted that to happen, he would have broken down the barrier himself."

"Nonsense," Mardon replied. "Elohim uses men to carry out his work. He called a man, Jesus, to break down the spiritual barrier, and now he has called another man, me, to break down the final, physical barrier." He peered at Ashley's work. "What are you doing with my bricks?"

She scowled at him and shoved the brick to the side. "A science experiment."

"The bricks are worthless now," Mardon said, wagging his finger at them. "They have no power over the Nephilim."

Ashley waved the photometer at him. "They told me what you're up to. All that radiation and magnetism over the years turned your giants into power generators. They are capable of making a gravity void that can rip the dimensional boundary."

"Quite right, and due to my genetic engineering, they are immune to the electrical charges as well as weapons like Excalibur. When the grid is fully maximized, Heaven and Earth will be joined in one dimension, and I will ascend my new stairway to God's kingdom."

Sapphira stalked toward him. Flames mixed in with her snowy hair, making her look like a walking torch. "And you'll get struck dead for your arrogance." She pressed her finger into his chest. "Then God will flick you back to Hades with his fingertip. Everything you've done will be destroyed."

305

Ashley pointed the photometer at Sapphira and shifted the dial through the different wavelengths, mentally noting every readout. The numbers looked familiar, very familiar. Shuffling the new data through her mind, she combined them with the readings from the bricks, crunching numbers madly until it felt like her brain was about to explode. Suddenly, everything clicked – the bricks, Sapphira's flames, Mardon's numerical code in the scroll – it all made sense.

"Death no longer has any power," Mardon said. "I have already united Hades and Earth. The dead are now alive again and spreading across the globe." Mardon pushed her away with a condescending tsk, tsk. "How little you understand. The first covenant was one of laws, which people could not obey because of their blindness. They could not see Elohim, so they had no concept of the Lawgiver. Jesus brought the second covenant, one that opened the spiritual eyes of those who believed. But even Jesus said that few people can find it. The path he provided is invisible, and billions are lost because they cannot clearly see the way."

While Mardon railed on, Ashley noticed Karen edging toward the door.

"My tower, on the other hand, creates a new path, a third covenant, allowing people to see Elohim with their own eyes. Now the entire world will know and understand when they behold his majesty. Surely the salvation I bring will gladden Elohim's heart as we inaugurate a covenant of full revelation. He will usher me to his side as he did Jesus, the author of the second covenant."

"You're mad!" Sapphira shouted. "God wants people to seek him by faith, and you're shredding the only veil that makes faith possible!"

"It's worse than madness," Ashley said, glancing at Karen as she cracked the door open. "If the gravity vacuum causes a lunar shift or even a change in Earth's orbit around the sun, millions or even billions of lives could be lost."

Mardon shook his head. "I have already proven the opposite. When I brought Hades and Earth together, far from killing billions, I brought people back to the world of the living."

"How did you do that?" Sapphira asked. "You had no tower."

He pointed at Sapphira. "I used you. Every time you crossed between Earth and Hades, you created a small void between the dimensions. Left alone, it would have dissipated, but I created a permanent link, an inter-dimensional rope that pulled the living and the dead closer together every time a void appeared."

Sapphira raised a hand to her cheek. "I caused the problem?"

"Unwittingly, of course, but, indeed, the merging of two dimensions was fuelled by your actions."

Throwing the door open, Karen ran outside. Her cries for Walter died away as the door closed again.

Mardon stalked toward the exit. "I believe I will check on my giant. Chazaq will be here soon to join him for the final step."

"I'd better follow him," Gabriel said, flapping his wings as he scooted across the floor.

When Ashley and Sapphira were alone, Ashley opened her hands and showed her palms to Sapphira. Each had a deep, bloody wound the size of her pennies, both with copper-coloured smears encircling them.

"What does it mean?" Sapphira asked.

Ashley's lips trembled. "It means I gave up my intelligence."

"You did what?"

"I figured out how we might be able to stop Mardon." Ashley shook her head slowly. "But my brain choked so hard, it doesn't work anymore, like my intelligence drained away."

Sapphira took Ashley's hands and clasped them inside her own. "You're just exhausted. After healing Roxil and making all those calculations, you really *are* drained." She caressed the gemstone in Ashley's ring with her thumb. The gem's colour had paled to a pearly white rather than its normal deep red.

307

"Ashley," Sapphira said shakily as she released her hands. "Look at your rubellite."

Ashley gave her a weak smile. "I know. I kind of thought that might happen." She displayed her palms again. "I gave my widow's mites to God, and my dragon powers are gone."

Karen spotted Walter in a huge open area and dashed toward him. "Mardon spilled his guts!" she called. "We know what's going on now!"

"If you can tell me in about five seconds, do it." He pulled out Excalibur and pointed it at the drizzling sky. "Roxil's coming, and I might have to help her."

Karen spoke rapid-fire. "He's making a gravity vacuum that'll destroy the barrier between Earth and Heaven so he can become some kind of messiah. Ashley says if we don't stop him, he might kill billions."

Walter glanced at the door to the control room. "Here comes Dr Delusional now." He took Karen's hand and hid behind a concrete pillar. "Stay here. So far Roxil's just been stalking from the clouds. I saw her peeking out to check on the giant, but she hasn't had a chance to see if he's going to take the bait."

Mardon scuttled back toward the wall the giant had punctured to get into the turbine room. He stood in the opening, glancing between the turbine and the exit, apparently waiting for someone.

Karen brushed her dampening hair back from her eyes. "Maybe Roxil's more scared than she was letting on. Remember she was worried about facing the giant alone."

"You're right. I'll go ahead and try to distract Mr Ugly, and maybe she'll be able to get closer."

"What are you going to do?"

"Work on his ego. I'm betting that he can't resist a challenge." He waved toward the control room door. "Look. It's Gabriel. He'll watch over you."

"Wait! I heard Mardon say that those magnetic bricks made the giants immune to the electrical charge." She pointed at herself with her thumb. "Maybe I'm immune, too. Why don't you let me climb up there and whack his legs off?"

"But they were in those chambers for years and years. You were there for what? Two hours at the most?"

"Maybe, but—"

"The answer is no!" Walter grasped her arm tightly. "You got it?"

Karen firmed her lips and nodded. What else could she do? As long as Walter was in charge, there wasn't much choice. Besides, he'd proven himself so many times and against such impossible odds, he could do it again, couldn't he?

Gabriel arrived, breathless. "What's going on?"

Walter guided Karen toward Gabriel. "Keep her safe, okay?"

"You got it!" Gabriel spread a wing over Karen's shoulders. "By the way, Mardon said Chazaq's coming."

Walter rolled his eyes. "Great! Just what we needed."

While Walter stalked away, Karen eyed Mardon until he ducked through the opening to the turbine room's antechamber. When he disappeared from sight, she turned her attention back to Walter. He marched out into the middle of the open-air room and shouted. "Hey, Mr Giant!"

The Naphil glared at him, his red eyebeams landing on Walter's chest. "What do you want, little man?"

"I want to issue a challenge."

Karen caught a glimpse of Roxil out of the corner of her eye, just her head peeking out of the clouds. She had circled behind the giant. Would she close in now that Walter had his attention?

The giant laughed. "How could a runt like you possibly challenge me?"

309

"Well, not a challenge to you directly. I heard that Chazaq is your commander and that he's coming here."

"He is my commander, and I expected his arrival." The shafts of light emanating from the Naphil's fingers grew slowly brighter. "So what?"

"If I can defeat him in one-on-one combat, will you surrender?"

"My surrender would be quite a prize for you. What could you possibly give me that is of equal value if you lose?"

"I'll be dead, and Excalibur will be yours." Walter spread out his arms. "What else could you want?"

The red eyebeams swept across the floor and landed on Karen.

"No!" Walter's face flushed bright red. "No deal!"

Gabriel planted his feet in front of Karen. "Over my dead body!" He pulled a dagger from his belt and held it high.

"And over my dead body, too." Walter lifted his sword. "She is not a bargaining chip."

"She is my choice, and Chazaq is now here to trample over your dead bodies."

Walter spun toward the sound of stomping feet. Chazaq hunched as he walked through the anteroom's punctured wall, but when he came out into the open area, he straightened to his full height and marched closer.

Mardon had to step quickly to stay at his side, his head only as high as Chazaq's elbows. "What are you two talking about?" Mardon asked.

"Nothing of consequence," the other giant said. He aimed his eyebeams at Walter. "The boy is a nuisance. I suggest that Chazaq dispose of him immediately."

"With pleasure." Mardon nodded toward Walter. "Chazaq, break him in half and bring the sword to me."

Gabriel stepped in front of Chazaq. "You'll have to go through me first." Beating his wings, he jumped high and swiped at Chazaq's face with his dagger but missed. The giant swung a fist. Gabriel darted back just in time, then struck again, this time plunging the dagger into Chazaq's eye. The giant roared and smacked Gabriel with the back of his hand, sending him flying toward Karen.

Karen tried to catch him, but his body flew by too quickly. Gabriel crashed into the pillar and sprawled around it.

Chazaq yanked out the dagger and threw it to the ground. With a hand covering his eye, he stalked toward Gabriel, screaming, "I will crush every bone in his body!"

"No!" Mardon shouted. "He is harmless now. Get the sword!"

Chazaq veered away from Gabriel and marched again toward Walter.

"Gabriel!" Karen knelt at his side, trembling as she pulled him away from the pillar. "Are you all right?"

He didn't answer. She laid a hand on his cold cheek and pressed a finger against his throat. "Come on! Give me a pulse!"

19

CHAPTER

THE OLDEST MEMORIES

Timothy awoke to the smell of roasting herbs, a hearty aroma that stung the back of his throat with a sharp, rousing bite. Sitting at his table, Abraham gazed at Enoch's Ghost while sipping from a steaming mug.

"Whatever that is," Timothy said, stretching, "I think I'll have some, if you don't mind."

"It is brown-leaf tea, a special blend I concocted many years ago." He nodded toward a fireplace where a silver kettle hung over fading embers. "Help yourself. There are mugs on the mantle."

Timothy rose from his straw-stuffed mattress and, still weary from his cathartic experience with the oracle, shuffled over to the fireplace, his companion bouncing up and down with his laboured gait. "What does Enoch's Ghost tell you this morning?" he asked, bringing the kettle back to the table by its wooden handle.

"That you have seen a great vision and carry an even greater burden."

Pouring the tea, a dark, pungent brew, Timothy sat in the opposite chair but said nothing while the aromatic vapour bathed his face. His companion hovered next to his nose as if taking in the aroma with him.

Abraham pushed his mug against Timothy's, making a quiet clinking sound. "I am willing to share that burden with you, if you care to move a bundle or two from your shoulders to mine."

Timothy swirled the tea around in his mug. "I think the greatest burden might be deciding who is reliable." He took a test sip, but it was too hot to drink. "I guess it's okay to tell you that the oracle said there's some kind of deceiver who is going to spread corruption. I'm not sure what she meant by that, but if this deceiver is already lurking, I have to be careful." He blew on the tea while keeping his gaze on Abraham. Of course, the oracle had said much more, but could he possibly reveal the plan about the sacrifice, even to Abraham?

After taking a long drink, Abraham fingered the mug's raised design, a dragon in mid-flight. "When a deceiver is in your midst," he said slowly, "it is difficult to trust anyone. Of course, I hope you will trust me, but if I am the deceiver, my pleas for your trust would be yet another deception. Therefore, until you get your bearings, you cannot reveal your mission to anyone, not me, not Angel, not even Candle or Listener, for a deceiver might pose as a child as easily as an adult."

Timothy sipped his tea and set the mug on the table. He watched three tiny black flecks spin in the rust-coloured liquid. As Abraham's words sank in, the tea itself took on a new character in his mind. Could even this drink be a ploy?

He picked up the pot and tipped it toward Abraham. "Freshen your cup?"

Abraham slid his mug over. "Please."

Timothy poured the rest of the tea, and as Abraham drained it without even waiting for it to cool, he scolded himself for his paranoia. His companion scooted in front of his eyes and flashed.

The seed for your lack of trust was planted by Abraham. Do not punish yourself for taking him at his word.

Timothy sighed. "You're right."

"Right about what?" Abraham asked.

Laughing, Timothy lifted his palm underneath his companion and let it rest there. "I'm not used to talking to these things yet. I have to learn to keep our conversation in my mind."

Abraham's fatherly eyes gleamed. "Some of our people speak out loud to their companions. It's not so unusual."

Timothy closed his fingers lightly around the little ovulum. "Since it attaches itself to the soul, what would happen if a companion were stolen while its owner was still alive?"

"A shadow person did just that. He took a small boy's companion. It caused immediate pain, and within minutes the boy's eyes glazed and he could no longer walk. By the time the news reached me, he was unconscious with a severe fever. Albatross and I hurried to the basin and searched all day until we found the culprit. If not for Enoch's Ghost, I never would have located the glimmer of light that always indicates a companion's presence."

His hands trembling, Timothy leaned closer to Abraham. "So, what happened to the boy?"

"By the time I returned ..." Abraham's voice pitched higher. "He had passed away."

Timothy hung his head low and tensed his jaw. "Cursed fiends!"

"Now you have more sympathy for my summary justice yesterday."

"I do." Timothy released his companion. It rose slowly and floated back to his shoulder. "I feel like I'm one of your people now, like I should just stay here under your rule."

Abraham raised an eyebrow. "And marry Angel?"

Timothy nodded, keeping his eyes on the table. "Not too hard to figure that one out."

"Not at all. Your face is still glowing from last night."

Timothy laid a palm on his cheek. "The light tunnel did that."

Abraham laughed. "Angel is a fine woman. I would have to look long and hard to find a more worthy lady, if I could at all."

He looked up at Abraham. "Do you think she'll have me?"

"Without a doubt. Without a doubt."

Timothy stroked his chin. "Of course, I have to know for sure that Hannah died and didn't come back to life, as I did, but how do I find out what happened to her? Can Enoch's Ghost tell me?"

"Perhaps." Abraham slid the ovulum between them. "Before we ask that question, there is other vital information you need to know. Now that much of your memory is restored, and now that I know who you are, it is time to fill in the gaps from the beginning." He waved a hand across the glass egg. "More memories should return as your distant past streams before your eyes."

Timothy slid his chair close and gazed into Enoch's Ghost. The fog evaporated, revealing a land awash in a heavy rainstorm. Low clouds swirled around an enormous boat as the downpour fed streams of rising water that rushed around the bow. Atop the deck, a red dragon perched on the parapet while a smaller, tawny dragon looked on from the deck's rain-slicked boards.

Tiny voices arose from Enoch's Ghost, giving life to the characters inside. At first, the language seemed odd but quickly grew more familiar. Soon, Timothy was able to translate every word as they sprang from the mouths within.

"I cannot leave my father!" The larger dragon stretched out his wings and lifted into the air.

"We must go!" The smaller one bit his tail and pulled him down.

"Don't make me fight you!" the red dragon said, jerking his tail away.

Scarlet light flashed all around. While a pulsing ball of fire descended from the clouds, an old man ran onto the deck, saying something, but the sound of rain drowned out his voice. Fingers of crimson flame sprouted from the ball, long tendrils that pierced the ground and gave birth to geysers of muddy water. A peal of thunder shook the ovulum. Torrents of rain veiled the boat, making it impossible to see the dragons or hear their voices.

Abraham rubbed the glass with one hand, seemingly turning the scene as if adjusting a camera angle. Now one of the rising streams came into view. Another red dragon, as large as the one on the boat, floundered in the water, black splotches covering his otherwise red scales. Beams from his ruby eyes pierced the misty breeze and the black clouds above. Shouting a dying call, he roared. "To you, Maker of All, I commit my spirit!" Then, he submerged.

Two winged humans, both bright and shining, descended from the storm. They plunged into the foaming water and lifted the great dragon, but, instead of trying to save him, they seemed to battle over him, struggling in mid-air while the dragon's limp wings and legs flopped from side to side.

"Give me the dragon, Michael!" one angel shouted. "You have no use for it."

"Jehovah's purposes are beyond your knowledge," Michael boomed.

As lightning flashed, Michael plunged a hand into the dragon's chest and pulled out its heart, then, with a flaming burst of power from his four wings, carried the heart away. The other angel shouted something in a different language, indecipherable but clearly words of outrage. It turned and flew in the opposite direction, lugging the huge body under one arm.

The scene in the ovulum faded, replaced by the red fog. Timothy looked up at the Prophet, his eyes blurred, his heart racing.

"Do you know what you just saw?" Abraham asked.

Trying to steady his breathing, Timothy spoke slowly in a near whisper. "I was there. I saw the rain, the red light, the old man on the deck. But I don't remember the battle between the angels."

"You wouldn't. You had already entered the protected part of the boat, Noah's ark."

"Noah? I remember Noah. He was a kind old man, gentle and good."

"Indeed he was. He rescued you and your soon-to-be mate."

"Thigocia? She was the other dragon?" A tear filled Timothy's eye. Memories rushed in – flying with other dragons, shooting fire at angelic beings, zooming with reckless abandon with two smaller dragons in playful dives and hairpin turns, then reclining with the tawny dragon, necks intertwined in blissful peace.

"Thigocia," Timothy said quietly. "My dear Thigocia." With each repetition of her name, the memories linked themselves together, fashioning a story chain that began thousands of years ago in a dim cave, where the dragon he had seen drowning in the flood boosted him with a loving wing, and the chain led through multiple millennia to this dim room and the chair in which he now rested. Finally, in breathless wonder, Timothy sat back. "I remember so much more! But every thought burns like fire!"

"Memories are the greatest torture of all, and the greatest solace." Abraham took Timothy's hand. "Now look into my eyes. What do you see?"

With their fingers locked, Timothy could feel the Prophet's rhythmic heartbeat. Trying to calm his own heartbeat, he first scanned Abraham's bushy red eyebrows, then focused on the gleaming orbs just below. The wise man's black pupils seemed to pulse as well, growing and shrinking slightly with every beat of his heart. The surrounding iris, the same colour as his eyebrows, suddenly flushed with a deeper red.

Pulling his hand away, Timothy almost toppled his chair. "The eyes," he said breathlessly. "The dragon in the flood. The red eyes."

Abraham stood and leaned forward. "What is my name, Makaidos?"

316

"I ... I do not know your name. I am a dragon, and I am unfamiliar with most humans." He got up and looked around the room, so confused he couldn't figure out where he was. "Where is Merlin? He might know who you are." He shook his head hard. "What am I saying? Who is Merlin?"

"Your memories are spilling together, and now you must speak the bind that ties." Abraham banged his fist on the table and shouted. "What is my name, Makaidos?"

The image of Angel bowing before Abraham flashed in his mind and the word she used to address him passed from his mind to his lips. "Fa ... Father?"

Abraham marched around the table and jerked Timothy into a tight embrace with his powerful arms. "Yes, son, but what is my name?"

Barely able to breathe, Timothy cried out, "Arramos!" Wrapping his arms around Abraham, he laid his head on his shoulder and wept. "My father! Oh, my father!"

Abraham kissed Timothy's neck and patted him on the back. "Yes, my son. And we will have many more revelations before the end of our journey."

Timothy slid away. "How did you get here? Is my mother here, too?"

"Since a picture is worth a thousand words ..." Abraham gestured toward the table and chairs. "Let us sit again, and I will let Enoch tell the story."

When they were both seated, Abraham touched the ovulum. Timothy scooted close again and gazed through the glass. As before, the red mist disappeared, and a movie-like scene materialized.

Michael cradled the heart, cold and lifeless in his hands, beating his wings furiously as he ascended through the swirling storm clouds, and later, a dense blanket of water vapour. When he

317

broke into the clear, he seemed to be in outer space, surrounded by inky blackness. He began to spin, and the black canopy shattered and swept to the side, as if the wind from his wings blew the pieces away.

When the spinning stopped, Michael, now surrounded by at least ten more angels in an enormous, church-like chamber, walked reverently to an altar where a human body lay, a man whose motionless chest proved his lifeless state. Tall white candles surrounded him, each one flickering yellow light over his bared skin.

When the other angels joined him, Michael glanced around, his gaze finally landing on the closest one. "Has his world been prepared, Uriel?"

Uriel nodded. "All is complete. Second Eden is ready to receive its king."

Raising both arms, Michael lifted the heart into the air. "Holy Spirit, breathe life into this creature and fulfil your wondrous plan. May the heart and soul of Arramos guide his people in this new creation and watch over his realm with eyes of wisdom."

Wind swirled through the room, invisible at first, but as it collected smoke from the candles around the altar, its shape became apparent, a narrow band that weaved its way through the angelic host and then poured into the heart.

Instantly, the heart began to beat. Michael plunged it into the man's chest, pausing for a few seconds like a surgeon attaching vessel to vessel. The body lurched and began to thrash. Michael withdrew his hands, and with a swipe of his fingers, closed the wound, leaving no perceptible scar.

The body settled down, the chest heaving at first until its breathing stabilized into an easy rhythm. Michael placed a hand over its eyes. "Awake, King of Second Eden, Father of the Forsaken. You will be called the Prophet, but the Holy One has named you Abraham, for you will be a father to the cast-offs of the wicked realm."

Abraham's eyes blinked open, and he sat up. "Where am I?" His head swivelled as he gazed at each angel.

"At Heaven's lower altar," Michael replied. "You died on the Earth as Arramos, but you are not called to ascend into the holy city. You will rule over a world God has created, but now in human form instead of your dragon body."

Abraham laid a hand on his chest and caressed his smooth skin. "Will I join my family? Shachar? Hilidan? Zera?"

"A day will come when you will be reunited, but for now, I will take you to your new world."

As Abraham sat up, Uriel laid a bundle of clothing on the altar. "Purity and innocence will not dress you adequately in this Eden," he said. "It is much colder than the first Paradise."

Michael and Uriel helped Abraham dress in multiple layers, finishing with a long-sleeved tunic, trousers tied at the waist, and soft leather shoes that rose above his ankles. Michael laid an arm over Abraham's back, and the other angels began to fly around them, orbiting faster and faster until they were a blur of faces and wings.

319

Soon, their surroundings faded away, and a new scene emerged – a bird's-eye view of a lush valley with a wide river meandering through thick greenery – grassy areas as well as dense forests. Now carrying Abraham, Michael flew to the ground and set him gently in an expansive basin where long-bladed grass emerged from dark, loamy soil.

"This is your garden," Michael said, "but you must not plant anything here. You will learn soon enough what fruit is to be harvested." An egg-shaped glass orb appeared in his hands. "Enoch's Ghost will teach you what you need to know. Take it. You will learn quickly."

When Abraham made a cradle with his hands, Michael rolled the egg into his grasp. Then, without another word, he lifted into the sky and flew away.

Abraham stood alone. As a stiff breeze flapped his tunic, he shivered. After surveying the landscape for a moment, he made his way to a nearby woods, marring the wet soil with the first footprint the virgin land had ever carried.

"So," Abraham said as the ovulum faded, "with only a few puzzling words and a strange glass orb to guide my way, I was commissioned to occupy this 'Second Eden'. Yet, I had no Eve to help me populate the world and no pair of trees to give me either eternal life or spiritual death. I had no idea what to do, though one of the first things I did was to name stars in the sky after my lost loved ones, including my mate, Shachar, and you and Thigocia."

"So that explains the stars." Timothy turned toward the open door. A pair of villagers passed by, a man followed by a woman on a donkey. "I see you found a way to forge a fine community. I am amazed at their gracious manner and kindness."

As another shadow crossed the light from the doorway, Abraham rose from his chair. "Angel!" he said, "you arrived almost before the sun! Welcome!"

Timothy shot up and smoothed out his hair and wrinkled clothes. "Yes! Welcome!"

Her head slightly bowed and her eyes trained on Timothy, she walked in, wearing a dress with sleeves that reached the heels of her hands and a skirt so long, its draught swept the floor. Two children followed – Candle, his dark face framing his brilliant smile, and Listener, pale and gaunt. Although her eyes sparkled, she neither smiled nor frowned. Their hovering companions also sparkled in the ray of sunlight passing over the three visitors' shoulders.

Timothy made a quick, silent count of the semi-transparent orbs. Four companions? Why would that be?

"You haven't been introduced to Listener," Angel said, nodding toward the girl. "Listener, this is our new friend, Timothy."

Timothy bent to one knee and took her hand. "It's my pleasure."

Listener just blinked and said nothing. Two companions whirled around her head and paused, one over each shoulder. The girl's skin was rough, with shallow lines dividing small leathery patches, even worse than it had seemed at the hospital.

"She doesn't talk," Candle explained. "But I think I already told you that."

"Yes, I remember." Timothy rose and lifted his eyebrows at Angel, mouthing his question silently, "Two?"

Angel curled her hands into fists. "She came from the pod that way, one companion in each hand. The Prophet tells us it means she has been placed here for a great purpose."

"A purpose yet to be determined." Abraham patted Listener on the head, then touched the lace on Angel's wrist. "You seem to be dressed for seasonal prayers. Have I misread the calendar?"

A slight blush coloured Angel's cheeks as she fanned the skirt. "I just thought you and Timothy might be tired of seeing me dressed for dragon riding."

"We walked all the way," Candle said. "Grackle whined like a baby until we got out of sight."

Listener slid her hand into Timothy's and walked toward the door, pulling him along. As he followed, he looked back at Angel, raising his eyebrows again.

"Listener?" Angel started toward them. "What are you doing?"

"Angel," Abraham called. "Let them go."

Angel halted in mid-step and merely followed with her gaze. "I left the bag by the door," she said to Listener, "if that's what you're going to show him."

Listener glanced back at her mother, but her face stayed sombre. When she reached the outside railing that bordered the road, she stopped and pulled Timothy down to his knees. Then, her eyes wide, she stared directly into his, gripping both of his hands tightly.

Timothy caressed the tops of her scaly hands with his thumbs. "What is it, Listener? What are you trying to tell me?"

Her lips trembled, but no words came out. Lifting a hand, she touched his cheek, then looked up toward the sun.

"Oh! You're wondering why my face glows." He covered her hand with his. "I saw this magnificent girl, an angel, I think, who told me an amazing story about a sacrificial lamb."

Listener drew in a quick breath and stepped back. She laid a hand on her chest, rubbing the gingham material.

Swallowing a painful lump, Timothy whispered, "Are you the lamb?"

She returned a single nod.

"Did someone come to you and tell you this?"

Again, a single nod.

Glancing left and right, Timothy leaned closer. "Someone from around here?"

Listener shook her head and pointed at a shoulder bag sitting by the door.

"Do you want me to look in the bag?"

She bobbed her head again.

Timothy hustled to the door and brought the bag. Reaching in, he found a spyglass and raised it to his eye. "Did you see something unusual through this?" With his other eye he caught her affirmative nod once again.

He lowered the spyglass. "Did you see a girl with white hair and a blue cloak over a white dress?"

Listener gasped. This time she grabbed his hand and nodded excitedly. Her two companions seemed to flash, mirroring her emotions.

Timothy glanced at the Prophet's door. Inside, Angel peered out, but Abraham closed the door in front of her.

Extending his hand slowly, Timothy brushed his finger against one of the companions. More opaque than the other, the faint eyes inside seemed older, weaker. With a quick snatch, he grasped the companion and pulled it behind him. It buzzed furiously in his grip, but he stiffened his fingers and pressed his fist against his back.

Listener shuddered, but instead of an expression of pain, a gentle smile grew on her face. Her skin smoothed, and a healthy blush refreshed her cheeks.

"Do you feel better?" he asked.

Glancing at the door, Listener cleared her throat. At first, her lips parted, and a raspy gurgle came out, but then a whispered phrase. "I ... I can talk?"

Timothy raised a finger to his lips. "Shhh ..." The companion in his hand heated up, stinging his palm as it lurched to get out. He had to hurry. "Do you want to be the sacrifice for my daughters?"

She formed each word carefully. "Yes. ... It is all ... I have dreamed of ... ever since the ... beautiful girl told me ... through that tube."

"But why? You are so young. You have so much to live for."

"I hurt. ... Always hurt." She angled her body to look behind his back where he held her missing companion. "But not now." She laid a hand on his chest. "I want to ... save your girls ... and stop *your* hurt."

Timothy wiped a tear from his eye. His throat twisting in a knot, he tried to speak. "Your mother ... and your brother ... will miss you."

Listener's voice strengthened. "The girl in white said ... my mummy killed me a long time ago in another world. Angel is my new mummy ... Only not really." She lowered her chin and shook her head sadly. "Her mummy killed her, too, but the girl in white said even our mummies could be forgiven. I was glad to hear that."

"But why you? Why should a little girl have to give her life for others?"

"It is my choice. The girl in white said if anyone else tried it, her companion would save the life of the one for whom she died, but she would lose her own soul, because she was not given the task." She held up two fingers. "I can save two lives, and since I already died once, God promised I could go straight to Heaven." She lifted her gaze. Her sparkling blue eyes seemed a reflection of the oracle's, dimmer, but still piercing. "So I want to do that," she said firmly.

Timothy could barely whisper. "And stop the pain."

Listener nodded. "I want to stop everyone's pain."

Timothy brought the companion to the front of his body and opened his hand. It sat on a reddened spot on his palm for a moment before floating up and drifting back to Listener's shoulder. As soon as it perched there, the colour drained from her cheeks. Her skin dried out, and cracks etched crusty new scales. Pain streaked her face, and her lips parted to speak again, but only a rasping whistle blew out.

324

Timothy swept her into his arms and hugged her close, weeping. "Oh, dear child! Dear, dear child! Your courage is beyond all others!"

Her weak fingers patted his shoulder, and her wheezing breath whistled into his ear. Carrying her back to the Prophet's door, he whispered, "We have to plan our departure secretly. Do you know how to fly Grackle?"

He felt her nod brush against his cheek.

"After your mother and brother are asleep tonight, bring him to the edge of the birthing garden. I will be waiting for you there, and we will fly to the land of the shadow people."

CHAPTER

20

HEAVEN'S ALTAR

As soon as Elam and Naamah passed between the blue curtains of Heaven's shield, the inner light seemed to fold them
in. Elam's eyes quickly adjusted, allowing him to lower the hand
he had been using as a barrier against the glare.

Still holding Naamah's hand, Elam stepped quietly across a
hardwood floor in what appeared to be the library of a humble
cottage. He picked up an old book at the top of one of the many
stacks that lined the stone walls on both sides. "I thought everything was supposed to be covered with gold and filled with per-
fume," he whispered. "This place is kind of cramped and stuffy."

"I don't know what Heaven is supposed to be like," Naamah
replied softly, "but I have never set foot in a holier place. I feel
cleaner than I have ever felt in my life."

Elam set the book down and turned back to their entryway.
A gap in the wall revealed Dikaios and a bank of dark storm
clouds behind him, billowing ever closer. The gap slowly narrowed until it disappeared, leaving a wall mural, a painting of a

narrow gate trimmed with clinging vines that bore golden kiwi fruit and purple grapes.

On the opposite wall, a small table and two benches sat next to a simple wooden door with an old-fashioned metal lift-latch. Elam set his hand on a lantern that rested in the middle of the table. "Still warm," he said.

"A quiet place to study," Naamah whispered. "The lord of this house might soon return."

Elam lifted the latch and swung open the door. A tender, sweet aroma instantly met his nostrils as he stepped through. Inside, row after row of prayer benches lined the floor of a massive chamber, and hundreds, maybe thousands of people in white robes knelt at the benches, their knees resting on soft pillows and their hands folded on chest-high, wooden shelves. Most kept their eyes pointed toward the far end of the room. Their words hummed through the sanctuary, thousands of prayers blending into a lovely harmony.

Elam followed the forward gazes to a raised platform where a giant altar – a high table covered with a white cloth – seemed to preside over the worshippers. With purple tassels sweeping the floor, it had to measure at least five hundred feet from one end to the other.

Overarching the entire chamber, enormous white drapes stretched from beam to beam. Animated pictures covered each drape, moving images of people and scenery, all unfamiliar to Elam. The images were so clear and realistic, they looked like digital movies played on high-definition monitors, but it seemed that only a few of the people ever ventured a glance at the action taking place overhead.

Elam took a step toward the closest kneeler. A colourful hologram floated in front of her. The three-dimensional image showed a young woman crying on her bed, blood pouring from her slashed throat. With her gaze locked on the scene, the kneeler's lips moved in prayer while tears dripped on her folded hands.

Clutching Elam's arm, Naamah drew close. "Is this a church?" she asked. "I have never been in one."

"Not exactly," another voice replied.

As a strong hand clasped Elam's shoulder, he turned around to find a tall, elderly man smiling at him. "I'm glad you could make it," the man said.

At first, Elam didn't recognize him, but as shrouded images of the past filtered through his mind, the man's name pushed to the forefront. He nodded reverently. "Master Enoch. I am blessed to see you." He wrinkled his brow. "But how did I know it was you? I've only seen you in the Ovulum, and you were more like a red ghost than a man."

Enoch extended his arm and waved it across the praying masses. "You will learn that you know everyone here, even if you have never seen them before. To return to Naamah's question, this is not a church; it is the martyrs' prayer room. They rest here praying for servants of God who are in danger of dying for their faith, even as they have died."

Naamah pointed at one of the holograms. "They pray for the people when they appear in front of them?"

"And they can also request to see and pray for whomever they wish."

Elam watched another image, a hooded man lying on the ground with another man poised over him with a machete. Elam's heart raced. He wanted to see the outcome, but he couldn't bear to watch. As the machete approached the victim's bare throat, Elam swung his head back to Enoch. "Do you join them in prayer, Master Enoch?"

"Although I join them from time to time, I am not a martyr. In fact, like you, I never died, so I am able to take on other assignments in addition to prayer. I have my own room and a special viewing screen that gives me a portal to other worlds. I spoke through the Ovulum from there, and I am able to project my

327

image or my voice wherever I wish. Often, those who see or hear me assume I am a ghost."

"So, do you have to stay here on this side of Heaven's shield?"

"Who would ever want to leave Heaven?" Enoch smiled, lifting his white moustache toward his deep brown eyes. "But you have a point. At times I have wanted to help the people I see on Earth, so God granted my special quarters to me, and I have been able to accomplish much there." He raised three fingers. "There were three recent occasions, however, when I was allowed to visit Earth in bodily form, but those opportunities are short-lived and rare. Fortunately, I was able to visit Ashley during her time of great need in a strange spiral staircase, though she had no idea who I really was."

"This is all so amazing!" Elam scanned the room, searching for Acacia. It didn't take long to find her – a girl with white locks trickling down over her folded hands as she watched the hologram in front of her. Unlike all the martyrs dressed in white, Acacia wore a dazzling blue cloak. Its cape spread over her kneeling bench like a royal robe, and the hood shadowed most of her lovely young face.

Enoch laughed gently and extended his arm toward the prayer bench. "You may go to her. This is a place of freedom, for all are holy. I will stay with Naamah. She and I have a few things to discuss."

After scurrying down an aisle between two long benches, Elam stopped behind Acacia and crouched, wondering if he should interrupt her prayer. Her hologram showed a girl with scaly-looking skin standing on a village road and looking at a hand-held telescope. Acacia reached into the hologram and touched the girl as though she were caressing a beloved sister.

"That's Enoch's spyglass," Elam said. "I lost it at the chasm. How did she get it?"

A little brown-haired girl kneeling beside Acacia wheeled around. "Elam?"

Elam smiled. "It's good to see you again, Paili."

Paili leaped into his arms. Acacia spun toward them, her blue eyes sparkling. Staying on her knees, she scooted over and kissed him on the cheek. "I'm so glad you made it! I've been watching and praying for you!"

Elam nodded at the hologram. "I see the girl. What's going on?"

Acacia stood and took Elam's hand. "Come. Father Enoch can explain it better than I can." He and Paili followed Acacia back to Enoch, but Naamah was no longer with him.

Elam searched the area for her. "Where's—"

"Shhh!" Enoch laid a finger over his lips and nodded toward Paili.

"Oh. Okay." Elam glanced at Paili. She seemed bewildered, but her smile never dimmed.

"Come," Enoch said, gesturing toward the anteroom. "I will explain our situation in here. Although the anthem of praying saints is always beautiful music, we should seek solitude and a better place to converse."

When all four had entered the library, Enoch closed the door, and everyone took a seat at the table, Enoch and Elam on the bench on one side, and Acacia and Paili on the other. Folding his hands next to a large, weather-worn book, Enoch smiled at Acacia. "I think a little more light is in order."

Acacia pointed at the lantern. "Ignite," she whispered.

When the wick caught fire, Paili grinned. "Someday, I'm going to learn how to do that."

As the flaming tongue rose into the lantern's glass, Enoch fixed his gaze on Elam. Yellow light bathed his face, casting shadows across wrinkle lines radiating from his deeply set eyes. "Many questions swirl in your mind," he said. "Would you like to ask some of them to settle your thoughts?"

"Okay ..." Elam rolled his eyes upward for a moment, and when the first question popped into his mind, he leaned close to Enoch and whispered. "Can I ask about Paili?"

"Certainly." Enoch patted her hand. "She has heard her own story countless times."

"Well, how did she get cured? And why is she a child again?"

"That is a long tale," Enoch replied, "so I will give you a shortened version. First, she and Acacia went on a very long journey through the grasslands of the second circle as well as Molech's forest."

"Me, too, but they must have had it worse. That would be awful, especially since her ankle was injured."

Enoch slipped his hand into Paili's. "Joseph was there to guide them and fend off the Caitiff, but, indeed, the journey was treacherous. In any case, after the gatekeeper allowed them into the Bridgelands, they crossed the bridge. As you might expect from your own experiences, that was quite a harrowing passage. I met them at this end of the chasm with a mash I concocted from the fruit of the tree of life. After much effort, we managed to get Paili to swallow it. As I predicted, the fruit revived her and brought complete healing, but she also shrank and reverted to her younger self, the same apparent age she was decades ago when Sapphira took her to her adoptive home. Although we have told her the stories of her history as a wife and mother, she remembers none of it. I have a theory as to why she regressed, but since it is pure speculation, there is no need to air it here."

Elam let out a low whistle. "I can't imagine carrying someone over that chasm! I had to crawl just to survive!"

"I know," Enoch said. "I watched you."

After a few more seconds of thought, Elam tapped his finger on the table. "Okay. Here's my next question. Merlin sang one of your prophecies that sounds like I'm supposed to take Acacia back to Earth. Is that true?" His voice grew more excited, and questions shot out in rapid-fire succession. "And if I take Acacia back, is Paili supposed to come? Will she still be healed there? And what about leading the martyrs to holy war? What's that all about?"

Enoch laughed and waved for Elam to calm down. "So many questions! I would have to write them all down!"

Leaning toward Elam, Acacia whispered, "Ask Father Enoch to sing the prophecy. I've never heard it."

Still laughing, Enoch pointed at Acacia. "But I heard you!"

Her brow lifted, and she gave him a sad, puppy-dog look. "Would you sing it? Please?"

Enoch's smile faded, but his eyes still twinkled. "I will sing the parts that pertain to you, fair one, but I think Elam needs no reminders." Clearing his throat, the old prophet stared at the lantern, humming for a moment before beginning his song.

> The tree that bears the ark of God
> Has flown to Heaven's narrow gate
> To purge the serpent's fatal bite,
> The fruit of Morgan's wicked hate.

The lantern's flame bent and twisted with every word, as if portraying the passion Enoch felt as he sang.

> A path of light will lead the way,
> A path the tree will soon ignite,
> A path of sorrows, pain, and death,
> A path to guide the mourning knight.

> Sapphira bends, but will she break?
> Depends on Elam's safe return.
> For if he fails to bring the ark,
> Her life is chaff and soon will burn.

When the last note died away, Elam folded his hands and sighed. "That was beautiful. And I thought Merlin sang it well."

With his head angled downward, Enoch glanced at Elam and gave him a sad sort of smile. "You are too kind."

Elam pressed his thumbs together. "The part I didn't understand at all was the path. What's that about?"

"Ever since Acacia arrived," Enoch said, "she has ministered to another realm through a portal that she maintains, but a time will soon come when she must illuminate that path for a tragic, but necessary, reason. And I suspect that you will be present to witness it." He opened the old book to a page near the end. "You may show him the chosen one, Acacia."

Acacia's countenance fell, and her solemn voice matched her sudden change in mood. "Your wish is my will, Father Enoch." As she rubbed her hands together over the book, a column of fire arose from the pages. She separated her hands, allowing the column to rise between her palms, and as she continued to draw her hands apart, the fire spread out into a thin oval. The flames scattered to the rim of the oval, revealing a face within the ring, a girl with a scaly pattern in her skin, the same girl who appeared in her prayer hologram. While keeping her hands in place at the sides of the oval, Acacia's eyes glistened with tears.

332

"Acacia has spoken to this girl," Enoch said to Elam, "and they both know what they must do to create your path into this other world where you will enter as its warrior chief. You will learn about your new role there soon enough, so I think I will tell you no more about that for now."

Acacia brought her hands together, compressing the image until it vanished. The flames dwindled and fell back into the page in a puff of smoke.

As Enoch closed the book, Elam drew an oval on the table with his finger. The girl seemed so forlorn, like a lost soul searching for help. But he couldn't dwell on it, not with Enoch stonewalling that topic. There were too many questions still remaining. "What about taking Acacia back to Earth?" he asked.

Enoch slid the book to the side. "As you have apparently guessed, Acacia is the tree that bears the ark of God, and Paili is that ark, but I perceive that we have run out of time for questions, so the answers to all other questions and riddles will have to wait until your first mission is complete."

"My first mission?"

"A great danger threatens this realm." Enoch nodded toward the gated garden painted on the opposite wall. "Beyond that shield, Mardon is in the process of pulling down the gates of Heaven in order to ascend to the throne of God as a mediator. If we don't stop him, he could very well succeed in dissolving the barrier between Heaven and Earth."

"Merlin told me about that." Elam folded his hands on the table. "I've been thinking about it ever since. How can any man endanger God?" As the lantern's flame flashed brighter, he raised a clenched fist. "Why doesn't God just crush him?"

Enoch waved a hand of dismissal. "God is in no danger. It is the created order that is threatened. If Mardon succeeds, God is quite capable of cleaning up the mess, but since Mardon is using the physical universe as it was created, God prefers to battle his enemy by employing his faithful servants. In other words, he wishes to use one part of his creation to save the rest." He set his finger on the book. "The girl Acacia showed you will provide a weapon we can use to fight against Mardon, and you will be an integral part of the battle."

333

As Elam uncurled his fingers, the lantern's flame settled. "What do you want me to do?"

"You must go back through the shield to the Bridgelands where you will find Dikaios and your other travelling partner. Once there, you must gather soldiers, ten wandering souls who wish to prove their worth, and bring them to the shield. When you return, Acacia and I will meet you, and I will give you further instructions."

"You want ten souls?" Elam asked, opening both hands to display his fingers. "Exactly ten?"

Enoch nodded. "Why do you act so surprised?"

"It's just that I already know where to find them. There are ten gentlemen who are hoping to get into Heaven, but they got lost somehow."

Enoch raised a finger and pressed it against his temple. "Take care that your enthusiasm does not overwhelm your discernment. We can hope for the deliverance of others, but the final barrier between them and this altar ultimately dwells in their own minds. And if they have died on Earth, their fate has already been decided."

Elam processed Enoch's mysterious comment but decided not to ask its meaning. The task at hand was too pressing. "So, do I go now? That storm was already getting close when I was last out there."

Enoch pointed at the mural. "Simply walk through it, and you will be on your way."

Elam took Acacia's hand and kissed it, then Paili's. "God willing, I will return." He rose and walked right into the wall. For a moment, the brilliant light blinded him again, but it faded away as the familiar Bridgelands reappeared.

Naamah stood next to Dikaios, her hair wrapping around her neck as the winds whipped across her face. She ran forward and hugged Elam. "I thought you might not come for me. When Enoch sent me away, I feared that I had been rejected from our father's house."

"He didn't tell me why exactly," Elam said, patting Naamah's back, "but I think it's because of Paili. She's still alive as a little girl, so her memories of how you treated her in the mines would probably scare her if she saw you again."

"I see." Naamah backed away and folded her hands in front of her. "My past sins are still a chain around my neck."

"Give it time," Elam said. "She's a special case."

Naamah bowed her head. "As much as she needs."

"Dikaios!" Elam shouted through the breeze. "We have to go back to the Skotos Woods. Enoch wants me to collect ten wanderers and bring them here."

The horse plodded to his side. "I can carry you and Naamah, but the ten will have to find other transport."

Elam set his hand above his eyes and scanned the horizon. "What's available around here? Can we find a carriage of some kind? More horses?"

"I know of other horses, but it would take hours to get to their grazing lands."

"Hours," Elam repeated. "We don't have hours." He stared at the gathering clouds. The stiff breeze dried out his eyes, and weariness flooded his bones, but he couldn't rest, not now, not when the storm was about to strike.

Out of the corner of his eye, he spotted movement in the field. A line of ragged men marched across the grasslands, Zane leading them. The last man in the procession grasped the shoulder of the man in front of him. As they closed in, they picked up their pace.

"Do you see what I see?" Elam asked Dikaios.

"Indeed. It seems that our nomadic soldiers have wandered right into our troop."

Elam crossed his arms over his chest. "But I told them to build a fire and wait. Could it have gone out so soon?"

"I suspect they built no fire at all," Dikaios said. "They have come a very long way, so they would have had to begin their journey as soon as we left the forest."

Naamah moved behind Elam and peeked around his side. "I think I recognize one of them. The last man in the line could be one of the men who tried to take advantage of me."

"Maybe you're right." Elam shielded his eyes again. "He's hanging on to the guy in front of him like he's blind."

When they came within earshot, Zane shouted gleefully, "We made it!"

As they drew closer, Naamah squeezed Elam's arm. "He is one of my attackers," she whispered. "I am sure of it! His name is Dawson."

All ten men quickly gathered around, the last one still grasping his guide. "You were difficult to follow," Zane continued, "but the horse's distinctive prints always put us back on your trail. When we reached a rockier path, we lost track, but I saw the lady in red waving for us to ascend a ridge. When we arrived, she was gone, but from that vantage point we could see you standing here."

Elam pointed a stiff finger at him. "I told you to build a fire and wait for me!"

"Well," Zane said, his smile unabated, "were you planning to come back soon and bring us here?"

"Yes. We were just leaving."

Zane spread out his hands and laughed. "Then we have arrived with the same result, only sooner. It seems that the lady in red has blessed us with another providential shortcut."

Elam stared at Zane, taking in his good-natured smile. He seemed so childlike, too excited to do what he was told. Maybe he was just desperate. Wouldn't anyone be desperate after all he'd been through? But what about his followers? At least one of them wasn't an innocent wanderer.

Elam touched the blind man's shoulder. "Naamah says this man attacked her."

The man stepped forward, his eyes wandering as he wrung his hands. "If Naamah is the beautiful lady I met in the forest, then, yes, it is true. When I saw her lovely form, the desires of my flesh overtook my senses, and I couldn't help myself." He blinked rapidly. "As you can see, God has chastised me for my sin, and I am deeply sorry."

Zane lowered his head. "It is sad that Dawson's sins were so vile and offensive, but, as you heard for yourself, he has repented. We are grateful that God looks upon our faith and not our evil deeds, so our eternal destiny is secure."

Pawing at the ground, Dikaios blew a flapping sound through his lips. "Your destiny is certainly secure."

Zane glared at Dikaios for a moment, but his cheery disposition quickly returned. "I'm glad we're in agreement. May we enter now?"

Elam glanced at Dikaios, but the horse swung his head away. Apparently, he had gone back to his "you-have-to-decide-for-yourself" mode. Elam sidestepped toward the blue wall. "I'll show you how I got in."

Naamah followed and ducked behind him, whispering. "Has God forgiven my attacker?"

He whispered back, "I think we'll soon find out." Naamah gave him a grim stare but said nothing.

"All I did," Elam continued, lifting his hand, "was lay my palm on Heaven's shield, and it covered me with the white clothes I'm wearing. Then it opened up and let me in."

Zane marched up to the wall. "Just as we expected all along. The scarlet key is simply our faith." He pressed his hand against the shield. In a splash of blue sparks, the wall threw him backwards. After rolling through the grass, he jumped to his feet and blew on his hand. "It feels like it's on fire!"

Elam ran to him. "It's blistered pretty badly," he said, examining Zane's burn. Thin streaks of dirt traced the fold lines in his skin, but no blood stained his palm. "There's a pool not far from here if you want to soak it."

"I can tolerate the physical pain." Zane blew on his hand again. "But the stress of not being able to enter Heaven is torture I cannot endure."

Elam patted him on the back. "There might still be a chance. I was told to find ten soldiers for an important mission. Maybe if you can accomplish it, you'll be able to get in."

Zane lowered his hand and glanced at his nine followers. "I am sure I speak for us all. We are troubled by these hoops we must jump through, but we are willing to do whatever it takes."

"Wait here," Elam said. "I have to check with Enoch to make sure it's okay for you to do the job he has in mind."

As he turned back to the wall, a robed arm and leg protruded from it, then the rest of Enoch's body popped through. Acacia followed, her blue hood down and her white hair flowing in the stormy wind.

Elam stepped back and gave each a head nod. When he smiled at Acacia, her return smile seemed forced, and her eyes were dimmer than usual.

"I was just coming in to see you," Elam said.

"Yes, I know. I watched you on my screen." Enoch glared at the ten men. "So these are the soldiers you have chosen?"

Elam shifted his weight from foot to foot. "I guess so. One of them is blind because of his own doing, but they're all I have."

With the breeze whipping his robe, Enoch walked slowly in front of each man, gazing into their eyes. When he reached Zane, he stared at the bespectacled leader long and hard. "Perhaps they are all blind," Enoch muttered.

338

"But I am not blind." Zane lowered himself to one knee and looked up at Enoch. "We are mere men, leaders of flocks of the faithful on the Earth, and we have journeyed through this land wondering why we have not been able to reach Heaven. Even now at the very gate of entry, it seems that we are unable to enter, so we are willing to do whatever we must."

"We shall see." Enoch gestured for him to rise and continued walking down the line of men until he reached the final one. Looking toward Heaven's shield he cried out, "Will ten blind or nearsighted men be able to accomplish this task?"

"Do you want me to send them away?" Elam asked. "I didn't know one of them attacked Naamah until they showed up."

Enoch waved his hand at Elam. "I was asking God, not you." He gazed at them from head to toe, then looked at Naamah, who tried to hide behind Elam. "We will let them stay. The word from on high is that they will serve God's ultimate purpose."

Zane clapped one of his followers on the back. "Excellent!"

"Father Enoch?" Acacia laid a hand on the prophet's elbow, her face streaked with pain. "Now that the participants have been approved, is the timing right for me to begin?"

"Yes, dear child." Enoch took her hand and patted the top. "I know how tragically dangerous and difficult your task will be. After all, the chosen one is a hybrid, much like yourself, yet thrown away before her birth. Still, every great sacrifice requires great suffering, and I know you will be able to carry out what you have been called to do."

Acacia walked to Heaven's shield and set her back against it. As she stretched her arms forward, fire erupted in her upturned hands, two egg-shaped flames that sat in the centre of her palms. Her lips thinning out and tears sparkling in her brilliant eyes, she looked at Enoch. "I await your signal, Father."

Your dragon powers are gone?" Sapphira caressed Ashley's hands. "Are you sure?"

339

Ashley nodded slowly. "I can't even remember the quadratic formula, and I feel sick to my stomach. I can usually make nausea go away in a few seconds, but I can't do it now."

Sapphira covered her eyes with her hand. "I feel it again."

"Feel what again?"

Blue light leaked between her fingers. "Remember when I looked inside you and saw a dragon?"

"Uh-huh. You scared me so bad, I was ready to slap you."

"I'm so sorry!" Sapphira closed the gaps between her fingers. "I think it will stop soon."

Ashley wrapped her fingers gently around Sapphira's wrist. "It's okay. I want to know what you see now." She slid Sapphira's hand away from her face.

Blue beams emanated from her eyes and spilled over Ashley, covering her in a blanket of azure light. Sapphira wheezed, breathing frantically. "I really don't like doing this. I don't like peeking at someone's soul. I have no right to do that."

"You have my permission." Ashley slid into the centre of the light. "Tell me what you see."

After a few seconds, the beams dimmed and blinked out. Sapphira closed her eyes and wept.

Ashley took her hand. "What's wrong? Did you see someone worse than a dragon inside me?"

"That's not the problem." Sapphira shook her head hard.

Ashley lifted Sapphira's chin. "Can you tell me what you saw?"

Wiping a tear, Sapphira leaned close and whispered, "The dragon's gone."

Ashley firmed her lips and nodded. "That's no surprise, I guess, since the traits are gone."

"But there was nothing there." Sapphira spread out her hands. "Nothing at all. No dragon and no angel."

Ashley winced at Sapphira's words but couldn't raise her voice above a whisper. "I'm just an empty shell?"

Sapphira shook her head. "Don't say that. It can't be true."

"But it *is* true. I feel the void, like my whole body is about to collapse." Ashley wrapped her arms weakly around herself. "I'm nothing inside. Nothing at all."

A loud clatter sounded from beyond the exit door. Ashley sat up straight. "What was that?"

"It came from where Walter and Karen went." Sapphira pushed her shoulder under Ashley's arm. "Lean on me, and we'll find out together."

CHAPTER

THE CALL OF THE CROSS

A pulse! Thank God!" Karen took off her jacket and covered Gabriel's head with the hood. With cold drizzle now pecking through her hair, she watched the battle, praying for Walter with all her might. What else could she do? She felt useless, too weak and small to make a difference.

With one hand covering his wounded eye, Chazaq stomped toward Walter, reaching for the young man's head. Walter leaped out of the way and charged toward the giant's blind side, raising Excalibur in attack position.

Spinning quickly, Chazaq dodged. Walter's feet slipped out from under him, and Excalibur flew from his grip, clattering to the stone as he slid past Chazaq's legs.

The giant leaped in the direction of the sword, but Walter caught the toe of Chazaq's oversized boot, tripping him and sending him toppling to the floor. Scrambling to his feet, Walter dove for Excalibur, snatched it off the ground, rolled away from the giant, then sprawled on the wet concrete, groaning.

Karen pressed her hands together. "Walter!" she shouted. "You can do it! I know you can do it!"

Walter pushed against the ground and rose slowly, nodding at Karen. "Thanks," he gasped. "I'm glad someone thinks so."

Ashley shuffled into the turbine room, her arm over Sapphira's shoulders.

"Ashley!" Walter raised his hand, still breathless. "Stand back! I don't want anyone to get hurt." He turned again and faced Chazaq, who had just climbed back to his feet.

Karen waved Ashley and Sapphira to the concrete pillar. When they huddled together on their knees, she whispered. "Gabriel's unconscious."

The three girls made a tent over Gabriel with Karen's jacket. "Walter's supposed to be distracting the giants while Roxil sneaks up on the one on the turbine," Karen said, "but I thought she would have attacked him by now." She pointed toward the covered portion of the turbine room. "Mardon's watching from over there. He's not so confident anymore."

Uncovering his bleeding eye, Chazaq raised a fist and roared. "I am going to grind you into dust!"

"Why don't you add a 'Fee-Fi-Fo-Fum' to that?" Walter shouted. "Then I'll really be scared!"

"What's Walter doing?" Karen asked. "Is he crazy?"

"He's taunting the giant," Ashley explained. "Anger in battle is a handicap, so Walter's trying to get him to do something stupid."

Chazaq dove at Walter in a flying rage. Leaping out of the way, Walter hacked at the giant's outstretched arm and sliced his wrist, drawing a new stream of blood. Chazaq grasped his wound and kicked at Walter, but he leaped away again, this time narrowly missing the giant's ankle with another swipe of his sword.

"Chazaq!" Mardon shouted from the turbine room exit. "Don't be such a fool! Remember what I taught you. A warrior has a will of iron. He cannot be seduced by a cunning opponent.

Your pride in your brawn will be your downfall if you don't change your tactics. Use your gifts, not your anger."

Growling deeply, Chazaq lifted a hand toward the sky. As though he were a lightning rod, energy from the other giant's beams streamed into Chazaq's arm, making his hair stand on end. He extended a thick finger on his other hand. A jagged yellow bolt shot out and sizzled into Walter's chest.

Walter flew backwards and slammed into a pillar, smacking his head against the concrete. Slumping to the side, he exhaled and his arms fell limply to the floor.

"Walter!" Karen screamed.

Ashley tried to get up, but Sapphira grabbed her arm. "No! Neither of you can do anything to help."

"But I have to," Ashley wheezed, trying to wiggle loose. "He's my friend. He's my ... my best friend."

"Get the sword," Mardon ordered, walking into the open area. "Then kill him."

Karen shook free and bolted from the pillar.

"Karen!" Ashley shouted. "No!"

Dashing into the battle zone with her head ducked low, Karen sprinted toward Walter. When Chazaq reached for Excalibur, she zipped past him and scooped it up as she ran. She straddled Walter, pointing the heavy blade at the huge, looming giant and screamed, "Get back, you creep!"

"She is mine!" the giant atop the generator shouted. "She is my prize!"

Covering his wounded eye again, Chazaq scowled at him. "Bagowd! Did you bargain for this puny wench?"

"There was no risk. I knew you would squash the runt."

Ashley struggled to get up, but Sapphira pushed her down and sprinted to Karen, sliding to a stop between her and Chazaq. Using both hands, she shoved Chazaq's thighs, but he barely moved an inch.

343

Chazaq laughed. "The little men are vanquished, and now the little women come to their rescue."

Sapphira raised her hands. Fire leaped from her palms and formed into balls of flame. "You absorb light energy, Chazaq, but I wager that you're still flammable. Want to test my theory?"

With a powerful swipe, Chazaq slapped her wrists, extinguishing her flames and knocking her to the side. Karen lunged and swung the sword at the giant's arm, missing badly. The momentum of her follow-through spun her around, nearly pulling her to the floor.

Chazaq grabbed a fistful of Karen's hair and dragged her toward the generator. Screaming, she kicked and tried to slash her captor with the sword, but to no avail. Suddenly, a stream of fire rocketed into Chazaq's face. Roxil swooped down on his blind side and slammed into his body, knocking him flat. As she swept back up, she roared. "Run! We must hit the other giant while we can!"

Chazaq, his face and beard sizzling, lay motionless on the ground. Mardon was nowhere in sight.

Dropping Excalibur, Karen leaped to her feet and darted back to Walter. Sapphira was already lifting his ankles. "Grab his wrists!" she yelled. "Let's get him under the roof." Struggling side by side, they half carried, half dragged him to the covered section of the turbine room. After laying him down, Sapphira pressed her ear on his chest. "He's alive, but he's barely breathing."

"Ashley will heal him." Trying to smile, Karen swiped back her dampened bangs. "I know she will."

"But Ashley lost—" Sapphira cut her words short.

Karen pulled on Sapphira's sleeve. "Come on! Let's get Ashley over here." Sapphira gave in to Karen's frantic pull, and they hurried back to the column.

When they arrived, Ashley's face was almost as white as Sapphira's hair as she rested her hand on Gabriel's chest. "He's breathing steadily now. I tried to get up to help you, but I just couldn't."

344

Karen pulled on Ashley's arm. "You have to come and heal Walter now."

Ashley jerked back. "I can't. I just—"

"Look!" Sapphira said, pointing.

Karen and Ashley tipped their heads up. Roxil blew a torrent of flames at Bagowd. As the tongues of fire penetrated his surrounding energy field, they fizzled into plumes of smoke. Two other dragons joined her, and all three spewed a barrage of yellow and orange jets.

"It's Arramos and my mother," Ashley said. "They're all working together!"

"Come on!" Karen pulled on her arm again. "Walter needs help!"

Ashley slid away. "I can't," she said, her voice cracking. "I want to … but I just can't."

"Why not? He's hurt really badly. I'll help you walk over there. I'll carry you if I have to."

"I can't!" Ashley buried her face in her hands and sobbed. "Please stop asking me. Please!"

Sapphira touched Karen's arm. "Ashley's too weak. Besides, there's no energy available. We need Excalibur's beam, and Walter's the only one who knows how to use it."

Tears blurred Karen's vision as she stroked Ashley's hair. "How about Ashley's mum? She has fire for energy. And she's a healer, so she could do it herself."

"She's busy trying to save the world." Sapphira wiped a tear from Karen's cheek. "We couldn't get her down here if we wanted to, and even if she could do it without Excalibur, we would need another dragon to heat her scales. We can't leave only one dragon up there to battle the giant. It won't be enough."

As the trio of dragons joined their flames, they flew in a tight circle, and the fire streams shot deeper into the Naphil's protective shield.

345

"They're making a firestorm," Sapphira said. "Do we want that to happen? What about the vortex?"

Ashley lowered her hands. Blood from her palms smeared the tear tracks on her cheeks. "I think that's exactly what Mardon wants. Arramos probably kept my mother away until this moment, and he convinced her and Roxil that this is the only way to stop Mardon."

Sapphira used her sleeve to wipe some of the blood from Ashley's face. "It probably wasn't hard to convince them, since that's what they did to the first tower. But you said you figured out how *we* can stop him."

"It's only a maybe, but I can't remember the probabilities." Ashley hooked her finger around Sapphira's collar and drew her close. "You have to do it yourself."

Sapphira pulled back. "Me? But how?"

"I analysed your light when you flamed up at Mardon. I remember thinking that the balance of frequencies was perfect."

"Perfect for what?"

Ashley opened her hand, exposing her wound. "To pierce the electromagnetic field the giants are creating. All it takes is a big enough interruption in the field, and it will collapse. Mardon's code, the one that was supposed to wake up the giants, was really a set of photometer readings, light intensities for seven different wavelengths. It looks like he matched the light waves that would shock the giants into wakefulness with the light that your fire creates. I guess he wanted to give you the ability to wake them if you needed to, but he never had the chance to tell you."

Sapphira's voice lowered to a whisper. "The other labourers and I were hiding from him. I didn't want him to find us."

"So he must have given up the idea and jotted it down so he could remember it himself if he needed it." Closing her eyes, Ashley ran her fingers through her hair. "I don't remember how I came up with it, but I think your fire light will interfere with their ability to store and produce power."

"Okay." Exhaling loud and long, Sapphira glanced at Walter, Gabriel, and Karen in turn. "What do I do?"

Ashley leaned toward her. "It's extremely dangerous, but you have to get close to the giant and make your light source penetrate his shield."

"Okay. How close? How much fire?"

"I'm not sure. Just get as close as you can and see what happens." Ashley touched Sapphira's fingers. "How much flame can you produce from your hands?"

"I can set my whole body on fire and make a pretty big cyclone."

"Good. Make the biggest inferno ever, but don't spin the flames. We don't want to help the dragons break down the dimensional barrier."

Karen tugged on Ashley's sleeve. "What about Walter?"

Ashley laid her fingers on Karen's cheeks. "The only way to save him is to get my mother down here. We can't do that until Sapphira destroys the field." She drew Karen close, almost nose to nose. "Do you understand?"

She sniffed and nodded. "I understand."

Ashley pulled her into a tight embrace and whispered into her ear. "I love him, too, Karen. But you know he would want us to save the world before we save him, right?" Ashley pushed her back and gazed into her eyes. "So we have to stop the giant. That's the most important thing to do right now."

"You're right." Karen straightened and trudged over the rain-slicked floor. "I'll get Excalibur."

After picking up the sword, she passed by the unconscious Chazaq. Shuffling up to his body, she lifted the blade and poised it over his neck. Her heart raced. It would be so easy to slice the

347

scoundrel's throat. So easy. She let the edge scratch his skin. A trickle of blood ran down and dripped into a puddle. She gazed at his swollen face, blackened from Roxil's fiery jets. *Would Walter do it?* she wondered. *Would he get rid of this beast once and for all?* She shook her head. He wouldn't. He always said you have to meet an enemy face to face. Killing someone when he's down is the coward's way out.

She hiked the sword up to her shoulder and hustled back. Sapphira now stood at the ladder that led up the turbine's exterior wall, while Ashley, looking pallid and limp, remained at the pillar with Gabriel.

The three dragons sprayed the giant's electric shield with fire, enveloping him in a flaming cocoon. As they flew closer, still shooting yellow streams, they used their wings to whip the fire into a frenzy as they zoomed around and around.

"No!" Sapphira yelled. "Don't create the vortex! That's what Mardon wants!"

The dragons continued their barrage. Either they didn't hear Sapphira's call, or they didn't believe her.

Sapphira climbed the ladder, speedily passing rung after rung. When she reached the fence, she scaled it quickly and hopped onto the roof of the generator. One more short ladder to go.

Karen followed, dragging Excalibur with her as she stepped up the rungs. She couldn't let Sapphira battle that hideous monster by herself. He made her look like a little white mouse.

After reaching the top rung, Karen stared up at Sapphira. With her hands raised and already flaming, she closed in on the pulsing electric field, the giant's surrounding glow.

Karen heaved the sword up to her shoulder and looked down at Gabriel and Walter, both unconscious. Firming her jaw, she tightened her grip on the hilt. The guys gave it everything they had. Now it was up to the girls.

Enoch joined Acacia at the shield. "Create the tunnel and hold it in place. We will add the fire and move you into position when the king returns with the sacrifice."

Acacia swirled her hands in front of her as if painting the air with her fiery palms. A shining orange oval emerged at the centre of her swirl and grew to twice her height and width. As she slowed her hands, the oval stopped growing and hovered over the ground. Still visible through the semi-transparent screen, Acacia looked at Enoch, her expression growing even gloomier. "The tunnel is ready, Father."

While Elam, Naamah, and the ten wanderers gathered to watch the hypnotizing aura, Enoch bent over and peered through the light from Acacia's side of the oval. "I'm not sure when the sacrifice will arrive. Can you hold it in place?"

As the swirling light pulsed, Acacia kept her hands moving in small circles. "For a while. It isn't hard."

"As you know, it will get harder." Enoch began pacing in front of the audience. "The storm clouds gathering overhead are the fingers of Earth reaching into this realm. As they grow, they will dissolve the Bridgelands, the dimensional barrier between Heaven and Earth, and bring the eternal kingdom into humankind's reach. Although such a result might sound appealing, you cannot imagine the catastrophe that would occur if the corrupt meets the holy."

He raised his finger toward the sky, still pacing. "If the passage between the two realms opens, it will seem as though an entire world is closing in on us. Some kind of energy-based connection will be made between Earth and Heaven's shield, a path between the two worlds that must be destroyed. Our weapon will be our own energy surge from Acacia's portal that should break the connection."

Enoch halted and nodded at Zane. "You and your fellows must stand in the path coming from Earth. Your goal is to keep the energy flow from striking Acacia when she moves into position to unleash our weapon."

Zane bowed his head. "We will be honoured."

Joining Zane at his side, Elam clenched his fist. "We'll make sure we block it. You can count on us."

"Not you, my son. Not yet." Enoch curled his finger, gesturing for Elam to come closer. "If you were to walk into a cross-dimensional path without protection, it could easily kill you. Zane and his followers are already dead, and the bodies they have now should not be affected by the connecting path."

Elam ground his teeth together. That wasn't what he wanted to hear. Leaning close, he whispered, "What do we do if they can't block the flow? I don't have enough confidence in them to risk Acacia's life. Since she's still alive, wouldn't the path hurt her, too?"

"Acacia is the only one who can accomplish her task," Enoch whispered back, "and she is aware of the risk. So, the connection beam must be broken at all costs. Otherwise, millions on the Earth could die."

"But if Zane and his men fail, is there any other option?"

Enoch glanced at the ten men once more before answering. "There is another option, a short prophecy I received last night, but I hope we don't have to face it." Drawing Elam even closer, Enoch sang quietly into his ear.

Son of man, O son of mine,
Your land has need of cleansing rain.
Conspiring teachers weave their lies
To make the holy foul, profane.

Art thou a son or just a hire?
Go stand before your land of sin
To stay my angels' swords of fire
And fill the gap from deep within.

Enoch pushed Elam back and laid a palm across his cheek. "Do you understand, Elam, my son?"

"Yes, Father Enoch." Elam let out a long sigh. "I think I do."

As daylight faded, Abraham and Timothy strolled along the road that led to the birthing garden. With the people of the village settling down for their evening meal, the two men had no need to assume the praying posture. As doors opened and closed in the humble homes to allow latecomers entry, firelight revealed fathers, mothers, and children gathered around stone tables, some with hands linked in prayer, others already enjoying the bounty of the harvest – food, warmth, and love.

The aroma of stewing vegetables hung in the chilled air. Timothy took a long sniff. Pepper and paprika spiced his nostrils and stung the back of his throat, a good sting that raised memories of Hannah's homemade sausages, hot and steaming on the plate as she gazed at him lovingly, waiting for him to take the first delicious bite.

The fragrance of the villagers' contentment carried both bliss and pain. Memories brought smiles, yet coated his heart with sorrow. With Hannah dead, that bliss was forever gone, burned away with the flames that ravaged their home. He blew a sigh and pushed his hands into his pockets. His companion nuzzled his ear but kept quiet.

As they reached the end of the road and stepped onto a dirt path, Abraham laid an arm over Timothy's shoulder. "You have held your tongue all day. Will you tell me nothing of your meditations?"

"I can tell you some." Timothy kicked a pebble to the side. "Since Enoch's Ghost didn't tell us anything about Hannah's fate, it wouldn't be right for me to live here. Angel would want to become my Eve, and I couldn't bear to say no, especially when I don't have a proven reason. She's an excellent woman, and if I could, I'd be her Adam in a heartbeat. But, as it stands, I can't, and torturing her any further would be a crime."

"Not to mention torturing yourself," Abraham said. "Still, I think she would understand. Your intentions are honourable."

Timothy nodded but said no more.

Abraham rubbed his son's back. "Can you tell me what you have been thinking about the prophecy?"

Timothy shook his head. "Just make sure the night guard knows I'm allowed to stay in the garden tonight, and I'll be fine."

Abraham stopped and faced Timothy, his expression grave. "Will you ever come back to us?"

Timothy couldn't bear to look at him. He just lowered his head and pressed on down the path. "No, Father. After I do what I am called to do, I could never come back."

Abraham caught up and marched at Timothy's side. "If you believe you have found the deceiver, then you need to tell me before you deliver judgment. As Prophet, I must first render a verdict, or there will be no justice in the land."

Timothy dared not look up at him. "Does God ever call us to do an injustice?"

"Of course not. He is the supreme judge."

"Then you have no concern." Timothy halted at the edge of the garden where a tall muscular man stepped in front of him.

"A fair evening," the man said. "What brings you to the garden after dark?"

Abraham waved his hand. "Matters of the heart, Cliffside. Please signal the other guards on the perimeter that my friend, Timothy, may stay here for the night."

Cliffside bowed. "Your will is mine, Father." He turned and whistled several short bursts, two long ones, and two more short ones. A high-pitched whistle answered from across the field, then two others, one from the left and one from the right. The guard extended his hand toward the rows of plants. "You are welcome here, my friend."

Timothy stepped toward the garden, but turned at the last second. He opened his mouth to speak to his father, but nothing came out. Heat surged into his cheeks. As he stared at Abraham's concerned eyes, Listener's pitiful face flashed across his mind. She was just a little girl! How could he possibly do such a thing to a sweet little girl?

Grabbing hold of Abraham's cloak, Timothy pulled him into an embrace. "Father!" he cried, shaking, "I ... I'm not really sure what I'm doing, but I have to do it." He pulled back, and clenched his hands together. His whole body quaked. "Please forgive me! It's ... it's for my daughters, my precious daughters."

Abraham nodded at the guard, who quickly retreated into the garden. He reached out and caressed the back of Timothy's head. "My son, I know how you feel. When I left you and Thigocia on the ark and flew into a storm of demons, I could only watch you float away as I faded into darkness. I had to act on what Enoch told me, and though it sounded like a fool's errand, my faith in God and in you was rewarded, and my obedience proved to save your life and the future of the dragon race." He drew back a step and nodded toward the garden. "You do what you must do, and even if I don't see you again until eternity's dawn, I will walk in confidence that you have followed the light. I taught you wisdom from the time you were born, and I believe you will hold to it now."

Timothy reached out again, but Abraham turned and strode away, his face set straight ahead as darkness enveloped him.

Drooping his shoulders, Timothy shuffled into the garden and sat at its edge. Without the benefit of nearby trees to break the wind, a cold breeze cut through his jacket and chilled his body. He shivered hard.

Hugging himself, both to warm his skin and to quiet his soul, he gazed at thin wisps of smoke rising from the village into Pegasus's pale yellow glow. The huge moon, now about a quarter of the way up its nightly ascension, was followed in its path by a smaller moon peeking above the distant tree line.

His companion orbited slowly, its eyes staying focused on his head. It hadn't spoken to his mind in hours, but he hadn't said a word to it, either. With only such a short time to get accustomed to this orbiting egg, it was hard to know its ways. Was he supposed to ask it questions or just wait for it to give advice like it did before?

As the night progressed, the delicate sounds of the deserted garden drizzled into his ears – the breeze petting the praying leaves, an occasional whistle from one of the guards, and gentle laughter from somewhere in the village, a happy family making ready for bed.

Timothy nodded. Bedtime. Soon Listener would come riding on Grackle. Soon he would complete this terrible task. Soon he would have the stain of innocent blood on his hands, an indelible mark that would scar his soul for all eternity.

354

He shook again, this time from sobs that heaved from deep within. Tears dripped into his lap, and, lifting his gaze toward the sky, he cried into the wind. "Father! Why have you brought me here? Why did you choose me? You need someone with a hard heart, someone who could plunge a dagger into the breast of a little girl without seeing his own daughters staring back at him as her life's blood drained away. For the rest of my life I will have to hide what I did, lest I hear them call out, 'Daddy, why did you do this? Why did you let an innocent lamb die in my place?'"

Heaving in a deep breath, he wept on. "If there is any way you can take this task away from me, Father, let it be so. You have already given your holy son for my daughters, why must anyone else make a sacrifice for them to see the light? Let someone else bear this burden. Let someone else give up their life force to show your grace. Not this precious lamb. Not this suffering little servant."

His companion brushed by his ear. *Who, Makaidos? Who has two life forces to sacrifice? Who but Listener has such a gift to offer?*

Timothy covered his face with his hands and directed his thoughts toward the ovulum. *Nobody has two. She is the chosen one.*

Then weep, dear Timothy. God will always listen. It glided in front of his face and hovered, its eyes flashing blue. *But will you despair?*

Timothy shook his head. *Never! I have seen too many miracles to despair. If I can watch from the prow of an ark while my father is murdered and not fly out to die with him in battle, I can carry out this sacrifice. I have to do my heavenly Father's will no matter what.*

The companion floated back to his shoulder and perched. *Then, so be it.*

As silence again descended on the garden, the moons shed light on the pregnant stalks. One of the plumper leaf pairs shifted, its walls bending and protruding in random spots. Timothy imagined a little elbow poking from near the middle, and a foot at the end of a stretching leg trying to find room as the precious life inside outgrew its temporary shell. Soon, maybe even tonight, it would leave that shell behind and fall into the arms of a loving mother or father where it would be safe from all harm.

Timothy searched the row for other mature pods and noticed Cliffside approaching, a torch in hand. Walking slowly, he paused at each of the bigger plants, obviously checking for imminent births. When he drew near, Timothy rose to his feet.

"This one is almost ready," Timothy said, pointing.

Cliffside smiled. "I've been watching that one. The chosen parents wanted to stay here tonight, but this baby won't come until tomorrow at the earliest. They probably can't sleep anyway. This child will be their first."

Watching the guard's earnest face drew a surge of emotion from Timothy's heart. "Thank you," he said.

Cliffside's brow arched. "For what?"

355

"For watching over the children. They need more guards like you where they came from."

A puzzled look flashed across Cliffside's face, but he just smiled again. "We have detected shadow people in the area," he said, withdrawing a dagger from his belt and extending it toward Timothy. "If one of them gets past our patrol, this blade is sharp enough to slice them."

Timothy grasped the hilt, silvery metal wrapped in a leather strap. Its eight-inch serrated blade gleamed in the moonlight. "Thank you," he said, blinking nervously.

Cliffside nodded and continued his watchful tour in the next row. After a minute or so, only his bobbing torch was visible in the dimness.

Clutching the dagger tightly, Timothy sat next to the wiggling plant again and imagined the squirming little boy or girl inside. He repeated his own words in his mind. *They need more guards like you where they came from.* Biting his lip, he lowered his head and spoke in his mind to his companion. *They certainly don't need hypocrites like me, right?*

The ovulum floated up to his ear and replied in a quiet tone. *You are not a hypocrite until you act against what you know to be right. Your deeds define what you are, and a hypocritical act will soil your character beyond your ability to cleanse. You only have one life to give to God, so give it to him without stain or blemish.*

"Easy for you to say," Timothy grumbled out loud, letting the moonlight flash on the blade. "You don't have any children you have to kill for."

I have only you to love and counsel. The companion perched again atop his shoulder. *I have no children to kill or die for.*

The plant wiggled violently. Setting the dagger on the ground, Timothy rose to his knees and caressed both leaves gently. "Shhhh ... It's going to be okay." As he rubbed the baby's back, it arched, and the little head shifted until it rested in Tim-

356

othy's palm. Tenderly massaging it with his thumb, he began to sing a lullaby he made up for Ashley years ago.

Your daddy slays the nightmare beasts
Who bring their sorrows to your mind.
Begone you monsters, take those fears
And never leave your ghosts behind.

Slowly, the baby settled down. As its steady heartbeat pulsed through the leaf 'and into his skin, Timothy wept. This child would be born tomorrow and cradled in loving arms, while another precious child would not awaken to another dawn. He snatched up the dagger again and gritted his teeth. There had to be another way! There just had to be!

A weak whistle spilled down from the sky. Timothy slid the dagger behind his belt and looked up. The silhouette of a great dragon passed in front of Pegasus and dove toward him. In a gust of wind and flapping wings, Grackle landed gracefully, Listener sitting in the control seat, dressed in purple sweatpants and a black leather jacket. She whistled again, and, while the dragon lowered its head to the ground, she waved Timothy aboard.

Timothy let go of the leaf and scrambled up the dragon's stairway. When he settled himself in the already warm passenger's seat, he reached around and hugged her from behind, his cheek nuzzling hers. "Are you absolutely sure you want to do this?"

She nodded forcefully.

"Then let's go." Just as he was about to pull back, her two companions buzzed around his eyes. The weaker one brushed against the stronger one, and they seemed for a moment to be annoyed with each other.

Listener whistled. Grackle spread out his wings.

"Wait!" Timothy called, falling back in his seat. "Wait just a minute."

357

Listener whistled again and massaged Grackle's warm scales, breathing a lower whistle to keep him calm.

"I have an idea." Breathing rapidly, Timothy ran his fingers through his hair. "It might work, but our timing has to be perfect."

A shout pierced the night. "Who goes there?"

"It's the guard!" Timothy clasped her shoulder. "Get us out of here!"

She pursed her lips and blew a shrill blast. Just as Cliffside came back into view, Grackle beat his wings and vaulted into the air. After gaining altitude in a tight circle over the garden, he shot away toward the land of the shadow people.

Timothy twisted and looked down. The torch streaked toward the village. Soon, Abraham would know. Brushing aside Listener's hair, he leaned forward and kissed her on her scaly cheek, whispering, "You are the bravest of the brave, little lass. I love you like my own daughter."

358

Listener nodded, rubbing their cheeks together. Warmth flooded Timothy's heart. Words weren't necessary ... She loved him, too.

As they approached the bowl-shaped valley, the wind grew colder and colder, stiffening his fingers and numbing his skin. He could barely extend his frigid arms to point the way or force out spoken directions into the biting wind.

Listener didn't seem to mind the cold. As she guided the dragon in the direction Timothy pointed, her little brow furrowed whenever a gust threw them slightly off course, but, other than an occasional shiver, she remained stoic.

Timothy leaned to see around Grackle's head, searching for the river's exit point. Now in darkness, except for the crossing rays of the two moons, the interlaced shadows seemed to blend together, making everything below a criss-crossed web of dark shapes. Since the light tunnel had gone out, there would be no beacon to guide them.

Finally, a glimmer arose from below, a sparkling ribbon. "The river!" Timothy shouted. "Follow it to the right!"

Listener whistled two short bursts and tapped the dragon's neck. With a sudden feeling of lost weight, Timothy retightened his belt and hung on as Grackle banked and dove at the same time.

Blistering cold wind flapped Timothy's hair and cheeks, bringing shivers so violent, he thought his bones might break. Even Listener trembled, but she kept her wits about her as she slapped each side of the dragon's neck in turn, taking him out of the dive.

Now below the tops of the surrounding ridge, the air tempered, allowing Timothy to speak without trembling. He pointed at the mouth of the river. "Over there. That clearing next to the clump of trees."

Listener guided the dragon to the spot, and they landed gracefully next to the river. As Grackle shuddered his wings, Timothy unstrapped his belt and glanced all around, whispering. "The light from the tunnel always kept the shadow people away, but now that it's dark, they could be lurking. Pegasus will likely keep them away from the river, but once we go into the forest, there's no telling what might happen."

He slid down to the ground and helped Listener dismount. Gazing up into the cold dark sky, he brushed his cheek against hers. "I will miss you," he said. "Your willingness to die for others will never be forgotten."

Listener's brow furrowed, and she squeezed his hand.

"Shhh. We have to wait a moment." Timothy stroked her hair. "Our timing has to be perfect. Without more than one witness, who will believe such a story?"

A faint roar rumbled in the sky from far away. Timothy looked up and scanned the darkness. "That sounded like Albatross."

Nodding, Listener pointed at a spot over the ridge. The white dragon, just a tiny blur in the moon's glow, was closing in fast.

359

CHAPTER

SACRIFICES

F acing the giant, Sapphira raised her flaming hands higher and whispered, "Jehovah-Shammah, I know you're here with me. Grant us victory over our enemies, for they extend their prideful fingers into your holy city and dare to touch what is sacred with their bloodstained hands."

She edged closer to Bagowd and leaned into his protective energy field. The giant's electricity buzzed across her skin, sending bullets of pain up and down her spine and through her limbs to her fingers and toes. Steeling herself, she called upon her internal fire. Flames leaped from her body, exploding outward from her head, hands, and torso. The fire ate away at the giant's electric shield, and his surrounding glow shrank as she pushed closer to his feet with her inferno-clad body.

Bagowd swung a foot at her but missed. "Begone, fiery demon!"

Thigocia swooped low and took advantage of the weakened field, sending a blast of flames that torched the giant's foot.

Bagowd roared, but he kept his hands in place. Using the turbine's output and the incoming light from the ten giants at the distant power plants, he refuelled his electric cocoon, making it grow wider and taller. The dragon's fire mixed with the shield again, and the combined energy grew into a twisting column that shot past the clouds. Sapphira trudged closer, and with each torturous step, the column dwindled.

Thigocia took aim at the giant's feet again, but a streak of red scales zoomed in front of her, making her swerve away. "No!" Arramos shouted. "Do not break off the central attack! We must keep the firestorm going. It is the only way to destroy the tower."

Sapphira screamed through her flames. "That's what Mardon wants you to do! The vortex will break down the dimensional barrier between Heaven and Earth!"

Thigocia looped back toward Sapphira. "How do you know this?" she asked as she swept by. She rose again into the air and began another orbit, too far away now to hear an answer.

The giant grunted. "The girl is degenerating the field! I must increase the power!" A new surge of electricity blasted from his body, brightening the upward column and rebuilding his electrified barrier.

As Thigocia approached again, Bagowd's electric cloak pushed down on Sapphira's flaming shield, making the orange tongues surrounding her body tremble. Pain knifing through her heart, Sapphira spat out her reply to Thigocia in short bursts. "I know this because ... I am an Oracle of Fire ... an underborn who saw the ancient days. ... I have made many firestorms ... so I know what they do."

Arramos dove down and barged in between Sapphira and Thigocia. "While we delay, our storm dwindles!" he said, making a tight orbit around the giant to stay in shouting distance. "Roxil and I destroyed Mardon's tower once before, so we know what we are doing."

Thigocia beat her wings furiously, trailing Arramos. "But what if she speaks the truth?"

"There is no time to argue. You said you would not doubt me when this hour came." With a burst of wing power, he launched higher into the sky.

Thigocia followed him, calling back to Sapphira, "I have no proof that what you say is true, so I must keep my word to Arramos."

Sapphira stretched her pain-racked body, reaching for the dragon in vain. "Noooo!"

The three dragons again stirred up the mix of fire and electricity. The brilliant column continued to rise. The clouds evaporated, leaving nothing but a clear blue ceiling that seemed to bend and wrinkle in the heat of the twisting cylinder that stabbed the sky. The blueness streamed away from the atmospheric wound, leaving a black hole that expanded with every second. Soon, black faded to grey, then white. Brilliant light shone through the hole, like a sunray penetrating the clouds.

363

Sapphira continued her relentless march toward Bagowd, bending at the waist as she strained to slide each foot forward. The electric shield pushed down on her like a thousand-pound load. A clanging sound of metal on metal made her glance back. A red-headed girl pushed up from the last rung on the ladder, dragging Excalibur behind her as she mounted the top of the generator.

"Karen!" Sapphira called through the flames. "Don't!"

Karen laid the sword on the roof and rested in a crouch, her arms dangling limply as she panted. "I just ... want to help."

A loud creaking sound erupted from the sky. The hole in the ceiling widened, revealing another land far above – a shimmering blue curtain bordered by a grassy field with several people and a horse standing nearby. The fiery tornado transformed into a cylindrical beam that solidified into a transparent tunnel of light.

The tunnel knifed through the hole in the sky and attached to the centre of the curtain, making a bridge between the two lands.

The newly formed tunnel of light surrounded the giant, giving him a sleeve of protection. With his hands still raised, he held the end of the tunnel steady, his palms pressing against the inner walls and his feet supporting the base.

Arramos shut off his fiery jets. "No more flames!" he ordered. "There is nothing more we can do. We have failed!"

Thigocia wheeled around and flew straight toward the vertical column. "Failure is not an option!" She smashed into the tunnel chest first. In an explosion of sparks, the barrier flung her away in a whirling backward somersault. Stunned, she flapped her wings awkwardly and spun slowly toward the waterfall.

"Mother!" Roxil zoomed under Thigocia's body and helped her spiral safely downward.

"Excellent!" a man called from the turbine room floor. "My new tower is complete! My father's dream of a stairway to Heaven is finally a reality!"

Sapphira cringed. Mardon's voice. Now he's going to try to climb up to Heaven! Her body still aflame, she crept close to Bagowd's legs and laid a fiery hand on the tunnel wall. With a spine-jarring jolt, her hand sizzled and bounced away. She gripped her wrist, holding back a cry of pain. It was useless. The tower was complete; she hadn't stopped it.

Shutting off her flames, she hurried back to Karen. The redhead's gaze was fixed on the sky. "What's up there?" Karen asked. "Who are those people?"

Sapphira looked up. The land in the sky drew closer, inch by inch, as if the tunnel were reeling it toward the Earth. The people in the small crowd near the curtain grew more detailed, but since they were moving around, it was hard to lock on any one of them. Finally, she caught a glimpse of a familiar face and followed it, a young man walking between a horse and the tunnel of light.

When he paused to speak to a much older man, his identity became clear.

Covering her mouth, Sapphira dropped to her knees. "Elam!"

A s gusty winds tossed his hair, Elam stood close to Dikaios and Naamah. "I think all we can do now is wait for the connection."

The horse nodded toward Zane and his nine followers. "Unless you have words of wisdom for our soldiers, I would agree."

The storm clouds thickened and descended, their feathery undersides brushing the treetops. Black funnels spun down. A dozen twisting tongues licked the ground before getting slurped back into the cloud bank only to be replaced by a dozen more. The ten wanderers huddled, the wide whites of their eyes a stark contrast to their soiled clothes. Though unable to see the looming catastrophe, the one blind man obviously felt and heard the rumbling storm and shaking ground. Only Zane seemed to try to keep a brave face as he firmed his chin and stared into the wind.

Elam sighed and shook his head. "I'll try to come up with a last-minute pep talk, but I don't know if it'll do any good."

"I sense that you have no faith in their abilities," Dikaios said. "Do you have an alternate plan?"

"Maybe." Elam looked back at Heaven's shield. "I need something to block the connection, a barrier of some kind."

Naamah picked up a cloak from the ground. "Perhaps this will work. You used it to cover me. Now it might serve another good purpose."

Elam took the cloak and slipped it on. "It might help, but something metal would probably be better."

"The only metal is inside Heaven," Dikaios said. "There is none in the Bridgelands, at least none that I have seen."

"Then this will have to do." Pulling the hood over his head, Elam approached his ten soldiers, but just as he opened his mouth to speak, the clouds lowered to the ground and enveloped them in soupy grey fog that swirled in a frantic dance. Damp misty hands slapped Elam's hood down and mopped his hair with dewy fingers. The fog gathered into streams and funnelled toward Heaven's shield in a twisting horizontal cylinder, clearing the rest of the air.

Like a huge spinning snake, the cylinder lunged at the shield, striking the blue wall just a couple of feet away from where Acacia stood, but she stayed put, still keeping her halo of light in place. As the rush of fog struck the shield, the mist evaporated as soon as it made contact, but the barrage of new fog continued unabated.

The cylinder grew thicker and thicker, until it finally became rigid and slowed its spin. At the point where the fog struck the shield, the grey streams extended tiny fingers that drilled minute holes and attached to the blue wall. Like a ten-foot-thick rope being pulled at one end, the cylinder drew taut and yanked at the shield. The wall groaned but didn't bend.

At first grey and opaque, the cylinder slowly cleared to a translucent yellow, then to pure bright crystal. Thousands of sparks of light zoomed toward the shield and splashed against it in tiny bursts of energy.

Elam patted Dikaios's neck. "Please stay with Naamah, no matter what happens."

"I will protect her as you would," the horse replied.

Elam edged close to the cylinder. It hovered over the ground just above his ankles and reached well over his head. As he extended his hand to touch it, a buzz of electricity tingled his skin, but he ignored it long enough to push a hand into the path. Several sparks zapped his fingers. "Ouch!" He jerked his hand back. "It's electrified."

Zane reached out and pushed his hand into the centre. "I feel a tickling sensation, but it seems harmless." He picked up a stone and released it inside the beam. It hovered near the centre for a moment, then floated toward the shield, accelerating through the beam until it smacked against the blue barrier.

"As I suspected," Enoch said, "it should be safe for you and your companions to enter. The idea is for all ten of you to stand in the gap between Earth and Heaven and disrupt the path of those electrified particles so that Acacia may stand safely at the connection point to the shield. For the sake of all unredeemed humans on Earth, the beam must be extinguished."

Zane waved to his followers. "Let's do this job quickly. Our eternal reward awaits!"

The men formed a chain, locking elbows as they entered the beam about ten feet in front of Heaven's shield. As soon as the light enveloped the last man, he called out, "I can see!"

Elam tugged on Enoch's sleeve. "Why can he see now?"

"To remove all potential excuses," Enoch replied.

367

Thousands of sparks bounced off the men's bodies and splashed to the ground, reducing the electrical attack on the shield. The men stood straight, pulling in their bellies and expanding their chests, like superheroes repelling bullets.

Enoch waved at Acacia. "Move the portal in front of the connection point. The time to unleash the weapon is almost here."

Keeping the fiery halo swirling around her hands, Acacia slid her feet sideways and edged into the beam. As soon as she entered, dozens of energy particles lashed her face. Dropping to her knees, she called out, "Father Enoch! Help!"

Enoch waved frantically at the ten men. "Too many of the particles are still getting through! Assemble in two rows and fill in the gaps!"

The men scrambled into staggered lines of five and raised their hands to block as many of the tiny sparks as they could, but hundreds still passed around them and through the halo, spattering against Acacia. She struggled back to her feet, tucking her chin against her chest. Some of the sparks adhered to her blue cloak, making her appear to be on fire, and her white hair began to rise in the electrified light. "It's not so bad now," she grunted, still keeping her head low. "I can stand it."

Far down the cylinder in the opposite direction, a bright hole opened in the distant sky. The horizon drew slowly nearer. Trees collapsed as if swallowed from underneath. Ponds splashed high as their shorelines clapped together and disappeared. It was as if the entire land had become a river tumbling into a chasm.

Elam backed away from the cylinder and laid one hand on Dikaios and the other on Naamah. In mere moments, they, too, would be washed into the void.

The hole widened to fill the entire horizon. An image coalesced within as if the sky had transformed into a movie theatre screen. A huge man stood with his arms upraised within the cylindrical tunnel of light as a river of water fell into a building beneath him. Two smaller people crouched at the man's feet, while another stooped near an inert body lying on the ground.

As the Earth drew closer, details coloured the people on its surface – the giant, furrows etched across his brow; a girl at his feet, red-headed and tear-streaked; and the other girl, white-haired and flaming.

Elam swallowed a lump. "Sapphira!"

Zane pointed through the tunnel. "I see a giant!"

The other nine fidgeted, breaking the links between them. Hundreds of sparks zoomed past and hammered Acacia. She fell to her knees again, holding up the portal with trembling arms, but she didn't cry out.

"Hold fast, men!" Enoch shouted. "Do not fear this son of the Earth! If you stand firm in your faith, you will defeat this demonic giant!"

The tunnel shuddered. A new pulse of energy shot millions of sparks into the barrier of men, half of them passing around and between their quaking bodies. As the particles riddled Acacia, she moaned but kept the portal in place.

Elam screamed at the men. "Form your lines! She can't take it much longer!"

As the ten men pushed closer together, the sound of the disappearing horizon crashed all around – trees splitting, water splashing, and rocks smashing together in a cacophony.

The giant let out a deafening roar. The strongest pulse yet shot through the tunnel. The men scattered, diving out of the connecting beam just before the wave of energy arrived. It smashed against Acacia and pinned her to the shield.

"It was a giant!" Zane shouted. "He shoots electricity from his fingers! We can't fight an enemy like that!" The other nine murmured their agreement.

"Cowards!" Naamah shouted. "You speak as men of heart, but passion flows only in your loins!" She lunged for the tunnel, but Dikaios grabbed her dress with his teeth and pulled her back.

"Father Enoch!" Elam screamed at the top of his lungs. "I have to help Acacia! I have to block the path!"

"You would die in less than a minute!" Enoch shouted back.

The tumbling earth roared closer. They had only seconds until it would swallow them all.

"Better me than her!" Elam ran toward Acacia. He leaped into the beam directly in front of her portal halo and spread out the cloak's cape as far as he could. Like bees from a hive, the sparks swarmed over Elam, adhering to his skin and clothes. Stinging with horrible pain, he turned and watched Acacia. Most of the particles that flew past him missed her, flying high or wide of her body.

Acacia rose slowly to her feet again, her legs and voice trembling. "Father Enoch! The sacrifice has arrived!"

The onslaught of energy pushed Elam back. He set his feet and leaned into the flow, suffering pure torture every second.

Enoch pointed at Acacia. "Create the pyre for our sacrificial lamb! We will go to battle with the only energy strong enough to counter this monster!"

Her body erupted in brilliance. She pointed into the halo with both arms and sent dazzling streams of light into its centre. Although the radiance streamed into the oval, it didn't come out on the other side.

Steadying her voice, Acacia spoke into the portal. "I am here. The sacrifice must enter alone, for as it approaches, the light will become flames and consume everything in its path."

The energy particles thrashed Elam's body mercilessly. His skin burned. His bones ripped against his muscles as the onslaught flogged him with thousands of electrified lashes, stinging, piercing, stabbing at every pore.

As he kept his pain-riddled arms outstretched, he shouted, "I can't last much longer!"

"Elam!" Naamah cried. She broke away from Dikaios and rushed toward him.

Elam heaved violently. Breath and life drained away, and darkness bled into his mind until he knew no more.

Cradling Listener, Timothy sprinted into the woods. As he leaped over brush and dodged protruding branches, he imagined the spindly limbs of altered ones stretching out to grab his ankles. He ran faster, stomping heavily on every moving shadow.

When he reached the tunnel, he set Listener down at the entrance and shouted into the cavity. "Oracle!"

The call echoed back. "Oracle! Oracle!"

Timothy cupped his hands around his mouth. "I have come with the sacrifice. Are you there?"

The tunnel's light flashed on, so bright, he had to leap away.

"I am here," came the lovely voice, reverberating through the woods. "The sacrifice must enter alone, for as it approaches, the light will become flames and consume everything in its path."

He looked up into the sky. In a flurry of wings, Albatross skimmed the treetops and disappeared toward the edge of the forest.

"They are landing at the river," Timothy said, caressing Listener's cheek. "There were two riders. I'm pretty sure they were Abraham and your mother."

As Listener nodded, her brow furrowed once again.

He pulled her into an embrace. "Don't worry. Neither one of them will be able to stop us."

As she rose from her knees, Sapphira helped Karen to her feet. Far above in the heavenly dimension, yet closing in on their world, Elam jumped toward a blue wall and stood in front of the tunnel of light. Sparks flew everywhere, veiling his face. The tunnel flickered and dimmed.

371

The giant yelled toward the floor. "Mardon! Someone is standing in the circuit. The connection is breaking, and I am running low on power!"

Mardon cupped his hands around his mouth. "Send one big wave of photons! That should kill him!"

Bagowd heaved in a breath. "Here it comes!"

A new blast of shining particles roared through the tunnel. Up above, a woman in a white dress ran toward Elam and jumped in front of him. She spread out her arms and blocked the light, shielding him from most of the new explosion of sparks. Riddling her body with bullets of electricity, the beam shook her like a rag doll.

Sapphira gasped. "That's Naamah!"

Karen bent low, snatched up Excalibur with both hands, and charged at the giant. "You wanted me?" she yelled. "You got me!" With a mighty lunge, she swung the sword and sliced into the tunnel's outer wall. Excalibur swept through Bagowd's ankles, cutting off his feet.

The blade welded to the tunnel's wall on the other side. Karen stiffened. As her fingers locked around the hilt, blue and yellow bolts of electricity arced across her body.

Letting out a scream that shook the entire turbine, the giant crumbled into a heap. His stump of a leg kicked Karen's hands, knocking Excalibur several feet away, then his arm slapped her down, pinning her to the generator's roof.

A second burst of energy rode up the beam and smashed into Naamah, lifting her into the air for a moment as her arms spread wide. Electricity shot from her hands and streaked into several men standing nearby. The men vaporized and disappeared. When the pulse dispersed, she dropped to the ground.

Although the waves of sparks had died away, the connecting tunnel itself remained, leaving a shimmering rope between Earth and the world above. The rope slowly contracted, pulling the two worlds closer every second.

372

Sapphira dashed to Karen. Lifting with all her might, she pushed Bagowd's arm away, exposing Karen's pale face. A trickle of blood oozed from Karen's nose and the corner of her mouth. A pain-filled grimace streaked her brow as she gasped, "Can't ... breathe!"

Sapphira dabbed the blood with her sweater. "I have to get you down from here!" She glanced at the ladder. Much too dangerous. But how else could she do it?

Karen clutched Sapphira's sleeve, new blood leaking from her mouth. "No," she said, gurgling. "Have to help the girl in white!"

"Naamah?"

Karen nodded. "I see her up there."

Sapphira took a quick look at the sky. A bolt of red lightning sizzled from the world above, closer than ever now, and zapped a tree on a nearby mountain, setting it on fire. A loud clap of thunder shot across the power plant, making Sapphira duck low. "I saw her, too," she said, "but I can't see her now."

Karen raised a weak hand. "She's up there. I have to go to her."

"Shhhh." Sapphira pressed a gentle finger on Karen's lips. "Just stay quiet. I'll call Thigocia." She stood and shouted. "Thigocia! Roxil! Where are you?"

A distant call sounded from far away. "I'm coming!" The voice was warped by the roar of tumbling water, but it was clearly a female dragon's, though Sapphira couldn't tell which one.

Another red lightning bolt streaked to Earth, zapping a transmission tower only a hundred yards away. The rifle-shot thunder clap shook the generator, nearly knocking Sapphira down. A few seconds later, Roxil landed on the turbine room floor. "Who called me?" she asked, her head swinging with her neck.

"Up here!" Sapphira waved her arms. "Karen's hurt badly. We need to get her to Thigocia!"

Roxil stretched her neck upward. "My mother is in the river spillway. Her wing is bruised, but she is slowly making her way back up here."

With a frantic wag of her head, Sapphira scanned the floor. "Where did Mardon go?"

"He ran when he saw me coming." Roxil flicked her tail toward the covered portion of the turbine room. "He's hiding behind a pillar like a yellow belly."

Suddenly, Mardon ran out into the open and waved both arms frantically. Arramos swooped down, shooting a barrage of fire at Roxil. She lunged to the side to dodge his attack, but he passed her by, caught Chazaq and Mardon in his claws, and flew away.

Roxil snuffed a stream of sparks. "Cowards! Betrayers!"

"Hurry!" Sapphira called. "Karen's in pain!"

"But we have no healer!" Roxil countered. "Ashley and Walter are in no shape to help."

373

Ashley shuffled out to Roxil and looked up. "Go ahead and bring Karen here. Walter's stirring, so maybe I can get him to wake up and use Excalibur."

Keeping her head low as she glanced at the darkening sky, Sapphira pressed a finger into her palm. "But what about your powers? Aren't they—"

"We have to try!" Ashley interrupted. "What else can we do?"

Sapphira leaned over and picked up the sword. "Roxil, can you carry us both, one in each claw?"

"I can, but there is not enough room to land up there. I will have to come in at your level and pick you up on the fly." Roxil vaulted into the air and began a wide circle.

Sapphira knelt and laid a hand on Karen's cheek. "Okay, get ready for a rough ride, but it will be short."

Karen's eyes stayed closed.

Sapphira gently patted her cheek. "Are you still with me?"

No response. Her head lolled to the side.

Sapphira laid her ear on Karen's chest. As another clap of thunder rumbled across the sky, she pressed down hard to listen.

No breathing.

She grabbed her wrist and squeezed it with her fingers.

No pulse.

"Roxil!" Sapphira screamed. "Hurry!"

Sapphira put the heel of her hand on Karen's chest and pushed – once, twice, three times. More blood oozed from her lips.

Sapphira cried out. "Jehovah-Yasha! What do I do?"

Roxil approached, her claws extended. Sapphira turned Karen over, then, clutching Excalibur, she rolled herself up, exposing her back to the dragon. Suddenly, she lifted off the ground. Karen dangled from the opposite claw, her arms and legs completely limp.

Seconds later, beating her wings furiously, Roxil laid them softly on the ground and landed in a run.

Still gripping Excalibur, Sapphira jumped to her feet and ran to the spot she had last seen Ashley, but she was gone.

"Over here!" Ashley called. She knelt close to Walter as he leaned against the column where Gabriel also rested. "I managed to drag him over here, and he woke up."

Sapphira sprinted to Walter's side and handed him the sword. "Can you use it? Can you and Ashley heal Karen?"

Walter blinked and slowly wrapped his fingers around the hilt. "I'll try," he whispered.

Sapphira looked at Ashley. "Can you do it? Do you have the gift back?"

Ashley opened her hands. The two wounds still dressed her palms in red. "I was hoping for a miracle," she said weakly, "but I don't think I got one."

Two fiery red lightning bolts crashed to the ground, rattling every window in the building. Sapphira grabbed Ashley's jacket. "You have to try!"

"Let's get her to a hospital, maybe she'll—"

"No!" Sapphira pulled so hard, she jerked Ashley up to her feet. "Karen's dead. You're her only hope!"

CHAPTER

HEAVEN'S BOUNTY

A wakened by a roar, Elam blinked his eyes open. Acacia stood in the connecting beam, her hands shooting a barrage of flames into the oval halo. Enoch and Dikaios stood close to her, peering into the halo from her vantage point. The sparks of energy that had racked her body were gone, allowing safe passage in and out of the tunnel, and the encroaching Earth had slowed, easing the horizon's flow into the void.

"Will he do it?" Enoch asked.

Dikaios shuddered his mane. "It is impossible to guess. Timothy has brought the girl, but I cannot imagine his turmoil. He is torn apart by conflicting forces of love."

"He must do it. The destruction of the giant has only bought us a little more time. As long as the connection between Earth and Heaven remains, the two will draw slowly together, and with every inch the gap closes, a holy wrath will build against the corruption of the earthly lands." Enoch looked into the halo again and clenched his fist. "If Timothy fails, Earth will perish."

Elam shook his head slowly, trying to make sense of his surroundings. He twisted his neck and looked back. A red translucent film coated the blue wall of Heaven's shield, sizzling and bubbling like oil on a hot pan. Slowly, the redness gathered toward the centre of the shield a foot or so above Acacia's head, creating a chaotic swirl of scarlet sparks. Then, in a rush, the red energy shot straight out. A jagged bolt hurtled toward Earth, following the connecting tunnel until it zapped the ground somewhere near the power plant that hovered above the horizon.

Several shadows crawled along the grass near Enoch's feet, oozing toward Acacia's halo like thick oil. One of the shadows streamed through the portal, but, although Enoch looked straight at it, he didn't react at all. The other shadows sank into the soil and vanished.

Still too confused to understand what was going on, Elam tried to rise, but a bulky weight pinned him to the ground. He blinked rapidly to clear his vision. A body lay across his waist, a small body dressed in a white gown with a circlet of flowers pressed around her head.

"Naamah?" he whispered.

"Ah!" Enoch said to Dikaios. "Elam has awakened. He was merely sleeping, just as you thought."

"Should I help him up now?" Dikaios peeked around the halo. "I still wonder why you would not allow me to move Naamah's body out of the way."

Enoch nodded at an approaching shadow. "I was waiting for the other faithful witness to arrive. The first one covered him, and the second will raise him up." He smiled and returned his gaze to the portal. "Elam has all the help he needs."

A pair of hands pulled Naamah away and helped Elam sit up. Dizzy and confused, his gaze followed the helping arms up to the shoulders and face of a red-headed girl no more than thirteen years old. "Who are you?" he asked. "I saw you down on Earth with Sapphira."

"I'm Karen." As she gently rolled Naamah face up, a gem-stone flashed on her finger — a rubellite.

"Are you a dragon child?" Elam asked.

"No. I don't know why this came with me." Karen twisted the gold band and pulled it off her finger. "I should give it back to its owner, but I don't know how."

"Who owned it?"

"Ashley Stalworth, my adoptive sister and daughter of Thigo-cia, queen of the dragons."

Elam held out his hand. "I will do everything in my power to take it to its rightful place."

"Isn't it strange," she said, laying the ring in his palm, "that I would still have it, even though I died?"

Elam slid it into his tunic's inner pocket. "You died?"

"Uh-huh. It hurt a lot at first, but then the pain suddenly stopped, and this shining man with wings ... an angel, I guess ... pulled me up to this place. It was all pretty cool." She pressed her ear against Naamah's chest. "But this isn't cool."

379

As another red lightning bolt zipped over his head, Elam crawled over to Naamah and took her limp hand. His own hand trembled. "She's asleep, right? Or unconscious?"

Karen caressed Naamah's cheek. "She passed away, too."

"Dead?" Elam pressed his fist against his lips. He wanted to say more, but he couldn't. He would cry, for sure.

"She saved your life," Karen continued. "I saw her do it. She blocked whatever that stuff was ... that energy beam. It was killing you."

Enoch walked over to them and set his hand on Karen's head. "And you destroyed the source."

"Father Enoch?" Elam's voice faltered. "What will become of Naamah? She was alive, wasn't she? I mean, still alive in my world."

Enoch stooped and stroked Naamah's black tresses. "What you see is the earthly shell that was restored to Naamah after she faced the angel in the halls of judgment." He straightened and waved toward Heaven's shield. "Naamah's spirit passed through the barrier while you were unconscious. She wanted to wait for you to awaken, but we had no idea when that would happen, so I told her I would deliver her message to you."

Elam's throat clamped so tightly, he could barely speak. "What's the message?"

"While you were lying there, she kissed your hand and said, 'Even though you saw every shadow of darkness in my soul, you are the only man who ever really loved me. Without your love, I never would have seen the light. Thank you for believing in me.'"

Elam stared at Enoch. He could hear Naamah's voice saying those exact words – meekly, barely above a whisper. Turning back to her, Elam shed his cloak and laid it on her body. "There is no longer any shadow in your soul," he said as he pulled the hood over her head. "Rest in peace, and may God grant me the pleasure of seeing you again." Another bolt shot out from the shield and rained crimson sparks on the cloak. Elam folded his hands over Naamah's body and wept.

Karen rose to her feet. "Is that Heaven in there?" she asked, pointing at the shimmering blue wall.

"Indeed, it is." Enoch took Karen's hand and bowed his head. "If not for you, my brave little heroine, all would have been lost, and billions would have died."

"We all fought the giant." She raised a finger for every person in her troop. "Walter and Ashley and Sapphira and Gabriel. They all gave it everything they had, too."

"And the youngest one felled the giant!" Enoch swept his arm toward Heaven's shield. "Are you ready to enter?"

"I think so. I believed everything Sapphira said about Jehovah-Yasha. Isn't that all I need?"

"A surrendered life is all he asks, and you gave it without question." Enoch led her to the blue wall, just a few paces from where Acacia stood. "Now touch the shield and be dressed in holy attire."

380

Karen stepped up close, raising her hand. "Like this? Just touch it?"

"Just a touch. Your passage has already been purchased."

Karen paused. A frown wilted her expression. "Something's wrong. I feel something pulling me, like arms grabbing me and trying to drag me away."

Enoch took her hand and patted it. "Your friends are trying to revive you down on Earth."

Karen looked at the image of Earth in the sky. Ashley knelt at the side of a red-headed girl, thrusting the heels of her hands into her chest. Karen shivered and turned back to Enoch. "Will it work?"

"It is hard to say, but if you enter the shield, it will be much more difficult for them to succeed. Yet, if God so chooses for you to return, you could still go back."

Karen moved her hand closer to the wall. "I really want to go in, but I guess they want me to come back, don't they?"

"Of course they do. They love you. Still, because they love you, though they would weep for you bitterly, they would ultimately be satisfied to know that you have entered Paradise."

Karen shook her head sadly. "They wouldn't know for sure. I just started believing today."

"A late-blooming faith is just as effectual for entering Heaven as one that has stood the test of time, but, as you say, it is less of a comfort to those on Earth." Enoch set his gaze on the horizon. Now Thigocia was spreading her wings across Karen's dead body while Roxil heated her scales with a blast of fire. Enoch sighed. "That is the lot of many who grieve."

"Not to influence your decision ..." Elam rose to his feet, wiping tears on his sleeve. "But if I get to go back to Earth, I'll tell them you went to Heaven. Sapphira knows who your friends are, so I'm sure I can find them."

Her smile returning, Karen leaned toward the shield, pulling hard against the invisible force dragging her back. First her fingers, then her palm touched the blue wall. It rippled, sending waves of shimmering sparks across the expanse. Pure light crawled along her arm and enveloped her body in white glitter. Seconds later, the sparks evaporated, revealing Karen in a long white dress, much like Naamah's. Somehow she looked older now, more refined than the young teenager she had been. A white crease appeared in the wall, an open door to Paradise. With a timid wave, she whispered, "Until I see you again," and she disappeared through the shield.

Bolts of red lightning continued to streak from the spot above Acacia's head, becoming more and more frequent as the two worlds slowly pulled together. A cataclysm beyond all measure was only minutes away. Even Enoch seemed troubled as he watched one of the bolts, the thickest and brightest yet, fling toward the planet.

Acacia called out, "Watch, if you dare to see the sacrifice of love! It is coming into the tunnel!"

Enoch put his arm around Elam, and the two hurried to Acacia's portal. "Even though I have watched a thousand sacrificial acts," Enoch said, "this is one that makes me shiver. Even I cannot predict what the outcome will be."

A s red streaks lit up the sky, Ashley hugged Karen's lifeless body, still warm from Thigocia's attempts to revive her. With her arms wrapped around Karen's torso from behind, Ashley tried to push blood into Karen's stiffening limbs. "Come on, sweet angel," she cried, shoving her doubled fists into Karen's chest. "Get your heart going!" With her ear against Karen's back, Ashley listened. Nothing. No heartbeat. No breathing.

Loud peals of thunder reverberated, one after another, a chorus of rumbling echoes bouncing from mountain to mountain.

A wail erupted from the depths of Ashley's soul. "Oh, Karen! Why do you have to go? I love you so much!" She sniffed and wiped her nose on her sleeve. "I'm so sorry! You were a sweet little orphan, and I made you a guinea pig, but you still loved me.

You even followed me across the country. If you hadn't come with me, you'd still be alive!" She rested her face on Karen's back, heaving. "I'm so, so sorry."

A familiar grip rested on Ashley's shoulder. Walter's hot cheek pressed against hers. His voice breaking, he whispered in her ear. "Ashley, it's over. She's gone."

Ashley sniffed again. "I just had to try one more time."

"Of course you did," Thigocia said. "I know exactly how you feel. Life is precious, and healers do all they can to preserve it."

Trembling, Ashley laid Karen down and, with Walter's help, pushed herself up to her feet. She brushed her hair back and looked around at the array of wounded and exhausted soldiers. Gabriel still lay unconscious at the pillar with Roxil sitting next to him caressing his head with the tip of her wing. Sapphira, her hand radiating heat, rubbed Thigocia's bruised wing.

"Does the warmth help?" Sapphira asked.

"It does," Thigocia replied. "I will soon be well. My injuries do not last long."

383

"Mother," Ashley said, her voice frail, "in all the excitement, I don't think you noticed that you have another person to heal."

"Another human?" Thigocia shook her head sadly. "I will try, but I have not had much success with humans."

"With this one you might." Ashley hobbled over to Gabriel, knelt next to him, and cradled his head. "Mother," she said, her tears streaming anew, "would you please try to heal my brother ... your son ... Gabriel?"

Thigocia's jaw opened slowly. Her red eyes sparkled. With a beat of her good wing, she shuffled close and extended her neck, gazing at the wounded boy's face and sniffing his body. Finally, she stared at Ashley. "It *is* Gabriel!" She lifted her head and trumpeted a joyful arpeggio, so loud the three humans had to cover their ears.

When she finished her call, Thigocia quickly scooted closer and covered Gabriel with her wings. "Who will heat my scales?"

Walter withdrew Excalibur and looked at Roxil. "We're both pretty tired. Want to give her a double dose to make sure?"

"It will be my pleasure." Roxil backed away a few steps and breathed a weak stream of fire over Thigocia's scales.

As Walter moved into position, Sapphira guided Ashley to a safe spot behind the pillar, then carefully dragged Karen's body there as well. Walter lit up Excalibur's beam and lowered it to the floor. The energy surged through the concrete and sizzled into Thigocia, combining the light with Roxil's fire and covering the dragon healer with a glittering mix of sparks and flaming tongues.

After a few seconds, Thigocia thumped her tail on the floor. "Stop! I feel him moving."

Walter doused the beam. Roxil snuffed her flames. As Thigocia uncovered Gabriel and reared back to give him breathing room, everyone drew closer.

384

Gabriel blinked at the five faces staring down at him. "What are you all looking at?" he asked, rubbing his cheek. "Am I on fire?"

"Close." Walter reached down and latched on to Gabriel's wrist. "Get up, lazybones. Your mother's been trying to get you out of bed."

Riding Walter's upward pull, Gabriel rose and stood on wobbly legs. After stabilizing his body, he spread out his wings and smiled at Thigocia. "Dragon or not, I'd recognize you anywhere." He took a tremulous step toward her and held out his arms.

With a quick sweep of her wing, she folded him in and nuzzled him cheek to cheek. "You're still a teenager! I expected you to be much older!"

"It's a long story. You see—"

"Better hold that story," Walter interrupted. "We have to get back to business." He looked up at the beam connecting Earth to the land in the sky. Ashley followed his gaze. A huge red bolt split into five fingers and knifed into Earth, raising violent splashes of sparks and flames. As thunder shook the ground, Walter set his feet to ride it out. "I've got a feeling that if we don't knock that tower down soon, we're gonna be at ground zero for some serious fireworks. Anybody got any ideas?"

"I don't, but maybe they do." Sapphira's blue eyes glistened as she watched the people up above. "I can still see Elam. I wish I knew what he was thinking. Maybe he could tell us what to do."

"Too far to yell." Walter picked up a splintered two-by-four. "And I don't think smoke signals would work, either."

"I could try to fly up there," Gabriel offered, "but something tells me it could be lethal to cross the dimensional boundary."

Taking Sapphira's hand, Ashley watched the scene at the far end of the tunnel. A girl with white hair, a teenaged boy, an old man, and a horse stood around a shimmering oval. Ashley pointed. "Is that Elam between the girl and the old man?"

"Yes, and the girl is my sister Acacia."

"She certainly resembles you, and the man looks familiar, like I've seen him—" Ashley took a quick breath and pointed. "Elam is staring straight at us."

Sapphira's grip tightened on Ashley's hand. "You're right! He is!" She took several steps forward and gazed up at her long-lost friend, so close, yet still separated by a barrier neither one could cross. She lifted a hand and wiggled her fingers, their sign of love that began many centuries ago when she fed him and saved his life. Slowly, he raised his hand and wiggled his fingers. Trembling, Sapphira pressed her lips together, trying not to cry. Would she ever see him again? Would she ever get to whisper in his ear the words she longed to say?

Elam jerked around and glanced at Acacia, then frantically waved both arms at Sapphira.

Walter pulled Sapphira back. "I don't like the looks of this. I think he's telling us to run for it!"

As Timothy and Listener huddled near the cave entrance, a rustling sound, then a frantic call, pierced the forest. "Timothy!"

Timothy whispered to Listener. "It is almost time. Are you ready?"

She kissed Timothy's cheek, and, after taking a deep breath, she leaned toward the tunnel.

He held her fast. "Not just yet. A few more seconds." He withdrew the dagger from his belt and held it close to her neck, whispering, "Are you frightened?"

She shook her head slowly, but, even in the dim moonlight, he could see her throat move up and down in a tight swallow.

"Timothy! No!" Abraham broke through the shadows, followed by Angel. They halted and shielded their eyes from the tunnel's blazing light. "Timothy! There has to be another way!"

Angel held out her arms for her daughter. "Listener! Come to me. He can't make you do this!"

Listener shook her head and interlocked her fingers with Timothy's. She rubbed her roughened cheek against his hand, then kissed his knuckles.

Angel's lips trembled. She dropped to her knees and stretched out her arms, her face twisting in agony. "Listener! No!"

Timothy poised the dagger in front of Listener's throat but kept the blade away from her skin. "Angel, I'm sorry to put you through this, but—"

"How could you!" she wailed, her eyes wild with terror. "How could you condemn an innocent little lamb? She loves you! Candle loves you! And I ..." She buried her face in her hands and wept bitterly, her head bobbing in time with her sobs.

Abraham knelt at her side and draped an arm around her shoulders. "Hush, my sweet child. I will put a stop to this."

Timothy shuffled back a step. "You don't understand. I have to do this. I had to bring Listener here and wait for you to witness the sacrifice. There is no other way."

"Son." Abraham stood and walked toward him, taking slow, careful steps, his hand extended. "Son, come back to the village. We will sort everything out. God would never ask—"

"A lamb to be sacrificed?" Timothy shook his head hard. "No, Father. You're wrong. God set this standard over two thousand years ago." Now crying, he held Listener in front of him, one hand on her shoulder and the other still propping the dagger as they edged closer to the cave entrance. "If his children go astray, a father has to give everything he has to bring them back."

Abraham shook his fist and shouted, "But Listener doesn't belong to you! She is not yours to give!"

"I know!" Timothy sidestepped into the tunnel's light. Its radiance washed over him, filtering through his skin and piercing his heart. Love flowed through his mind and seemed to spill out through every pore. He bent over and wrapped Listener in his arms from behind. "She didn't belong to me," he replied softly, as he backed with her under the cave's yawning arch, "but she has given herself to me freely."

Angel reached out her clenched hands, shuffling forward on her knees. "Don't take my little girl! Please don't take my little girl!"

"I haven't taken Listener from you," Timothy said, slowly pulling his arms away from her. "I brought her here so her willingness to die would be proven in front of witnesses. I want her sacrificial love to be remembered among your people forever." Letting the dagger slip from his fingers, he grabbed one of Listener's companions in one hand and his own in the other. With one last look at Abraham, he said, "Farewell, Father. I hope you understand why I have to do this." He pushed Listener toward Angel, then ran into the tunnel, his eyes wide open. Frantic shouts of "Timothy! No!" faded away behind him. As the barrier came into view, the light turned to heat, then to fire. The beautiful white-haired girl stood behind the crystal wall, half smiling, half weeping. Extending an arm toward the scene behind her, she stepped out of the way.

As searing heat streamed all around, and as the companions scorched his palms, a view of a river and a power plant appeared behind the barrier. It seemed as though he were flying above it, floating perhaps a hundred feet in the air. On an exposed concrete floor, Ashley and Roxil stood together, both gazing at him.

Timothy gasped. They saw him! He was sure of it!

The fire burned away his skin, the pain so awful he could only spread out his arms, his hands opening as he fell to his knees, but he managed a weak smile as the vision of his lovely daughters faded away.

A n explosion boomed from the sky. Flames gushed from the oval in front of Acacia and hurtled through the tunnel of light, cascading toward Earth like a fiery avalanche.

Thigocia and Roxil spread their wings. The humans ducked underneath and peeked out. A torrent of fire poured through the tunnel in a violent storm, incinerating the electrified walls of Mardon's tower. The flames splashed against the top of the generator. Hundreds of fiery streams arced into the air, some landing on the dragons, but they easily shook them off.

388

After a few seconds, the fire fall ceased. A number of spotty flames remained, burning piles of debris as well as the Naphil on top of the generator. Still visible up above, Acacia held the shining oval. It expanded, stretching out in every direction until it filled half the sky with flames.

Ashley pushed Roxil's wing out of the way. "I see a man's face in that fire!"

"I see a red dragon," Roxil said, "and he's coming closer."

"A dragon? He has skin and hair." Ashley took Roxil's clawed hand and held it against her chest. "I've seen him before ... like in a dream. Do you recognize him?"

Roxil spewed out a weak stream of sparks. "Father! It is Makaidos! My father!"

"It is! It is our father!" Ashley's knees buckled. "Daddy!"

As Walter and Gabriel scrambled out from under her wings, Thigocia gazed at the sky. "Do you see my husband up there? I don't see anything."

"He's there, Mother!" Ashley cried. "He's there!"

The man in the sky smiled and spread out his arms. In each palm, a wound blistered open. Blood poured out, fading from red to white to clear. It rained down on Ashley and Roxil as diamond-like crystals that scattered on the floor around them.

Ashley fell to her knees and lifted her own bleeding hands in the air. "Daddy!" she cried as she tried to catch the precious crystals. "I love you! Come back to me!"

Roxil roared a low lament, moans too deep for words. Hot dragon tears dripped to the ground.

Flames consumed their father's body, charring his flesh to a black silhouette until only a joyful smile remained ... and bones, a skeleton that flashed against the dark body until it finally crumbled as the vision in the sky evaporated and disappeared.

389

Ashley buried her face in her hands. "Daddy! Oh, dear God, my Daddy!" She sobbed uncontrollably, heaving so hard her ribs ached.

"What happened?" Thigocia called. "What happened?"

Roxil let out another wail before answering. "He burned, Mother! My father burned! He is gone!"

Thigocia trumpeted a soulful note and collapsed to the floor. "Makaidos! My Makaidos! What have you done?"

With a loud boom, the world above reeled back as if slung away by a rubber band. The hole between the two realms closed with a resounding clap, leaving a clear blue sky.

As Ashley continued weeping, warm hands pressed on her shoulders. "Ashley?" Sapphira's fiery touch and satin voice caressed her aching heart. "Ashley, I have to show you something."

Lowering her hands, Ashley turned her head. Sapphira knelt at her side, her snow white hair and blue eyes shining. The aged oracle scooped up a handful of tiny diamonds. As her limbs transformed into flaming tongs, she moulded the crystals like clay. Opening her fingers, now flesh once again, she displayed a crystalline egg. It rocked back and forth in her palm, glowing with a brilliant white light.

"A gift from your father," Sapphira whispered. "During your vision, Enoch spoke to me from Heaven. He said your father gave his life so that you might believe in the ultimate sacrifice."

Her hands trembling, Ashley took the egg and caressed it with the tips of her fingers. As its warmth penetrated her skin, she clasped her hands around it and clutched it against her chest. Kissing her fingers, she wept again, quietly this time as the Oracle of Fire backed away.

Sapphira glided to Roxil and did the same with the diamonds that surrounded her, moulding another egg that shone like a full moon. As she presented it to the weeping dragon, she said, "Release your bitterness and hostility toward the image of God and take hold of the ultimate gift that your father treasured and now bestows to you."

Roxil extended her foreleg. "Do you mean I will ..."

Nodding, Sapphira raised the egg to her fingertips. "If that is what you have embraced in your heart."

As Roxil's red eyes flashed, new tears fell in trails of steam. She enclosed the crystal in her claws. Its glow leaked through her grip and covered her scales, bathing them in an ivory wash. The scales flattened and smoothed over. The tawny colouring eased into Caucasian flesh tones. Crawling up her foreleg, the transforming glow created an arm, elbow, and shoulder, silky and creamy white.

Walter yanked off his borrowed coat and tossed it on the floor near Roxil. "I think you might need this," he said, turning his back. Gabriel, too, faced the other way and stood next to Walter.

Thigocia raised her head and struggled to her haunches, her red eyes flashing. "I cannot believe what I am seeing!"

As the glow covered Roxil's body, her frame shrank to human size. Scales vanished and spines morphed into auburn hair. Soon, an adult woman stood barefoot in front of Sapphira, her eyes wide as she ran a hand up and down her new body, the other still clutching the crystal. "I'm ... I'm human again!"

Sapphira grabbed the coat and helped Roxil put it on. "Yes, you're human, but you look very little like the Jasmine I once knew."

After pushing her fist through the sleeve, she opened her hand. The egg, though remaining a beautiful crystalline gem, no longer glowed. "I am not Jasmine," she said softly. "I want to be called ..." Her eyes rolled upward for a moment, then returned to Sapphira. "I want to be called Abigail."

Tears filled Sapphira's eyes. "Abigail means, 'My father is joy'."

Ashley rose to her feet, still clasping her egg. She joined Sapphira and Abigail and spread out her hands. Her egg, too, had lost its glow.

391

Sapphira wrapped her fingers around Ashley's wrist. "Your wounds are gone! And so are the stains!"

Shaking too hard to speak, she nodded. She reached into her pocket and withdrew the dime, the only remaining coin of the original three. As soon as she opened her hand and exposed it to the breeze, it crumbled to dust and blew away.

Intertwining her fingers with Abigail's, Ashley pressed close and kissed her cheek. "I'm glad to have an older sister," she whispered. "I need someone to keep me in line sometimes."

Abigail smiled. "I will try to live up to your newfound confidence in me. I certainly deserved none before today."

Thigocia lumbered to Abigail's side. She spread a wing around each of her human daughters. "This is too much to take in. I have no idea what to say."

"Hey!" Gabriel called. "Can we turn around now?"

Ashley laughed. "Our brother wants to join in."

Zipping her bulky coat and pulling the bottom hem down near her knees, Abigail sang out, "You gentlemen may behold the new and improved dragon in your midst."

When Walter and Gabriel turned, Abigail posed, dramatically spreading her arms. Gabriel laughed, but Walter just nodded grimly and slid his foot on the damp concrete. "That's really cool. I guess with every disaster, we need something to give us hope." He shuffled over to Karen and knelt beside her. "We'd better get out of here. No telling if Mardon will come back with his overgrown apes."

Sapphira heaved a sigh. "You're right. We'd better figure out who can ride with whom."

Walter clutched Karen's limp hand. "Thigocia's in no shape to fly, so we'll have to hoof it. Maybe we can find a cart and try to get Karen to a morgue or a funeral home."

392

Sapphira continued her massage on Thigocia's wing. "Abigail and I are the only uninjured ones here, so we won't have a problem, but some of us are too weak to go very far."

Walter set his thumb in a hitchhiker's pose. "Then we might have to bum a smoother ride, if anyone's brave enough to be driving on the highways right now."

"And pick up someone who's carting a dead body?" Ashley shook her head. "Not likely."

"There was a truck at the guardhouse," Gabriel said. "Finding the keys shouldn't be a problem."

Ashley leaned against Gabriel. "Does anyone else know how to drive? I think I'm too dizzy."

"I have a learner's permit." Walter patted the wallet in his rear pocket. "But it's not valid in this state."

Gabriel stretched out his wing and gave Walter a light tap on the back of his head. "The state we're in is the state of emergency, so it's valid. If you can push the pedals and steer the wheel, you're our driver."

Walter shrugged. "Maybe, but if it's not an automatic transmission, we might not get very far." He scooped Karen's limp body into his arms and stalked toward the turbine room's exit. "Let's get to the truck. We still have a lot of work to do."

Sapphira ran toward the control room. "I'll be right back. Ashley's bag is still in there."

As Walter shuffled away, Karen's head bobbed limply over his arm. Ashley's jaw trembled. She was dead. Her sweet, adorable little sister was dead. The ecstasy of the miraculous in the wake of tragedy stirred her emotions into a stormy sea. In the span of a few minutes she lost a father and an adoptive sister, but she gained a new sister, a dragon reborn. She opened her hands and gazed at her freshly healed palms, one with a diamond egg staring back at her. Most important of all, she had found the faith she had been seeking all her life. Her fear of Hell was gone forever.

Still weak in her knees, she followed Walter slowly, her feet heavy as she clumped along. Gabriel flew to one side and propped her up, while Abigail hustled to support her other side.

Last of all, Thigocia slid along at the rear, fluttering her wings to help push her body. As they neared the turbine room door, she stopped. "The passages through the building will be much too small for me. I will attempt to fly around and meet you at the entrance."

Ashley turned and touched her mother's cheek. "If you're not there soon, we'll come looking for you."

"My wing is almost healed. I will probably be waiting for you." Thigocia shifted around and beat her wings slowly. After a few seconds, she gradually lifted into the air.

As Ashley watched her mother elevate and begin an arc toward the front of the power plant, she let out a sigh. "Do you think Karen has wings now?"

Gabriel draped an arm over Ashley's back. "I don't know about wings, but I'm sure she's in Heaven."

393

Tightening her lips, Ashley nodded but said nothing. Something in Gabriel's words rang true. Was it his confidence? No. It was something else, an impression more than anything.

As they pushed on, the image of Elam slowly materialized in her mind. Though his details were vague, his stance and his countenance poured comfort and solace into her heart. Everything was okay. Karen was alive.

Sapphira hustled back to the group, Ashley's bag over her shoulder. She joined Walter and supported Karen's head as he walked.

"Sapphira?" Gabriel called. "You said you heard Enoch. Did he say anything else?"

Turning back, Sapphira shook her head. "Enoch is just that way. He only tells me what I need to know."

Gabriel paused for a moment and picked up the dagger he had used against the giant. "Well," he said, sliding it behind his belt, "if you hear from him again, can you ask if he's seen Karen up there?"

Ashley piped up, her voice pitching high. "There's no need to ask him."

Sapphira ran her fingers through Karen's tangled red hair. "Why not? Enoch won't mind."

Pulling Gabriel closer, Ashley leaned her head against his shoulder. "Because I already know the answer."

CHAPTER

Clasping Hands

Flames rocketed from the cave entrance. Abraham twisted away and flattened himself against the face of the mountain. "I cannot enter!"

Kneeling close by and holding Listener in her arms, Angel cried out, "What can we do? We can't give up!"

Listener buried her face in her mother's shoulder, sobbing, but she managed to squeak out, "Let me go in there."

Angel pushed Listener to arms' length. "You talked!" Her fingers trembling, she caressed the girl's cheek. "What happened to your face? It's smooth!"

With fire still pouring from the cave, Abraham leaned toward them. "The companion my son took from her somehow carried her frailties with it."

Suddenly, a fireball burst from the cave, and the flames died away. Carrying his torch, Abraham dashed inside. As intense heat drew sweat from his pores, he stripped away his outer garments and pressed on. The stench of burnt flesh assaulted his nostrils and churned his stomach. Finally arriving at the barrier, his skin drenched and dripping, he pushed his hand against the flexible wall. His own reflection stared back at him, rippled by his touch. In the crystalline mirror, the torch's flame illuminated the floor at his feet, a floor littered with charred bones.

He knelt and waved the torch across the scattered skeleton. Reaching down with an unsteady hand, he picked up a long bone, mostly white, but blackened at the ends. As he stared at it, a gentle sob rocked his body. He closed his eyes. Grief flooded his heart, and the sobs took control.

He threw the bone and the torch to the floor. Grabbing his thin undershirt, he ripped it at the breast. "My son! My son!" he cried. "My dear son! Why have you done this?"

As the torch lay on the ground, its flame dwindled, leaving only a small tongue of fire lighting the cave. He rifled his fingers through his hair and screamed, "You came back to me after all these millennia, and now you're gone!" He fell to his backside and wept, his shoulders heaving.

After a few minutes passed, the sound of grinding pebbles popped in the hot cave, drawing closer. Two dark frames appeared, one much smaller than the other. As they crept into the torch's dying glow, the faces of Angel and Listener became clear. They, too, had stripped their outer garments, leaving them with knee-length leggings and sleeveless undershirts. Their sweat-slicked bare arms gleamed in the firelight.

"Is he here?" Angel asked. "Did you find Timothy?"

Lifting a bone, Abraham nodded. "What's left of him."

Angel leaped forward and dropped to her knees. "No!" she wailed. She reached for the bone but jerked back and wrung her hands together. "It can't be true! It just can't be true!"

Listener leaned her head against her mother's shoulder. "I was supposed to die instead of him. I wanted to save his daughters, and I wanted the pain to stop. The girl with white hair said all pain would end after the sacrifice."

"And what of my son?" Abraham asked. "What has become of his soul?"

"I think he gave it up," Listener said. "He wasn't the chosen one, so I think he can't go to Heaven now."

Abraham shook his head, his frown deepening as his voice lowered to a growl. "I can believe that my son would give his life for another, but I cannot believe that God would send his soul to Hell in return."

Angel guided her companion into her palm and held it in front of Abraham. "You have always taught us, Father, that if our companions are destroyed, our anchor in the afterlife is uprooted, and our souls would be set adrift. Listener explained to me that Timothy gave his adopted anchor as well as one of hers to his daughters. Perhaps the key to his destination lies with them. But I also must wonder what has become of Dragon. That companion was first his, and I am again bereft of my Adam's memory."

397

"Maybe I can look through that tube again," Listener said. "Maybe the girl will come back, and I will ask her what has become of my father."

Abraham climbed to his feet and picked up his torch. "You may ask her, precious child, but I think this mystery will remain until the warrior chief comes." He nodded toward the cave entrance. "In the meantime, we have to avoid the shadow people and keep watch for a coming deceiver."

Angel caressed a bone with her finger. "Perhaps we should collect these and bury them."

"In the daylight." Abraham reached for her. "Come. Every second increases our danger."

Taking a helping hand from Abraham and Listener, Angel rose to her feet. Sweat slickened each pair of clasped hands as they walked toward the entrance.

Angel sighed. "Father?" she said, her voice trembling.

As their footsteps echoed in the tunnel, Abraham waited for a moment to answer as he struggled to gain control of his voice. Finally, he gave her hand a gentle squeeze. "Yes, my child?"

"I loved him." She, too, paused. Her words came slowly. "We needed each other. I thought he would be my Adam."

Abraham nodded. "I loved him, too, but I don't think he was ever meant to be your Adam." He picked up his outer shirt and laid it over his shoulder. "Perhaps someday I'll tell you the whole story, but I don't think you can bear it so soon after this tragedy."

Now in cooler air, Angel and Listener gathered their outer dresses and put them on. "Father Abraham," Angel said, "I think it would be best if you hold on to your secrets. If Timothy and I ever meet again, he can tell me the story himself."

398

Acacia clapped her hands together, snuffing the flames. The shining halo quivered and slowly shrank into nothingness. Dropping to her knees, she covered her face and cried, "Father Enoch! Timothy sacrificed himself!"

Enoch laid his hands on her shoulders. "Does this surprise you?"

Acacia didn't answer. Her body just kept heaving as she sobbed on and on.

Elam drew near to Enoch, followed by Dikaios. "It doesn't surprise me," Elam said. "I met Timothy in Dragons' Rest. I could tell he loved his daughter, no matter how much she rebelled against him. He would have done anything for her." He nodded at the spot where the halo used to be. "Even that."

Enoch helped Acacia rise to her feet. He turned her around and pushed her snowy hair from her lovely face, revealing tiny burns that marred her skin. "Your journey is just beginning," he said. "Is the ark prepared?"

Acacia heaved once more, catching her breath. "Yes ... Father Enoch. ... I will go and get her." She walked into the shield and disappeared in a flash of blue.

"Do you mean the ark from the prophecy?" Elam asked. "Are we ready to go on the next mission?"

"You are. The first is complete. The second, a far more complex assignment, awaits. You must leave immediately."

Elam knelt at Naamah's body and took her hand. "How will I get her back to Earth? We can't just leave her here."

"I will see to her proper burial. For now, you and Dikaios must take Acacia and Paili on a journey." Enoch lowered his hand to Elam. "Are you well enough to travel?"

Elam accepted the help and pulled to his feet. "I'm pretty sore," he said, lifting his legs in turn, "but I can manage."

"Good. Then there is no reason to delay."

Elam gazed at the restored horizon. Lush trees and grass once again blanketed the Bridgelands. He scuffed his shoe across the grass where the shadows had seeped into the soil. "When I blacked out, Zane and the others were still here, but when I woke up they were gone."

399

"They fell victim to their own fears." Enoch raised nine fingers. "For all but one, their wandering is over. They have gone to their final destination."

Crossing his arms over his chest, Elam stared at the beautiful scenery. In his mind's eye, he saw Sapphira, wet and trembling next to that giant. Taking in a deep breath, he closed his eyes. How he longed to be with her again! Friends for thousands of years, yet he had never told her what he really felt about her. If only he could talk to her, tell her how proud of her he was for battling the giant. He would take her in his arms and –

Dikaios snorted. "I told you he wouldn't ask."

"You were right." Enoch sighed. "It's a good thing I'm not a betting man and did not accept your wager."

Elam swung his head around. "Ask about what?"

"The nine wanderers," Enoch explained. "Just about every human on Earth would ask what their final destination was, and you did not."

Dikaios smacked Elam with his tail. "His curiosity wouldn't kill a sick kitten, much less a cat."

"And you didn't ask about the tenth," Enoch added. "He has gone to yet another land."

Elam shrugged. "I just assumed it wasn't my place to know. They weren't family, friends, or loved ones, so it's really none of my business."

"Yet, earlier," Enoch said, raising a finger, "you asked about Naamah."

As a new tear welled in his eye, his voice faltered again. "She *is* a loved one, so I guess I thought ..." He turned away, shaking his head.

Acacia reemerged from the altar, followed by Paili. Swinging their clasped hands, they stopped in front of Enoch. "We're ready," Acacia said, keeping Paili's face pointed away from Naamah's body.

"Does she bear the words?" Enoch asked.

400

Acacia smiled and patted the little girl on the head. "Her mind is a steel trap. She won't forget."

Elam slid his hand into Acacia's. "So do we just go back the way we came? And what do we do when we get to Earth?"

"You will return to Earth in time," Enoch said, "but first you must travel to a completely different realm, one you have neither seen nor heard of. When you arrive there, you will learn about the rest of your journey."

Intertwining fingers with Acacia, Elam smiled. "I think we can handle it."

"We'll have lots of help." Acacia nodded toward Heaven's shield and whispered to Elam. "I saw Naamah in there. She's already at a prayer bench, and she has her hologram tuned in right on you."

Elam glanced at Naamah's body but quickly turned toward Enoch. "Can I see her for a minute, just to say thank you?"

"No, my son. The time for your departure is upon us." Enoch waved at Dikaios. "Come now, my fine horse. You're going, too."

"With pleasure, good prophet." Dikaios loped to Elam's side.

Enoch set his hands on Elam's shoulders. "Acacia, reopen the tunnel to Second Eden, and let the warrior chief, his two oracles, and his brilliant steed enter the new realm."

Sitting in an overstuffed chair in a motel lobby, Walter propped his feet on a coffee table as he closed the cell phone. "My dad says that power's been restored in most places, and" – he flipped the phone into the air and caught it – "obviously cell service."

Leaning forward to make room for his hiking-style backpack, Gabriel grabbed a French fry from a McDonald's bag. "Any other news?"

Walter tossed the phone to Ashley, who sat on a sofa on the other side of the table, her head resting on Abigail's shoulder. "Larry wants you to call him," he said. "His transmitter got fried by a power surge." He nodded at the lobby counter. "Dad phoned in his credit card number, so the bill's taken care of, but we have to find a good disguise for Sapphira as soon as possible. Sleeping in the woods with Thigocia won't be as cosy as a motel room."

401

"Mother will keep her warm and dry," Abigail said. "You can count on that."

"We should have gotten a disguise at the outfitter's store," Walter continued. "They had backpacks, so they're sure to have sunglasses and a floppy hat she could stuff her hair into."

Gabriel raised a finger. "The clerk said there's a Wal-Mart a couple of miles from our motel. I think that's closer. If they'll take your dad's card, we'll be in business."

Ashley keyed a number into the phone. "You're not taking the truck, are you?"

"No. I can hike that far." Walter half closed one eye. "Are you saying my driving's bad?"

Ashley lifted her eyebrows. "Don't ask me. Ask those chickens you scattered."

"There was traffic ahead, and I didn't want anyone to see us." Walter shrugged his shoulders. "So I had to invent a new road."

Ashley lifted a shushing finger to her lips. "Hello, Larry. ... Of course you knew it was me. Who else would call this number? Any news? ... Okay. ... Okay. ... Anything else? ... Got it. ... I'm not sure yet. Want to test me? ... A fourth root? In my head? ... Okay. But no more than three digits. I'm tired. ... Seven hundred, seventy-nine?" She rolled her eyes upward. "Let's see, five point ... two ... eight ... three." She laid her hand on her head and winced. "What? ... No, that's all the digits you're going to get. If you hear any news, give me a call on Walter's phone."

Gabriel grabbed another French fry. "It looks like you got your smarts back. I only knew it to two decimal places."

"Really?" Ashley said, her brow lifting again, "I couldn't do fourth roots until—" She caught Gabriel smirking at Walter. "Brothers!" She threw a pillow at him and snatched away the bag of fries, but she couldn't hide her grin.

Walter pointed at her closed fist. "Does that mean your healing power is back, too?"

"I guess so." Ashley opened her hand, revealing the crystalline egg. "But I haven't had a chance to try it yet."

"I hope we don't need it," Walter said, "but if it's back, it might come in handy."

Her smile faded. "It's too late for Karen," she said softly as she looped her arm around Abigail's. "I hope Sapphira and my mother can figure out how to get her body into the morgue."

Walter drooped his head. "Yeah. That'll be tricky. Maybe they should just bury her themselves or have Thigocia incinerate her."

Ashley covered her eyes with a trembling hand. "Please. Talk about something else."

Stroking her hair gently, Abigail kissed Ashley's cheek. "We will."

Everyone stayed quiet for more than a minute, nibbling fries and sipping drinks from straws. Finally, Gabriel spoke up. "So, did Larry have any news?"

Ashley wiped a tear and began counting on her fingers. "First, there's no news anywhere about the giants or Arramos, so it's a good bet that Mardon's hiding out with them somewhere plotting his next move. Second, there's a lot of creepy things going on, weird hairy creatures stalking the streets, sort of like ape men who don't die when they're shot, and people who are supposed to be dead showing up at their old homes, even a couple of murderers who were executed decades ago."

"Wow!" Walter picked up a soft drink cup and loudly slurped the last drops. "That sounds like a bad zombie movie."

"Tell me about it!" Ashley pointed at a third finger. "Finally, Sir Patrick is coming to the States with Sir Barlow and his knights. If we can get back to West Virginia, he'll meet us at Walter's house. Otherwise, he'll figure out a way to get out here."

403

"Why is he coming?" Walter asked.

"Larry didn't say, but knowing Sir Patrick, I'm sure he'll be able to help us straighten out this mess."

Gabriel stood up and adjusted his backpack. "We don't have much experience separating Earth and Hades. Time to call in the pros." He stretched and turned to Walter. "I need some sleep. You coming?"

"Yeah." Walter said, rising from his chair. "I'm beat."

"Wait!" Ashley reached out a hand. "Walter, can you walk Abigail and me to our room first?"

"Uh, sure. No problem." Walter nodded at Gabriel. "You go ahead. I'll be there in a minute."

After helping the ladies to their feet, Gabriel shuffled down the hall in one direction, while Walter and Abigail supported Ashley as she hobbled down the other.

When she stopped at her room, Ashley swiped the key card through the reader and opened the door. "You go on in," she said to Abigail. "I want to talk to Walter for a minute."

"Sure. Take your time." Abigail smiled and disappeared into the room, closing the door behind her.

Ashley took one of Walter's hands into hers and displayed the egg in her palm. A pained expression wrinkled her face. "I think I figured out what this thing is all about." She pulled in her bottom lip and pressed her teeth down on it.

Walter caressed her hand with his thumb. "It's okay. Take your time."

"I think ..." She closed her eyes and tried to steady her voice. "I think my father sacrificed his life for me. What I saw in the sky was him dying so that I could believe." She opened her eyes and raised the egg higher. "This is his gift, a symbol of faith that I never really had. He opened the sky and showed me a heavenly Father. He painted a picture of God, a father who is willing to die to give me life."

"But your grandfather explained all that to you. You told me that yourself."

Ashley nodded. "My grandfather sang 'Amazing Grace' to me for years, but I never really listened. Now I finally understand that verse."

"Which verse is that?"

"Do you mind if I sing it?" Ashley shifted her weight from foot to foot. "One of the last things my grandfather ever said to me was, 'Maybe someday you'll sing it with me, even if it's in Heaven.'"

"So you want to sing it for him now?"

"Because ..." Her jaw quivered. "Because I know he's listening."

Walter nodded at her. "Go ahead. I'd love to hear it."

Ashley folded her hands and, tilting her head upward, whispered, "This is for you, Daddy." After clearing her throat, she sang in a trembling voice.

404

Amazing grace, how sweet the sound,
That saved a wretch like me.
I once was lost but now am found,
Was blind, but now, I see.

She sniffed and wiped her eye. "That's the verse. That's the one I finally understand."

"I'm sure he loved hearing it." Walter brushed away his own tear. "What made the difference?"

"I always knew what it felt like to be lost, but not to be found. And, worst of all, I had no clue how blind I was." She lifted a finger and pressed it against Walter's shoulder. "And you're the one who helped me see it first."

Walter stared at her finger. "Me? How?"

"When I saw you fighting that giant, I knew you were willing to die. I'll never forget your love for Karen, Sapphira, and me for as long as I live." She opened her hand and gazed at her crystal. "That's the kind of love that'll open anyone's eyes."

Walter trembled, but he quickly recovered. "Maybe you can wear the egg on a necklace, like some people wear a cross. Isn't it a symbol of your faith?"

Ashley pressed it against her chest. "It's more than that. As long as I keep my father's gift close, I feel like I have a connection with him, like I know his heart and his thoughts."

Walter nodded. "Then a necklace would be perfect. It would be touching you near your heart all the time."

"True, but there's more to it than that." Ashley tapped a finger on her head. "You remember how I used to talk about people thinking I can read their minds?"

"Yeah. I remember."

"Maybe it's more real than I thought. Now that you and my father opened my eyes, I feel like I can see everything a lot more clearly, like I can even imagine what people are thinking."

Walter closed his eyes. "Okay," he said, grinning. "What am I thinking?"

"No, silly. It's not like I can read the words in your mind. I see images in my head and feel emotions that help me know what people are worried about or happy about."

Walter's face slowly took on a serious expression. "Do you see any images now?"

"You want to test it? Right here?"

"Sure. Why not?"

"Okay. ... I'll try." She closed her eyes and concentrated. After a few seconds, she raised a finger. "I see Karen ... and that's making you sad. ... I see you standing next to her and holding Excalibur, and that makes you feel strong and brave but kind of useless since she died. And over to the side, I see ..." She opened her eyes, now blurred by tears. "I see me, and that makes you feel ..." She paused, biting her lip again.

406

"Go ahead." Walter cleared his throat nervously. His voice grew soft and tender. "How do you, Ashley Stalworth, make me feel?"

She squeezed his hand. "Loved?"

"Yes." He touched the crystalline egg. "Loved by my new sister, born today because of her father's love."

Ashley lifted her brow. "Just a sister? Nothing more?"

"I wouldn't say *just* a sister." He interlocked his fingers with hers. "You're my partner. And we have a lot of scary stuff to do together before this is all over."

Ashley smiled. "Together. That's what's important." She raised their clasped hands. "As long as we're together, I'm not afraid of anything."

Recap of *Eye of the Oracle* and *Dragons in our Midst*

B ack in the days just after Adam and Eve sinned in the Garden of Eden, Lilith, an ancient sorceress, found the leftover seeds from two trees, the tree of life and the tree of the knowledge of good and evil. As the wife of one of the Watchers, a powerful race of fallen angels, she had learned the secrets of the dark magical arts, so, along with Lucifer, she plotted a scheme that would use those seeds to deliver into her hands the power to rule the world.

One obstacle stood in Lilith's path – the impending flood that would destroy every creature on Earth, including her. Using genetic material stolen from her demonic husband, Lilith implanted within her sister, Naamah, the ability to produce a hybrid race of humans – a cross between normal humans and fallen angels, thus allowing the Nephilim, a race of evil giants, to survive the great flood. Naamah married Ham, a son of Noah, thereby allowing her to escape on the ark.

In order to conceal her identity, Lilith took the name Morgan and asked to be allowed on board Noah's ark, but she was unmasked during a cataclysmic battle between the Watchers, who wanted to destroy the ark, and a host of dragons, including Arramos, the king of the dragons, who were trying to protect it. During the battle, a strange egg-shaped glass orb called an ovulum, from which the prophet Enoch spoke, helped Noah overcome the evil Watchers and banish them to a prison called Tartarus, the lowest level of Hades. While on the ark, Naamah gave birth to Ham's son Canaan, a hybrid who carried the genetic code of the Nephilim.

Two of the dragons who helped secure the ark, Makaidos, son of Arramos, and Thigocia, stayed on board as the only survivors of their species. Morgan died in the flood, but, because of her sorcery, she became a wraith, a quasi-physical phantom who could shift her shape, often appearing as herself, as a raven, or as other humans. Promising Naamah eternal life and beauty through her sorcery, Morgan pushed Naamah off the ark and turned her into a wraithlike creature who could become a bat as well as other forms.

Naamah and Ham stole Chereb, the sword an angel had used to guard the tree of life, and, after Noah cursed Canaan, Naamah took her son into exile. This sword could shoot out a laser-like beam that would transform any organic matter into light energy, thus killing any living creature unless someone captured the light energy and saved it until the creature could be restored. The sword could only be used by a king with holy hands or by his heir or designate who also had holy hands. This property, however, could be counterfeited if the user smeared his hands with the blood of someone pure and innocent.

Morgan and a brilliant scientist named Mardon used Canaan's genetic material to fashion a new genome, a cross between a plant and a human. These new creatures began as plant seedlings but later matured into humans. Many of the males blossomed into giants, new members of the Nephilim race, while the females became simple labourers called underborns who worked in the caverns far beneath the third circle of Hades.

One of those labourers was Mara, a girl with special traits – intelligence superior to the other labourers, eyes that shone with an unearthly blue radiance, and stark white hair. Her sister, Acacia, another labourer with the same traits, had been cast into a river of magma, punishment delivered by Morgan, though Acacia did

408

nothing to deserve it. Mara later learned that she and Acacia were Oracles of Fire, twins who were supposed to disrupt Morgan's plan to kill the dragons, a plan that included releasing the Watchers from their prison and growing Nephilim as soldiers who would march on Earth as a conquering army.

Meanwhile, the two surviving dragons, Makaidos and Thigocia, procreated quickly, producing Goliath, their firstborn male, and Roxil, a female. As the young dragons grew, and as the human race began repopulating Earth, a great leader arose, Nimrod, the son of Canaan, who became the king of Shinar. Nimrod, with the help of his son, Mardon the scientist, built the Tower of Babel, hoping to reach into Heaven.

Mara worked with Mardon in the lower realms of the underworld. She carved out a growth chamber, a recess in the cavern wall where the seedling of a giant would hover in apparent weightlessness and grow into a human form. Magnetic bricks lining the arch around the seedling would shine coloured lights, giving photo-nutrients to the plant while providing antigravity forces to allow it to be suspended in mid-air.

While Mara helped Mardon as a laboratory assistant, the other girls dug in the cavern, mining the magnetite ore used in the bricks. One of those girls was the young and verbally challenged Paili, whom Mara took under her wing to protect her from Nabal, their cruel taskmaster.

At a lower level in the maze of underground tunnels and chambers, two boy labourers fashioned and baked the bricks. One of those boys, Elam, had been kidnapped from his father, Shem, son of Noah, and forced to work in the mines. Maltreated by Nabal, Morgan, and Naamah, Elam barely survived on the morsels he could scrounge. Mara befriended him and later, when he was near starvation, fed him by hand through a hole in the wall. From that time forward, whenever they wiggled their fingers at each other, they were reminded of her gift of love.

409

Elam found the tree of life Morgan had grown from the seeds she discovered in the Garden of Eden. After eating its fruit he no longer hungered and never aged. Mara, since she was born and lived in the land of the dead, also never aged, so she and Elam retained the appearance of teenagers. He later stopped showing up at their meeting place, so their friendship seemed to have abruptly ended.

Because of her excellent work, Mara earned the opportunity to temporarily leave her home to visit Earth, the land of the living. Mardon had another reason for allowing this visit. He had found Enoch's ovulum, but he had no idea what it was. The ovulum indicated that it would communicate only with a maiden of nimble mind, and Mardon guessed that Mara could easily be that maiden. When he showed it to her, the ovulum told her to visit Nimrod, Mardon's father, an idea to which Mardon readily agreed.

Mardon, with the help of Morgan, transported Mara to Shinar through a portal. When King Nimrod met her, he was so taken with her beauty and sparkling sapphire eyes, he called her Sapphira Adi, a blue gem, a name she took as her own. When Sapphira showed Nimrod the ovulum, it spoke a prophecy of destruction upon the king and his tower to Heaven.

Makaidos and Roxil, along with several other dragons, attacked the tower and created a spinning column of fire around it. One of the other dragons was Arramos, who supposedly died in the great flood. He encouraged Roxil and the others to follow him in rebelling against the humans, who had corrupted the newly reinhabited world. All but Makaidos and Thigocia joined Arramos, leaving only two dragons who were faithful to their calling.

As Sapphira, still carrying the ovulum, raced away from the destruction, the bottom third of the tower sank into the ground. When she reached the place where she had emerged from Hades, Sapphira used an escape trick she had learned. She spun a fire-topped stick over her head, thereby creating a vortex that sliced through the dimensional barrier and allowed her to return to the land of the dead.

The huge vortex the dragons spun had also created a rift in the barrier. The bottom portion of the tower, a museum that held a great library of scrolls, transported to a massive underground portion of Hades near where Sapphira lived. A residual portal, a swirling column of light, remained in that chamber as an easy way to transport from Hades to another dimension.

Sapphira kept the ovulum. The voice inside comforted her by teaching her about Elohim, the God for whom the prophet within the ovulum spoke. Soon, she learned to love this God. Though her knowledge of him was lacking and immature, her love for him was pure and very real.

Mardon later returned to Hades as a dead spirit and went back to his work with the Nephilim. In an underground chamber called the mobility room, he taught the maturing giants how to walk and become powerful soldiers, including a growing seedling Sapphira had raised on her own, a plant she named Yereq. Sapphira and Yereq had become fond of each other, but Morgan taught Yereq to hate Sapphira and recruited him into Mardon's army.

Sapphira missed Elam and wanted to search for him. Paili tried to convince her that Elam had to be long dead, but Sapphira didn't believe it and set out to find him. Although she was forbidden by Morgan to use the residual portal, Sapphira learned how to circumvent that problem. She used her power as an Oracle of Fire to ignite anything that would burn. Then, by creating a spin with her fire, she could create her own portal wherever the dimensional barrier was thin. She found such a place at the top of the tower museum and frequently travelled back and forth between her home deep underground and the surface lands of Hades.

This portal atop the museum led to Morgan's domain, a castle-like house on an island surrounded by a snake-infested swamp. Searching for Elam there proved fruitless, though she found other

411

portals in Morgan's dungeon-like basement. Most of these led to other parts of Hades that also revealed no trace of Elam, while one seemed to be a bottomless pit. Sapphira didn't dare jump into it.

Morgan had taken Elam to the sixth circle of Hades and was keeping him prisoner there, hoping to use him to betray Sapphira. Since she was an Oracle of Fire, she could not be safely killed unless someone betrayed her. Using Morgan's sorceries, Naamah sang songs of hatred for Sapphira that constantly repeated in Elam's ears, songs so horrible they tortured his mind. By refusing to betray his friend, he spoiled Morgan's plan to obtain the oracle's blood for use with the sword of Eden.

Roxil, the dragon daughter of Makaidos and Thigocia, rebelled against her father's commands to serve humankind. Her brother Goliath, also a rebel, took her as his mate and produced a son named Clefspeare, who sided with Makaidos when he came of age. Morgan hatched a plan to create war between humans and dragons, using Sir Devin, one of King Arthur's knights, as a dragon slayer. Devin murdered Makaidos and Roxil and claimed that the dragons wanted to kill all humans.

Meanwhile, Sapphira, because she was trying to escape a ferocious dog in Morgan's basement, dropped into the dark portal hole she had feared, leading her into the sixth circle of Hades, which looked to her like the ruins of the ancient city of Shinar. There she found Elam and also the dead spirits of Makaidos and Roxil, who had transformed into humans. Strangely, Sapphira was unable to communicate with the former dragons. They appeared to be deaf and mute ghosts wandering through the ruins.

Sapphira created another portal that led her and Elam back to a place she had never visited in her underground home, the edge of a magma river at the bottom of a chasm into which Morgan threw labourers she wished to punish or dispose of. Sapphira and Elam arrived at the precise moment Morgan and Mardon cast Paili into the chasm and the river of fire.

After figuring out that the river would not harm them, Sapphira and Elam dove after Paili. A whirlpool in the river created a vortex that sent them into a completely new dimension, Dragons' Rest, a place similar to Hades, yet created for the spirits of dead dragons. They found Paili and were able to communicate with Makaidos and Roxil. Makaidos learned that he was to build a whole new village in Dragons' Rest in preparation for the spirits of many more dragons who would soon join him and Roxil.

While in Dragons' Rest, Sapphira found a way to restore some of her labourer friends who had been cast into the same magma river, including Acacia, her twin Oracle of Fire. Although Makaidos was friendly to the humans, he told them they had to leave, because this realm was meant only for dragons. Sapphira and Elam departed, taking Acacia, Paili, and several other underborn girls with them.

Shortly thereafter, Sapphira and Acacia figured out a way to hide a portal entry and keep Morgan out of their underground caverns, and, with the help of Enoch's ovulum, Elam escaped to the world of the living. Since his family had died centuries ago, he made a new life for himself with a descendant of Joseph of Arimathea. Sapphira, however, had to return to her caverns in Hades, but she was comforted when she learned that her underground portal could expand into a viewing screen through which she could watch Elam and follow his adventures.

Merlin, a prophet of God and descendant of Enoch, intervened in the war between dragons and humans and convinced the king to wage war only against the dragons who were not loyal to Makaidos. Devin had other ideas and connived to show the king that no dragons could be trusted.

Merlin gathered the remaining twelve dragons he believed were loyal to Makaidos and asked God to transform them into humans. In theory, they would be safe in their disguises, and since they would retain their dragon genetics, they would survive

413

for centuries and outlive Devin and any other slayer. Unfortunately for the dragons, Devin learned of the plan and began searching for and killing these newly formed humans. He found the candlestone, a gem that could weaken dragons, and used it to slay every dragon he could find.

Merlin assigned Elam the task of following and guarding Hannah, who had once been Thigocia. Her departed mate Makaidos, after building a new village in Dragons' Rest, escaped through a portal and lived inside the ovulum Elam now carried. Since Elam never aged, he was able to secretly follow Hannah for centuries, and he successfully duped Sir Devin into seeking her elsewhere.

Sapphira and Acacia discovered a secret entrance into Mardon's mobility room, a tunnel vent that led to a trapdoor in the room's ceiling. After climbing down a rope, they found a long line of Nephilim growth chambers and a sleeping giant in each one, including Yereq. A note on a scroll left behind by Mardon indicated that he would try to find a way for his giants to escape. He also left digital counters on each chamber that indicated how long it would be until the giants awakened. Sapphira took one of those counters and kept it with her, giving her an easy way to know when that time would arrive.

After many years passed, Hannah discovered Elam while he was checking up on her in Scotland. On the same day, Devin attacked, destroying the ovulum in the process. Timothy, the human form of Makaidos, emerged from the broken egg and helped Hannah and Elam escape. Hannah and Timothy went into hiding, while Elam learned of his new assignment to befriend and help a man named Patrick, who was once Valcor, a dragon son of Thigocia and Makaidos. Elam stayed with Patrick in England for years and took on the name of Markus in order to protect himself from Sir Devin.

Timothy and Hannah had a son they named Gabriel, fully human except for a set of dragon wings sprouting from his back. Thirteen years after his birth, as Devin closed in on them, Timothy and Hannah decided to hide Gabriel with Patrick and lead Devin to the United States. The slayer, however, stayed in Europe and tried to kill Gabriel. As it turned out, Patrick used the sword of Eden, now called Excalibur, and transformed Gabriel into light energy. Elam and Sapphira created a portal that took Gabriel's energy to Hades where he maintained a physical form. Whenever he went to the living world, however, he again became a phantom, consisting of energy particles visible only to Sapphira's eyes.

Patrick and his wife, the now grown-up Paili, had a daughter named Shiloh. Morgan, who was trying to gain a host body for herself, kidnapped Shiloh and kept her prisoner in Hades. Sapphira and Acacia searched for Shiloh, but, in the process, one of the snakes in Morgan's swamp bit Acacia. Since Acacia was no longer able to help in the search, Sapphira sent her to Sir Patrick's house. While she was there, Morgan, in the guise of Sapphira, poisoned Paili. Acacia, under the direction of Joseph of Arimathea, carried Paili into Hades in search of a way into Heaven to find a cure.

415

Merlin, now living as light energy within the candlestone, assigned Gabriel guardianship of Ashley, Timothy's and Hannah's newly born daughter. Devin killed Ashley's parents, but her adoptive grandfather helped her escape, not allowing the slayer to know she even existed. Since Ashley's danger had passed, Gabriel was assigned by Merlin to watch over Bonnie Conner, the daughter of another dragon-turned-human. This girl also had dragon wings as well as an amazing gift of eloquence and later became Bonnie Silver when Devin murdered her mother.

Ashley grew into a super genius and later learned that she had the gift of healing. As her grandfather aged and fell into ill health, she cared for him, though she would never believe in the God her grandfather worshipped. Her intellectual pride always got in the way.

During these guardianships, Sapphira watched every event through her portal screen, trapped in Hades' grip. Through watching Bonnie's amazing faith in God, Sapphira learned to take hold of that faith herself. She escaped Hades and helped Merlin rescue the dragon spirits in Dragons' Rest as they learned about and followed a dragon messiah, Billy Bannister, the human son of Clefspeare.

This messiah had already restored to dragon form all of the dragons-turned-human that Devin had killed since their transformation, including Thigocia, who had once been Hannah. Each dragon had the opportunity to become human again, if they wished, and all but Thigocia chose to do so. She believed she could more easily search for Gabriel and Makaidos in her dragon form. After reuniting, Thigocia and Ashley set off in search of their lost family members, taking with them a boy named Walter and a girl named Karen.

Walter, Billy's best friend, was already experienced in interdimensional travel, having helped Billy in one of his journeys into Hades where he battled Watchers and an evil dragon. Karen, Ashley's adoptive sister, had proven a great help in programming and maintaining a supercomputer they had named Larry.

416

The exodus of dragon spirits from Dragons' Rest brought about its imminent destruction. Roxil, who refused to believe in the dragon messiah, stayed behind. Sapphira and Gabriel entered Dragons' Rest, hoping to convince Roxil to leave before it was too late. They escaped through a portal Acacia created from Heaven and wound up back in one of Hades' underground chambers, the same chamber that held the tower museum and Sapphira's portal screen.

The new story begins with Thigocia's search and Sapphira's decision on how to help the dragon find her lost loved ones. Sapphira's heart, however, yearned to find someone else, the friend she had saved from starvation centuries ago, her beloved Elam.

ORACLES OF FIRE®
SERIES

ISBN 978-1-85985-796-0

ISBN 978-1-85985-872-1

ISBN 978-1-85985-873-8

Available in August, 2010

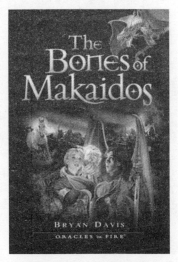

ISBN 978-1-85985-874-5

Available in October, 2010

DRAGONS IN OUR MIDST ®
SERIES

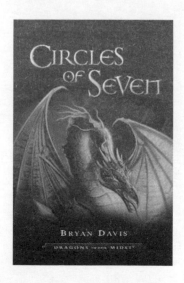

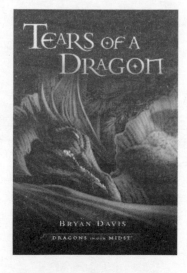